THREE UNCLES
AND A LAWMAN

THREE UNCLES
AND A LAWMAN

Keith G. Scott

Ordering Information:

For orders and inquiries, please contact:
1-888-404-1388
www.goldtouchpress.com
book.orders@goldtouchpress.com

Printed in the United States of America

Keith G Scott@geterdone.54

AUTHOR'S NOTE

A famous outlaw and bank robber in the old west once said, "I am a hard man living in a hard land, this simple statement pretty much sums up how things really were, you were either strong and hard or you were likely to expire sudden like. Life was hard carving civilization out of the western wilderness there were dangers at every turn, outlaws, natives, animals, weather, accidents, but the strong did survive and built western North America.

With my writing I like to portray the west as I wished is was white hats against black hats, living by the code and keeping with the fantasy that was the wild west. My hope is that my readers will enjoy the read, find it fun and a nice escape from nasty reality, even for a short time, we all need our distractions to survive.

Saddle up and enjoy the wild ride, be seeing you down the trail.

KG

DEDICATION

Dedicated to all those who run towards danger.

Thanks

CONTENTS

CHAPTER 1

BLOOD, SMOKE AND TEARS

FEAR- grips me in its tight bonds the beast tightens its hold on me until I am finding it hard to breath, my mind and body numb. Overwhelmed by shock and grief and how life can change, a few hours ago I was just a boy with a good family leading a happy normal life, now all is lost including hope and my living out the day unlikely. Sitting on a small knoll looking over the open plains of Montana, I am scared to death, tears flow down my face, dread fills me as I turn to look upon once was my family, death and destruction fills me with new horror. The smell of smoke from our covered wagon stings my nostrils and makes my eyes water, I am overwhelmed by my sense of loss, and at this moment I do not care if I live or die everyone I love is gone.

My name is Hardin Thomas Steele, I am a large lad for only being 12 years old, dark skinned with light brown hair and eyes that are almost emerald green, strong for my age life on the trail is hard and Pa expected me to do my share and more if needed. Ma was Irish and from the old country always talking about good and evil spirits and the magic of the Green Isle, always serious she told me many times my eyes were a gift from Hibernia the land where magic still lurks in the shadows, she would tell me often I will be a known man of importance and am destined to accomplish great things

Finally with great reluctance, I turn to look at the grizzly scene behind me our wagon is still smolderin g the flames out now burning wagon, my parents and sister Bess all lay dead, the horses and mules gone, taken by the renegades who had committed this most horrific and brutal of crime, I am only alive because Pa sent me out with his .56 spencer rifle to a stand of trees and brush about a half mile away from camp to try my hand at getting a deer for some fresh meat fresh meat fowl or fish are always welcome treats on the trail.

Lost in my grief and sorrow I did not hear or see the 2 men riding towards me until they were within a few feet of me, startled and afraid I fumble with Pa's seven shot .56 spencer rifle, shaking badly I almost drop the heavy weapon, I will make my stand, and die standing and strong.

Before I could bring my rifle up, a very huge man wearing beautiful beaded and fringed buckskins and has the look of a mountain man calls out" Whoa there Button we are not going to do you harm, we are not the villains who committed this evil deed". The man riding with the big man is a Mexican, slim and sleek like a cougar, very dark eyes had on the most beautiful high topped black soft leather boots with a set of big Mexican silver spurs. Both men were heavily armed and riding magnificent animals, the mountain man sat atop a long-legged mouse coloured mule with a mean look in its eye, the Mexican on a beautiful almost totally black Spanish gelding that would stand close to seventeen hands.

The big man looking down off the huge mule "boy my name is Angus Macdonald most people call me Bear, and this is my Pard Ramon Valdez, we saw the buzzards and smoke knowing that mostly means trouble in the wilderness we figured we best come have a look see, what happened here lad"?

I look up at the 2 men, realizing I have little choice and in urgent need of help I put my trust in these big men tough looking men but I recon makes no difference nothing left to steal and I cannot stop them from killing me if that is their aim. Taking in a deep breath I tell the men of how Pa had sent me out to try and fetch some fresh meat and was a fair distance from camp, I had just found a deer trail when I heard gunshots and saw smoke rising from where I figured our camp was. I took to running back to camp but coming up on a small hill close to the camp I see the bodies of my kin sprawled on the ground, the wagon smoking and in the far distance 4 men leading our horses and mules away at a fast pace. When I get back to the wagon, I see Pa's body first, he had been shot to in the body three times and twice in the head. On the other side of the wagon I found Ma and my sister Bess, I knew they were both dead their clothing ripped and torn, I could not stand to look at them, it was to terrible. Then I tell the men I was praying the outlaws would come back so I could kill a couple of the bastards before the put me under. Bear says in a gentle voice "how long ago did this happen boy". Not liking being called boy I said" Sir I do not like to be called boy, putting my chin up," my name is Hardin Thomas Steele, time seems so much different today but I think it has been many hours, sorry sir but my mind just ain't right".

The man named Bear gives a small gentle smile, "Hardin "we must go into the camp and tend to your family check for sign to trail and kill or capture the villains who done this evil thing". Both men dismount, Bear looks even bigger on the ground dwarfing Ramon, putting his huge hand gently on my shoulder "come Hardin, we have much to do". Walking back to camp with the 2 men I begin to feel safer and stronger, tears of grief and hate are still flowing, thankfully my shaking has stopped I do not want to show fear in front of these big men.

When we near the camp, Ramon makes the sign of the cross, speaking softly in Spanish which I figured is a prayer, Bear looks around a look the look in his eyes that sends shivers through me, I knew then these were good men but very dangerous when angered or threatened. Just at the edge of camp Bear tells me to wait, they need to check for sign while they were fresh.

I watch as they walk to Pa's body, squatting down looking closely at the ground the talk in low tones, they then go around back of the wagon to where Ma and Bess were laying, from the rear of the wagon I hear the men cursing in angry voices Bear cursing. Ramon then walks out from the wagon in the direction of which the bandits went, looking closely at the tracks he studies and memorizes the horseshoe prints of the outlaws horses.

Bear comes back to me and kneels in front of me and in a gentle voice says "Hardin with your permission we will bury your kinfolks then we gather up your belonging and start out after those varmints, but Indians might have seen the smoke and injuns can get mighty curious. "I need you to take your spencer and keep a lookout on that small hill yonder and keep watch we will call you when we have finished our work, keep a sharp eye out Hardin the wildness is filled with dangers." Before I leave for the hill Ramon gives me a hand full of jerky and his canteen then with a gentle squeeze on my shoulder which for some reason near brought tears, gently he gives me a nudge to get me going.

I know there was little danger from Indians and Bear wants me away from camp so not to see the carnage that was once my family. Upon reaching the hill I find a good spot and lay down putting the canteen and rifle beside me, without thinking I start chewing on the jerky suddenly hungry. Looking out over the plains I notice the beauty of them, endless open blue sky, the rich green grass with yellow, blue and purple wildflowers waving in the breeze, it was then I knew I am going to be a man of the west, the big sky and wilderness have already captured my soul.

I watch as Bear tend to Pa, gently he covers him with a blanket and picks him up as you would a sleeping child, he then carries him a short distance from the wagon. After he puts Pa down he goes around to the other side of the wagon to help Ramon prepare Ma and Bess for burial at this moment I am so grateful the 2 men are with me I am not sure I could stand putting dirt on their still faces.

After what seems an eternity they come back around with Ma and sister wrapped up and place them next to Pa's body. Rummaging through the partially burnt wagon and finding a shovel that escaped the fire they commence to dig the 3 graves, working in turns silent and solemn.

After the graves were dug, the bodies are placed in them and covered Bear waves for me to return to camp suddenly I am afraid again but damn if I will show it. Arriving at the grave site I notice Ramon making 3 grave markers, he asks me what names I want on the markers. I tell him the names which he cuts into the crude wooden monuments with a beautiful but deadly looking blade, finishing the markers, he and Bear drive them deep into the ground at the head of the graves.

Bear says to me" sorry we could not do more for your family son but it is to far to take them for a proper burial, hope you understand", I just nod my head and say I understand. The men remove their hats and Ramon in his beautiful voice starts praying in Spanish, not yet knowing the language I do not understand the words but the tone and the genuine tenderness of his words touch me deeply, Bear looking down at me says in a surprisingly tender voice for such a big man, "Hardin would you care to say a few words over your kinfolk"?

I look at the lonely graves, fighting back tears and finding my voice I speak "Lord please look over my family they were good hard working peace loving folks doing the best they could, noticing Ramon was holding Ma's bible, I hold my out for it, when it was in my hands I continued in a much steadier voice, Lord, I swear on this bible to find the men who did this evil, and send them to hell, Amen."

Suddenly not scared anymore I am mad, killing mad, with both of these magnificent men looking at me Bear says with a small grin," you will do to ride the river with Hardin, now let's see what we can save from the wagon, then we will begin the hunt and by God there will be a reckoning". Ramon said nothing but his eyes I notice have gone hard and dark the softness gone it reminds me of a lobo wolf

I once come upon, young as I am I realize the quiet soft speaking Ramon is a very dangerous man.

"I don't know where I am going
but I am on my way"
Voltaire

CHAPTER 2

THE CHASE

There is not much left of our worldly items everything pretty much went in the fire of our covered wagon, and for the last few months my home on wheels, I had my bedroll, Ma's bible, the big .56 spencer, in a hidden compartment the bandits missed a small satchel of money hidden under the floor boards of the wagon about 200 dollars in gold coin Pa kept for emergencies. Looking at the leather pouch of gold coins I remember Pa saying money corrupts be sure of the people you trust with it. Holding the bag not sure of what I should with it, then I look to Bear, he smiles and nods knowingly "Hardin put that money in my saddlebags, it will be safe you have my word on it Pard", I hand him the bag which he stows away. "Crawl up behind Ramon, my old mule has enough of a load to carry, letting out a laugh that would shake the mountains, still carrying my spencer I mount up behind Ramon, unknown to me at the time that these two men will impact my life in ways I can not even imagine.

It is getting late in the day but not wishing to remain near the ruined camp we ride until we find a nice spot with a small stream of sweet water and is was well protected with a good field of fire in case of uninvited visitors. During our ride to our night camp Ramon starts to talk "Jouencito you are young and have much to learn and this wilderness it is not like where you came from the ways of survival are much more important, put trust in your instincts and never stop learning, watch and learn from men like Bear, there is no better woodsman or tracker in the west, a ghost in the woods or on the plains, watch nd listen Hardin, and Jouencito a person listens better when the mouth is shut now it is getting late we need to find a place to camp, this is where the lessons start.

When we finally dismount an intense weariness washezs over me, I can not remember a longer or more difficult day, I shrug it off the best I could I begin to gather wood for the campfire, not wanting the men to think poorly of me for not holding up my end. Ramon takes the horses to the stream, waters then picketed them on a nice piece of grass close to camp, I notice that Ramon filling the canteens, I have learned my first lesson, always get water first the plains in some ways are not much different then the deserts water is precious. Bear has the camp and set up and fire going coming back to the fire with my second arm load of wood Bear tells me that is plenty after supper and coffee the fire will be out not to draw unwanted attention, I watch Bear set up camp everything is smooth no unnecessary noise or wasted movement the huge man moves like cat and then every so often he would stand and listen survey the land, always alert always watching. Ramon cooks up some bacon and some fry bread in the hot grease, as the smells of the cooking reach my nose my stomach starts to growl, I realize it had been some time since my last meal, after inhaling my meal and feeling the comfort of a full stomach Bear hands me a cup of coffee, hot as hades and black as a deep well "here Hardin drink this will put hair on your chest", laughing to himself, well let me tell you the black brew has a kick like a mule. Coffee finished I gather the plates to take them to the stream to wash them, weariness weighs on my like a heavy stone I rise staggering a bit I hope the men did not notice my weakness, Bear rises and takes the plates from me saying" young Master Steele you have had yourself a long and difficult day, I will do that, then we will move camp back away from the stream". Confused I ask Bear why we had to move the camp. "A right good question Hardin, he explains that if we stayed close the animals would not come for water and all critters need water, and being we were in rough untamed country a person must think of Indians or bandits who would rob or kill you for the gold in your teeth, never make it easy for them Amigo". After moving the camp and move the horses back away from the stream we settle in a small stand of cedar with good cover and protection.

Ramon sets up a place for me to sleep, I almost fall into it, just before falling asleep I heard Bear say," that is one tough little man Pard, "Si Amigo, mucho hombre, with those words in my mind I fall into a deep sleep hearing nothing until morning.

The smell of breakfast and coffee wakes me, shaking off the sleep I see Bear with his hands wrapped around a cup of his horseshoe floating coffee from last evening. Saying good morning I then apologize for sleeping in but then I notice the sun was not up yet, the men both chuckle quietly, sound carries on the plains. I ask if it was alright to go to the stream to wash up, Ma was a stickler on keeping clean, Bear told me to go ahead but keep a sharp eye go ahead Hardin and make it quick, we are going to ride fast and hard today, make up some ground on them villains. Upon returning from the stream and shivering from the skin numbing cold water I realize Bear and Ramon are both standing alert standing rifles in hand, I walk over and pick up my rifle, hoping there will be no more trouble. A horse comes with no rider says Ramon, the horse walks up to the stream dipping its velvet muzzle into the cold clear water, seeing the horse my heart pounds wildly in my chest, it is my horse old Hammerhead himself, still bridled and saddled, I clicke my tongue and that old horse trots right up to me, without any shame I wrap my arms around his neck and cry, he is the one thing I have left of my former life. That old horse just stood there seeming to be as happy to see me as him, Bear smiling says to Ramon, "looks like they know each other, Amigo what form of critter do you think it is? "both men smiling. A bit annoyed at the teasing I say "Sir I will not have you making fun of my horse, he is all horse pure mustang, he may not be the fastest or very pretty but will go all day and night, no quit in him, climbs like a mountain goat and a fights like a tiger, a time back we came across a cougar looking for trouble, old hammerhead went at him with hoof and teeth, and that old cat took off like its tail was on fire. The men were still smiling but nodding their approval. Still chuckling Bear puts his massive paw on my shoulder, "Just teasing you a might son, we will see what he is made of other than ugly, let's get ready boys were burning daylight."

We then clean up the camp and get the horses ready, Ramon made a sling of leather for my spencer which I could sling across my back making it easier to carry. When all was, ready Ramon leads off in the direction of the outlaws, it was a beautiful morning, I feel much stronger today sitting atop my own horse, riding with 2 good and strong men, the hunt begins, I will have my vengeance.

We ride in relative quiet for a couple hours both men studying the ground carefully. Ramon brings his horse to a stop and points at a lone rider heading towards us at a walking pace. Both my protectors become cautious and watchful, Ramon removes the thong on his holster and Bear pulls his rifle from the scabbard, it was a 50 caliber sharps buffalo gun, it was the biggest damn gun I ever seen, looked like it should have wheels attached.

This as it would turn out would be another day I will remember for the rest of my life, today I meet a living legend. The rider begins to take shape with the sun shining in blazing light behind the rider the appearance giving off an aura around him reminding me of one of the old gods Ma used to tell stories about around the nightly campfires. Taking my eyes off the rider I notice both Bear and Ramon relaxing then put their weapons back in their holsters. The man pulls up his big beautiful buckskin horse in front of us, his hair is long shoulder length and wavy it hung down to his broad shoulders, he has a large groomed moustache, square jaw, large prominent nose and pale penetrating grey eyes I even as young as I am I see death in this big mans eyes. He was dressed in a beautiful fringed buckskin jacket, high top black boots, black flat top hat, but what caught my eye was the red sash around his waist with 2 beautiful ivory handled pistols tucked in for a cross draw with either hand, and a United States Marshal's badge shining brightly on his chest.

"Howdy boys" he says, looking at Ramon," still riding with this old horse thief Ramon", Bear interjects loudly "I ain't that old James Hickok and you know it, you damn sheep herder", all the men laugh and shake hands all around.

Mr. Hickok looks at me with those flat grey eyes, "now who would this youngster be and why is he riding with you two wild men". Bear replied" Hardin Thomas Steele meet James Hickok, better known as Wild Bill" Walking up to me looking so tall and strong extends his hand in greeting. With a smile, "pleasure to meet you Hardin, I was in such awe of meeting a legend I could barely speak but managed to say what a pleasure it is to meet him. Ramon asks Senior Hickok where he is heading, "Riding dispatch for the army, heading to fort Whoop up in Canada, looks like there me more trouble with the whiskey traders and the Indians. Where are you boys off to". Bear answers," James we are on a ride of vengeance and justice, 4 outlaws killed the boy's family and stole all they had, we thought we would follow them and read them from the book".

Mr. Hickok's face took on a hard serious look, "Sorry to hear of your loss Hardin, I would very much like to join you boys but am committed to delivering these dispatches". Bear understanding nods, "Would enjoy your company old Hoss but I recon the three of us are up to running these polecats into the ground and skinning them."

We dismount, Mr. Hickok hands out cigars, the men talk in low and serious tones. After a few minutes of war talk Mr. Hickok goes to his horse and rummages through his saddlebags and returns with a short barreled .38 caliber six shot revolvers rigged up in a shoulder holster rig. Putting his hand on my shoulder he leads me off a short distance to talk. Before handing me the weapon he in a serious no nonsense tone says to me," the man who owned this was a bit slow and has no need of it now, remember Hardin it is not the gun but the man behind it, never draw it unless you mean to use it, and once drawn never hesitate, accuracy is more important than speed, make sure your first shot scores or you may not get a second. "I am giving this weapon to a man not a boy, make sure you are standing on the right side of the law if you need to use it, do you understand young Mr. Steele?". "Thank you, sir, I will remember what you said and will do my best to live up to it". Mr. Hickok smiles, "well said son, you are riding with 2 of the best, hard but good men, pay close attention and you will learn a much from them". We walk back to the horses, Mr. Hickok mounts his horse," got to get moving on, good luck boys be seeing you down the trail, turning his big horse leaves without another word.

I show the pistol to my friends, it had a nice curved handle which fit my hand real good, Ramon helps me to put on the shoulder rig and adjusts it to ride smooth under my left arm. The weight of the revolver under my arm feels good and gives me a feeling of confidence and safety.

We resume our journey and after a bit Bear starts talking about Mr. Hickok," that man you just met is one of the good ones but a hard man if crossed, a real fire eater, and a whiz with them hog legs, never a step back and if hunting someone would follow them into the very gates of hell. I start to laugh, they both looked at me a bit puzzled, I tell them that is just about what the marshal said about you two, after a moment of reflection we all begin laughing.

Ramon again takes the lead, both men were studying the ground for tracks, we ride for hours before Bear calls a halt, we all dismount, Ramon leans over and outlines the tracks with his fingers, "these ones are lazy and think they have escaped, they are only a short day ahead", Bear nods in agreement," we will have them soon", chuckling a bit Bear asks me how old hammerhead holding up, smiling I reply," ain't even got the rust off yet sir". Smiling we hit the trail again, I am getting that scared feeling again knowing I would soon meet the men who murdered my family, my fear fades replaced with a coldness deep within me and a resolve to punish to see these evil men punished.

Coming up on a good place to camp for the night we stop, I take the horses to water and refill the canteens, I glimpse a nod of approval from Ramon. While waiting for the horses to drink their fill I spot th some blackberry bushes just heavy with ripe purple fruit a true treat then close to the stream I dig up some wild onions, filling my bandana with the dark juicy berries and onions i return to camp. The camp is already set up when I get back, as usual Bear has his coffee on the brew, that man surely did enjoy that black varnish he made. I take it upon myself to cook supper, I must not be a drone and show these men I will carry my end of the load. My supper meal of venison steaks and onions for flavour in the grease I make some fry bread the way Ma showed me, I save the the blackberries for dessert when all was ready we sit down and commence to chow down, I notice western men take their eating right serious and never do much talking while eating, when the meal was finished I bring out the blackberries which are quickly inhaled to the pleasure of us all. Bear rubbing his stomach looking most content said" Hardin that was a right fine meal, did your Ma learn you how?" Yes, sir I says, Ma always said a man needs to know how to cook for a lot of times there will be no woman to do it for you. Ramon interjected "your Mamma, Nino was a wise woman, and it was wise of you to listen". Well Bear says if nothing else son you can always be a ranch cook, them cowboys appreciate and respect a good hand with a frying pan, both men smiling. I am very much pleased with the compliment feeling I had earned a bit of respect, I gathered up the plates and head down to the stream to wash them. I am beginning to understand the routine and as previous nights moved to a spot further back with good cover and field of fire.

Ramon decides that there was little chance of danger and we will not set up a guard, but brings the horses in close, I bring old hammerhead in close to me, that old horse would warn me better that any old watch dog. We all craw into our bedrolls, my hands clasped behind my head I look up at the night sky, I love looking at the stars, it is a clear and beautiful night, the thousands of stars twinkling with the occasional shooting star arking across the night sky, it somehow gives me great peace and humbles me at the same time. My star gazing was interrupted by Bear," Boys from here we will have have to dry camp we will be getting close to our prey I rather them not knowing we are after them, Ramon and I just nod in agreement, I snuggle up in my bedding and drop into a deep sleep.

Just as the sun was rising we are on the trail again, Bear leads of a good pace, I ride up beside the big mountain man," Hardin, he asks,"did your pa have any liquor in the wagon"?, yes sir had a case of whiskey for medicine and maybe trade for goods we may need". "Good says he it will be much easier to take them if they have been hitting the bust skull."

Two days hard riding around about sundown we arriive we come to a thicket of poplar, Bear lifts his hand to stop, indicating to make no noise, I watch him as he smells the air and looks over the landscape," I smell smoke and I believe they are in that grove, we will move the horses back to the hill yonder and look see when it gets dark, Hardin keep your voice low sound travels far out here". We move back and picket the horses, Bear tells me to rest if I could it would be a few hours before we move in to capture or kill the fugitives, using my saddle as a pillow I try to relax, but have to many emotions running through me, but I am mostly scared but determined not to show it.

After what seemed an eternity Bear rises, whispering that he is going to scout the outlaw camp and we were to wait until he returns. He leaves his cannon rifle behind not wanting it to catch in the branches, I watch him as he enter the trees, vanishing like a ghost, it amazed me how a big man like him could move so damn quiet, a bit scary knowing the Bear was on your trail. Ramon and I sit quiet, occasionally he will look at me and give a reassuring smile but sitting relaxed calm as in Sunday church. I look up and Bear is standing beside me, I had not heard a sound, I jumped startled by his sudden appearance.

In quiet tones, he tells us what he saw, "it is the outlaws camp with 4 men, he saw the mules and horses, and the pondscum were hitting the sauce hard and quarreling over the last of it, they had 1 guard out but he has been drinking as well and would not be a problem". Bear then went to his horse and removes a wicked looking sawed off shotgun. I take the .38 from its holster and check the loads making sure all chambers were filled, satisfied I return it and strap it in. Both men then checked their weapons, Bear with the shotgun and sidearm, Ramon with pistol and blade. Bear says to me, "stay right behind me and be careful where you put your feet, a breaking branch is like a gunshot at night, we want to take them by surprise".

Slowly we move into the trees, I try my best to do what Bear told me, I follow him closely with Ramon behind me, a short time later I begin to see the glow of a campfire and can hear the men in camp talking loudly, a couple of the outlaws are quarreling over the remaining bottle of liquor. Ramon touches Bears shoulder and with silent communication indicated he is going to take out the guard, then he like Bear vanishes like smoke. Bear and I stand quiet watching the camp, waiting for Ramon to get in position. We are on the very edge of the trees only a few yards away from the killers, seconds later we hear a started yelp from the guard, as the outlaws turned to see what is happening Bear and I step out from the trees, leveling his shotgun and with a menacing tone yells, "Hands up boys or the devil will take you", now a man may take a chance against a pistol or rifle, but a greener at this distance means certain death, the remaining 3 men stand a bit wobbly from the drink but sobering up fast reluctantly raise their hands, Ramon enters the camp half dragging the 4th outlaw who was holding his head which was bleeding from the whack Ramon had happily provided him.

Ramon herds the outlaws together and making sure not to get between them and Bears shotgun and disarms them, checking for hideout guns or knives. Then taking thin cords of leather he ties their hands behind their backs and then not gently shoves them to the ground. The biggest of the outlaws looks like a real hard case, tall thin, mean beady eyes and a scar running down from his left eye to his jaw, I figure him to be the leader of this murderous crew.

Looking up at us and with a mean surly tone starts flapping his beak, "What is the meaning of this we done you men no harm, you have no call to treat honest travelers this away". Bear looks down at the outlaw with a look of utter disgust, then says to the scare faced man," there is not a lick of honesty in this here whole bunch, honest men do not kill innocent people, assault their womenfolk and steal their animals". The leader responds, "we done no such thing, say who is that pup you got with you?' finally noticing me. Ramon answers in his quiet but menacing voice, "this is Senor Steele, it was his family you butchered, and stole from, you are men most evil "then spits in disgust at them. The other outlaws begin to proclaim their innocence, the big leader tells them all to shut up. With an evil glint in his eyes he laughs, "you got nothing but the word of this whelp". I look to Bear "Sir those mules over yonder are mine, the Morgan horse and that shotgun on the ground was Pa's, his initials are carved in the stock". Bear nods to me, "well you boys done missed a witness and this is an honest lad, whose life you destroyed, and now you will pay a heavy price for your wrong doing".

The scar faced man named Evans, known around the camps as a back shooter and thief, even men riding the outlaw trails will have no truck with him. Knowing they had been caught red handed the other three men remained quiet but Evans looks right at me with those hard eyes and smiling says, "so we missed you boy, to bad, but we sure enjoyed your women folk, the bitches were just begging for it ", giving off an evil grin. My mind explodes in a terrible rage, without realizing it I pull my pistol and walk up close to Evans, the gun shaking a bit in my hand, I am going to kill this evil man. My finger was tightening on the trigger, from behind me I heard a calm voice of reason, "Jouencito this is not the way, it would make you as bad as them, think of your Papa and Wild Bill", Bear grunts his agreement. I slowly release the pressure off the trigger, remembering Mr. Hickocks words I lower my gun and return it to its holster. Bear says to me "Hardin these are your prisoners, you must decide what needs doing, if it were me, I would hang them all and leave them for the buzzards to feed on. I walk over to a tree and sat down to think things out, Bear and Ramon wait patiently and keeping a close eye on the prisoners.

After a spell, I walk up to the tied-up men, in a strong voice which surprised me I tell them, "my Pa was a law and order man, as is Mr. Hickok who gave me this here gun. You will be taken to the law and put on trial so folks will know the evil men you are, you will be hanged and I will be there to start you on your way to hell". The prisoners all had an astonished look, Evans says" you know wild Bill.? Bear answers for me, "the lad is known to him and I am a thinking if anything happens to him, he would take it right personal, and you know Bill got no give in him,". Unnoticed Ramon with that beautiful knife in his hand squats in front of Evans looking him directly in the eyes, then faster than the eye could follow he flicks the razor-sharp blade slices open the right nostril of the big outlaw's nose, blood gushes from the cut Evans screams, then in his quiet voice says, "you will not talk again of the Nino's family or talk bad of him, for next time I will cut off your ears", and he meant it. Bear interjects "we promised the lad to get you to trail, but how much of you gets there is up to you", his eyes are hard and had grin that would scare the devil, leaving no doubt he meant what he said.

There is no hunting like the hunting of man and
those who have hunted armed men long enough and
like it, never care for anything else thereafter
- Ernest Hemingway

CHAPTER 3

DANGEROUS JOURNEY

It came time to parley on what to do next, Bear makes coffee from the prisoner's food sacks, sitting together sipping the black steaming lava that is Bears brew, the two men talk over their options and where to take the prisoners. They both agree that Glasgow would be best, they know the town had marshal and a jail, it is going to take at least 2 days of hard riding to get there probably a bit longer with the prisoners in tow. It is coming around to sunrise, Bear says" we best be moving, Hardin go round up the stock and bring them in". I head over to the livestock, Pa's Morgan nickered as I came close, as I was stroking his neck, I remember how much Pa loved this horse, thinking of Ma and Bess laying buried like many other victims of the lonesome prairie, shaking my head as to shake the thoughts away, I buckle down and get to work. the prisoner's horses are fine animals, I remember hearing one time, outlaws always wanted good horses so to get out of trouble faster than they got into it. Checking check over the mules they all looked fat and sassy, I swear them ornery critters were honestly happy to see me. Bear came over to help with the animals, Ramon is smashing the prisoner's rifles against a tree, them outlaws were some pissed off, then he places all the pistols in a burlap bag, Pa's shotgun he leaves out for me, I roll it up in my bedroll, thanking him. As we get ready Bear looks down at me serious look on his face says "Son we have a long hard ride ahead the stock and prisoners are going to slow us up some, out here you must always be alert for danger at all times there be injuns, grizz, cougar, outlaws, the weather, all can kill you, use your eyes and ears, trust your instincts and always expect danger, might just keep you alive for a spell "I will remember sir, thank you". "Your pa raised you right Hardin, right good manners, but just call me Bear, sir does not sound right in my ears, holding out his ham sized hand deal? Shaking his hand "deal "I say with a big smile.

We lead the animals to where Ramon and the prisoners are waiting, looking at the men they are a sober and quiet bunch this morning, Ramon cuts their leg bindings then checks that their wrists were secured tight and snug. Bear crawls into the saddle, "are we ready to ride Senor Valdez? "Si Bear we are ready".

Ramon leads off, the outlaws behind him and Bear and I riding rear guard with the extra livestock. After we get into the rhythm of the trail I ask Bear, "do you know any of the prisoners Bear"? "I know Evans, he is a bad one, robber, killer when has the edge, would rob a man for the gold in his teeth, comes from feuding hill stock, may be some trouble there, Ramon knows the half breed, they call him Crow, a scalp hunter, worse than Evans, never particular where he gets his scalps, the other two I believe are brothers, Clem and Sam Hathaway from down Texas way, both killers and not a bit of mercy in either of them".

Looking at the prisoners ahead of me, I can not understand how men could create and use such cruelty and violence are they born evil or has the world broke them. They, for the most part ride quiet but I notice Evans scanning the horizon as if expecting company, looking a bit to smug for my liking.

Unknown to us me 3 rough and dirty men are laying in the deep grass of a knoll watching our small company. "Shit "one of the men exclaim, "that there is Bear Macdonald and Ramon Valdez with some kid". The other 2 men had not heard of Bear and Ramon, one of the men with a coyote face and drooping eye says "there are only two of them we can take them easy". "You go ahead and try then, I would rather tackle a full-grown grizzly with a club than those two, and they have a lot of friends like Hickok and the Traveller. Well old droopy eyes now looking at things in a safer manner says, "well what are we going to do Boss?" "Well says the boss," I am going to get word to the Pa Evans and his clan, then I am heading west fast, this climate just got plum unhealthy, without another word they mount and ride off. Mr. Evans is going to be right disappointed. Getting on towards sundown Ramon pulls off into a stand of cedar by a fair sized beaver pond, a beautiful spot in the wilderness, thick green grass for the horses and mules, evidence of many old campfires. After I water and picket the animals, I head back towards camp picking up small dry branches that would burn with little smoke, I am learning, Ramon earlier in the day, killed a deer with a beautiful long rifle shot, Bear skinned and cut the choice parts. Feeling like I am not pulling my weight I tell the boys I will be the cookie, with some faked reluctance they agreed, so in grease I fried up the venison steaks added the wild onions I had saved, then made fry bread in the remaining grease. When the food ready I dish up plates for Bear, Ramon and myself, sitting we proceeded to eat what I think is a fine meal. Evans in his surly tone asks if we were going to feed them or make them starve. Bear says to the prisoner, "You will get fed after we eat, and given a chance for the privy, we want you pilgrims well fed for the hangman, I recon it might even be old George Maledon using his ropes, they call him the Prince, does a right fine hanging". Looking amused Bear settles in and gets to eating.

The prisoners are fed and had their time in the bushes to relieve themselves, then re-tied for the night, Bear and Ramon decided to keep watch overnight, I said to them I would take my turn on watch, this load was mine as well, they agree and I would have the first watch. Bear stands" grab your spencer and we will set you up", he leads me to a spot that had a good view of the prisoners and the landscape. "Listen close Hardin, this is a man's job and never forget these are desperate and dangerous men, and desperate men are capable of anything". He then started to instruct me on what needed doing, "never look into the fire you will not be able to see what is in the darkness, scan with your eyes never look at anything directly unless it is moving, watch and listen to the animals, if the crickets or frogs stop their noises be on your guard and watch the horses, they can smell trouble faster than we can. If you think something is not right wake me, just put your hand on my shoulder, do not speak, do you understand son". "Yes, Bear I do and will hold up my end." "One last thing Hardin, if you feel you cannot keep awake come and wake me, we cannot take chances, otherwise when you see that bright star is over that hill yonder it will be my turn on watch".

Without another word moves back to camp and both men crawl into their bedrolls, I am alone now, Bears instructions running through my mind, I am very proud of the trust these two fine men put in me, I am consumed with learning the ways of the west and how to become a big man like Bear or Ramon, hope when the time comes I do not let them down.

I must admit I am a bit scared at first, things look so much different at night, eerie and distorted, but also a quiet that is comfortable and peaceful natures night song. My confidence grows throughout my shift, I spend my time watching the prisoners who seemed to be asleep I keep my ears and eyes open for possible intruders or trouble. It is a beautiful evening, the crickets chirping their song, I am beginning to love this wild and lonely country, vowing one day I will travel and see much more of it. When the star was in position over the hill Bear told me I get up and head back to camp, bending over I put my hand on Bears shoulder, as men who live in the wilds trains themselves to do to survive he opens his eyes not making a sound, listening before moving, we then move back near the fire Bear pours a coffee, in low tones I tell Bear all was quiet. "Hardin, time for you to bunk down and get some rest, long day tomorrow", taking his coffee and sharps he then moves to my previous spot and settles in,I crawl into my blankets, falling into a deep sleep almost instantly, after what I thought was only minutes I wake to the smells of coffee and bacon.

It takes us the most part of three days to reach Glasgow, our unusual cavalcade draws a lot of attention as we lead the criminals down the main street to the Marshal's office, not every day a person sees a huge mountain man a Mexican and a kid leading in 4 hardcase outlaws to jail. Pulling up in front of the marshal's office a tall pleasant looking man, who is well dressed and sporting a small mousestash there is a well used but finely kept .45 revolver tied to his hip, a tin 5 star Marshals star pinned to his vest. With a bit of a smile he looks and us and asks howdy boys nasty looking bunch you got there and I recon that one is an Evan's.

The only thing necessary for the triumph of evil is for
good men to do nothing
- Edmund Burke

CHAPTER 4

WAITING FOR JUSTICE

The Marshall was not Mr. Thompson as Bear expected, after dismounting Bear says" Howdy Marshal thought Ben Thompson was marshalling here". "He still is" the still unknown marshal stated. "He got into a shooting scrap with two would be bad men trying to rob the bank, they sure picked the wrong town and a tough marshal. If you now him you know Ben he is a man without fear, the two outlaws got right nice spots in boot hill, but the marshal got shot up a might, I am holding down the fort until he is on his feet again, my name is Seth Bullock". I am guessing from Ben's yarns you are Bear MacDonald and this is your Pard and the famous pistolero Ramon Valdez". Old Bear chuckling a might responds, "That would be a right smart guess marshal, we have heard of you as well they call you the Canadian gunfighter Seth Bullock and it is said you have nerve and are a man of the code, we heard of you backing down that lynch mob with a sawed off awhile back, I have no problem with hanging's but I do not care for lynching's". Smiling the Marshal replies"not sure about the gunfighter handle but I am a stubborn SOB, a Canadian and damn proud of it." "So, what have we here" looking over at the four restrained outlaws. Bear takes the lead and answers that they were killers and evil men who have been brought here for justice, the outlaws are taken off their mounts led into the jail and put immediately into jail cells, once secured we all go back to the marshal's office, and coffee was poured. Bear looks to the Marshal,"Mr. Bullock this is Hardin Thomas Steele it was his family that was done in by them back in your cells'. Rising and extending his hand we shake hands "sorry about your kinfolk Hardin, I promise you justice will be served." sitting back down, "looking at Bear says "tell me your story Mr. Macdonald". Bear begins with him and Ramon finding me and the remains of my family, then about the burial and taking up the hunt. He continues with the meeting with Hickok, and him giving me the 38, the eventual capture of these outlaws and finding the stolen animals and some of my family's possessions in their camp ending the story with the ride in. Marshal Bullock, looks at me, and with a sincere look says "sorry about your troubles son, it was very lucky it was that these two scoundrels found you first," giving off a small chuckle. "Do you know the names of the men you captured, that one with the slit nose looks like an Evans I think Tom, bad family clannish and large they could be trouble, I don't recognize the other three." Bear shaking his head in a negative matter responds "You got Evans pegged Marshal, the half breed we believe is called Crow, the other two are Sam and Clem Hathaway from down Texas way, every man jack of them vile and pure evil, I would like to give them all to the Blackfoot to play with, them Blackfoot are some damn mean injuns." Bear then asks if there is a judge in town explaining how I wanted a trial and hanging. Marshal Bullock said there was a circuit judge and he would send word immediately, would likely get here in a week or so.

After leaving the marshals office we head to the town livery stable, in front is an old codger in bib overalls and smoking a foul smelling pipe. Turns out he is an old friend of Bears named Ivan, they trapped in Indian country together when only the very brave dared enter. Howdy's and some good natured rough talk and bragging are bantered back and forth before putting the mules in the corral and the horses in their stalls feeding and rubbing them down, I give old hammerhead some extra corn Ivan had on hand. Promising Ivan they would get together for a drink later Bear leads us in search of some grub and about damn time, my stomach is beginning to think my throat was cut.

We stop in front of front of a rooming and eating house named Megs, the owner was a woman named Megan Rogers she served best food in town and has the cleanest rooms in the territory, but if anyone caused her trouble they went out on their ear fast and were never allowed back. As we entered Meg comes out from the kitchen then seeing us gives a big smile and hugs both Bear and Ramon. Bear says" Meg I would like you to meet Mr. Hardin Steele, Meg being a full figured busty woman bid me welcome and enveloped me in a big hug, I almost cried feeling and smelling Meg reminded me of Ma. "You boys must be hungry you sit I will bring some coffee and get you fed shortly". She is back in a flash with coffee for the men and a large glass of buttermilk for me. Well sir let me tell you Meg cancook, loaded platters of steak, eggs, fresh bread and jam were brought out from the kitchen, she joined us and after eating and brought a fresh pot coffee with some bear sign, known to some as as donuts, we all complimented her on the fine meal, then Ramon told her as briefly as possible of our adventures and hard ride. Meg I can tell shows steel on the outside but is a sweet and sensitive earth Angle, a few tears in her eyes expressed the sorrow for my loss and hardship. Bear inquires if she had a room for me, she said she had rooms for us all, but Ramon had friends in town and Bear would camp not liking town roofs, so it was arranged that I would stay at Megs until the trial was over, I reckoned I would be gaining weight within no time and liking the thought. I thank Meg and say I have money to pay, just tell Bear how much she needed "Hardin do not worry about paying you are a quest in my house for as ;ong as you like and it is a pleasure to have you here to keep me company".

Meanwhile many miles down the trial Mr. Hickok is eating up the miles towards his destination when he spies a rider in the distance heading towards him riding slow Indian style. Not being a trusting man he removes his rifle from its boot he checks that the Henry rifle is fully loaded and ready for quick action, holding it across his saddle he rides slowly forward to meet the rider, recognition brings a rare smile to the Marshal's face he replaces the rifle in the saddle boot. The lone rider is not a big man but tough and rough looking, dark skinned as any Indian, dressed in a combination of western and Indian dress, beautiful beadwork decorating on both his high-topped moccasins and buckskin fringed jacket, carrying a well used henry repeating rifle, it did not take a second look by anyone to know that this was a man not to be trifled with. Marshal Hickok recognizes the man as Jerry Potts a Metis, known as a Trailblazer, exceptional Scout, maybe most important the savior of the NWMP on their trek west. It was said he killed more men than the plague killing a man for every year of his life and he was over 30, but a very mean drunk and to be avoided when he was on the hooch.

Meeting up both men dismount Potts with a huge smile and with a French accent greets his friend "Bonjour mon Ami how is my good friend Hickok?". "Howdy Jerry how has the road been treating you, are you on the scout?" "No, my friend I am traveling maybe visit my Blackfoot cousins, and you my friend where do you go?". "I am headed to Fort Whoop Up with dispatches, seems like more trouble with the whiskey traders". As they were talking Hickok tells him of his encounter with our group and the trouble that had been brought upon me. "Very bad ", says Jerry, "I have heard of this Evans, big family very clannish and mean, there is talk on the wind and in the blowing grass it speaks of trouble for the boy, I believe they will try and bust out Evans out of jail, kill the boy and anyone that tries to stop them, they are many and all will fight if Pa Evans says it is to be". With a frown of concern the Marshal tells Potts, "I am greatly distressed something may happen to the lad. Jerry, you are a man I can trust, you would be doing me a personal favour if you could take these dispatches to the fort, they know you there., if I ride fast and hard I may get back in time to help out the lad." Smiling hugely and with no hesitation responds, "Of course I will do this for my good friend, you can rely on Jerry but you owe me a bottle of the good whiskey ". Handing the dispatches to Jerry promising they would pop the cork and pull the tigers tail soon, Hickock once again mounts his magnificent steed shaking hands says, "I am in your debt and much obliged, you are welcome at my fire anytime Scout". Both men then ride on with a wave of goodbye.

Meg leads me to my room, it is furnished with a soft looking single bed, a chair and writing table and a small dresser, bright sunlight comes through a single window with bright yellow curtains floating tin the breeze of the open window, nicest room I had ever been in and I have it all to myself, strangely it gives me a feeling of safety and home. I have very little to unpack, so after putting my gear away I lay on the bed, it was a most comfortable feeling, I had not been in a real bed for a very long time. I lay with my hands clasped behind my head, thinking of the recent events and with much worry about my future, it is scary and overwhelming, not being able to rest I decide to stretch my legs and check out the town.

Glasgow was in the new territory on which had been taken from the Dakota and Lakota bands, typical of western towns, consisting of stables, a couple of saloons, general store, a single hotel, jail, the Bon Ton eatery and assorted houses folks was living in. Not a large town just starting to grow, but busy with farmers, ranchers and drifters coming and going. As I walk by a store window I caught a reflection of myself, I stop suddenly, hardly recognizing myself in the reflection, I look shabby, my clothing are pretty used up, I decide to go to the general store to see if I can find some new duds and necessities. The general stores at the time carried everything from canned milk to weapons, but it is the smell of them I love most, smells of, gun oil, leather, coffee, assorted spices, and they have a whole shelve of candy jars, a dark comforting interior where people would gather mostly men solving the problems of the day over the cracker barrel. The store is quiet as I look around, the man running the counter finished serving a couple of women and comes over to me, a kindly looking older man with a friendly smile. "How can I be of assistance young man?" I tell him I am looking for some new clothes, he leads me over to where the clothing is stacked and as he is showing me the clothing when he asks, "are you the lad that came in with Bear and Ramon leading in those outlaws?" in western towns there were no secrets and news traveles fast, within hours everyone in the area would know my story. I tell the man who called himself Pernisky, I was, and give him a short version of my story, he expresses his sorrow for my loss and says call on him if I needed anything. I Thank him and say I will be back soon. I am back out into the street intending to go back to Megs and see if I can find Bear to get a bit of Pa's gold coin to purchase the new cloths.

Looking down the dusty street I notice 3 boys about my age, so I start drifting over in their direction, as I near them I notice 1 of the of the boys was a bit older and the obvious leader, the other 2 were a bit younger follower types. The older boy has a mean aggressive look, obviously, the town bully, not wanting trouble I turn to walk away, but just then the bully calls to me to come join them, against my better judgement I stroll over to the boys. The older boy almost immediately begins digging his spurs into me, trying to intimidate me with his size. Pa always told me most bullies are cowards, standing up to them was the best way of dealing with them. When I figure I have taken as much abuse as I intend so I rear back and let my right fist go, catching the bully square on the nose, knocking him to the ground his nose gushing blood. I doubt if anyone had stood up to him before, he has a most shocked and hurt look on his face, getting to his feet he yells at the other 2 boys get me, now I am in for it, they all rush me, I get in a couple good licks before their sheer numbers overwhelm me, knocking me to the ground all of them punching and kicking me. From behind me I hear a voice "leave that boy alone" the three stop there assault and look up at the speaker, the bully says "stay out of this Bill Mathers this is none of your affair", Bill looked about 15 a big good looking lad, dark hair and eyes, and he is smiling at them as if inviting them to attack, looking at the three townies says "I am making it my affair you cowardly pumpkin rollers", looking at the older boy said and" remember Jimbo I whopped you once and will do it again". The town boys think better of it and with curses and empty threats walk away. Bill came over to me helped dust me off and checking I was not hurt, held out his hand," my name is Bill, shaking his hand I said I "my name is Hardin thanks for your help I was surely up against it before you showed".

From that day, Bill Mathers and I became good friends and in time close like brothers, but the Gods would have their amusement with the two of us before the end comes. Bill tells me he was the son of a farmer and their farm was a couple hours' ride from town, feeling I had a friend to talk to I told him my story, we walked around town talking as young men do of our hopes for the future. He askes me what my plans were after the trial was over, I say I have not had it figured out yet, but when I was of age I was going to be a lawman like Mr. Hickok and Bullock, he laughs and says, you will never get rich that way and will be a target for every bad man in the west. I ask his intentions, well he says" I ain't going to be any damn dirt farmer that's for certain, I want the finer things in life, fine clothes, a good horse, straight shooting guns and money in his pockets". It was getting on to supper time and I have a mighty strong hunger, I invite Bill to join me but he said his Pa would be heading back to the farm soon but he would be coming back to town again in a few days, I thanked him again for his help and hoped to see him again soon.

After we part I head back to Meg's, entering I see Bear sitting and chatting with Meg, I join them, Bear who misses very little smiling asks" laddie, what sort of mischief I had been up to, looks like been in a scuffle." I tell them of my encounter with the bullies and how Bill came to my rescue, Meg shaking her head got up and said she had to get supper ready her boarders would be wanting their suppers soon, then was off to the kitchen. Bear looks at me, "you did right son, I doubt if they will be bothering you again, also Marshal Bullock had got a wire back from the circuit judge and he will be here next week to start the trial, seems word has got around and you are the talk of the territory, going to be many strangers coming to town we must be careful, we best not be forgetting them Evans bastards".

I had not noticed before that Meg had a man helping her, he is wide shouldered with the narrow hips of a rider, blond but dark from the sun, like me emerald green eyes, soft spoken but has a presence of confidence and is a watchful man, who will dig his spurs in deep if pushed, he and Bear nod a silent greeting of recognition, no words are spoke, Bear I asked "do you know that man". "You betcha I do and he is one of the good ones, but deadly, only man I know that could come close to swinging iron with him would be Ramon and it would be a damn close thing". "I will not be telling you his name, that is for him to say", intrigued and mystified I let the matter drop for the moment for it is time for supper.

Meg comes out of the kitchen with 2 steaming bowls of beef stew and a plate of hot biscuits, that woman can surely cook, I eat slowly enjoying the meal and watching the other boarders coming in for their supper, she returns a bit later with 2 huge slices of fresh apple pie, despite myself I was getting hooked on coffee and with a bit a frown sweet Meg brings coffee for the both of us. I am so full, the was excellent meal I almost have to be rolled away from the table. After finishing his coffee Bear gets up and says he was heading over to the Red Dog saloon for a couple drinks and some socializing, before leaving he tells me to stay in my room for I it was not safe to be out after dark. Just as I am getting up to go back up to my room, Meg's mysterious helper comes up to me, "Howdy Hardin", extending his hand in friendship we shake," my name is Wade, pleasure to meet you Pard, no offence to you but can you read lad?". I nod yes but explain I have had not much time for reading lately Pa would sometime read stories when we camped, handing me a week-old newspaper says "something to pass the time, call on me anytime if you need anything." "thanks Wade, greatly appreciate it I recon I need all the friends I can get.' I then go up to my room and get ready for bed, I scan the paper for a short time but am weary and climb under the blankets and quickly fall into a deep comfortable sleep.

The next morning, I am up early and went down for breakfast, other than Meg I was the only one in the dining room, I walk over to the coffeepot and poured myself a cup, Meg brings me breakfast and a glass of milk, I see Wade come in he gives a quick good morning then goes directly to the kitchen and begin cleaning up the cups and few dishes. After my second cup of coffee and some idle chat with the other boarders coming down for their breakfast'ds, I leave Meg's and slowly walk down to the Marshal's office. Marshal Bullock is sitting at his desk going through wanted posters coffee cup in hand. "Morning Marshal, how are you sir?" "I am well Harden what can I do for you"? "Marshal I want to see the prisoners and I intent to be in here every day until they are dead at the end of the rope, I want them to see me looking in at them caged like the animals they are, reminding them every day of their evil deeds." After some thought he says," ok by me but do not get to close to the bars, he got up and unlocked the door leading to the cells. I admit I am scared to near death am but determined i hesitate building up my nerve to entre the cell area. The marshal must have noticed my reluctance," I believe I shall have to in with you in the cells Hardin, be safer, I nod n a quick yes much relieved we then enter together the cells. The half breeds Crow cell is at the end I walk and stand in front of him he just stares at me with dark mean eyes reminding me of a rattler I had once come upon, the to brothers just hang their heads in shame of the evil they have done, but Evans being the evil man begins to mouth off." "This is far from over you little shit, Pa will not let me hang even if he has to burn this one horse town to the ground, and I aim to kill you boy, slow Apache style', his face a mask of hatred and a bit of insanity. Marshal Bullock looks at Evans, "If any harm comes to this lad and you miss the noose I will hunt you to ground and fill your black heart with lead", and there was no doubt by anyone including Evans that he would do as he promised. Before leaving I tell the prisoners,"I will be back tomorrow and every day until you bastards are hung and 6 feet under in boot hill".

Returning to the office the Marshals office he offers me a coffee which I accept gladly, "That took nerve Hardin, do you really mean to do as you say" "Yes sir I have vowed to it," smiling he said drop in anytime. As I have stated before news travels fast in western towns and by noon the whole town knew of my visit to the jail and my promise I made to the prisoners.

The greatest gift of life is friendship,
and I have received it
- Hubert H. Humphrey

CHAPTER 5

PA EVANS GATHERS THE CLAN

Pa Evans is a tall lean sour looking man, mean as sin and tough as wang leather, unwashed dressed out in dirty greasy buckskins. He is the unchallenged leader of the clan, originally from Tennessee, before being run out for various crimes including assaulting women and robbery, he always carries a 12 inch Arkansas toothpick, preferring the feel of the cold sharp steel deep in a mans guts slicing his vitals to the bullet. The clan overall are dirty, lazy hard drinking men who through intimidation and fear receive and live off their ill-gotten gains. As with most hill men they are all excellent shots with the long guns, cutting their teeth on them, but prefer to kill when there is little danger to themselves, very few of them would face another man straight up. Pa Evans has sent out word that all the clan is to at his homestead, he figures he would have about 20 men armed for bear riding with him on this deadly mission to save his worthless son from hanging, but kin is kin. Once gathered they would ride to Glasgow and free his boy Tom and would kill any living critter that resisted, meanwhile he is getting some of the boys preparing the animals and gathering provisions ready for some hard riding.

Unaware of the unfolding events I wander the town meeting people and exploring all was new and exciting things to see for I have not spent much time in towns. Looking down the main street I see Bear, I cross the street to meet him, he askes me about my time at the jail, and what I said to the killers of my family. "Hardin that took sand, making you a lot of friends in town and a name for yourself." I will be going to the jail with you tomorrow Laddie", laughing, "the men in town are lining up to volunteer to go with you, never seen anything like it, never."

I ask Bear if I can have some of Pa's money I needed me some new duds, but I am clean at least, Meg insisted I bath, I learned fast you did not argue with that woman. Bear agreed and said we will go over to Pernisky's and see what we could find. The store owner, Mr. Pernisky greets us with a big natural smile then shakes hands Bear and me. I pick out several items, two checkered shirts, couple pairs denim black pants, a nice tan leather jacket, a new pair of high top black boots, a blue bandana and a few toilet items, when we finished it was a fair stack I am worried greatly about the cost, but Bear shows no concern and tells me not to worry. Bear pays for the items then remembering something Mr. Pernisky asks us to wait a moment and went to the back room, he returns carrying a fine-looking black felt hat, he had me try it on, fit right nice, reluctantly I handed it back knowing it would cost to much. "A gift son, man should have a good hat and I recon you earned it", after thanking him greatly Bear and I head back to Megs with my new cloths and I feel better now than I have in days. When we get to Megs I take my items and immediately go up to my room to change, throwing my rags in the corner, about to dress Meg calls through the door tells me I am to bath again before putting on my new clothes, frustrated but knowing I was doomed I bathed. Taking my time dressing liking the feel and enjoying the smells of the new cloths, then I leave my room and go downstairs to the dining room thinking to myself that I am one damn sharp dressed young man. Meg sees me and immediately and with much fuss makes a big deal of how handsome I look, making me blush, Bear mentioned that I cleaned up pretty good, that got a smile and nod from Wade you gives me a smiling wink.

Feeling good I leave them to take a stroll around town, stopping occasionally to talk with some of the townspeople, receiving many compliments, as I approach the Red Dog saloon, I notice a man outside, a somewhat short but handsome man, dressed in a tailored black suit, a beautiful white frilly shirt, sting tie with high polished black boots, carrying a 45 colt in a hand tooled holster. "Morning Mr. Steele my name is Luke, beautiful day would you agree?". "I would indeed sir, very pleased to meet you, would you be Luke Short the gambler?" "Yes, I am gambling is my trade how I earn a living, Hardin I would be honoured if you would allow me to have a turn escorting you to the jail." Thanking him for his kindness, I say Bear would go with me tomorrow so we agreed he would meet me at Megs the day after we would go together. He looks the true gentleman, but his eyes have the look of a hunter, Bear said he was honest as the day is long and way to good at cards to cheat, proved his bravery over the felt of a card table no fear cool as a mountain stream. I have a feeling anyone pushing this man will find they have a tiger by the tail, everything is fine hunting a tiger until you catch.

When I get back to Megs, Wade is alone at the table reading a paper, I join him and tell him of my encounter with Mr. Short, he gave me a rare smile and says" I know Luke, a good man, very handy with that smoke wagon he carries, easy going unless pushed or insulted, an honest and skilled card player, never cheats, a good friend but a dangerous enemy". "Now to you, if there is any trouble or you feel something is not right find me always trust your instincts Hardin, keep you above the flowers". I knew he meant what he said, and I thank him, it gives me great comfort, not knowing why but my instincts are telling me this mystery man may be the very best and most dangerous most capable of a very tough group of men.

During the days while waiting for the circuit judge to arrive Bill came to town a couple times and we quickly become fast friends, we spend a lot of time at Meg's eating pie and drinking coffee, people drop in talking and giving me their support, Bill I can tell is impressed and a bit jealous of my popularity. Every morning a new man escorts me to the jail, I am beginning to greatly annoy and distress the prisoners just as I hoped it would, today Wade comes with me, the half breed sees me and explodes in a mad rage screaming and pulling on the iron bars, he screams insults and cursing at me, with a quick step Wade grabs the half breeds shirt and with a quick pull forward slams the prisoners face into the bars, then pushes him back into the cell, the half breed holding his bloody face looks into Wades eyes and wisely says nothing more, the Hathaway brothers still quiet but looking pale,shakey and scared. Evans just leers at me, "your time is coming kid, you will be dead within the week and I will be piss on your grave". He then seemed to recognize Wade or his type of man he is and for the first time his face shows fear. Marshal Thompson was far from being healed but is up and on crutches and sitting with Mr. Bullock when we came back to the office. Seth introduces me and shaking hands with me says" you are the talk of territory son, that can be good and bad, be careful this Evans crowd are pure coyote, be on your guard lad, always.". I am getting an uneasy feeling some would say this is instinct so I decide I am going to start carrying Mrasal Hickok's revolver, which will be hidden by my jacket, there are times a man must saddle his own broncs.

The next day I was to learn how fast trouble can happen and how a person will fight to survive I am wandering the town alone just killing time, most of my protectors were all busy with one thing or another. I decide to cut through the ally to get to the corral and check on the mules horses and of course brush down old Hammer head. Out of nowhere a large mean looking filthy man dressed in filthy blue overalls steps out in front of me, he grabs me by my jacket collar "I got you squirt, I be Bob Evans and I aim to kill you dead", he then points his big handgun directly at my face. I am trapped the only way out was through him, my mind goes numb with fear, beyond scared in fact, being evil and sly like the coyote he holsters his gun knowing a shot will bring some tough men quick, he then pulls from his belt a wicked looking Arkansas toothpick old nicked and deadly looking. With pure malice, he advances on me "I am going to gut you like a fish boy,"now laughing and waving the knife in front of my face with deadly intent. I know there was no choice it is "kill or be killed, hoping to make him hesitate I say with a confidence I do not feel, "please mister do not make me kill you sir", as I hoped he stops and begins laughing, "well boy you sure got grit I will say that for you but I got to take your life, Adios boy". Reaching under my jacket I pull the .38 from its shoulder holster, point it dead centre on is dirty blue overalls and then without hesitation I close my eyes and start cocking the hammer back and pour lead into him, even though my gun is empty I cannot stop cocking back the hammer and pulling the the trigger the smoke wagon just clicks on empty chambers. It is all very surreal and seconds seem like minutes, I watch as the would be killer slides to the ground, a queer look of surprise on his face, "damn, kilt by a kid, but there are more of my kin coming along behind me you ain't got a chance". I watch him as the life leaves his eyes his evil ways finished forever come, I have killed my first man. I just stand there stunned and feeling sick, within moments people running towards me, I cannot take my eyes off the dead man frozen in shock. Marshall Bullock is one of the first to arrive, he grabs me looks me over, "You alright hardin are you hurt?", still in a daze I could not answer him, deciding Iam not physically injured he checks ov er the dead man. "Another one of the Evans crowd, you did right Hardin, that was a very bad man and he would have killed you sure".

The realization of what just happened hits me like a bucket of ice cold water, feeling sick, dizzy, I am trying not to pass out, I hear Megs voice asking Wade to get me to my room, she then sends one of the town boys to fetch the doctor. Staggering back to my room Wade more or less carries me, once they got me to my room Meg takes off my boots and has me lay down, both stay with me until the doc comes, after he checked me over to make sure I did not incur any injury he gives me some drops to help me sleep. I am just starting to drop off when there is a clamouring on the stairs, Wades hand came up fast with a gun in his hand, and I do mean fast. Bear and Ramon rush in looking like two old worried grannies, I smile "howdy boys good to see you," then I pass out into a deep drug induced sleep.

While I am in dreamland, there was a council of war downstairs, including both Marshals, Wade, Luke, Bear and Ramon, Bear was fit to be tied I was told later no one had ever seen him this angry. It was decided that I would never go out alone and there would always be a man at Megs, Meg came from the kitchen with 2, .44 caliber derringers, loading them she then put them in the pockets of her apron, sweet as she was Meg would fight, rumors were spreading that the Evans clan was on the move and are closing in on Glasgow. The fighting men at the table discuss where the best place for themselves if the attack did come, but all the men had been tested and have survived many gun battles, the meeting breaks upWade says he would take the first night, and if they heard gunshots, they are to come a running.

It is full dark when I wake up, still feeling the effects of the drug, I finally take notice the man sitting in my room, startled I moved quickly, I hear the calm voice of Wade telling me everything was alright, and I was safe, I look at him, it was Wade but not Wade. He had changed his clothing, now he is wearing a large black flat topped hat, black shining boots with big rowel spurs, like the vaquero's wear, but what got my attention was the 2-gun rig strapped around his waist, the guns showing care and use, I knew immediately this man was much more than a cooks helper. He brings me over a big mug of water knowing I will be thirsty, as I drink and enjoy the coolness of the water Wade tells me of the meeting and the decisions made and that I am never to go anywhere alone for awhile from the tone of his voice I knew he was not asking. "How do you feel about killing that man Hardin"? After a moment of thought I tell him the truth of it, how it made me sick, and ittroubled me greatly, how I watched the life drain from the mans eyes knowing it will haunt my nights. "Killing a man is serious, always avoid it if you can, but never hesitate if it needs doing, only draw your gun if you are going to use it, any man who enjoys killing is insane and worse then a hydrophobic dog." Just then we heard Megs footsteps on the stairs, my earth Angel is carrying a plate of sandwich's and coffee, I smile at her and tell her I am alright and that I was very pleased to see her and the food. Wade and I just inhale those sandwiches then coffee and enjoy some small talk with Meg. When coffee is finished, Meg said I was to try to get some more rest, Wade tells me to rest easy, he would close by. After my friends leave, I lay staring at the ceiling for a long while the thinking of the killing, the great, amazing men and women I have met recently. I notice my .38 is hanging on the bedpost close at hand for a quick grab, snapping it open I check and find fully loaded, the gun gives me a certain sense of I now thankfully fall back into a deep restful sleep.

To survive it is often necessary to fight and to fight
you have to dirty yourself
- George Orwell

CHAPTER 6

DEATH IN THE STREETS OF GLASGOW

Waking early I watch the sun coming up over the foothills, I always enjoy the peace of the morning before the world comes alive. On this day two great men will arrive in town, Marshal Hickok and Judge Hawthorne dam n big men in a big country. The judge was not a big man a bit on the lean side, pale blue eyes that missed very little, he carried himself with dignity and speaks in low and intelligent a well educated man and a man who was well respected by both good and bad men.

As I am enjoying Megs strong morning coffee Bear and Ramon come in, both are looking a bit worried, Meg brin both men coffee, Bear asks how I am holding up and if I would be going to the jail today. I tell them I am alright, just a bit worn, and damn right I am going, I gave my word, both men smile, Ramon said that he would be with me today, I notice he was carrying and extra gun today. A short time later Hickok rides in and talks with both marshals about the news from he got from Scout Jerry Potts, about the threats on my life. Marshal Thompson tells Hickok of my killing of the Evans brother Bob. Hickok smiled" I knew the moment I saw that lad he had sand he will be a known man all over the west one day you mark my words." "Count me in boys if you are needing me, I will be at the Red Dog playing some stud." Later that morning the stage gets in from Helena and the good judge dis embarked and goes directly to the jail. The marshals immediately brief him on recent events and the threats made towards me and their plans for keeping me alive.

Satisfied for the moment the Judge lugs his duffle over to Megs and requests a room, he usually stayed at the hotel but being a true western man wanted to be close in case of trouble, Meg happily welcomes him and shows him to his room just down the hall from mine.

Bear, Ramon and I take a stroll around town before heading to the jail, I get a lot of waves, smiles, and well dones, as we start walk our again I notice that a lot of the townspeople are now wearing weapons or had them close at hand, Ramon and I arrive at the jail and are waved into the cell area by Marshal Thompson. The half breed Crow is pacing this cell like a caged animal, muttering or praying in Ute, insanity creeping into his eyes, the two brothers are telling me how sorry they were begging me to forgive them, I look at them with hard eyes an say nothing. When I get to Evans cell, he looks at me with pure hatred, he had been told of my killing his brother, but is not accepting it as fact. Ramon showing his hard side tells Evans "Your pig of a brother made his try at killing the Jouencito and failed, Hardin filled him full of lead, we buried that brother of yours on boot hill and dug a second grave for you Senor so you can meet the devil together." Evans jumps to his feet in a frenzy screaming at us that he will not hang, his clan would get him out and burn the town down, smiling Ramon says" I do hope it is soon we got a reception committee waiting for them, if this town is attacked there will be many Evans souls for the diablo". We meet my friend Bill as we were coming out of the jail, I am feeling a bit shaky, I always feel this way after coming from the jail, as if waking from a nightmare or narrowly escaping a horrible death. Knowing it was just him and his Dad at the farm and his Pa is not a good hand with a skillet so I invite him to join me for lunch on which with a smile he immediately accepts. Our little group enters Meg's, the Judge is eating his lunch looking up he smiles and nods to us. Meg is really trying to fatten me upwith, venison steaks, potatoes and fresh bread and butter, and a huge pieces of apple pie. Western men take eating very serious and talk little eating their chuck, as on cue Meg brings out the coffee, the Judge finishing his meal walks over to our table coffee in hand introduces himself and asks if he can join us, not waiting for a response he grabs a chair over and sits down. Looking directly at me says, "would you be Hardin Steele young Sir," I nod a yes a bit fearful I might be in some sort of trouble for the killing of Bob Evans, "Master Steele I have spoken with the Marshals and seen the prisoners, the trail will start in a couple days we have to find an attorney for the accused, and I will be calling you to the witness stand to tell your story, I sadly cannot say more until the trail begins." "Young sir I am just down the hall, call on me anytime if you need assistance." I thank the Judge and ask shyly if am I in any trouble for killing that Evans man? Chuckling to himself, "Marshal Bullock has told me of the events a pure case of self defence, if it were me I would give you a medal, that villain needed killing, no more will be said on the matter". After he departs Meg said she is glad he is here now this ugly matter could finally be settled. "Hardin" Bear says to me," that there Judge is one tough old cob, done more then his share of Indian fighting, trailblazer in the big Rockies, he may not look it but like old Kit Carson he is a holy terror in a scrap".

After coffee, I ask Bear if Bill and I can go to the corals I wanted to check on old Hammerhead, Ramon said we could go but he would tag along and keep an eye on us. Bill and I head out Ramon a short distance behind, Bill starts asking lots questions on the shooting, I answer but leaving out the part of my terror and cowardness, "are you going to notch your gun Hardin?" "Not me Bill, none of the real gunfighting men do, only a tinhorn would notch his pistol, and anyway I did not care to keep count. He seems mildly disappointed but does not push it any further, we arrive at the livery, the livery man bids us welcome and tells me he is pleased that I was alive and kicking, not more than me I said, laughing. I brought Hammerhead a carrot, then spent some extra time time currying him being close to him gives me a comfortable feeling it is always the small things that are important, I then check on Pa's horse and the mules, all are getting fat and sassy, the livery man takes real good care of the stock, can tell a lot about a man how he treats horses and dogs.

Bill and I are now strolling the town, the bullies I had trouble with avoid us, and wisely so, Ramon is always within seeing distance, after a bit Bill says he has to head for home, I see him off and head to Meg's for supper. Luke was there talking to Meg," Howdy Hardin, looks like you are stuck with me tonight". Smiling I reply" suits me just fine Mr. Short, but I know most of the card playing is done at night, hope I am not keeping you from fleecing the sheep." Laughing loudly, "Hardin you sure are something, it is no bother at all, I need a night out of a smoky saloon, and it is nice here, kind of homey", I believe I see a quick touch of sadness reach his eyes. After another delicious meal and good coffee, Luke pulls out a deck of cards and we pass the evening away with him teaching me the different types of poker, and some card tricks, his slim hands working their magic with the cards. I am fascinated absorbing as much as I could, Meg came to the table and in her motherly voice says it was time I was hitting the hay, knowing better than to argue I get up to head to my room saying good night to them both. Luke hands me the cards, "you practice handling these cards and practice daily it will keep both your hands and mind sharp." Promising him I would I head to my room.

As it is my habit I wake early and after washing up and dressing go downstairs, Luke had gone but Wade was in the kitchen, I always felt safe when the quiet man with the 2 guns was near. Sitting over coffee and talking with the local breakfast crowd when we hear a horse thundering down the street horse the rider pulls up sharply in front of the marshal's office. Watching Wade, I see him take off his apron, then check both his guns and puts another short barrelled revolver in his belt at the back, he looks now like a man anxious for a scrap. A short time later Marshal Bullock arrives and tells us the Evans clan is close and will be here within a couple hours, word of the clan's arrival spreads quickly, within half an hour all my protectors and friends are all gathered at Meg's. After a short discussion these men being all being first rate fighters and professionals make their call, Hickok and Bullock would meet them in the street, Luke and Ramon would outside the saloon, Wade would be in front of Megs, this would put the riders in a deadly crossfire. Bear announced loudly and in a commanding voice" Pa Evans is my meat, you boys take care of the small fry let old Bear take the head of the snake" seems no one was willing to argue. Marshal Thompson unable to walk well pulls a chair just outside the jail door and places 2 shotguns against the wall behind him. The citizens were scurrying to shelter or their homes, all knowing the air soon would be heavy with lead. The jail is built of stone and was the most secure place in town it is decided where I would be and not to be left out Meg said she would go with me. The boys tried to talk her out of it, concerned for her safety, she held her ground and being a strong-willed woman the toughest most dangerous men in the west failed to sway her and reluctantly agree she can stay at the jail with me. I put on my shoulder holster and check my .38, it was fully loaded and ready. Meg and I are escorted to the jais over to the jail and greeted by Marshal Thompson, smiling he says" looks like it might be a right interesting day". I ask him if I could see the prisoners, Meg insisted on joining me, the men looked at Meg, the half breed just stares at us, a look of total brutal sanity on his face, the 2 brothers removed their hats and said nothing but as usual Evans was all mouth saying we will all be dead soon, he learsat Meg "hiding behind a woman's skirts now I see you whelp, I am going to enjoy taking your life boy". Meg reaches into her pocket and pulls a derringer cocking it and with a steady hand points it at the outlaws belly "you make your try and I will kill you, and you will not be the first man I killed." Calmly she un-cocks the weapon and replaces it in her apron, I just stand there my mouth hanging open. We rejoin the marshal who is pouring coffees we then and sit on move outside sit on the porch, Looking over the main street i can see all the men but Bear are in position, I tell the Marshal how much I respect these brave men and am fearful for their lives I do not want any of my friends dying today. The marshal says to me "it is much more than that Hardin, it is about law and order, good over evil, men and women sticking by their friends, part of the unwritten code of the west, it is what makes us strong one day it will be your role as leader and protector".

Waiting calmly in front in front of Megs Wade watches with a smile as a tough looking red headed man in need of a shave and haircut, with wide powerful shoulders and wearing a well worn two-gun rig walking over to him. "Howdy Red, if you are looking for action you are standing in the right spot, but son let me tell you she is going to get bloody today." Red smiles and hooks his thumbs in his belt, replies," Howdy Wade old scout, some friend you are, hogging all the fun in what may be the biggest scrap ever seen in the territory, I figure I will just keep you company for a spell, always did like watching you work."

The waiting is hard on me I am edgy and scared not for myself but the brave men out in the street willingly facing danger and maybe death all because of me. Finally, we see a cloud of dust from many horses which will be riding down the street within minutes, the men take up their positions and make a final check of their weapons, the smiles are gone now replaced with a look of hard determination, hunter's eyes, the Marshal then orders Meg and I inside.

Pa Evans is leading the pack, including him there were 16 hard cases to back his authority they ride boldly down main street. Marshal Bullock holds up his hand indicating for them stop, just as they all pull up the Judge comes out holding a big pistol by his side. The Judge speaks first, telling them who he was and would not permit taking of prisoners or any foul play. Old Pa Evans is as cool as ice, his eyes scan the setup, "I have come for my boy, I do not care of the others but my boy goes free or we will burn this here town down around your ears. "Before anyone could respond a savage wild scream splits the air, what I was to learn later was a Sioux war cry, all heads turned, Bear is walking down the middle of the street holding 2 Sioux 6 foot long war lances. "Evans, you low down mangy dog my name is Angus MacDonald they call me Bear, if you are man enough for it I am going to rip down your wheelhouse and rid the territory of you and your foul smell." Bear then rears back and with a mighty heave hurls the right hand spear which arches high in the air, heading directly at Pa Evans, the blade of the spear bites the ground quivering not more than 6 inches in front of Evan's horse.

Pa Evans looks at the spear and smiles thinking to himself finally a man worth fighting, he has never been beaten by any man with any form of weapon, killing or crippling all comers, he is going enjoy having the big man on his spear, he would get him low in the guts, watch him suffer and beg. Dismounting he pulls the spear from the dry ground lets out a fiendish almost insane laugh, "I know of ye Macdonald, you think yourself the big he wolf here about, well you don't scare me none, I have killed all sort of critters, today I recon it will be Bear meat for dinner." Bear does not respond, holding the spear in a 2 handed attacking position he starts walking slowly towards his enemy, the blood lust now almost overpowering the 2 big deadly men.

Now there is a time for talking and a time for fighting, both men go quiet now being in spear range, Pa knew his way around a spear, spent many years in Indian camps mostly Crow, what Pa did not know is that Bear chose his weapons carefully, he had been taught by the Sioux who were masters of the spear and before crossing the ocean had served with a distinguished Scottish regiment and was highly trained in the use of the bayonet. Suddenly Evans feints and quickly thrusts his spear forward aimed at Bears stomach, Bear barely steps aside in time, Evan's is fast, but Bear still gets a shallow cut along his ribs drawing blood for being sloppy. Pa Evans laughing now feeling it was going to be an easy kill, with incredible speed for a big man Bear aims his spear low then quickly slices up at Evans head, putting a 4-inch cut bellow his eye. Shocked Evans touches his hand to the cut, blood flowing freely on his fingers, he is not laughing anymore, he now knows he was fighting a man who can and will gladly kill him. Bear gives off a bit of a smile seeing Evans distress, Evans is in a blind fury now charges Bear hoping to overwhelm him and get the big man on the ground, it proves to be his last earthly mistake. Bear calmly waits, poised and ready, suddenly he adopts the on guard position, he then thrust the spear straight forward impaling Pa Evans deep in the stomach, Bear then pushes the spear head deeper into Evans and turns it before he pulls the spear head from his enemies dying body, blood and guts cover the now gory weapon . Kneeling beside the dying man the former Scottish officer takes his huge wicked looking tomahawk from his belt and with two mighty strokes he removes Pa's head clean off his body, picking up Pa's head by the hair he walks about 20 paces towards the attackers then rolls it towards the clan. With a chuckle address the combatants, 'Well boys I done cut off the head of the snake, now you boys will have to get er done."

All eyes had been on the titanic battle, now the clan members look towards each other, not sure what to do next. Four men faced Wade and Red, one looked out of place, slender, clean, wearing a black suit had gunfighter written all over him. Both Red and Wade knew him to be Ross Evans and that his gun was expensive to hire and he is not fussy on who he works for, rumoured to be one of the fastest an A rate gunslick. Ross looks down from his horse looks at Red, "Howdy Red, been awhile, you with this so called gunfighting bunch?" Red with his usual grim humour looks Evans over as if measuring for the slab, "Evans I never figured you to be this low down as to ride with this sorry looking bunch, kin or no kin." "Got to stick by your folks but I only came because there is a rumour the Traveller is here and if he is I aim to kill him." Red now outwardly chuckles "Ross old son it is your lucky day, turning his head to Wade, the Traveller just happens to be standing beside me." The men all go quiet, the Traveller is very well known, more than a gunfighter a man of mystery, a champion for those in need, his name given to him because he was always riding off to some distant destination, a living legend. Ross now turns his attention to Wade looking directly into the Traveller's intense penetrating green eyes knowing this was the man he is seeking, and after his brag has no choice but to face this man with a gun.

Calmly without even raising his voice the Traveller looks Evans directly in the eye says, "I will be waiting in the street, come and get some Ross", he then flicks his still smoking quirly into the street and moves to an open place in the street, both good and bad men moved back to give them room. Wade turns looking relaxed his arms by his side looking relaxed but muscles are coiled tight ready for fast action, then waits for his opponent. Evans climbs of his horse Red with a huge grin bids the gunfighter farewell, Ross frowns and then moves into the street stopping about forty paces from his opponent. For a moment, the duellists just stood quiet, getting themselves ready, Evans face showing nothing but a small sneer on his thin lips giving his facial features have a hawkish look, "So you are the great Traveller, figured by folks talking you would be seven-foot-tall breathing fire", chuckling at his humour," always figured them stories for bullshit." The Traveller just stands and waits, looking relaxed as if about to go for supper, his silence is beginning to unnerve Evans. "I recon it is, "Evans in mid sentence hoping to catch Wade off guard makes his draw it was very fast and extremely smooth, but as the barrel of his revolver clears his holster a .44 lead slug shreds his heart and a second enters his skull over his left eye, he did not even have time to know he was dead just folded and fell to the ground. The Traveller never taking his eyes off the clansmen ejects his empty shell casings and reloads returning his .44 to its well-worn holster.

There is a moment of stunned silence at the suddeness of Evans death, then as if by some unheard signal all the defenders quickly draw their weapons and point them at the grouped clansman, getting the drop on them, the Evans boys know now one mistake and they will all die on the dusty street.

The Judge breaks the silence "We do not want to kill anymore of you men and it is to nice of a day to die, surrender your weapons and pick up your dead, leave and never return, Tom is a rapist and mad dog killer do you really want to die for him?" One of the older men who looked more like a farmer than killer tells the other men to drop their weapons and to load up Pa and Ross. "you be right in your thinking we want no more truck with Tom we will be leaving and to hell with him and the hell with you." Hickok gives them one last word of warning "if I see any of you boys again I will shoot you on sight, you have my word on it." After the headless body of Pa and the deceased gunfighter were put over their saddles the new clan leader turns and slowly rides out of town the others following close behind, not one looked back as they rode out of sight.

Unknown Quaker to an intruder
-- I would'st not harm thee brother but thou standest
where I am about to shoot.

CHAPTER 7

THE TRIAL

There is no celebrating the victory the fighters collect themselves as a person must do after conflict, I think the whole town felt as I did, a vast sense of relieve and a genuine feeling of safety and security at last. The judge said he had much to do and the trail would begin at 9 tomorrow morning sharp latecomers will not be permitted in the cortroom.

Marshal Thompson hobbles back into the cell area and with a huge grin tells Evans and the rest that his Pappy and gunfighter cousin were both dead and the rest of the clan have been run out of town for good and the trail would be starting tomorrow morning. Evans sat on his bed a look of disbelief and fear on his scarred face, the brutal realization that he and his crew's fates are sealed, a chill went through him as he thinks of his last 13 steps.

Although the trouble seemed past it was decided until the trial is over I would be accompanied always in case a few of the varmints decide to sneak into town to do evil. The judge decides due to the size of audience for the trial he would hold court in the Red Dog saloon. Folks from all over the territory are starting to flood into town everyone is excited about the biggest trial and probable hanging in the territories history. The saloon fills quickly is packed to the rafters many people crowded by the doors and windows outside try to get a peak inside. I see my friend Bill at the door trying to get in, I go to the door and tell the deputy on guard that he is a friend and he could let him in. He just nods and held the door for my friend to enter, we sit together in front, I am overwhelmed by the fast-moving events around me, it is a great comfort to have Bill here supporting me.

The judge enters and we all rise he sits banging his gavel saying the bar is closed, men are to remove their hats and he would toss out anyone who caused a disturbance, and to make his point placed the big horse pistol on the table in front of him. A seedy lawyer most times drunk named John Franklin was chosen to defend the prisoners no other lawyer wanted to touch the case. My lawyer is a good looking strong young man, up from Texas, a gifted speaker with a sharp mind and wit, he volunteered his services after hearing the horror of my story, his name was Houston, the son of the legendary Texican Sam Houston.

Court is now in session and 12 good men from town were selected as the jury, and the charges of murder, rape robbery and destruction of property.

I am really nervous knowing I will be called to the stand to testify very shortly, when called to tell my story, Bill gives me one of his big smiles, "get er done Hardin." When I am seated, Mr. Houston askes me to tell my tale, looking around the room seeing all my new friends there gave me the confidence to speak up, I tell my story as clear as I could remember it, there were no questions from lawyer Franklin, Bear and Ramon were called up and said their piece, Mr. Houston said he had no further questions or witnesses, Mr. Franklin put Evans on the stand and he told a bunch of lies as to having nothing to do with charges against him saying they found the horses and mules wandering and gathered up to bring in to find the owner. Mr. Houston then asks him how then my Pa's shotgun and belongings that were found in their camp, Evans gives a weak excuse, he was then excused and returned to his seat. Each lawyer gave a final summation, Lawyer Franklin gave it a good try but the evidence is to damning to be effective. Mr. Houston a superior public speaker gives a rousing speech of evil and injustice, the evils of these men and then pounding his fist on the table demanded the defendants be took out and hung as soon as possible, the crowd erupted in cheers and applause, the judge is banging his gavel demanding order.

After order is maintained Judge Hawthorne issues strong threats of jail anyone if there are anymore disturbances in his courtroom. He then turns to the jury explaining to them their options and responsibilities, he said the jury was to go to the back empty storeroom and find a verdict. The men of the jury hesitated to rise, the 12 men looked at each other and all nodded in agreement. The foreman stood and addressed the judge "your honour I recon we all agree that these prisoners are guilty as sin on all charges and we find them guilty as hell they all be hung until dead and good riddance.

The judge has the prisoners stand "You four men have been found quilty on all charges brought against you, I sentence you all to death by hanging to be executed at 10 am in 3 days hence, Marshal Bullock will oversee the preparations, may God have mercy on your worthless souls" The half breed Crow goes berserk took 3 men to restrain him, the brothers did not speak but were white faced shakey and scared looking, Evans stares at me cursing me out, making useless threats, pure hatred in his voice. The judge then ordered the marshal to return the prisoners to their cells, the trial was over.

Just as soon as the prisoners were taken away and people got up to leave the Judge pounds his gavel loudly and tells them to sit down there is one more important matter to be taken care of before court is dismissed and the bar opened. With that statement people returned to their seats most curious as to what the judge has on his mind, Bill and I looked at each other neither one of us having a clue what was happening.

When all is quiet he looks at me and asks me in a gentle voice to come up and we will have a talk. Taking the chair, I had testified in I look to the judge, all was deathly quiet in the room. "Hardin, I first want to say that you are a brave and intelligent lad, you have showed a lot of nerve for someone your age", he then asks me" So mister Steele where do you go from here do you have plans for your future". Looking to Marshal Hickok I reply "your Honour I want to one day become a lawman like the Mr. Hickok and Mr. Bullock, and Marshal Thompson, bring justice and safety to the territory", there was a general sound of approval from the audience the Judge smiled and gives me an approving nod. Next, he asks me if I had any kin, I told him no that all my family was dead on the plains. "with a very serious look he continues "What are we going to do with you Hardin, you need schooling and a home, safety until you can saddle your own broncs which I believe will not be long", I interject "Judge do I have any say in the matter of my future?". Smiling again says "of course you do son, say your piece".

I hesitate, nervous, then throwing all caution to the wind say," I would like to stick with Mr. Macdonald and Senior Valdez, they are right smart and good men I could learn much from them." Well old Bear sputters and just about falls off his seat, Ramon has an amused but shocked smile on his face, sittingsitting speechless. The saloon then erupts with loud laughter and many shouts of encouragement, old Bear is looking a bit ill. The judge orders quiet, and has Bear and Ramon stand, "well men what say you, will you take responsibility for the lad, you would be officially his adopted uncles." Old Bear a man prepared for almost anything was caught totally flat footed, finally answers "Judge I believe there are much better folks than me for this job, but I have come to know the lad, he has sand and skill, I am honoured and willingly accept the role of uncle, and swear I will always do what I think best for him." Nodding the Judge directs his attention to Ramon, "well Senior Valdez will you agree to be this lad's guardian." "Si Judge I will do my very best to make him a strong and man of knowledge, I am much pleased with this great honour". Judge Hawthorne smiles "all settled then Bear Macdonald and Ramon Valdez are officially charged with the upbringing of

Mr. Hardin Tomas Steele, case closed, court dismissed, bar is open". There was a loud cheer and loud laughter, much hand shaking and congratulations, everyone seems to be very pleased with the decision, even Wade gives a rare smile and laugh, Meg of course is smiling and crying.

When the student is ready the Teacher will appear
- The Buddha

CHAPTER 8

THE HANGING AND THE
MEETING OF BLACKHAND

That evening Bear, Ramon and I sit over coffee and discuss matters, as soon as the hanging was over we are going to head to a cabin by the Yellowstone river, spend the upcoming winter days there, I have been thinking some on it and say to them I would like to sell 3 of the mules and keep my favorite horse Blackjack, he mean as sin, smart as a fox and as fast jackrabbit quick and Pa's big chestnut Morgan. The selling of the mules was agreed to and Bear says he will damn well get me good price from the old cheapskate at the livery, later we will stroll over to Perninsky's and get outfitted. I always carry the .38 now, it gives me a feeling of security and now I considered it my good luck charm, Bear heads to the livery to dicker on the mules, I feel he enjoys the haggling, Ramon said he needed to pick up some teaching tools, that got me wondering some about what I would be learning. I go up to my room and get Pa's shotgun checking it over and making sure it is unloaded I head for the blacksmith shop. The blacksmiths name is Will Sampson huge but kind looking man with an easy smile, as I enter he looks up from his work" Howdy lad what can I do for you?" "Mr. Sampson, could you cut down the barrels on this here shotgun? I can pay." Taking the shotgun looking it over and checking it was empty nodded "sure son I will take care of it right away." "You would be the Steele boy, that sure was some trial, giving off a booming laugh. "I hear you got yer self tied up with that old knot head Bear, he and I go way back, trapped, fought Indians, rapids and critters together, no better man to be in a scrap with. "Other than old Panther I recon Bear is the best plainsman and woodsman in the territory or most anywhere else, be sure to learn all you can from him, he knows more about scouting and survival than any man I know and I know a few, even the Indians respect his skill and fear him". I knew what Will was saying is true, these were things I will need to know to survive the western lands, when the job on the shotgun is done I offer to pay, "no need son, letting out a laugh, "watching Bear yesterday was pay enough, I figure that is the first time I ever saw the Bear treed like an old he coon" still laughing to himself walks off towards the livery.

The next 2 days pass quickly there is plenty to do, finally the day of the hanging arrived, a crude platform has been built a large beam with 4 rope nooses attached to it, the floor of the platform was rigged to open when the pin holding the trap door it was removed, and then below a short brutal neck snapping drop. I get dress in my best Sunday duds, shine up my boots, not sure why but getting properly dressed seemed appropriate for the event. When I come down for breakfast the whole gang is there, Meg in her glory feeding and bringing coffee, I am jittery and on edge, but seeing my hero's there lightened my mood for a short while, the men are talking among themselves but in quiet serious tones. The time comes to go, we all get up and upon leaving Meg's see there is a large crowd already gathered we head as a group to the gallows, I meet Bill on the way and he joins us, he is very excited about the big doings. I have mixed feelings, I am pleased the end is finally near and the four men who killed my family will die publicly and horribly, but with there deaths there is no more of my past or family, that chapter in my life will be closed forever.

When we get to the site people respectfully move aside to let me and my group of friends move to the front, Meg would not come, she told us she had seen a man hung before and did not wish to see another. It was almost a carnival atmosphere, people came in from everywhere, kids playing and running through the crowd, vendors selling beer and treats, hangings were big entertainment in those days. Finally the four doomed men are led out and placed standing before the nooses, then are asked if they had any final words. The half breed Crow has gone totally insane under restraint just curses and spits drool running down his chin, the 2 brothers tell me how sorry they are then said goodbye to each other before the hoods were placed over their heads, Evans looks right into my eyes, the sneer is back, "well looks like you won kid, but I ain't sorry at all, and one day one my kin will put you under, now you just watch how a real man dies". The prince of the hangmen George Maledon then placed the hood over Evans head and the four nooses were placed around their necks and set to the proper so to snap the neck when the rope stopped. The town preacher said a quick prayer, after the amen the Prince pulls the lever the men drop together, the half breed and one of brothers die quick necks snapping cleanly, the other 2 take a long time, their necks did not break and struggled and strangled, Evans went last of course, a brute and pure evil man but he died game.

The sight sickens me I ask Bear to get me away, he leads me away quickly but as I get to an alley I had to run in to puke, I keep throwing up until there was nothing left in my stomach, I come out of the alley shame faced, but feeling much better we then continue down the street. Bear said we would be leaving town in 2 days, and like a mother hen suggested I get rest, Meg walks me up and after fussing over me a bit leaves me alone with my thoughts. I lay there on the bed my hands clasped behind my head, my Ma used to say a door closes and a window opens, it was just how I felt, my family and former life is gone with the hangings, and the start of my new life with Bear and Ramon was about to begin and I can not wait to get on the trail. Time in town is getting short, I seek out all my new friends to say my goodbyes and thank them, inviting them to come visit anytime, Luke gave me a couple decks of new cards and tells me practice, Mr. Pernisky gave me a sling for my shotgun so I could carry it easy like a sling over my back, I mosey over to the Marshal's office and said my goodbyes over a cup of their horrible coffee.

Finally, the morning comes to depart, I am terribly excited but trying not to show it, I talk to Wade over breakfast, he tells me he would be riding by ever so often for a visit and see how my education was coming along. The most difficult to say goodbye to is Meg, I love the woman as a son would his own mother, she packed me a lunch figuring I might starve to death on the trail, we hug and cry, then composing herself stands back and hands me one of her derringers, always good to have some insurance she tells me, smiling with tears in her eyes. Befor leaving I say to myself this is my town now and if asked this is my home station, "you need anything Meg anything at all you just holler I will come a running." I walked through the door hearing it slam behind me for the last time I knew it was time to be going

Everything is ready I just have to crawl up on old Hammerhead, he gave me a bit of a frisky bucking for ignoring him then forgives me, we ride out heading west to the mountains, I surely want to see those high snows covered peaks

We make good time, the horses adjusting quick all seemed happy to be traveling, it was going take us awhile to get to the cabin, we fall in to a camp routine quickly, seems I was volunteered as cook, but I did not mind, I enjoy cooking. We are three days from Glasgow when around mid morning we ran smack dab into a bunch of Indians about 8 strong. I have never seen a wild Indian before and am both scared and curious, I see Bear and Ramon draw their rifles I pulled my shotgun from its sheath with sweating hands, Bear tells me they were Sioux and he knew this bunch but be careful and never show fear, Indians only respect courage. I will never forget as I watch them ride towards us, proud, strong, somewhat dignified heads held high riding on good looking mustangs, all are dressed in fine looking leather, holding spears with decorations and scalps hanging from them some looking real fresh. A very large feathered headed Indian catches my eye, I suspect he is the big man of the bunch, his manner left no doubt he is a great man and fearsome. Greeting us in Sioux and using some form of hand talk, which left me with no idea as to what he was saying but got the impression he was doing some old-fashioned bragging, the leaders name I learn name was Black Hand and is a great warrior and leader of his people. Then switching to broken English, he asks Bear what a small man like him was doing in Sioux country, only big men should ride on his peopless lands. I have no idea what the hell was going on, but I watch Ramon he is calm, but Ramon was always calm, the 2 big men dismount and walk towards each other, looking sternly at each other, it was Bear who broke first, roaring out a laugh clasps Black Hands arm in greeting, Black hand is smiling also, seems they are old friends and I just witnessed Indian humour, I am much relieved. The younger braves ride over to me checking me out, bumping their horses into old Hammerhead, remembering what Bear told me I looked at them and put on my best brave face, Hammerhead having little patience screams out a challenge and charges hitting the horse closest full on then lets them other horses now he is up for more fight, the Indians wisely decide to give us a bit of room. Black Hand invites us to his camp, they were hunting meat and had much food in the village, Bear accepts immediately so we all ride off together this will my first experience in an Indian village.

Just short of the Indian camp we pull up looking down on the village, it was set up in a ravine or known to some as a coulee, not a big camp I counted 14 tepees, a small slow moving river flows close by, the buffalo hide tepees are decorated in brightly coloured and Sioux symbols, I can see children playing, women going about their tasks, men lounging but always alert for danger. We start down the slope, by now they know of our coming and the whole bunch has gathered to greet us, Bear is waving and talking Sioux, seems them Indians hold old Bear in high regard. After we dismount and strip our gear, we let the animals join the pony herd, then we go over to Black Hands tepee, Bear brings out coffee and a big bag of sugar knowing the Indians like their coffee sweet. Ramon is well known to Sioux as a wise and powerful warrior, but they seemed most curious about me, I figure they were wondering what a pup like me was doing with the big dogs. Introductions are formally made, up close Black Hand looks even more imposing, a fine-looking man, 2 long black braids run down past his shoulders, he has some terrible looking scares I figure a bear attack, his dark eyes seem to penetrate into a persons soul, I know without being told he is a great man and admired amongst his people. Black Hand has a son named Grey Wolf, who is a couple years older than me, we look each other over then for some unknown reason I smile and he smiles back, laughing together he takes me on a tour me around the camp, as with most Indian camps it was the smells that gets your attention first, bear grease and smells I could not identify have me breathing through my mouth a bit, but as most things you get used to it, the camp is set up neatly and cleaner than many future villages I would be in later in life. Grey Wolf could speak a bit of English, as we walk he tells me they were Oglala Sioux and his father was Chief and an honoured warrior which he will be one day. We come up to a bunch of young braves playing games, but these games are used as training to become warriors and take coup. I watch them practice with the bow and arrow, amazed by their skill, some are running foot races, and there is an unorganized game with sticks and a ball going on and it looked mighty rough and tumble looks like great fun . Grey Wolf leads me over to others and invites me to join them, I try the bow and arrow first, I have never used one before, Grey Wolf shows me how to hold and aim it, my first arrow missed the target by a mile, that got a lot of laughs, my second was close, and with the third I hit the edge of the target, I figured best quit while I was ahead. It was the footrace I want to have a go at, back home I was the best, I love to run. Grey Wolf and 3 other boys say they will run against, off we go Grey Wolf is the fastest but I am sticking with him, with about 20 yards from the finish I open er up and beat Grey Wolf by 3 strides, there are a few approving nods and maybe a bit of respect. After catching my wind, I ask my new friend if we could join the game, I slightly regretted it a few minutes later, those Sioux boys like it rough, I strip off my shirt and we get into it, seems everything was legal except punching, I got knocked down more than a few times, did some knocking down myself, hitting with the stick was ok, so I took a few wacks which I will feel later. I never had so much fun in my short life, I realized I liked and embraced the rough and tumble lifestyle of the Sioux.

It was getting on to supper time and we head back to Black Hands lodge, the men are outside sitting in a circle, speaking in a mixture of Sioux, Spanish, sign and whatever language Bear spoke. Grey Wolf and I join the circle but do not speak, he explains a bit of what was being said, I figure they are all on the brag and swapping lies. Black Hand's wife and daughter bring out food in wooden bowls, the guests are always served first, food is eaten with our fingers, it is a buffalo type of stew and a flat bread, after all the exercise I got I am famished, but watching the others eating slowly I do the same. When the meal is finished, Black Hand asks Grey Wolf how the games went, he responds in Sioux and with much embellishment tells him of it, I believe I saw his eyes sparkle a couple times but,his face impassive as if made of stone. Black Hand stands and in a voice, that would make the ground shake says that there would be a council fire, and all would hear a great story by Bear and they would smoke the pipe. The Sioux enjoy a good story and were very good story tellers and very eloquent speakers, there was great excitement in the camp, the drumming and chanting started and the whole village gathered around the big fire, Grey Wolf sat with me we talk and he translates best he can, I know this may sound strange but I could almost taste the magic in the air, Ma would have loved this .

Black Hand rises first and tells the story of how he and Bear became blood brothers and how he got his name of Bear Killer. Years back when Black Hand was a young brave he suddenly came face to face with a huge grizzly, the bear charged him, he got 2 arrows into the bear but it did not even slow the huge animal down, leaving him only his knife to fight with, he was starting to chant his death song as he fought a losing battle with the beast, then the great spirit sent Bear Killer.

Bear was unable to use his rifle in fear of hitting Black Hand in the swirling battle so he up and grabs his big knife and they both battle the animal, steel against huge sharp claws and teeth that bear, both men taking many wounds but finally finish off the grizzly. Black Hand had been seriously wounded and near death, although hurt badly Bear Killer made a travois and brings him back to the village. It was mesmerizing listening to the chief speak, listening to the drums, the big fire, some of the women dancing and chanting, felt like I have entered a place of fantasy and magic.

Bear rises and the 2 brothers grab each other forearms in friendship and brotherhood. Black Hand takes his seat and Bear speaking Sioux begins his tale, which was of all things about me, he tells of my family, the outlaws, my killing of the Evans man, with that there was a gasp from the audience and Grey Wolf was now looking at me in a new light, he tells of the gun battle and how he and Ramon were now Uncles and would raise me to be strong and proud like our Sioux brothers, they all seem very delighted with the story. Black Hand looks to me and nods his regal head in approval, and in English says," you will be known as a great Sioux warrior one day, I have sen it in my visions". I am very proud at that moment my chest is stuck out like a strutting rooster. The stories end and the drums changed to a faster tempo all the native ladies are starting to dance in a circle chanting and singing, I notice a couple young and most beautiful maidens keep looking my way, Ramon who misses nothing is smiling hugely looks at me", careful now Hardin they will lure you into marriage", many in the circle giggled, I just sat there glad it was night so they could not see my blushing and red ears.

When the festivities are over we go to Black Hand's lodge and settle in for some rest, there were so many new things running through my mind it took me a long awhile to drop off to sleep, damn I love the wilderness.

The next morning, we get the stock and gear together and say our goodbyes, Grey Wolf and I have become immediate friends, I tell him I would like to come back and visit again. Yes, he says you are Kola to Grey Wolf, good friend, come often we will go hunting. While riding away I keep looking back to the village as if by magic it would disappear, I was surely enjoying this new life. I ride up to Bear, asking did you and Black Hand really kill that Grizzly, he then shows me a very large bear tooth on a leather string hanging around his neck, sure enough he says and old Black Hand has the other, I tell him I thought he was called Bear because he was as big and hairy as one, Ramon and I laugh so hard we almost fell off our horses, Bear looked back at us with grump then a smile.

A few more days traveling brings us to Bears cabin, we were just on the edge of the mountains, a sweet water creek runs close to the cabin, beyond lay small lakes, beaver ponds and huge stands of trees. The cabin was mostly built of stone, good protection from 3 sides and a good field of fire for shooting downhill. The corral is behind the cabin and provides good protection for the animals, old Bear sure knew what he was about. After unloading our packs, I lead the horses and mule to the corral, not only is it a safe spot but opened into a small meadow with plenty of grass and water. Entering the cabin, I find it is dark and cool, a good comfortable place, handmade furniture and beds, I realize I am now a long way from Megs comfortable home. I am finally home.

May the stars carry your sadness away, May the
flowers fill your heart with beauty, may hope forever
wipe away your tears, and above all,
may silence make you strong.
- Chief Dan George

CHAPTER 9

MY EDUCATION BEGINS

Ramon as it turns out is an educated man, taught by the priests in old Mexico, well read with an excellent knowledge of history and literature, can speak Spanish and English fluently, also understands Latin and some western Indian dialects. As if that is not enough, he is an excellent rifle shot, a master with a blade and a lightning fast dangerous pistolero. Bear although formally educated has a totally different set of skills and they had nothing to do with books, he can track a skeeter through a rain storm, excellent hunter and marksman, knew things like how to survive in bad weather, could talk sign as well as any Indian he is a man that is in his element travelling the plains or woods. I have much to learn and determined to learn as much as I can, but the thing of it all I am learning from the very best.

I am certainly earning my keep, Bear sees to that, my chores are many, cutting and storing wood for the upcoming winter, looking after the livestock, bringing water to the cabin, Bear insists we keep a couple barrels of water inside the house in case of attack, this is Blackfoot and Crow country and they can get right ornary. On top of all that there is book learning, mathematics, and am encouraged to read every night before bed. Most days I spend in the woods with Bear, learning new skills every time we go out on the hunt. As an example we were hunting a white tailed deer and sneaking up downwind of him, Bear tells me to watch his tail if it flicks tail just stop dead still they will look around before eating again, the surest shot is just behind the shoulder where the heart and lungs are but they can still run a fair distance before dropping, the neck shot the best, he teaches me how to skin and cut up the meat, and over the winter teaches me how to make buckskin clothing and moccasins from the dear hides and animal pelts. I am getting pretty handy with the spencer .56, it holds 7 shots and can knock down about anything, Bear makes me do most of the shooting, half jokingly saying I miss I do not eat.

Ramon he is very patient and will keep explaining until I understand this learning stuff ain't so bad, I have learned of the Greeks, Romans, Spanish cultures and of learned men, like Plato, Epictetus and Aristotle, the planets and stars and constellations become known to me. Math is my most difficult subject, I recon I have no mind for figures, practicing with the cards Luke gave me helps a great deal with my sums, Bear shows me of all the cheating tricks of cardplayers, I get to where I can read and remember cards, can bottom deal or set up a deck with the best of them, knowledge is power.

One day late fall I can see Bear is becoming more watchful and is scanning the hills more often, telling me says we would stick close to the cabin today. "What is it Bear, Indians?" "Blackfeet I recon but they may just pass us by we have run em off a few times before, them damn Blackfeet always like a good scrap". I went and bring extra wood in, check the water barrels, they are both full we all then checked to make sure our weapons are all fully loaded, and extra ammunition was close at hand. Bear feels they were close and decides it was time to secure the door and close the window shutters, the shutters have slits like crosses cut into them to fire through. Bear puts me by one of the windows and tells me to keep my aim low because I will be shooting down hill. As I stand at the window I start feeling fear, mouth is dry and my hands sweating, just then I see a slight movement to my left, I tell Bear, "will not be long now Hardin, stay calm, pick your targets and shoot straight". I look outside again and as if by magic 20 warriors come out of the grass, shrieking war cries firing bows and rifles. I am anxious to fire but Bear says to wait until they are closer, I figured they were close enough for a sit down dinner now. Bear fires dropping a brave, all of us are firing now, an Indian runs directly at me I let go with the right barrel of the shotgun he drops to the ground in mid stride he screams as the flesh from his face is ripped away by jagged lead. Overwhelmed by our firepower and accuracy the Blackfeet braves retreat, 4 lay still in front of the cabin, I knew others had been wounded. I ask Bear if they would be back, "Maybe but I don't recon, their medicine was not good today, it is almost tradition to try to catch us once before the snow flies, by evening we knew they were gone, I had killed my second man.

There is no more Indian trouble, shortly after the raid the temperature drops and the snow startes, winter is upon us. The work and education never stopped, there were many skills to learn about winter survival, Bear shows me how to make snowshoes, and helps me with making my buckskin cloths and moccasins. The most important lesson is never rush or panic in cold weather, if you worked up a sweat, it would freeze to your skin and you were a goner. Montana winters can be brutal you learn to adapt to survive or you die. We still hunt most days but go far afield as we did not want to scare the game close to the cabin, there may a need if the winter went long. As we hunt Bear never stops passing on his what seemed unlimited knowledge of the wilderness. I now knew things like how to select a camp, where to make a fire, the different animal tracks, the building of a snow cave if no other shelter could be found in a blizzard, keep your senses sharp for danger there is always danger from, Indians, outlaws, nature and animals in untamed country. Hunting is good but we are running short on supplies, most importantly the coffee is getting low. There is the town of Red Creek about a 4-hour ride in good weather, about 2 weeks before Christmas we all saddle up and head for town, I still have money left from selling the mules and I want to get the boys presents and have a real family type Christmas. We arrive in the small town it is a sunny but cool day, Ramon went for the supplies, leaving Bear I go in search of presents. Surprisingly there is a small shop that had books for sale, this is a rare thing I enter and after a long search I find a book written in Spanish by a monk on the Aztecs and pyramids of Mexico I purchase it hoping Ramon has not read it yet, I have been racking my brains on what to get Bear, what does one buy a uncivilized man, remembering that Bear said his kin came from Scotland, I return to the book store and find him a book of poems by the great Scottish poet Thomas Aird then I mosey over to the general store. As I enter the smells remind me of Mr Perniskys general store, all general stores have the pleasant smells of leather oil, and spices, I look around and find a beautiful solid silver belt buckle I think Ramon might like. I was about to give up on Bear when I spotted a big ceramic mug with a scenic picture of a Grizzly on the front, after picking up some stick candy for myself and asking for some extra paper for wrapping I leave the store my presents hidden in a burlap bag, I am feeling very pleased with my choices hope the boys like them. I find Bear and Ramon outside the marshal's office palavering with a couple locals, we decide to treat ourselves to a home cooked meal and then leave right after our meal head back to the cabin, Bear senses weather may change and he is rarely wrong, I sure enjoy my meal and not having to cook, we finish with dried apple pie and coffee.

The days are passing quickly Christmas day finally arrives, Bear had gone out the day before and brought back a couple nice fat geese, they will make a great supper. After chores and morning coffee I bring out my presents wrapped the best I could do. I watch the men opening their gifts both smiling like big kids, Bear is very pleased with the mug, but I really hit the nail on the head, Bear holds the book fondly as if it were fragile big man big heart. Ramon to my pleasure has not read the book I got him, and makes a big deal about the silver buckle Ramon has a great fondness for silver, Bear says a big thanks, they were very thoughtful gifts and the nicest presents he ever got. I am beginning to feel a bit rejected when both men start to laugh and bring out my gifts. With great excitement, I open Ramon's gifts first, my first gift is a beautiful double edged knife with an ivory handle and a beautiful leather sheath to hold it on my belt it, also he gives me a book called the The Republic written by Plato, a type of book a man has to read 3 or 4 times before comprehending any of it but once it sinks it it is worth the time. Bear hands me a brand-new Russian .44 handgun, one of the best sidearms of the day and with it a hand tooled belt and holster, and to make the day even sweeter a huge bag of mixed candy for my sweet tooth. I am totally overwhelmed and thank them both many times over. We spend the day loafing around cooking the goose for supper, sing a few Christmas carol in a mixture of Spanish, Scottish and English, everyone has a favorite Christmas memory this will always be mine.

A couple years slide by, I have grown considerable, almost 6 feet in moccasins, wide shoulders, narrow hips, a bit lean not filled out to my man weight only yet, dressed now in clothing I hand made, my hair is a dark blond needing a cut and my skin is deeply tanned front frontier living. I am learning my lessons well, Ramon and practice with the blade and side arms, the Mexicans are artists with a knife. Bear is now letting me hunt alone, I know every inch of country within 50 miles, and have become skilled in hunting and tracking, very rarely coming home without meat. It is such a day in the bush I am tracking a big buck, but feeling uneasy, my instincts are telling me to be cautious, my senses alert to trouble. Staying in the treeline I move slowly then I backtrack my trail for a bit, finding nothing but still feeling a threat was near I remain cautious. Suddenly there is the scrape of buckskin on a branch and sensing movement behind me, I sidestep quickly, a spear tip go by my stomach just missing slicing open my gut by mere inches, I swing my rifle butt catching a young Blackfoot brave in the stomach doubling him over then i butt stoke him a hard blow to the chin, he was now out colder than a January morning. Looking down at the young brave I see he is about my age, slightly built, I imagine he thought I was a pilgrim and an easy scalp. It is not in my nature to kill so I place the young warrior on his back, remove his moccasins and place them on his chest then take his spear as a throphy and head back to the barn quick he may have friends around close by.

When I get back I tell the old boys of my encounter, they are pleased and proud, Bear pats me on the back, "you were lucky it was a young one a more experienced brave might have got that fine long hair". I did understand if the brave had been older it would have been a close thing, very close, I vowed to work harder until all my skills are honed to a fine point.

We will on occasion get visitors, old mountain men, come to drink corn licker and swap stories, I always listen close wanting to learn more but for the most part heard just the outlandish windy stories mountain men brag normal as breathing. One day a Kickapoo Indian comes to the cabin, they are traveling Indians always headed someplace, always searching and learning, he tells stories of the many things he had seen, strange places of magic and mystery, of the bones of animals of giant size, old civilizations. I would have enjoyed talking more with that Kickapoo.

One day while Ramon and I are practicing with the blades, Bear says there is a rider coming, although still a long distance away Ramon looks shrugs and said it is the Traveller, no rider sits a better horse. He rides in and howdy's are shared all around, looking at me I think he was surprised at how much I have grown, "Howdy Hardin you have grown some, getting near man sized ", I take it as a great compliment, he looks much the same lean and dangerous maybe a few more wrinkles around the eyes. After supper, he tells of his adventures, he cleaned up a tough mining town in Colorado, had a couple Indian fights scouting for the Calvary, took a trail herd from Texas to Kansas. He stays with us a couple weeks, doing his share of chores and hunting. He notices my .44 and asks if I was any good with it, Ramon answered for me that I was a pretty good with fast hands and a steady eye. For the next 2 weeks Wade and I practice with the pistols, I was good but no where near his caliber, but he teaches me a lot about gunfighting. Things like in close quarters just point like you would your finger and fire fast, make sure you are never have the sun in your eyes, how to recognize boxed in setup. "Watch the eyes and how a man stands it will tell you much, in bars or saloons put your back to the wall and do not sit in chairs with arms as they can get in the way of your draw, at night try to stay in the shadows, always be watchful Hardin" It was great to have Wade at the cabin, I like this quiet mysterious man, and wanted to be like him in many ways. As is his way one morning without notice saddles up says some quick goodbyes and with a wave, says "see you down the trial boys" and is off to his next adventure. My life pretty much fell into a routine of work, practice and my studies. By the time, I was 16 my skills were honed fine and I figured I can hold my own with any man, not knowing at the time these very skills will be severely tested andin the very near future.

To improve is to change;
to be perfect is to change often.
- Winston Churchill

CHAPTER 10

THE POSSE

I am sitting in front of the cabin enjoying a little lazy sun time, Bear and Ramon are both away for a few days and I was minding the store. Around mid morning I spy a lone rider riding dead straight towards the cabin be he nears the cabin, I duck inside and grab my sawed of shotgun, I fill both big tubes with nasty lead buckshot holding the big gun I point it at the ground and wait outside enjoying the warm sun.

I look him over as he stops in front of me, a man of medium build, fair haired, showing some sunburn on his neck, the only thing that was not ordinary about this man is he had very pale blue eyes almost grey and he was wearing a town marshals badge.

Pulling up in front of me he looks down at me he asks, "I am looking for Bear Macdonald, I am Marshal Sam Teale out of Silver Creek, banks been robbed and couple town folks got killed, in need of a guide, heard he was the best." "You are right there but old Bear is away may be gone a week or more, I know this country like the back of my hand I could guide for you." Frowning looking as if he needed to cuss some replies, "you look a bit wet behind the ears boy, I cannot have youngsters guiding this posse these are dangerous men, wiped out to a man two other town posses, don't think I can chance it." "Marshal if you recon you do not need me fine, but I have been taught by Bear and I am near as good as him on the prairie or the woods, I been in an Indian Attack killing me a Blackfoot." "In fact, you might have heard of me, I am Hardin Steele, nephew to Bear and Ramon, and if you ever call me boy again I will pull you off that nag and pin your ears back, now do you want me to guide or not?"

My name struck him like he had been slapped, everyone in the Territory had heard my story and over the years it has grown into legend and gets more embellished with every telling.

Thinking it over for a few minutes made his decision "grab up your gear Mr. Steele, we need to be riding", I did not miss the sarcasm but I choose to ignore it.

I decide to ride Sampson a long-legged fast mule, fast sturdy and could go all day and night, me and him we got along right fine but he did not take to strangers and is a damn fine watch dog I will be keeping him close at night, trusting him to alert me of trouble. I put the sling over my back and slide the shotgun in, I had sold Pa's .56 and bought a new 44.40 Winchester had it in a rifle holster ready to be attached to the saddle, I strap on my Russian .44 and belt knife, I then stuff extra shells into my pockets. Got out my bed sheet and rolled my slicker and put my extra moccasins in it, with my canteen and some travelling jerky I was ready to go.

The Marshal did not look to pleased seeing old Sampson and more than a little surprised how well I was armed being a townsman he knew little the value of mules, but wisely said nothing.

Within twenty minutes after I agreed to guide we are riding back to meet up with the posse, I leave the boys a note, GONE SCOUTING FOR POSSE BE BACK DIRECTLY

H.

so, they would not worry, old grannies, the both of them.

A short time later we hook with the posse, there are eight men plus the marshal and myself, I am not interested in their names but I quickly to size up each and everyone of them. Something I learned from Luke Short, use your eyes and your mind, you can read most people like cards, and as is in poker keep your mouth shut and ears open, play it close to the vest, amazing what a feller can learn.

A couple of the men looked like town toughs there hoping to hang or kill someone the bigger and dumber looking of the two is named Ned, he winks at his buddy and with a mean grin starts right off digging in the spurs, "Marshal, could you not find any grown men for this here posse, this here youngster may be calling for his mommy if we run into them robbers," letting out a horse laugh, his buddy laughing with him as followers do, the other men stay quiet and wait to see what I will do. Reachingback and casually pull out the shotgun cocking both barrels I lay it across my saddle, looking at Ned and in a low dangerous tone say, "Well Ned, I recon this old shotgun does not care how old a man is to pull the trigger, be right nasty at this range, I will say this once only, leave me be, I am going to be to busy for these games, but I promise you one thing Neddy boy, after this is over I am going to give you a licking and send you home tail between your legs." Neddy looks displeased "I can wait, if you fight me and I will cripple you youngster, and I am looking forward to, I hate uppity youngsters."

I say no more but ride out front of the posse to check for any sign of the outlaw band, and I find sign of them within minutes, the tracks show a very clumsy attempt to conceal their direction, making it easy to follow it was to easy and I did not care for it one damn bit, my instincts scream trap. I am almost positive we are being led into a trap I say nothing for the moment needing to think on how them varmits plan to kill this many man, and by the freshness of the tracks I better start thinking fast.

Around mid afternoon we were by a small creek resting the horses and having coffee, suddenly the quiet is broken by a hellish scream coming from the wilderness that sent shivers down my back, it was a Panther scream smiling I recon I knew who this panther was. The posse all had their guns out all looking skittish, chuckling "what's the matter boys you never heard a panther scream before, sounded like big one, meaner then sin they are." "Now boys you can put away your guns, you will be meeting a real ringtailed wild mountain man here right directly", I then walk over pour another coffee move to the shade and wait.

Minutes later a voice comes from the distance, but he was not wanting to be seen just yet, "don't shoot boys I am friendly, smelled your coffee be obliged for a cup." Before the others could answer I called out, "Nobody is going to shoot you Mr. Martin, be right pleased if you joined us for coffee." I heard chuckling I had the old cob guessing, then not more than 40 feet from the camp he shows himself, with rifle in hand as if were part of him he walks in looking every part the wild man he is.

Walking by me, he gives me the look see and I smile back was causing him some distress, "Howdy their young feller, by chance have we met?" "No sir Panther Martin, but Bear Macdonald is my uncle and he has spoken of you, Hardin Steele at your service" now I can not contain my laughter. "I bet that overgrown knot head had plenty to say, just cause I be the best man and the he wolf of the mountain, but that old Bear is a right good man to have at your side in a scrap and we had a plenty." "Extending his hand pleased to meet you Hardin, so what goes on here then?"

The Marshal came over to us and without hesitation confronts me, "I recon you can head home now youngster, with old Panther here we will not be needing you." Well Panther is not a man of tact but straight talk, "Marshal you recon wrong I just stopped by for a cup of real coffee been a spell since I had me a cup. As to young Mr. Steele here, I know for a purdee fact that he be better than any Indian at tracking, may just be the best rifle shot in the territory, and will stand." Looking at the marshal I tell him "alright I am a going but before Panther be obliged for a few private words then give Neddy his whipping I gave my word then back to the barn".

Panther and I walk out of hearing distance away from the group, I tell him of the tracks and my suspicions as to a trap waiting, "old timer I overheard they got two other posses this way just make sure you ain't with number three." Looking up at me in a thoughtful manner then without a word turns and walks back to the marshal. "Marshal, Mr. Steele and I will guide for you, take it or leave it, time is a wasting and daylight is fading fast". Having no choice, the marshal agrees, riding by Ned I look him dead straight in the eye, "sorry Neddy I recon the beating must wait a spell." Neddy was not happy.

Panther and I mount and take the point, we are riding slowly Panther is reading the ground and not liking it any better than I. "Hardin there is surely something wrong with this here set up, when a man hunts men he is not just reading tracks, he must think like the critter he is hunting, like a game of cat and mouse, watch things like how they treat their horses, how and where they make camp, and when in doubt go with your gut." "What does your gut tell you Hoss?"

These were very familiar and wise words I hear from Bear often, but I appreciate old Panther taking the time to pass on some of his vast knowledge of the hunt. "Well friend Panther I believe we are being led by the nose to the slaughter house, I have been looking over the posse, mostly townsmen and a couple would be toughs but there are two cowboys that tend to talk real close and quiet and always seem to be near the back of the bunch, I think we need a palaver with the Marshal." "I know he will not come if I ask, but I figure he will talk to us if you take the lead, and we need to talk to him alone." "Good thinking old son I am going to mosey back and bring Sam up, tell the boys to take a stretch and smoke, wait here be back lickity split." I keep riding slowly studying the tracks, Panther slows up and waits for the posse. Minutes later the two men ride up to where I am waiting, the Marshal is looking confused and concerned, "so what do you boys have to show me?" Panther did the talking, "well Sam we think we are being guided into a trap of the outlaws making, we want to talk about your posse, how well do you know these men?" Resenting the question, as if we were questioning his judgement of the men who rode with him snapped back, "Damn good men, each one, a couple boys are a bit rough but honest." I interrupted, "Marshal them two cowhands riding with you, how long have you known them, they seem a bit out of place with this bunch?" That gives him pause, scratching his chin, "they are just off a drive been in town just over a week, well behaved caused no trouble, seeing we were short of men like good citizens volunteered to ride the culprits down, the man in the black hat calls himself John Tate, his Pard is Pecos, Texas boys." "Marshal, I have been doing some hard thinking on this and I may know how the other posses were wiped out. "Now just suppose these two men were planted in town before the robbery, get known by a few people, when their comrades rob the bank they join an unsuspecting posse, now I figure the bank robbers are waiting in a good ambush spot, them Texas boys hang back and when the shooting starts we are caught in a crossfire, and our goose is cooked but good."

Panther joins in, "Sam I recon the lad may be right, would explain how the others got planted, and I plan on keeping my shooting eye on them cowboys and staying above the grass." Nodding thoughtfully the marshal is not so sure, "I ain't saying you boys are on to something but I am responsible for these men, I believe I will be keeping a closer track on them Texas boys, well I better be getting back." Before he rides off Panther advises "Sam I recon we should keep this amongst us three or we will either end up dead or with an empty sack and there will be more robbing and killing." Nodding his agreement, the Marshal rides back and joins the posse we again take up the scout but now we are looking for a camp as it was getting on to supper time and I am right hungry and in need of coffee.

We find a good spot in some spruce trees, good water and grass, Panther tells the men to eat and get their coffee before it got dark, there would be no fire tonight, a fire at night on the plains can be seen a long distance off and we did not want to draw the outlaws or any renegade Indians attention.

Although there was little danger of attack, Panther and I decide to stand watch, maybe catch a glimpse of the outlaw's fire and keep an eye on our two suspects. One of the Posse men came over and introduced himself, he is a pleasant looking man about twenty, although in western gear had a look of an educated eastern man. Shaking hands smiling he says" been hoping to talk with you, my name is Steven Leacock I am starting up a newspaper naming it the Mercury, I have heard a lot about you and you have had a lot of adventures for one so young, I hope to hear about some during the ride." I immediately took to this well spoken young gentleman, figuring him for a peace-loving man but would willingly fight and die for a principle. "Anything I can do to help, just call on me although I must admit I am a bit lost this being my first posse." Smiling back, "Appreciate it pard, lets hope it is not your last and you get a great front page story," then in a serious tone I told him, "keep your senses about you and stay sharp, if you see anything out of the ordinary you come see me or old Panther, now you better get some rest I think tomorrow is going to be a right interesting day."

After Steven leaves me Panther said he would take first watch and call me in a few hours, which was good by me I loved the mornings and watching the sun rising the light giving life to the land, the few moments before the world wakes is my favorite time of day. I feel I had just been asleep a few minutes when I feel a hand on my shoulder, as I was taught by Bear I did not stir just opened my eyes, looking around before moving. "Time for your watch Hoss, all is quiet out yonder and in camp ", nodding towards the two sleeping cowboys, going to catch me a might of shuteye."

I crawl out of my blankets the night is cool grabbing my coat and rifle I settle in to a good spot to watch both front and back. It was a quiet night but just as pre-dawn was waking up the birds I am fair certain I spotted the flicker of a fire far off in the distance. I am pondering if those bandits are getting lazy or being clever, but certain whatever was going to happen was going to happen quick, and good by me I do not like waiting.

As the camp comes to life I notice Steven is doing his share gathering wood and getting water, I am hoping he brought some books from back east and we could swap, hard to find reading in the wild lands. After a quick breakfast and coffee, we mount up, Panther leads off at a fast pace, we were going to do some hard riding, old Sampson is fresh as a daisy and raring to go, he would survive the hard riding better than any of the horses, damn tough mule and I like them tough.

Panther figures might be a good idea if one of us scouts and one rides in the rear keeping an eye on the posse that one of us would be up front and one behind the posse keeping an eye on things especially the two Texas boys. Pecos and John did not like us behind them, they grew quiet and seemed to be getting edgy, sensing this ambush might not be so easy as the others.

I am up front, I keep the pace fast but slow enough not to not to tire the horses, there was little need for tracking a blind man could follow the trail the robbers left and we are gaining on them fast, to fast.

The countryside is becoming more hilly, with small stands of trees dotting the landscape, looking over the country in front of me I am thinking to myself this a group of men in the trees or on top of one of these hills would put them in a perfect ambush position. I stop Sampson and wave Panther forward, it was his experience we needed most now. There is no fooling the old he coon, he took one look at the tracks and the hills is thinking the same as me, just as he was about to speak we catch a quick reflection of sunlight off a possible rifle barrel. "Well youngster I do believe them killing rats is up on that hill waiting to take our hair, but old Panther has tangled with worse then them and still got most of his hair and plans on keeping it." We will need a plan, ye got any ideas lad?"

Smiling at him I say "Well first off I recon that no self-respecting savage would want those few stray grey hairs on is lance or coup stick, better get the Marshal up here I may have a plan but we need to act quick."

The Marshal came up and intentionally not looking at the hill we tell the marshal our thinking on the trap, this time he did not argue, "Hardin has him a plan Sam I think we should hear him out." Sam looks over at me, "I hope it is a good one lad or we may all be buzzard meat by nightfall."

Without hesitation, I outline my plan, "alright then the first thing we do is disarm and tie up those two Texas boys, I will bet my spurs they are part of the gang." "Panther and I are going to swing wide left and I figure we can sneak up behind them varmints, there are some blind spots we can make good use of. Marshal that leaves it to you and the boys to cause a diversion need to get them watching you, and not watching for us. "About a quarter mile to the right there is a god spot to rest the horses and have coffee, we will ride in slow making a show of taking a rest." Panther and I will take care of the Texas boys, looking at Panther I figure we will need close to an hour to get in position." the old boy rubs his chin in thought and confirms my timing. "After we leave give us an hour then start for the hill slow put the Texicans up front, if you hear gunshots you come a running Marshal we do not know how many men are waiting for us but I recon no more than five." "Well boys there she is the best I can figure how to do er, your thoughts gentlemen."

We talk it over quickly knowing time is getting short, it was time to act, the marshal goes back to the posse and we slowly lead them to the resting area in sight of the bandits.

When we get to the grove of trees Panther and I waste no time each drawing our razor-sharp knives put them to the Texas boy's throats as soon as their feet touch the ground, I tell them if they call out we will lay their throats wide open and they would be dead. They make an unconvincing argument that they were just trying to help and we had them all wrong, they should not be treated in this manner. Old Panther not being a patient man at times slaps Pecos across the ear, "You boys just relax if we are wrong we will be apologizing and standing to drinks but if we are right we will have the pleasure of hanging ye, best sit still and do what the Marshal says."

With that we prepare to leave, I retrieve my canteen and some extra shotgun shells, I would not take the long gun this would be close in work, Panther left his big 50, bringing only his wicked looking knife and his huge modified walker colt.

With a quick nod to the marshal we sneak out of camp, Panther is in the lead keeping low but moving with confidence that comes with experience, this was not his first roundup, a has a grin of pure pleasure on his face. For the most part we stay low and have fair fair cover, we now move now with great stealth there was little cover our buckskins blend in well with the dry grass, we mke better time than we had gauged arriving at the bottom of the hill in less than 45 minutes.

There are a couple of shallow crevices at the bottom of the hill the bandits waited on carved out by years of flooding rains, using hand talk we decide we would each take one depression and meet up at the top hopefully surprising the killer bandits. We can hear them talking, one is nervous and saying they should ride, a gruff voice who we suspected was the leader told the man to shut up and relax, they would move when he said, then threatened to kill any man that did not follow his orders, it got real quiet after that.

Shaking hands just in case we separate, I take the right-hand trough my shotgun in my right hand in front of me I slowly crawl my way up the hill hugging the ground. Man, I am scared my hands are sweating sweat runs down my neck and into my eyes I worry of making to much noise my rapid heartbeat sounds like a drum in my ears if noticed they would have me dead to rights then it would be as easy as shooting fish in a barrel, looking over I see Panther moving smoothly up the hill, I take confidence and continue up.

When only a few feet from the top the leader I hear the leader he is angry at the delay and cursing his men, his voice covering the sound of my shotgun hammers being cocked back, looking at Panther he signals for us to announce ourselves. Panther lets out one of his fiendish screams I jump up, there are 5 men laying all in a line their rifles pointed towards the posse, now all looking a bit pale in Panthers direction. Then in my best firm voice say" hands up boys or the devil may take you." They all looked up at me shocked unable to believe the reality of their predicament, a man at the far right was the first to react, he began to swing his rifle around fast trying to get a shot into me, I hold my sawed off in my large right hand and swung it over a might and squeezed the right-hand trigger. Buckshot is a nasty thing especially up close those soft lead pellets each the size of a 32-caliber bullet causes brutal damage. The man took the blast in the neck and face, the hot lead ripping large holes in his neck, breaking teeth and face bones, with 2 pellets smashing through his skull going deep into the brain, after a few muscle spasms he did not or would ever move again. "I got me another barrel boys anybody want some", Panther shows himself, his big revolver in his hand and ready. The survivors look at the mutilated corpse of their fellow killer and know it is surrender or die on this hill, they drop their weapons and choose life surrendering without anymore fuss.

Panther comes over to me, "that was right fine work lad old Bear will be some proud when I tell him of your deeds, well here comes the marshal and his bunch ready to claim glory and fame", chuckling.

Looking at the captives I point my shotgun down the hill, "alright down the hill the lot of you and you go real slow, you do not want to be dead and I do not like killing more than one man a day." Old Panther cackling loudly now says" you will do to ride the river with scout, that was some damn slick work."

If everyone is thinking alike,
then someone isn't thinking.
- George S. Patton

CHAPTER 11

A POSSE DIVIDED,
KEEPING A PROMISE

All parties meet at the bottom of the hill, the two Texas boys were tied to their horses looking right unhappy, the gruff voiced man on the hill was in fact the leader, Lon Tate a rough customer on the run from the Nations, Texas and Colorado. He looks at the two secured men and starts cursing them for being fools and incompetents, Pecos livid with rage curses him back and struggles to no avail against his bonds. This left no doubt that our guess had been correct they were in cahoots, there would now be 6 for trail and hanging.

"Panther I am going to take Steven and go get their horses, they got to be close by, Marshal there is one good outlaw on the hill that needs bringing down for burial." To my satisfaction, he sent Ned and his sidekick, again Neddy is not happy.

I pick up my rifle and with Steven we work our way around the hill in search of the outlaw's stock, as we walk Steven askes, "Hardin how does it feel to kill a man, these types of things rarely happen back East?" "Hard to explain Pard, but I do not enjoy killing, anyone who does is insane, strangely I always feel a bit ashamed, when you kill a man you take everything he ever has and everything he was going to have." Minutes later we find the horses in a small thicket, saddles on but cinches loose ready for a quick get away, I went to each horse and removed the saddlebags putting them over one of the horses then we head back our conversation turns to books which is one of my favorite topicS. To quickly we are back in camp and immediately I can sense trouble brewing.

Ned in a loud voice is saying that he nor any others of the posse would be working up a sweat to plant the dead outlaw, let the scavengers have him. "Marshal I said, I sure would feel badly if these town boys got any blisters on their lily hands, I will bury the man, you boys better check out our prisoners, I suspect a couple have hideout guns or knives, and I think we should move out as soon as the burial is done, this is Crow country and them damn Crows can be a brutal bunch."

The Marshal feeling his authority challenged makes a quick retort, "I do not need a youngster telling me my job, and I doubt there is a redskin within 50 miles." Panther laughs drawing attention to himself, "No injuns you say Sam, now just what would you call them 2 on that yonder hill," all heads turned looking in the direction he was pointing and sure enough 2 braves on horseback, skylined, looking down at our group. Every time I see mounted natives it reminds me of the stories of Genghis Khan and his warrior tribes, both wild, free and superior mounted fighters.

The Marshal said no more to me but turned to the others and starts the preparation for travel, when travelling I always carry a short-handled spade with me, always proved to be a most useful tool. Moving away to a spot a few yards from the group I start to dig, Panther and Steve come over and take a few turns letting me catch my breath, in no time at all we have a fair-sized hole dug. Panther and I roll the dead man in his dirty blanket and placed him in the lonely hole, then fill it quickly. There was nothing to make a marker so I turn to the outlaws, "he road and died with you men, any of you want to say words over him." Tate responds, Jim was never good for much, I just brought him along because he was kin, dumb as shit, goodbye and good riddance I say," spitting towards the grave.

Nothing more is said, the prisoners are mounted and have their hands tied to their saddle horns, I lead off, it was getting to be late afternoon so I head straight for a good spot I know of about 8 miles' easy ride, nice stream, sweet cold water, loaded with trout with good grass for the animals.

With 6 very desperate and dangerous criminals the Marshal wisely decides on 2 man watches, one to watch the prisoners and the other to watch for intruders. I ask Steve if he would like to stand watch with me, hoping to continue our talk, it is not commonplace to talk with a well read classically educated men, he readily agrees, I let Panther know we would take the last shift,

After a sparse meal rations were getting a bit low but there was lots of coffee and jerky which I can survive on for days, rinsing out my cup I head right to my blankets I am exhausted, spent from the actions and stress of the day.

Morning comes to soon as I feel Panthers hand on my shoulder, but I feel good and rested, youth does have its advantages, with no need to hide we keep the fire going and the coffee on, cup in hand I head for the what is sure to be a wicked black brew and I am not disappointed. Steve and I pass a couple quiet hours on watch mostly talking of great books, great leaders warriors peace keepers, we agree to get together after this and see about swapping a few books. "Hardin, you have a high-quality education, knowledge not expected at your age and in the wild lands no less you must have a very good teacher." Smiling "Steve I am the product of the teaching of one Ramon Valdez, I will bring him with me I think you two educated men should meet".

Time passes quickly as it does when doing things you enjoy, the camp is beginning to stir, it is a beautiful morning, the meadowlarks are singing their soft song, but I am uneasy there is tension in the camp, men are more surely and less patient this morning, only old Panther seems undisturbed.

Unknown to me during their watch Ned and his sidekick snuck through the prisoner's saddlebags looking for loot as neither man liking to work for his eating and drinking money. Most of the bags carried normal items a western man would need, spare shells, pieces of rope or leather pigging strings, needle and thread maybe some with pictures or mementos. In the last saddlebag, their efforts are rewarded finding 2 full bottles of good rye whisky, smiling hugely Ned stashes the bottles in his saddlebags.

I check the prisoners ropes and they are secure, rolling up my bedding I saddle Samson and head to the fire in need of more coffee, after pouring myself a cup I squat down beside Panther, slowly sipping the scalding hot brew, I am just about to grab a second cup when Ned and his sidekick arrive at the fire joking loudly and a partial bottle of whiskey in Ned's big paw. "Hold out you cups boys old Ned has an eye opener for you, the town boys were quick to get a share of the bust skull, Panther myself and Steve refuse the offer, this is no time for drinking and getting sloppy. Panther looks to the drinking Marshal, "Sam, you know this ain't no time for the panther piss, betwixt the robber gang and the Crows I recon we need are wits about us, marshal you need to confiscate that hooch." Panther you mind your own damn affairs, nothing wrong with a man having a few drinks to get the day going, ok boys drink up and mount up we are riding."

Panther and I take charge of the prisoners, leading their horses, looking back I say to Tate, "If you boys want to make it through this day you need to be very quiet and well behaved, I will do what I can for you if the time comes." Tate looking pale and just nods he had been down the trail and knew what the townsmen were getting boozed up for, a 6-man necktie party.

Ben pulls up sharply, "lookie there marshal some live ok trees big strong limbs, good a place as any", taking a pull from the second bottle. The Marshal was half corked swings his mount towards the oak trees, "ok men lets ride em over and get er done."

I reach behind me and pull out the sawed off, then made sure my belly gun is ready for fast action, Panther pulls his giant walker pistol from his belt and holds it at his side.

I do not move with the prisoners and Panther is right behind me more than ready to tangle with the drunken posse the lead party finally notices we are not following and turn back towards us. Before any could speak I declare, "There will be no lynching, this swine will be taken in for trail and proper hanging, now ", cocking the right hammer of my shotgun, "I am willing to die keeping them are you vigilantes are you willing to die trying to take them"? I then swing my shotgun in the direction of the posse but at no one in particular. Now drunk or not every man there remembers what the dead outlaw looked like all torn to sheds, they were full of respect of the shotguns power. Old Panther gives the posse a hard look over and expresses his support, "I will be backing my Pard Hardin, I recon we can empty plenty of saddles afore you get us, open the ball anytime you cowards," spitting. Steve rides over and joins us his rifle out and ready, addressing the marshal says "Listen Marshal, if you hang these men you are the criminals, no better than the criminals we are taking in. "Now if you bring them in you will be Marshal Sam Teale the man who brought in the notorious Tate gang, you and the other men even Ned will be famous", I interject pointing the shotgun right directly at the Marshal's midsection, my green eyes blazing, "there will be no more talk about lynching the prisoners go to Silver Creek."

With my speaking done I slowly start Sampson leading the prisoners back on the trail, intentionally I put my back to the posse, I am plenty scared but I kept my shoulders straight and do not look back.

I knew Panther had my back, Ned with a look of almost insane hatred put his hand on his six-gun, before he could pull it Panther gives him warning, "I sure would not want to be the feller who kills that Lad, for I would shoot them dead on the spot, even if I went down men like Bear Macdonald, Ramon Valdez, Wild Bill and the Traveller would be on the hunt for his scalp, Bear would hunt you into the deepest of hells, a right dangerous man and Uncle to the

Lad." Every man had heard of these legends and knew what Panther said was true, without another word the posse falls in behind me with Panther and Steve brining up the drag. We should make Silver Creek by late afternoon next day, I am going to be very relieved when the evil 6 are securely locked up in jail.

The remainder of the journey is fairly uneventful Silver Creek comes into sight about 3 in the afternoon, reining in old Sampson I call a halt, time to keep my promise to big   Neddy. "Be getting off your horse Ned I promised you a licking and I always keep my word, I am going to tear down your wheelhouse you trouble making big asshole." Ned dismounts smiling knowing he had an inch of height and over 25 lbs on me, and has been in many a hardscrabble fight, "well punk I am surely being going to enjoy pinning your ears back, I am going to give you a beating you will never forget."

Spitting on his hands he goes into a crouch his hands balled into fists, I am easy on my feet and ready for him, these local brawlers mostly won by brute strength or intimidation, no real fighting skills. I had spared with Bear who had done his share of fighting, I love the rough and tumble and know all the dirty tricks, working with Ramon he taught me balance and how to anticipate an counter an attack.

Ned with a huge smile and without warning throws a hard-looping left hand, I easily see it coming and blocking it with my left arm I threw a straight right hand into Ned's solar plexes, his mouth opens and he stops looking shocked. Before he could recover I let my left fist go catching him just behind the ear making him stagger, stepping back smiling I give old Ned some time to recover "I hope you can do better than that, these pilgrims figure you for a bad hombre, all you bullies are of the same mold, cowards", laughing. Ben regroups and charges his arms out to trying to grab me and crush me with his strength and weight, I let him come then pop him with a straight right hand to the mouth making a bloody mess of his lips, then threw a left hook to his ribs, it is a powerful and vicious blow, I can hear the sickening sound of live bones cracking. Well about the only good thing I have to say about Ned he had no quit in him, my fighting blood is up now so I invited him in, now it was legs spread and punching time to see who the better man is, I feel a couple of his heavy blows but I am very strong from living the outdoor life, little by little Ned gives ground. I know he was about done so I feint a left hand then hit him with another straight right to his nose crushing the bone then bring up a left uppercut catching him square on the chin old Ned then went to sleep crashing heavily to the ground and did not move.

After I recover a bit I go over to Ned who was starting to come around, kneeling beside him I check him out to make sure there is no serious injuries, looking at him smiling, "How you holding up Hoss, hoping there is no hard feelings I will stand to drinks when we get into town." Ben tenderly felt his face and although it must have hurt he smiles, "Damn Hardin you hit damn hard for a youngster, I recon you whipped me but good, be a pleasure to drink with one tough SOB", laughing. Steve helps him to his horse, once aboard we head for town and within minutes are riding down Main street with the captured outlaws in tow.

Panther and I are going to spend the night in town get a home cooked meal, have a couple drinks then both head back to Bears cabin the next morning. I can feel the stress falling off me as the Marshal secures the outlaws in their cells, I am a bit proud of myself, I did some man-sized work in capturing the Tate gang, I also found out that I was good on the trail and I very much liked the hunt.

What I perceive, is above all justice,
where everyone has the same law.
- Imran Khan

CHAPTER 12

UNCLE BLACKHAND AND THE BIRTH OF CROW KILLER

Just after I turn 17, Bear and I ride out to visit Black Hand and Grey Wolf for a few weeks to do some hunting and story telling around the council fires. We bring gifts with us, some red cloth and beads for Black hand's wife and daughter, coffee sugar and tobacco, I brought my Kola, Grey Wolf a new knife of good steel that has a razor sharp edge.

When we ride into the village we receive a great reception, they are going to have a feast tonight held in our honour to celebrate our arrival. Bear and I formally greet the great Leader Black Hand, Indians are big on ceremony, after we finish Bear and Black Hand were back to their old ways both telling windies and trying to outdo each other. Grey Wolf came running up smiling, we look at each other amazed at how much we had grown since last seeing each other. He is now a full-grown warrior still a few inches shorter than me, but lean and hard, he is well respected by the band and following in Black Hand's large footsteps. Holding out my arm to him, I say it is very good to see my Kola again, smiling we grab each other forearms in greeting. I present him with the knife, he was reluctant to accept he had nothing for me, I tell him it was a gift to my Kola and is given in friendship, I can see he is greatly impressed with the beautiful blade, I knew would add to his status amoung his fellow warriors. I also brought with me a big bag of stick candy and during the evening give a stick to each of the children, saving 2 for me and Grey Wolf. Those kids just attacked the candy, huge smiles all around, my small gesture made a great impression on all in the village, as I have said before Indians love their sweets.

Bear had made me make a bow and arrows before leaving the cabin telling me I was to hunt with them while in camp, I needed practice for sometimes you need to hunt real quiet, not risking the sound of a rifle. We have been at the village about a week when Bear and a couple older braves go off hunting, Grey Wolf and I set off with our bows heading out a different direction to hunt and show those old men up, the foolishness of youth. We had not gone from the camp and are now standing on a rise overlooking a stand cedar and a small valley, looking down we see movement, it was a big war party of Crow warriors painted for war and eager to slaughter, there were around 30, heading directly to the village, without hesitation we run back to camp screaming Crow and attack. With men out hunting we are short handed and outnumbered almost 2 to 1, the Braves grab up their weapons put themselves in position to defend as the women and children run for their lives to hide in the hills and trees. I run into Black Hand's tent and quickly throw on my belted .44 and knife, quickly grab both my long gun and the sawed off shotgun I come out just as the Crow are hitting the camp, I toss the rifle to Grey Wolf, lookin g around quickly I catch a quick glance at Black Hand, looking like a demi god, the anchor which we all relied on. Grey Wolf drops an enemy with his first shot, I am facing 3 very angry Indians charging, now only feet away so I just let go with both barrels, at that close range I get part of all 3 killing 2. I drop the shotgun and pull my handgun picking targets until the handgun is empty, before I have a chance to reload a Crow thrusts his spear at me from behind cutting the side of my buckskins and slicing deep into my side, quickly drop and roll picking up the empty shotgun I rise and rush in swinging, I batter that Crow into a gory mess. I look to Black Hand he is against 3 enemy, he taunts them screaming insults calling them cowards, Grey Wolf and I look at each other and draw our knives, screaming the Sioux war cry we charge right into them. Thank the gods for Ramon's training, my opponent was big, strong and very fast, fresh blood is dripping off the blade of his knife, he feints over extending himself showing his side at which I deliver two quick thrusts into his kidney, he lets out an animal scream of pain, before he could recover I drive my razor sharp blade into his exposed throat, his blood covers me, he bled out quick and died within minutes.

Bear and the warriors come charging back into the camp letting loose a barrage of bullets and arrows, it is just too much for them Crow warriors they hightailed it leaving their dead behind. Quickly I look for Grey Wolf, relieved to see he survived a dead Crow at his feet, we are both smiling like idiots. The Crow left 8 dead behind, 2 Sioux were killed and about 6 with wounds. I go to move a great pain red pain explodes in my side, when my battle blood was running hot I forgot about the spear wound in my side, now I am feeling a bit dizzy and fall to the ground blackness overwhelms me.

I wake in Black Hand's tent under a blanket, without thinking I try to move, the pain and tightness of the stitches Bear had put in while I was out restricting my movement. I lay back down broth and water are brought to me by Black Hands daughter, I am very thirsty, seems strange how a man is how a man isalways gets thirsty after a battle. Bear is beside me looking concerned" How goes it lad, gave us a bit of a scare," I am alright you old mother hen, quit your frettin" laughing even though it hurt like hell. "Black Hand and Grey Wolf both say you were a holy terror in the scrap, fought as well as any Sioux warrior, in a couple days when you are up and about there is to be a ceremony, they are bringing you into the tribe Hardin, it is a very rare and great honour". After a couple days I was up but moving very carefully not wanting to rip open my stitches, the ceremony is this evening and I am most curious about the ceremony.

Evening finally comes all the village members are dressed in their finery, Black Hand in beautiful decorated fringed leather and full headdress made from eagle feathers. Black Hand like many Indian leaders are great orators, equal or better than most politicians or poets would have been right at home with Plato or Socrates. He spoke of the great victory over the Crow and how the Sioux were the most powerful of the tribes, feared by all tribes the bravery and skill of a Sioux warrior, then thanks the Manitou for his favour in their victory over their long hated enemy.

He then calls Grey Wolf to stand and proclaims with great pride he is now a full-fledged warrior for having killed an enemy in battle, now this is a big thing with the Sioux, if you have not killed an enemy in battle or stole horses you were not given warrior status and could not go on raids or marry. Grey Wolf stood very proud and thanked Black Hand, no longer just father and son, but as warriors. He sits and Black Hand has me stand, he then recounts my part of the battle how through bravery and skill equal to a Sioux warrior killed many of the Crow enemy, I would now be known through out all the Sioux villages as Crow Killer, and I am now the adopted nephew of Black Hand. Humbled and very proud, I thank the great chief and say how proud I am to be among the People, I will carry the name with pride and my enemies will come to fear it. When I finish speaking he calls his son and I to the circle, now being warriors we can smoke the pipe.

We stay around for a few more days, mostly to let my wound knit before riding out, but the day comes for us to leave. Grey Wolf comes up to me with a serious face, takes out his knife and cuts his palm, bleeding he hands me the knife I do the same, we clasp hands, He says "our blood is now one we are brothers, the Crow killer and the Wolf, it was an emotional moment for me, I now had a brother, it is a good feeling to have family.

Just as we are saddling up the Shaman of the tribe shambles forward, looked like he is at least a hundred, very thin, he has me bend my head down and places a leather pouch on a rawhide string over my head, he tells me it is big medicine it will protect me and always wear it. "Thank-you Grandfather, I will keep it always and remember my Sioux family when it is over my heart." Looking greatly pleased he shuffles off again. With that we mount and head back to the cabin, not knowing soon Bear would be taking me north.

Wars may be fought with weapons, but they are won by men. It is the spirit of the men who follow and the man that leads that gains the victory.
- George S. Patton

CHAPTER 13

CANADA AND THE NORTH WEST MOUNTED POLICE

In early spring after the Crow battle Bear announced that he and I are heading for Fort Whoop Up in Canada, so that I can be trained and learn the ways of a lawman by men of the North West Mounted Police, acknowledged as the best police force in North America. As we ride Bear gives me a brief history of the fort, originally called Fort Hamilton, built by J.J. Healy and A.B. Hamilton traders from Montana as a trading post at the belly of the Oldman and St Mary rivers. The post served as a centre for many illegal activities to include the selling of whiskey to the Indians at very high prices, the Mounties were sent west to stop this activity and provide a Canadian presence in the west. The post went by many names one of the more unusual was Whoop Up Bug Juice for the type of firewater whiskey locally made and was highly prized.

The NWMP are acknowledged as one of the best police forces in the world and if I was to be a lawman I should learn from the best. Their motto is, **always get their man**, they rarely sent more than one man after one or more outlaws, if he is killed they would send another, and another if necessary dogging them to the ends of the earth or into the gates of hell to make an arrest. Stories tell it that some villains hearing the Mounties were on their trail found the first constable and turned themselves in, others preferred not to face jail or make a futile run took the quick way out, eating their own bullet.

The foothills and mountains of Montana and Canada are some of the prettiest country in all the world, rolling hills with deep green grass and many coloured wildflowers, deep coulees with rivers running through them, lakes and ponds by the mountains, stands of aspen cedar and pine, the mountains high solid and imposing, snow on some peaks year-round, it is certainly a paradise we are riding through.

After a comfortable and pleasant ride, we get to the Canadian border, Bear tells me to take off my sidearm and put it in my saddlebags, the shotgun and rifle are allowed, but they do not allow the carrying of handguns in Canada. It took us most of the day to get to the fort, as we near I see the fort itself, it did not look like much of a fort to me, four long low log buildings, large stables, tents and huts for shelter, a few tepees in close I assume for the natives protection. Inspector Sam Steele was in command of the detachment, a man of strength, honesty and a complete devotion to duty, imposing in both size and bearing, strict but fair with his men and if not liked, respected. We enter the headquarters building a constable greets us then led us into the inspector's office, he without rising greets us with politeness and a formal detachment. "Master Steele, Constable Finn O'Shea will oversee your training while you are with us, you will take your orders from him, and young sir keep in mind it will be an order and obeyed, have you any questions?" Without thinking I came to somewhat of attention, "no Sir, I appreciate the chance to learn". Constable O'Shea is summoned to the office, marching in smartly and coming to attention in front of the inspector's desk, he had on the famous scarlet tunic of the mounted police. Inspector

Steele briefed him and puts me under his care, and with a wave we are dismissed, when we got outside, I say to Finn, "the Inspector appears to be a very hard man", laughing he replies "you have no idea Hardin, he relates a story of when the Inspector was in Dawson City in the Yukon during the gold rush, a northern town that was half on the American side and the other Canadian, from the American side it was lawless, with men shooting, robbing and killing. Miners were in constant fear of being robbed and killed, the Inspector had a small detachment of only 3 constables but did not allow any lawlessness, miners would bring him their gold for safe keeping, the Inspector would just throw the gold under his bunk, he never lost even a flake of their gold, a man of strong will and totally honest".

He then leads me to his quarters where I will be bunking with him and another Sgt named Maurice, a Prussian, ex soldier and is rumored that he came from nobility, he has a scar of a saber cut just below his left eye. After I stow my gear we go out and he shows me around the fort, even though it was only a short distance to the American border, it was a whole different world, much more regimented and has a feeling of peace and order. The Mounties are always undermanned, a few doing the work of many, covering an area larger than most states and some countries. I am amazed on how a few good men could mostly through courage and determination control and keep order in such a vast area.

The fort is not that large but held a general store, blacksmith, armory, what they called a mess hall where everyone ate together, a jail which for a reason no one could be explain is called it a hoosegow, there were many types of people in and around the fort, natives, Metis, mountain men, a large group of Chinese who had been railroad workers, all going about their business in relative peace.

Bear is talking to a group of tough looking mountain men and trappers, all laughing and swapping tales of their adventures with Indians, dangerous animals and weather that they have survived, telling tales of those that crossed over or vanished in the wilderness. Constable O'Shea and I wander over and join them, in the group is Jerry Potts, I immediately go over to him shaking his hand and thanking him for helping in saving my life years ago, "Mon Ami he says, it is a good thing, you have grown strong and your bravery is already known Crow Killer, seems everyone already heard the stories of the capture of the Tate gang and the battle with the Crow, we will go hunting one day you and I". We leave the group to their confab, but as we depart O'Shea said "no drinking Jerry or it will be jail, seems Mr. Potts was a man to be avoided when hitting the bust skull, tending to turn mean and sometimes violent when intoxicated. Bear is heading into to the Rockies to do some trapping and hunting with a couple other mountain men, although it was Canada it was still Blackfoot country and Bear would be big coup to the Blackfeet, I warn him of it before they depart, as usual he just laughs and they head out as if going to a church social, for those old mountain men, it was just short of heaven.

Constable O'Shea gives me a book on Canadian law to study, I realize now there is a great deal of difference in democracy between Canada and the United States, with Canada relying more on their Government for protection and guidance, no vigilantly justice, citizens call the law when needed.

I was told the stories of the trek west, a tough journey saved just before disaster by the scout Jerry Potts. The fort was originated to stop the American whiskey traders coming into Canada, and providing law and order to all including the Sioux who whipped Custer and are now residing in Canada. They were larger than life men working in wild country, big men doing a big job and doing it well. They never drew a weapon unless they were going to use it, using their authority, common sense, and adherence to duty as weapons, and most were good at hand to hand combat, using arm locks restraining holds and the odd rap on the skull for the more aggressive criminals. But everyone who knew if the Mounties drew their weapon they shoot fast and to kill. The Texas Rangers had a saying 1 town 1 Ranger, the Mounted Police creed was They always get their man, one crime one Mountie.

I enjoy the evenings listening to O'Shea and Maurice talk of distant lands such as India, Afghanistan, even China, Maurice had once been a general for a Chinese lord. O'Shea one evening says "Hardin do you how to fight, like boxing or wresting"? "I can fight but just rough and tumble, a bit of Indian wrestling and some tricks Bear showed me". He smiles at Maurice" we will visit Mr. Li tomorrow, be part of your education", both men smile and chuckle to a private joke that has me just a might concerned.

The next morning after breakfast O'Shea and Maurice take me behind the main building where the Chinese have a small camp, everyone is hustling about there is a wonderful aroma of cooking and strong odor of lye. Maurice approaches a thin old man and bows to him respectfully, the 2 men talk in a sing song language which like Spanish sounded good in my ears. After some discussion, they walk up to me, Mr. Li was an old man about 5 ft. 2, a could not weigh no more than 110 lbs soaking wet but he has a look confidence and a smooth movement about him. Mr. Li walks right up to be and looks me over like he is buying a horse, studying me as if he was deciding if I was worth of his time. I look to Maurice questions written all over my face, Maurice says" Mr. Li is deciding weather to train you in his martial arts skills, he does not like wasting time on weaklings or quitters, "I ain't no quitter nor a weakling" getting a little angry about it all. Mr. Li walks away about 10 feet and talks to Maurice, Mr. Li says to attack him and do not hold back, I was astonished 1 hit of my large fist would break the little man in pieces, after some prodding I threw a half hearted punch, I see Li make a slight move, then I see the sky, and then I impact the ground with great force, it knocks the wind out of me, today I learn gravity is a bitch. Mr. Li seems right displeased and motioned for me to try again, well this time I go in low, well that did not work much better, but I am learning to bounce better. In the next few minutes I must have hit the ground 10 times, but I keep getting up even smiling a bit, the last attack I came in cautious threw a straight right hand, he blocked it with ease then steps back with an open hand stabs me with his fingers on my shoulder which goes numb immediately then with a sweep of his feet I am once again looking at the clouds, but as a Sioux brave I refuse to utter any sound of pain, Mr. Li bows to me and I do my best to return the bow without falling on my face. He speaks a few words to Maurice and leaves us, he looks much bigger to me now walking away. As we are leaving Maurice tells me Mr. Li was impressed not by your skill but my heart, and if I desire to learn you are to see him tomorrow to start your training. "I hope you boys got plenty of liniment I have a feeling I will be needing it, smiling I walk slowly and tenderly back to the barracks.

Thus started my learning of the martial arts and how to defend or attack, use your enemy's strength against them, where to find the bodies pressure points to hurt or maim and of the philosophy on how to calm your mind in times of stress. Mr. Li's English was good but heavily accented when he wanted to use it, we practice 4 hours a day and after we would sit and eat, I just love the food, noodles, rice, exotic flavors, I even learn how to use chop sticks. He tells me old stories of China and the hero's and gods, I tell him of the mountains, the people I had met, how I became a Sioux warrior, Mr. Li seemed very interested in the Indians and their gods, he once told me it was believed that the Indians and Chinese were related many centuries before.

One morning O'Shea tells me to get mounted we were going to a Cree village to recover 2 horses stolen from a local farmer and bring the thieves in, I am not to bring any weapons but my rifle. He looks me directly in the eyes his voice now full of authority, "Hardin you will not draw your weapon unless I order it, and that sir is an order". With us rode 1 other constable, the village was a large one, the Cree gathered around us crowding us as we ride in, O'Shea pulls up and in a loud commanding voice tells them that 2 horses were stolen and he would be taking the horses and returning them to the farmer and thieves to the fort for trail. The Cree are getting mean and begin crowding and pushing our horses, cursing us out in Cree and English, I must admit I am getting more than a little scared, I look to O'Shea, he is sitting tall and still in his scarlet jacket. The Cree are getting angrier and more aggressive, I am near pulled off my horse, then O'Shea orders the constable to draw his rifle, just then the Indians part and their Chief named Mouse comes running up to O'Shea talking nervously. O'Shea tells Mouse he was a bad and weak Chief and the Queen mother across the big water is displeased, any who break the queen's laws white or Indian will be arrested. The names of the 2 braves names were known O'Shea tells Mouse that both braves and the horses were to come to the fort tomorrow morning or he would come for them. Mouse looked like a whipped dog but said it would be as O'Shea ordered. We ride out of there as easy as pie, I knew I had just witnessed my most important lesson, I now know the importance of the use of proper authority, it would remain with me for the rest of my life and career as a lawman.

My time at the fort goes quickly, most of it is spent with Mr. Li, and on occasion O'Shea, Potts and I went hunting, O'Shea was a good shot but Jerry Potts was a whiz with his Winchester, it was almost like the rifle was an extension of the man. I enjoy our outing, out hunting Jerry was cheerful and O'Shea lost some of the stuffiness, conversation and company is good, and again both men provide me with knowledge always teaching.

My training with Mr. Li is coming along and I am not defying gravity as often and using less liniment. I acquire knowledge on pressure points, things such as where to strike to create great pain, stun, throw off a man's balance and reflexes. Mr. Li teaches me the near chock technique, how to put pressure on a man's neck and where to strike, the eyes, ears, temple, nose, chin and solar plexes of your opponent. Further instruction teaches me how to use a man's size against him, different styles of punches and chops, how to place my feet to be balanced from any angle, I could have spent years with him never learned near enough. but the fighting skills he taught me would save my ass many a time in the future. We have our final tea together I thank him and wished him the blessing of Buddha before I leave him he says "Hardin you were a fine pupil, practice much, and always keep peace in your heart" he bowed we separate for the last time.

I will miss Canada; the people were overall friendly and polite with a live and let live attitude in a multi cultured country. Beautiful country with impressive views of the rolling grassy foothills and the tall jagged mountains to the west both mysterious and with majesty. One thing I will not miss is the damn skeeters, nasty blood sucking insects, and in countless numbers, netting for horses and people is needed, they can kill a tied up uncovered horse overnight and could drive a man to insanity or even death. But what I admire most of the

Canadians was that they were tough, the climate alone was brutal at times, winters going down to 40 below, summers could reach well over 100 degrees, but as with all new societies the strong stayed and survived, the weak perished.

Bear and I make our departure and return to the cabin both Ramon and old Panther are there, it is good to be home, but now I was considered a man full grown and it was about time I saddled my own broncs. A few days later Bill Mathers rides in and within a couple weeks Bill and I would be off to blaze our own trails.

Education is the most powerful weapon which you
can use to change the world.
- Nelson Mandela

CHAPTER 14

DANGEROUS WORK

Bill looks good, we were very near the same size me a might taller and a bit leaner being mostly muscle, Bill is dressed in new store bought clothes, has a .45 colt and bowie knife hanging off his black leather gun belt, and a good henry rifle in the rifle boot. After supper, he tells me he is heading to Colorado, they are looking for men some tough men to protect gold shipments, there has been a lot of robberies with about every outlaw gang looking to get rich, the gold shippers were paying top dollar plus bonuses. "Hardin, he says," I think you and I could handle that game and make some money doing it", "Well Bill only 1 small thing we got to live long enough to collect it,". smiling, we both have a good laugh over it. That evening we all gathered around the table and with coffee talk it over, old Panther said, "I hope you youngsters are not in the deep water, a tough job starting out, but if it can be done I recon you lads can do it". After more discussion, I knew it was time for me to decide,

Bear and Ramon even if they did not like it, would not try and stop me, like them I had to take the step into manhood like they all had done. I tell the group I will be heading out with Bill, and we would be leaving as soon as arrangements could be made, I need to get my gear ready, and by the sounds of it I better be ready.

Many decisions had to be made as on what to take on the trail and what weapons would be needed for this job, this would be work where your tools would be hammering out death. For my weapons, I take of course my Russian .44 and the beautiful razor sharp blade Ramon gave me, I will also take the greener in the sling over my back shotguns come in right handy at times, my new Winchester 44 40, shells working both in the pistol and rifle, my good luck charm Hickok's .38 in its shoulder holster, and lastly Megs derringer just in case.

Bear had studded his Appy with a beautiful big mustang mare, they produced a fine colt now 3 years old, the most beautiful blue roan you ever did see, tall close to 17 hands with unlimited speed and bottom, a horse a man could be right proud to ride. Bear trained him to be a war horse who in battle would attack other horses and men with tooth and hoof a touch of wildness made him an excellent watchdog, horses can sense and smell things long before we can, watching your horse can save your life.

I get all chocked up as Bear handed me the reins, taking them from him I say tearfully with no shame," I want to thank you boys, I surely do not know what would have become of me if you 2 had not found me and took me in, a man never had better uncles, hope I can make you both proud." Bear grabs me up in a sweeping bearhug squeezing the wind clear out of me, wiping a tear from his eye" we are already proud of you son, keep your powder dry and your ass down, this here horse should get you out of trouble about as fast as you get into it, outlaws and lawmen always ride the best." Ramon smiles a sad smile "Adios Buena suerte Sobrino, may the virgin mother watch over you, do not forget your uncles and if you need us send word". No more was said or needed saying, looking over and getting familiar with my animal brother and warrior I decided to call him Apollo after the god of war, I figured a fitting name for this magnificent animal.

It takes me most of the day to get everything ready, it was a fair long trail ahead, all had been said and the silence was speaking for us to part company, I look back a couple times, the boys were still standing watching us leave. Time to put my experience and training to use, I just hope I learned my lessons well enough to stay alive.

Apollo likes the trail as much as I do and steps out at a brisk pace as we travel Bill and I talk of many things mostly about our futures, but always watching the skyline and selecting our camps carefully danger on the trail is never far away. Bill still wants to get rich, have the finest, talks constantly about travel to Europe, New Orleans and New York and living the good life. I had never been much interested in money, I always like to have some for a few comforts, my path is still the law and I ride to this job more for the experience and credentials than for the money. Our destination was a new gold mining city called of all things Golden, still mostly tents and green wood shelters, tents for bars, planks for counters, a rough town in its finest. When we reached Colorado, we came on a place called the Painted or Magic valley, there were old Indian writing and drawing from long before the memory of todays tribes it is a place of worship by the native tribes, a place where you can feel the magic, I vow to return to study it more carefully one day.

We ride into Golden and although its not even noon there were drunken men staggering in the muddy street, and some occasional gunfire, we dismount taking our rifles from there boots and enter the office of the Denver Gold and Shipping Company and ask to speak to the manager. A smallish sour looking man checks us over carefully and frown "what do you want to see him about". Bill replied we were looking for work as guards for the gold shipments, he gives off a nasty laugh," you 2 could not guard a chicken coop," just then the manager steps out, a friendly looking man, who looked like he enjoyed his meals big and is going a bit bald, but his voice is strong and holds a tone of authority. I say "Sir could we have a few minutes of your time we just arrived from Montana and are looking for honest work, after a moment he said he knew that Montana country and invited us into the office, the little rat face looks unhappy.

We are seated the manager introduces himself as Charles Pearson, I said "this here knucklehead is Bill Mathers and I am Hardin Steele, "Steele he says I believe I have heard that name, Bill interjects, "Mr. Pearson old Hardin was the one with Panther Martin brought in the Tate gang and he was years younger. He looks at me again I believe in a different light, "are you familiar with old Bear Killer", I laughed "yes him and Ramon are my adopted uncles, and my teachers". After some thought "I am going to give you men a chance, but it is dangerous for you, almost every shipment gets hit".

He went on to explain that it was about a 30-mile trip leaving from this office and arriving at the train station at Clear Springs where it will be taken by train to Denver. He asked if we had any questions and I have many, we are going to do this right. First, I ask him how many people knew about the timings of the shipments, it seemed it was 4 including old ratface, I suggest only he the bank manager, Bill and I know when the gold is going out, to which he agreed. I ask then when the next shipment was going out and was it already known to the other 3, he said yes and in 3 days. I tell him we would be hit for sure but we will be ready, then lastly, I ask him who his best meanest and toughest driver was, that brought on a chuckle, "that would-be Whiplash Smith, best driver tough as wang leather and fearless, honest and best man with a bull whip you ever did see". I request permission to talk to Whiplash to handling the driving of the shipment. Just before leaving our new boss Mr. Pearson we would be out of town for a bit and would be scouting the trail would appreciate no to many people knowing about it. Showing us to the door, shaking our hands welcomes us to the company then tells old rat face to add our names to the payroll as guards, rat face looks unhappy.

We walk our horses down to the livery, I give Apollo a good rubdown and a bait of corn, then we head over to the only hotel, we were lucky to get a room to share, there was an eating room but the food was bad. I noticed riding in a Chinese tent serving food, been awhile since I had some good noodles, Bill and I wander over and sat at some planks being used serving as tables, a young man comes over smiling hugely, in my very primitive Mandarin I order for us, I ask for chopsticks and for my friend a fork. Shortly he returns with many bowls on a tray, placing the steaming dishes in front of us, before he leaves he asks very respectably my name, after I tell him I am Hardin Steele, he says his name is Sam, he is the nephew of Chin Li and he knew of me asking if my bruises have healed yet smiling hugely, the Chinese had a hell of a good system of information. After we pay and thank Sam for what was a delicious meal, he leans in and just above a whisper says" many bad man in town, kill, steal, we are friends you need something you come see Sam, bowing with thanks we head out.

Bill convinces me to join him for one at the saloon, I do not much like saloons but it is a good place to gather information. We make our way to the bar, although early in the evening the saloon is packed with miners and cowboys. Bill has rye I order a beer and I start to survey the smoke-filled room, couple tables of poker going, many sharks in the water, Keno, roulette, most of the working gals looked tired. I notice a tough old codger sitting alone, with one look I knew it to be Whiplash Smith. I nudge Bill and we head over to his table, with a smile I ask him if we can join him, "set, no ones using them chairs". I look right at him and tell him we just signed on with the company, "Mr. Pearson says you are the one the lazies most timid easy going man in the outfit, tea drinking sort of us, but a fair to middling mule skinner." Bill and I were both smiling now and s barely able to contain our laughter waiting for old Whiplash to start to bucking and snorting. After a moment, the hard-old boy laughs, "yes that would be me but never cared much for tea." I inform him we need the best and I had volunteered him to make the next gold run, in a dry voice askes me not to be so thoughtful in the future future.. "I like your talk Hardin, count me in, should be right interesting trip hope you youngsters can keep up "laughing. We agree before separating that we would have another war talk before taking the shipment out, I am very pleased Whiplash is driving, he is of the same mold of Bear or old Panther his word is his bond and he will never shirk on a job. I tell Bill I was heading back to the room, he said he was staying for a bit, not to late I tell him we are on the road before sunrise.

We are 3 miles down the road before the sun was up, from here on in we were on the scout for ambush sites, like tracking you have to get inside the outlaw's heads, think if you were them where would be the most likely spots, as in chess you always want to be thinking a few moves ahead. We find 3 spots that would be good spots for a holdup, all on the top of grades where the wagon must slow down or stop to rest the horses, good hiding spots for men and horses. We stop and check each spot for sign, and in all 3 there were boot prints and evidence where the horses were kept, we would have to be very crafty and careful to survive the run.

We arrive at the Train Depot and check out where men could easily hide to take the gold as it was being loaded on the train, there were only a couple other buildings around the station, we agree on where we could best provide covering fire if needed. The station agent prepares us a much appreciated meal a talkative man who lacked for company, we sleep in the stable and on our way back to Golden checking for anything we might have missed and plan our course of action.

Arriving back at the livery I ask the stable boy if anyone had been asking for us, he was hesitant and would not divulge much but a couple tough looking men came by asking questions, I thanked him and gave him a dollar.

We find Whiplash by the wagon and we all mosey over to the office for a final meeting with Mr. Pearson. Pearson said they would be loading the gold at 7 in the morning and there would be 3 strong boxes worth more than 20 thousand dollars, a heap of money, he tells us to all be ready and report to office at 6 am, with nothing more to say we leave the boss.

After supper at Sam's we go back to the room, clean our weapons, then fully load them all, storing extra ammunition in our pockets, there would be more in our saddlebags, we were loaded for bear and ready for a fight. Our plan is for me to ride Apollo up front, Bill would be on the seat with Whiplash, all of us would be carrying shotguns, I would hit the ambush sites first and try to discourage them lost souls before the wagon arrived, if that fails we will just keep driving and blast our way through. Not much of a plan but with a little luck we might just pull it off.

The morning came fast, Bill heads for the office, I head to the livery to saddle Apollo, Whiplash is getting the wagon ready, at the appointed time we all gather in front of the shipping office drinking hot black coffee and talking in hushed tones. Ratface is there a smug expression on his face, looking at us like we were already dead men. Mr. Pearson supervises the loading, then we shake hands just in case, then he wishes us luck, a look at worry on his face, I smile down at him astride Apollo, "don't go to worrying boss, old Whiplash, Bill and I will get er done". With that Whiplash cracks his whip and lets out a loud curse the team hits the braces moving out lively, Whiplash has Chosen fast strong mules, 4 strong, it is the man knows his work a wise decision, mules were stronger on the hills, he seems pleased when I agree with his choice of animals. Whiplash is a wizard with a team and a whip, knew how to not use up their strength knowing it might be needed later.

I ride back to the boys and tell them I was heading to the first site, horse tracks showed that 4 riders were riding ahead in our direction, we will have to show them the error of their ways before the day is out. Smiling riding fast the warrior fighting blood begins to stir in me, I clutch my medicine bag I feel its power. I stop just out of sight of the first ambush site, after ground hitching Apollo I grab the Winchester and start to injun up to a spot I selected previous, about 50 yards away and in direct line of fire with the hideout. Now not all outlaws are the sharpest sticks in the pile, this bunch had a solid wall of jagged rock directly behind them, perfect for ricochets, I could easily tear them to pieces with my rifle. Not being bloodthirsty, I holler at them to drop their weapons and come out with their hands up. My response is a blast of gun fire, so I just up and let go with my rifle, bullets screaming off the rocks, sounds of pain and curses fill the air. "Last chance boys, I will kill you all, now come out and I better see empty hands, then fired in another round to make my point. Within seconds 4 tough looking but scared men came out with hands held high, I can from here the wagon coming, "drop your gun belts and walk towards me, when they were separated from their artillery I have them sit and we waitfor the wagon, they were a quiet bunch, I just stand there smiling at the disgruntled bunch. Whiplash pulls the team up, looking like a man in his element, teasing and cursing them pitiful outlaws for fools. Bill turns their horses loose, we gathered their weapons put them in the wagon, then sent them walking, I tell them we knew their faces now and if we ever see them again we would shoot on sight, I realize I was smiling, feeling it a good day for battle.

The same strategy is used at the next 2 sites but no one was waiting for us, I feel it had been to easy and have a strong feeling they are going to hit us at the station, just try to shoot us down and just drive the gold away. About a mile from the station I had the wagon pull up and express my concerns, we all are of the same mind we need a plan. After jawing a bit, I finally say" I read once no matter if outmanned or outgunned always attack, attack, we are going to ride in nice and slow showing no concern, when we get close to the train we are going to let loose and run the wagon up beside the train and will fight from behind the wagon, maybe upset their plans". On my signal, Whiplash let them loose and be damn careful, laughing with a glint in the eye, "do not worry about me I will be right behind you.

Well that's how we play it, about 50 yards from the train shouting a Sioux war cry we charge the train, Whiplash has those mules running hard. Shots ring out from everywhere but they were caught flatfooted, rifle in hand I jump off Apollo and with a slap on the ass send him running down the track out of danger. My feet just hit the ground when Whiplash pulls the wagon to a stop, both men quickly get off the seat, Bill and I put down heavy and accurate fire as Whiplash quickly cut the mules loose. Suddenly the shooting stopped, we can her men arguing on what to do next, Bill calls to them," we brought the gold for you boys, now come and collect, but there will not be many of you shitheads to collect on it".

About 10 minutes later we hear horses leaving, waiting until we sure they had left we then search for the station agent and the railroad men. We find them all tied and gagged inside the station but otherwise unhurt, we release them and after a brief period the gold is loaded and we watch the train smoking down the tracks, our job was done, we have succeeded and done what many could have not, it gave me a sense of pride, taking on a mans job and doing it well.

We return to a hero's welcome in Golden, miners cheering, Mr. Pearson smiling hugely, old rat face looking surprised and angry. Pulling up to the shipping company, looking at Mr. Pearson, I say "Well Sir we got it done as promised, they heard old Whiplash was driving and they all skedaddled". Pearson said after we got settled to come to his office to get paid and talk about upcoming shipments.

We head to Sam's for a bite to eat, he seemed happy that we had survived, and chatters away as we eat, and that Chin Li says to practice more, laughing to himself.

When we get to Pearson's office he is waiting and calls us in, after we are seated, I give him a brief description on the attempted robberies and the receipt for the gold, I think he was a bit in awe. He goes to the safe and took out some cash, placing 200 plus a 50-dollar bonus for both Bill and I, good money when cowhands were drawing about 30 a month. I look at him, "What about Whiplash, he had the toughest job without him we might not have made it. Pearson says Whiplash was on salary and got monthly pay, he was just doing his job. I am not at all pleased, so with a smile I tell Pearson "Whiplash will get a 100-dollar bonus for every shipment he drives through including this one, and we will not have any other driver but him, if not Bill and I might have moseyed along, recon lots of work for men of our skills. "Now don't be hasty Hardin, I will agree with your terms", quickly counting out a hundred more and hands it to Whiplash, who is now smiling hugely. Before we depart I talk to Pearson and told him flat out I believed there was an inside man tipping off the robbers, only he and the bank manager should know, and give us the shipment date at least 2 days in advance, the room was in total agreement when we left. Once outside the office old Whiplash could not contain himself, laughing and slapping his leg, "Hardin you are a wonder, getting the biggest skinflint in town to almost throw money at you, come on boys I will stand for drinks". I always believe in fair play and tell him honestly it took more nerve to sit on that exposed seat than me riding ahead. "Well boys off we go to the Red Rooster, got to tell the fellers what hero I am and buy a round, they sure are going to get a kick out this."

I tell the boys I will catch up with him later I needed a shave and a bath, instead of going to the crude bath house I went to Sam's knowing he could accommodate my needs. He is extremely pleased that I came to him, taking me around back ordered a bath going and had people scurrying, as I suspected Sam was the leader of these people, and a damn good one. While I wait for my bath, I undress and have a big soft towel around me, Sam's wife then with her gentle skilled hands gave me a very relaxing massage, and I realize it had been awhile since I relaxed, I would work more on Mr. Li's training. Then I had a long luxurious bath with scented water, never wanting to get out, but my toes started wrinkling before I finish with my bath my cloths were returned brushed off and my boots cleaned up.

When I was all set, I went I went to pay Sam, but he would not take my money, he told me we were good friends and family now. I bowed low and humbly thanking him before leaving, people will always surprise you.

—

If you fail to plan, you plan to fail.
- Benjamin Franklin

CHAPTER 15

THE INVENTION OF SUDDEN STEELE

I am feeling good, cleaned up and smelling good time to go see the boys for a quick drink head over to the saloon I find Bill sitting in on a few hands of stud and Whiplash is at the end of the bar talking a blue streak and doing some downright sinful bragging, I join the boys at the bar and order a beer. Now in Whiplashes version of our adventure we had whipped 40 deadly outlaws and Indians to boot, Whiplash has knack of stretching the truth to its far limits.

    Lifting my beer and about to take a drink I get pushed from the side and spill half of it all over the bar, I look over and see a huge half drunk Irish miner wearing a worn brown derby. It only takes a glance to recognize he is a man looking for a fight. Ignoring him I go back to talking to Whiplash, but the minerwill not let matter lay, after the second push he sure enough gets my attention. The bar gets quite they all know what's coming, Sneering the miner says" if it ain't the great Hardin Steele, heard you was right tough, well boy you do not look so tough to me", a few of his buddies are egging him on, he was a bruiser alright, has the look of a battle proven warrior and a tough customer, "" if you have the guts drop your gun belt and we will have a wee us a bit of fun". I smile at him my green eyes flashing feeling the warrior blood rising, "Well Paddy I'll oblige you, I recon you are all mouth and I will be teaching you your manners buckoo, bring it on big man this boy is going to clean your plow." From the end of the bar I hear Bill say," I got 100 that says old Hardin whips him", he was covered quickly.

Unbuckling my gun belt I put it on the bar the turn to face the big man, without a word he rushes in fast hoping to catch me off guard, I easily side step him and as he goes by me I hit him with a chop between the neck and shoulder hitting a pressure point, it did not slow him up much but he knew now I could hurt him and he may have caught the tiger by the tai. Paddy smiles but comes in slow hands up ready to throw punches with those huge fists, he throws a looping left hook which I easily block on my forearm, with my fingers extended palm facing up I drive my fingers deep into his solar plexes, with a gasp the miner stops in his tracks, I slide to my left and with a hard left I stab him in the kidney causing him to let scream, moving quickly in front of my gasping opponent I then let go with a left hook and upcut to the chin catching him right on the point of the chin, the sweet spot. The big mans eyes roll back in his head he falls like a tall oak tree, but it was lights out, he does not feel his face crashing into the hard-dirty sawdust covered floor. There is stunned silence at the unexpected outcome, one of Whiplashes cronies is heard saying, "Damn that was Sudden". Bill picked up on that immediately "Sudden Steele, it has a good ring to it", and that is how I got the name Sudden, people seemed to like it, and out west when you are tagged with a name it sticks like it or not, reminds me of old Wild Bill.

Bill comes over smiling and laughing, "well done Mr. Sudden Steele, thanks Hoss I made good money betting on you ", damn fools" he says loudly. "Pleased I can help your financial situation, I recon you can buy supper then." Whiplash comes over looking almost sober, "that was some fighting Hardin, I do not think you will be bothered much after that there massacre ", chuckling loudly. I check on the big Irishman, he will be alright, slowly he is coming around, I held no grudge, some men just like to fight, I put 20 dollars on the bar and tell the bartender to give the defeated man and his friends some grand Irish whiskey when he comes to.

About a week later the Denver paper gets to town, I open it before breakfast, there in big bold print on the front page was my name, shocked I almost spit out my coffee. After the initial shock wears off, I read the article, it was all about bringing the gold shipment through despite 2 attempted hold ups, I suspect the station operator at the train depot had something to do with this. Soon as Bill comes in I show him the newspaper, he was greatly impressed with himself, damn show-off. But it gives me an idea on how to handle the next shipment, but I will have to mull it over a bit.

The town now has a small newspaper and I plan on using it as one of my chess pieces in this deadly game, always plan and keep a step ahead, never let your enemies get set. Convincing myself it was a clever idea I meet up with Whiplash and Bill and tell them my idea. We are going to publish in the paper our next trip with warnings to any would be hold up men. They both kind of look at me funny, I then explain to them my reasoning to why I think this plan will help get the next gold shipment through. Right off the get it will deter the dumb and small time crooks, and the smart ones will likely think it is a trap, I think they will wait for each other to act, "Boys I believe we can bluff em good and leave them villains with an empty sack. They sit silent mulling over the information, Bill is thoughtful, Whiplash a bit confused, but a moment later he says, "that might just be bold enough to work, you got some brass balls Sudden." We all agreed to give er a go, with that I go to see the newspaper editor. The editors name is Franklin Felix a young intelligent pleasant man full of pride and principle, was educated in Boston, I tell him I want to put a full front page add and would pay good for it. The page is to read exactly as follows.

ATTENTION TO ALL BANDITS AND
HOLD UP MEN

Mr. Bill Mathers, Whiplash Smith and Hardin Steele with be will be escorting the next gold shipment on the 25th of this month. Any attempts to rob or delay this shipment will be dealt with aggressive violence and hot lead.

For those unfortunates who disregard this warning, we have dug 5 fresh graves on boot hill, more will be dug if required.

Signed
H Steele

Franklin the young editor is just in bliss, "this will surely hit all the big papers, you are taking significant risk Mr. Steele, and please no fee required this will make great print and it will be damn fun to watch the outcome." "Thank you, Franklin, appreciate it, I am hoping if we survive to that you and I can get together for a few drinks of good scotch and talk a little literature and politics." Frank readily agrees to the idea, he also very much enjoys intellectual discussions and good scotch.

Well the news spreads like wildfire, Pearson was livid as I had not told him of it yet, I thought the old boy was going to explode, but he finally calmed him down after I explained my thinking. "Well you got the first one through I will trust your judgement and savvy, but damn slick trick if it works, be careful and good luck Hardin if you get yourself killed lad old Bear will skin me alive. On the 25th we loaded the gold in the wagon, making a point to look ready, relaxed and confident, other than our weapons you would think we were heading out for a picnic lunch. We keep the same setup with me on

Apollo up front on the scout, with a careful eye I scout every possible ambush site, not a single outlaw to be found, we make it to the train in ahead of schedule, I check the station it is safe and secure workers attending their duties, we quickly unload get a signed receipt and head back to the barn, damn, we fooled em again.

When we arrive back in town I head straight for Pearson's office, Whiplash heads to the barn to unhitch the team and Bill takes the horses to the livery. Walking into the office I notice old rat face is gone and a new man was behind the counter, smiling he sends me immediately into Pearson's office. I give Mr. Pearson the receipt, "Well boss I recon the bluff worked, learned that a good bluff comes in right handy at time, Luke Short taught me that." Pearson went to the safe asked me to sit for a moment as he drew our pay. Looking across the desk at me with some concern on his face proceeds to fill me in on the next shipment. "Hardin within the next 2 weeks we will be taking the biggest shipment ever in the territory, close to 75 thousand dollars", well I knew immediately this one was it, there was going to be trouble and lots of it, it was just too much money for the outlaws not to have to try for it or they must leave the Territory in disgrace, even outlaws have a code of honour. My thoughts turn to what I read on the great general Alexander, what would Alexander do I thought to myself.

Alexander the Great was a master at war but in the beginning, he was always outnumbered so used skill, tactics and most importantly deception to defeat his enemy he just a smart commander you could react as the battle changes as they always do and that's the way we will plan the big run with tactics and deception.

I call on Pearson and request a secret meeting with him at his home, Pearson had power and connections, I am hoping to use them. We sit in the parlor enjoying a glass of scotch I tell him of my plan and ask if he could convince the railroad to cooperate but it all must be done in secret, he tells me there will be no trouble with the railroad and he would see what he could arrange then let me know in a day or two. After finishing my fine glass of scotch I leave Pearson I need to talk with Whiplash we need another driver and a good one, tough and honest. "I will talk with Dutch Herman, a Pard of mine a good man keeps his word and has no give in him. The next day Pearson tells me all is in order and arranged, the shipment is to be delivered in 2 days' time. Pearson, Dutch, Whiplash, Bill and I have one final meeting to make sure we missed nothing, one mistake will most certainly lead to death and tragedy.

I had already made the decision this was going to be my last trip, word has it that they were needing Rangers in Arizona, I am hoping to get on with them. I will tell Pearson when I get back, now it is time to get to work and load up. I again lead us out of town setting a slow easy pace, no use ever rushing towards death. We take our time staying vigilant, there are a few very smart robbers you just never know what they may do. Just before we hit the first ambush spot, we stop the wagon just out of rifle distance, then proceed to have lunch that Sam had packed for us. As I am eating my sandwich I can feel eyes upon me smiling I wonder what the would-be robbers were thinking, I am getting great amusement out of it. We sit there for about an hour talking away then we all mount turn the wagon around and head back to Golden.

We are met by Pearson outside his office, he tells us Dutch made it through and the gold was already safely on the train. What I done was get Pearson to do was talk to the railroad and have them stop at a crossing about 20 miles in the opposite direction, then loaded up Dutch late at night and very quietly sent him and 2 deputies on their way. We acted like the decoy and we did are acting well, the robbers once again holding an empty bag, and any waiting at the station could only watch as the train high balled it right by them. When we head over to get paid, I tell Mr. Pearson this was my last run, I am heading to Arizona to hook up with the Rangers, he then asks Bill if he would stay but Bill declines saying he was heading to California, hoping to get rich. He said he was sorry to see us go but understood how young men need to find their nitch in life.

Shaking hands, we say our good- byes and thank him for the entertainment. I ask old Whiplash if he was staying on with the company, he explodes" hell no, be to damn boring and civilized with you boys gone, Hardin I know that Arizona country and some of the Indians, might make a good guide for a wet behind the ears Ranger boy". I immediately saw the logic of it and reply to him I would enjoy his company and to get ready, we are riding in 2 days.

What the ancients called a clever fighter is one that
not only wins, but excels in winning with ease.
- Sun Tzu

CHAPTER 16

MY FIRST BADGE

After saying a sad good- bye to Bill I wish him well and tell him I hope he makes his fortune, Whiplash and I with excitement and apprehension head for Arizona country to new adventures and unknown dangers. It became my habit to read in the evening by the fire, Whiplash who had not been as lucky had no formal education and could barely read but is fascinated by books, so I read aloud, the first book I read to him was Ivanhoe by Walter Scott, about Normans, Saxons, jousting and combat, old Whiplash and I will explore many books in our travels. As we ride I have Whiplash explain the country to me, the Indians we may encounter, most important were to find water in this dry country. The old he wolf was not bragging he knew a lot of the country, the Apache and Paiutes and probably the most dangerous the Puma's being the troublesome types in the territory, mean, invisible until wanting to be seen, run down a horse over a day, if they captured an unfortunate they would be tortured for days as sport, but they respect bravery and only bravery.

We finally arrive in Tucson, looking down at the town I first notice is the majestic church a bright white Spanish built structure with two steeples, beautiful workmanship, in front of the church was an open plaza with a water fountain with a couple shade trees. Adobe buildings dotted the town, ideal being low solid keeping it dark and cool inside, most had small pens in to hold the goats and other animals, some with gardens. There were few people about, we arrived during the heat of the day, being intelligent folks most were taking their siesta's letting it cool down before continuing their day, looking over at Whiplash we ride down into the pleasant looking small town.

After stabling our horses and stowing our gear we head over to the Ranger office to talk with the Captain. When we enter the Captain is sitting behind the desk feet on the table reviewing wanted posters, looking up he recognizes old Whiplash and after some good-natured ribbing Whiplash introduces me to the Captain who goes by the handle Tom Ford, he reminded me of Inspector Steele, both hard honest men cut from the same cloth. After we sit down and over coffee he asks what he can do for us, I let Whiplash do most of the talking, Captain this here is Mr. Hardin Steele, in Colorado known as Sudden Steele, he has come to join up and I would sign on as scout. The Captain looked me over, "you seem to be a bit young for the work, tough dangerous country out here, especially for lawmen, but seems I have heard that name somewhere. Whiplash again takes the lead, telling him of how we hoodwinked the bandits in Colorado, not loosing an ounce of gold, and it was me who did all the planning. Smiling the Captain now remembered reading of our exploits, I give him a short talk of my background and the training I had received from men like Bear, Ramon, Black hand and others, also I could read and write and was fluent in Spanish and better than average pistolero. Whiplash jumps back in telling the Captain of my tracking skills and I was a fighter, and real handy with gun, knife and hand to hand combat, telling him the story how I took out the big miner.

I finally manage to get a few words in tell him of my brotherhood with my uncle Black Hand and brother Grey Wolf, great Sioux warriors and the battle with the Crow.

The Captain after thinking the matter over for a few minutes, says "welcome to the Arizona Rangers boys, the pay is 55dollars a month and found, the bunkhouse is next door store your gear and get settled, come back tomorrow morning and I will swear you in "thanking him we head back into the street, gathered our gear and took it to the bunkhouse. It is empty when we arrive so finding a couple extra beds set up in our new home, I have a good feeling about it, and just hope I am up to the task. It was hot dry country, rugged mountains wild and mysterious, I liked it for its beauty and challenges, I am becoming anxious to go to work.

We stroll over to a cantina run by a man called Manuel and his family, it has a pleasant atmosphere, dark and cool inside, basic wooden furniture very clean. Manual is a short round man with a big smile, his wife was a large sweet woman, he comes to our table and welcomes us with great fanfare, his English was not strong so we speak Spanish and we ask for coffee and whatever there was to eat. The cooking smells delicious making my stomach grumble reminding me been awhile since we ate last and the coffee is real good, shortly after he brings out heaping platters of food, I took to Mexican food right off liking the spices and the heat, we dig in and eat hardy, after the meal he brings more coffee and a desert of a fried dough with honey, almost as good as Megs pies. I invite him to sit and have coffee with us, after telling him how much we enjoyed the meal, I start asking him questions of the town, the people, local customs and so forth, as with the Chinese the Mexicans always seemed to know what was going on, and are for the most part good and loyal friends.

We leave Manuel telling him we will be around for awhile and keep the coffee on for we would be back often.

After a quick stroll around the small community and greeting a few of the locals and introducing ourselves, we then head back to the bunkhouse. When we get back there are a couple Rangers loafing outside, both tough and capable looking men, not gunfighters but determined hunters, solid, tough and killers if need be. Surprisingly they have both heard of me and Whiplash, the Ranger with the pale intense blue eyes is named Tom **Wilkes**, the other ranger was a tall galoot with an easy going way about him was called Lanky **Bellows**. Sitting in the shade out front of the bunkhouse I begin to check over and clean all my guns, then commence asking questions of the Rangers seeking information on the land, the outlaws in the area, the natives, I learned young to listen to men of experience, they had already learned the hard lessons of survival. Other men came in through the evening, all seemed like good steady men, including Whiplash and myself there were 8 Rangers to cover an immense area, a few good men doing the job of many. That evening when things settled down I pull out a book written by a man named Marco Polo who was the first outsider to visit previously unknown China and he wrote of his adventures, most of the boys though this was amusing and started calling me the Professor, all good-natured humour with no mean in it.

The next morning, we report to the Captains office and are sworn in and I receive my first lawman's badge, after the short ceremony, wasting no time he orders us to head to a town called Sabino Canyon, there was trouble with the robbing, claim jumping and killing of miners. Before we depart the Captain says to me "Ranger Steele we clean things up and fast, try to bring them in sitting a saddle but there is no problem with them if they are wrapped up laying across it, good luck to you and if you need help just holler, good luck". After he dismisses, us we gather up our gear and are on the road within the hour, riding towards my first test as a Ranger and Lawman.

Life is full of surprises and I got my first test as a lawman before we even reached Sabino, riding into a small meadow we came across 4 men who were mistreating a young Mexican sheep herder youth roughing him up. One of the cowboys is holding the boy and another punching him, all of them thinking it was great fun. I pull the shotgun from my back sling and casually lay it across the saddle, Whiplash pulls his rifle we then ride up to the men. They stop their entertainment looking us over, I shift the scattergun to cover them and then in a commanding tone spoke," You men release that boy and step away, seems damn cowardly to me it takes 4 big men to beat up one young lad, now do as I say and let the boy go.". There is always a mouth in every group this was no exception mouth he quickly speaks up in a surly threatening voice," you boys should mind your own affairs isn't none of your concern what we do to this filthy Mexican sheep herder, damn sheep stinking up the whole country, light out or you will get the same.

Well sir any form of abuse does not sit right with me, so smiling I level the greener on them, men may argue with a pistol or rifle but no one goes against a shotgun at close range. Looking down at the men I announced myself", my name is Arizona Ranger Steele drop your weapons or you may be having dinner with the devil tonight," 'I then cocked both barrels of the shotgun, grumbling they all dropped their gun belts. My fighting blood is up and it angers me when the strong hurt the weak, with Whiplash covering them with his rifle I dismount and walked up to the 2 who were beating the boy, ordering the other 2 to stand back. "Well I can I see you can fight boys now let's see how you 2 fight a man," I am feeling mean and craving action, so I up and backhand the closest man and tear into those boys. I hit, chopped and grabbed pressure points I wanted them to feel pain with every hit or throw, they must have felt they had run into a twister, I show little mercy and punish them maybe a bit more than I should have, now both men are on the ground groaning in pain and bruised up bad before the lesson was over. I then go over and checked the young sheepherder, he is bruised up a bit but being a tough lad had no further injuries, after his thanks I send him on his way, and held the cowboys there until he and the herd were out of site. The 2 cowboys on the ground are slowly recovering, old Whiplash thinks this is great fun and is laughing at them, calling them all sorts of unflattering names. After mounting up I say to the roughnecks" if you follow or hurt that boy I will hunt every one of you coyotes down and kill you on sight, you have my word on that", my flashing green eyes signaling deadly intent, they all knew I meant what I said.

Without another word, we turn and ride away towards to our destination, after a bit Whiplash breaks the silence" that was some slick work Hardin, you done good, word will spread now that Ranger Steele is one mean hombre and not a man to go to war with". I tell him that it would probably be a help in the future, but I did it because it was right, and I will not tolerate abuse, he nods his agreement. The next morning, we are riding into Sabino Canyon.

We are rough men and used to rough ways.
- Bob Younger

Chapter 17

RANGER WORK

Our first stop upon arriving in town is Sheriffs office, my first impression is not a good one, the office was dirty a couple liquor bottles littering the floor, we find a grubby looking hard case behind the desk, not even to bothering to take his feet off the desk as we came in. Looking up he in a surly tone says, "what do you two want"? I tell him we want to speak to the Sheriff and quick. He laughs "the Sheriff is in back sleeping one off and does not want to be disturbed", without hesitation I enter into the cell area and find the passed out Sheriff, I grab him roughly by the collar and accidently smash his face into the bars, quickly put him in an arm lock and push him back into his office. Whiplash has his pistol casually pointed at the deputy, after taking their guns I release the shocked man. They are very unhappy complaining they were the law should not be treated this way. I smile and Whiplash chuckles "My name is Ranger Hardin Steele and this is my Pard Whiplash Smith, the

Captain sent us down to sort out this trouble you are having with the robbing and killing of the miners, and believe me we are going to get it done hard and fast. "I was going to ask for your help but now I am going to tell you to stay out of our way, now go tell your Boss we are here and his time is short and he should pack up and leave the country, taking his pack of rats with him. The dirty lawman is getting some of his nerve back "you will not be living long ranger, Pago Jones, Black John, and Kid Riess are in town and they eat Rangers for breakfast. I laugh, "you just tell them they might find this ranger damn tough chewing".

I give them back their guns and order them out of the office, going to the door I watch as the 2-dirty lawman beeline it straight to the Blue Ox saloon to announce our arrival.

Wasting no time, we mount up and head directly for the mines that sit on the edge of town, as I near the first diggings 2 men put down their tools and pick up their rifles, riding up slowly and stopping in front of the men I announce ourselves as the law, flashing my badge while doing so, and tell them we were going roust out those villains and stop the stealing and claim jumping and killings. I ask the men to gather as many men as they can I need their help and information before I can get to work. Within a half an hour about 20 miners are gathered, when I asked who was responsible for the robbing and killing there is always a top dog. The overall opinion was it is the leader called the Reverend, no one knew his real name, but claims he was a preacher at one time, a man with no morals or compassion, they tell me Pago, Black John and the kid were his henchmen and a mighty salty crew, not caring which direction their bullets come from. I inquire how they operated, seems they just bust in at night, wearing masks that fooled no one, and stole whatever gold they could find, most times not wanting witnesses kill the owner. I tell the men to keep their guard up and we were going rid the town of these snakes, I had already stirred the nest, the miners are all looking somewhat relieved.

On the way, back into town we spot a Mexican family sitting in the front of their adobe, we ride over hoping for a good meal. A man his wife and 3 kids are in the yard watching us ride up, suddenly there was great commotion, seems the oldest boy is the boy I saved from the cowboys, he is telling his story to his father in quick and animated fashion. All of them are smiling as we pull up, "Welcome Senor's, my house is your house come in and refresh yourselves", we all go inside it was nice to be around a family again, gives a man a certain feeling of comfort. Finding the house had no coffee, I go to my saddlebags and bring a bag of arbuckles into the kitchen, a man needs his coffee. The Father is a talkative man and insists on us telling us the story of his son's rescue, I let old Whiplash do the talking, that man could spin a yarn and soon has them all enthralled. I had also brought out some sheets of paper, I am going give the outlaws fair warning and an ultimatum.

Meanwhile the Sheriff tells the Reverend and his cronies what I had done to him and of my warning the Reverend finds this right amusing, just then 2 outlaws recent of Colorado get up and tell the Reverend they were pulling out, and advise him to do the same. The kid snickers, "you boys scare easy over 2 men", the older of the outlaws replied, "they do not call him Sudden Steele for nothing, salty with any weapon and gets mean when riled, I would rather rassle a cougar than have Sudden after me, be seeing you boys, climate just ain't healthy here anymore, take it from me boys, leave the territory and do not look back"." The Reverend is not smiling any longer, the men who left him were both tough and had proven their courage many times over.

The kid looks over at the Reverend, "not to worry Rev, I will kill him, I am going gut shoot that star packer and watch him die slow and hard, the kid liked killing it excites him, if he were a tinhorn and notched his gun handle he would have 7 notches filed.

We had finish our coffee and are now going out to find a camp, thinking we would not be welcome in town, we were invited to stay by the father but I tell them it was to dangerous do not want innocents hurt, the father than informs us of a small cabin that is hidden behind the house, good place for the horses to. We spend a quiet and comfortable night, the morning would most likely will be filled with blood and death.

We ride in early and go directly to the Sheriffs office, only the deputy was there, I tell him to get out and stay out we would be using this office while we were in town, he did not like it but did as he was told, uttering more threats as he walks away. I mosey around town and put up my notices while Whiplash cleaned up the office. The signs are printed in plain language, leaving no doubt leave surrender or it will be a showdown.

NOTICE

THE NAMES ON THIS LIST ARE TO LEAVE TOWN BY SUNDOW TOMORROW

THE REVERAND

PAGO JONE

BLACK JOHN

KID RIESS

SHERIFF BLAKE

DEPUTY ANDERSON

THOSE NOT OUT OF TOWN BY THE ALOTTED TIME WILL BE ARRESTED OR SHOT IF RESISTING ARREST.

H STEELE

RANGER.

The Kid Riess gets plumb upset reading the notice, swearing to kill me on site, as he is ranting, just then Whiplash enters by the front door with his shotgun, as I enter through the back of the saloon. With everyone's attention on Whiplash I enter unseen and in a sharp tone say "Hi Kid I said, hear your looking for my hide" all heads turn. The Kid is across the saloon directly in front of me, a look of malice on his face, "why yes Ranger "and begins drawing his hogleg, my first bullet nails the third pearl button on his shirt through his heart the second notching his shirt pocket, both killing shots, his gun had just barely cleared leather, he falls forward a look of fear and surprise on his face, dead before he hit the floor. Just then Whiplash swinging the greener tells everyone to just take it easy, "one killing a morning is more than enough, now you boys sit and relax". I look directly at the Reverend, "the notice stands and time is getting short, time you boys leave Arizona, if not you will be arrested and taken back to Tucson either sitting in or over your saddle. I later find out later 4 more outlaws leave quietly in the night the ex Sheriff and deputy among them.

It has always been my intention to arrest the leaders, cut off the head and the body will die, the miners seeing them locked up will bring witnesses forward to testify. I spot the young Mexican boy I saved and ask him to do me a favour, he is most anxious to help, I tell him I want him to watch the saloon and after an hour come back and tell me what he saw, and be careful not be seen. An hour later he comes back and tells us the men were drinking much, and arguing, thanking him I gave him a silver dollar, he left with a big grin. Just as I hoped they were drinking heavy and in the wee hours of the morning we were going to take them in their beds and have them locked up by morning. The three we were after were the Reverend, Pago and Black John, which all had rooms above the saloon. We wait until close to 3 am the town was graveyard quiet, then crossing over the street we quietly go up back stair of the saloon to the criminals rooms, we knew which rooms they were in and it is the Reverend we needed most, quietly moving down the hall we came to his door, the Reverend was getting sloppy he did not even bother to lock it, Whiplash had rags with him for gags and I had pigging strings for hog tying them, the Reverend did not wake up until we had him gagged and tied, his liquor fueled mind trying to figure out was happening to him. Next we approach Pago's room, it was locked but the locks on the doors were useless in these places, we easily sneak in, just as we get near the bed he wakes up without hesitation I whack him a good one on his thick skull with my pistol barrel, we leave the bleeding man secured, Black John will be the most dangerous, with the other 2 outlaws out of the game I take the direct approach, kicking the door in Whiplash rams the shotgun in Black Johns belly hammers cocking with deadly clicks, he has no choice but to give up. We leave the gags on and their hands tied walking them across the street to the jail, they were a might chilly in only their long johns. Once we have them behind bars we take the gags and binding off, they look right pitiful sitting there in their underwear. The Reverend looks up" what's this Ranger you gave us 24 hours, seems you cannot trust no one these days", smiling at him I answer, "Well I lied Reverend but I figure I am still in good with the big man on high, you could always call a Ranger if you feel you were treated unfairly". Whiplash was just beside himself with laughter and knowing he had a mighty good tale to tell when we got back to headquarters.

We then grab a couple hours sleep in the office, after coffee I send Whiplash to go to the mining site and tell the miners what happened and ask them to come to come over to the jail, I had something to show them. Whiplash returns shortly, said the miners would be drifting in directly. Within no time at all there is a fair sized group of miners outside the jail and more are coming. I go to the cells and wake the prisoners, then with the sawed off I prod them outside. When the miners see the outlaws standing embarrassed in their underwear, there was much laughter and applause. I call for quiet and then address the crowd

"I asked you men here today to show you that these outlaws have been skinned and will be taken back to Tucson for trail, as you can see they are no where near as tough as you thought. I want everyone who witnessed or has been robbed to sign sworn statements, we will clean out the rest of unfortunate ones that have not left town yet, we did our duty now it is up to you to do yours." With that Whiplash escorts the unhappy chilly prisoners back to their cells and the miners head to the saloon to talk things over. My next duty was to talk to the mayor and try to find a solid Sheriff to now keep the town and miners safe, the mayor told me of a man named Bret Hart, ex army officer and had worked keeping the peace in a few cow towns, tough and steady a good man who knows when not to use a gun. The mayor then tells me Bret is currently working as foreman for a rancher about 10 miles from town, I thank the Mayor and head directly back to the jail.

During the next 2 days 6 miners came in and signed sworn statements charging the prisoners with robbery and intimidation, unfortunately there were no witnesses left alive to charge them with murder. I now had more than enough evidence against them, leaving Whiplash in charge of the prisoners I ride out to talk with Bret Hart.

I find the ranch with no problem and as I am riding up to the ranch house there is a tall man with a military bearing is standing on the porch, a well used but clean six gun on his hip. When I pull up in front of the ranch house he looks over Apollo, "Howdy stranger damn fine looking animal you got yourself, get on down the coffee is on ". "I never turn down a coffee pard, obliged". Over coffee I introduce myself and tell him of the events of the last few days, the killing of the Kid and the capture of the Reverand and his gang, and I have come out to talk to him about taking on the Sheriffs job, further telling him I thought he was the right man for it. "I heard of you when I was up Colorado way when you were hauling gold out of Golden, I figured you to be a might older, you must be mighty good with that handgun, the Kid was no slouch, and that was some pretty slick work catching the Reverend and his bunch. I look to him" that Kid was nowhere near fast, a lawman's work was mostly using his mind and trusting your instincts not guns, never enjoy killing". "Brent, they need a good man, a man who knows when not to use his gun, I believe they need you old son, the money is pretty good and much easier than punching cows". Being a ex army officer he was used to making decisions and after a some thought he smiles and says he will take the job, but would be a week or so until he could make it in, he could not leave his boss until the roundup and branding was finished. I said that would be fine and I would tell the Mayor of his coming. Shaking hands, I climb back up on Apollo and knowing I had chosen the right man and ride away satisfied.

Things are calm in town when I get back, the honest and good folks are enjoying new freedoms, women can walk the streets again without fear. My first stop back is to the Mayor and let him know Bret would be assuming the duties of Sheriff and would be in town within the week, he is greatly pleased.

When I get back to the jail, I tell Whiplash of my meetings with the Mayor and Bret Hart, then sent him over to the Saloon to get the prisoners clothing, I had made my point and did not want those boys catching cold, the Captain might be down right displeased if I bring em back ailing. After we check all the clothing for weapons and such I throw them into the cells and inform the prisoners we will be heading back to Tucson in 2 days' time.

There were 4 saloons in town, grabbing my shotgun leaving Whiplash to guard the prisoners I visit each saloon and announce that all card sharps, grafters and lawbreakers were to leave town right quick, there is a stage leaving that evening and if they were not on it, they would be arrested. Well sir, when that stage left it was packed to the rafters, men were fighting to get on it.

The next morning, I have Whiplash get our gear ready and prepare for our departure tomorrow, I am sitting outside sitting with my feet resting on the rail when I spot 2 young men in buckskins both carrying rifles looking like they were part of them. On a hunch, I invite them for coffee and conversation, they had a look of being from the Tennessee Blue mountains, men who did not look for trouble but would will never walk around it. I introduce myself and Whiplash, they had both heard the stories and seemed to be right pleased to meet me. As I thought they were brothers, Peter and Paul Hennessy, I make my offer to them, asking them to keep an eye on the town until the Sheriff took over it would pay 20 dollars apiece for a week's work.

They discuss it for a few minutes and being short of cash take the job, I tell them they would start tomorrow morning and I would like to treat them to supper at Manuel's later this evening, they readily accept my offer.

The Hennessy brothers show up bright and early next morning raring to get to work, I have the Mayor swear them in as deputies, with everything ready for our return trip we once again hit the trail with prisoners in tow, and knowing the town is in good hands, I was feeling good about the job we had done, only one killing and 3 hard evil men in soon to be residing in Yuma prison or walking the 13 steps.

I ask you to judge me by the enemies I have made.
- Franklin D. Roosevelt

CHAPTER 18

THE HUNT FOR TEX FOWLER

There are no problems on the trail back, I had learned from Bear and Ramon on our first meeting how to handle prisoners, and I am a man of caution and vigilance, old Whiplash is as steady as they come,I have the right man covering my back, another lesson learned. As we ride into the Ranger compound with our prisoners in tow the Capt. comes from his office looking a bit surprised at our speedy return and our bringing in 3 of the most dangerous outlaws in Arizona. After I lock up the prisoners, I quickly brief the Captain on our activities and hand him the signed statements from the witnesses, anticipating he would want a written report I had taken the time on the road to write one up and presented it to him. He quickly looks it over, this is where Ramon's teaching comes in handy, the Captain is very much impressed with the well written report and excellent penmanship. We are dismissed and told to take it easy get some rest he would have another job for us soon.

That evening in the bunkhouse as I am reading the Republic written by Plato, Whiplash with his flare for the dramatic tells the other Rangers of our adventures, and my gunfight with the Kid Reiss, they are all looking at me with a bit of awe and a new-found respect and I feel I earned some. After a bit, I tell the boys that is was not much of a ruckus like most outlaws they were none to smart, I just went in and told them old Whiplash was in town and they scurried like gophers into there holes, this getst a great laugh from all in the room.

A few days later the Captain sends Whiplash out with Lanky to hunt down a couple of renegades that were causing havoc, stealing livestock and killing homesteaders looks like the next job I stand on my own.

I am sitting around reading and getting a bit bored wanting some action when I get summoned to the Captains office bouncing off my bunk right up I make my way quickly over to his office. "Ranger I am sending you to bring in a man named Tex Fowler for bank robbery he robbed a bank in Oxbow, the Captain said Tex is not a bad man but the just a damn impulsive fool who after losing his spread to the bank got drunk and robbed the damn bank. He went on to warn me that Tex could hide his trail like an Indian, an excellent shot with any weapon, and knows the country well, it will not be an easy job, I was to get ready to depart immediately and head to Oxbow to pick up the trail, just as I am leaving he says, "Ranger Steele, bring him in alive if you can". "I always hope to bring them in alive Captain I do not care for killing folks, I will try my best Boss, but it will be up to Tex" Nodding the Captain dismisses me.

I do not want to waste time going to Oxbow but I need information, instead I found out the location of his former spread and pointed Apollo towards it figuring he would stock up on supplies and ammunition and head out from there. When I get to the small ranch it is deserted and after checking the cabin I confirm my suspicions, the pantry has been cleaned out and his clothing and guns are gone, the corral is empty, but after searching a bit I find tracks where he mounted up, and headed north into the mountain country, also noticing there is a distinct mark of a crack on his horses front left horse shoe.

Tracking down a man is not just following tracks in the sand, you had to think like your prey, know where he would have to go to find water and shelter, then try to figure what his destination might be. Just before I left Tucson, just to make things a little more interesting I am told the Apaches have broke from the reservation and were on the warpath killing raping and burnin. I hope Lanky and old Whiplash are keeping a sharp eye on the skyline, I seem to have grown quite fond of old Whiplash.

Apollo is raring to go so I set off north at a fast pace, it will be brutal hard riding for the next few days I need to make up some distance, damn I am grateful to have a horse like Apollo who is more than up for the challenges I am going to put him through I hate it but my animal brother will suffer some before this hunt is done. I basically headed north, figuring he will head for the north country and the border, but always I keep an sharp eye out for the renegade Apaches. Tex is good and I mean Apache good, I have to use all my skills to keep on his trail, I find his horse in a corral on a small ranch, it had a bruised hoof so he was forced to trade his fine big horse for a smaller mustang cross. Looking over the ground for the shape of the mustangs tracks I warn the rancher of the Apaches busting out of the Reservation and to keep his guns close better yet, climb on your fastest horse and make run for town, once again I set off at a good pace, Apollo is still showing no signs of wear he is one in a thousand. I can tell by the freshness of the tracks and his well concealed campsites that I am making up ground and I figure old Tex would know someone is on his trail by now one thing sure I ain't going to low rate this man he is all Hombre. There vis a slight change in his riding he is stopping and checking his back trail more often, using every trick in the trying to hide his trail, Bears training has prepared me for just this scout, Tex is good but there is no shaking me I am on him now lick a tick on a coon dog.

We are getting well into the mountains, knowing now I must be getting close, Tex I recon is about through running and will make his stand soon, he is no longer trying to hide his trail, Tex I figured being a fighter like myself and will always at some point say the hell with it and make his stand, go out slugging.

The next day around noon I finally spot him, hazy through the heat waves, riding into a valley slow and careful I watch as he carefully sweeps the area looking back he sees me sitting high up on the rocks, he turns and puts his horse into a trot. I work Apollo down into the valley and hit the flat ground running full out, I can see his horse is tiring, I run Apollo until I feel he had enough then reined him back into a fast ground eating trot. The distance is closing he sees me gaining on him and even from this distance he knows there is no chance in hell outrunning Apollon, he suddenly turns and heads for the rocks I know he will be looking for a good shooting position. I turn Apollo into a cleft in the rocks and ride in until a wall of jagged rock stops me short, but I am close enough now, Apollo is safe from bullets and close enough I can get back to him fast.

Grabbing my rifle, I crawl up to the rim, crawling slowly until I find what I think is a good position, slowly I raise my head, my hat is whipped from my head followed by a rifle shot and a chuckle, I roll quickly pulling up fast and let go a quick shot, tickling his left exposed shoulder, it is my turn to chuckle. I call over, "Howdy Tex, nice morning, I am Ranger Steele and the Captain sent me to fetch you in, I figure you should come along peaceable, come back get a good lawyer maybe only get a year or two". Laughing he says "You must be the one they call Sudden, I heard of you, don't be so sure I will be the one killed here, sending a shot close to my head to emphasize his point. I hold my fire, "Think it over Tex, come back with me, give the money back, the Captain and I will speak up to you, get you a short sentence", then I put a bullet by his ear, making my point, "besides the Captain said he wanted you alive". We sat there quiet for a spell, I am giving Tex time to figure things out. Suddenly I see movement and dust moving in the valley, "Tex?", "I see them Ranger" as they get nearer we see it is a boy and a girl on a horse riding full out with 8 Apaches on Indian ponies giving chase. Without hesitation, I tell Tex to cover me I am going to try to bring them in here we got ground here to hold them off. I run to Apollo

and charge into the he valley heading at the Apaches from an angle
to keep the lead horse with the woman and boy out of the line of fire.
I charge them screaming the Sioux war cry, cutting loose with my
long gun, not hitting much but between the war cries from a white
man and the firepower they slowed up, I turn and charge to the
youngsters horse slapping it on the butt with my rifle barrel getting
everything that horse had to give, we run full out until we come up
to Tex's position, securing our horses with Tex's we scurry up and
get behind cover fast. When I look back the Apaches have already
vanished into the landscape, but they are not about to give up, looks
like it is going to be a scrap. Taking a moment from looking over
the landscape I turn my attention to our new arrivals they are very
scared and quiet. Introducing myself and Tex I tell them Tex and
I can handle these pesky Indians no problem at all. The girl in a
shakey voice tells us her name is Carol she was coming on 17, and
the boy was her brother Billy 10 years old, they had gone for a ride
and when the Indians came upon them and they had made a run
for it, Carol did the talking "thank God you were here, they would
have got us for sure, I was real scared I did not have a gun or knife
to kill myself before the caught us". Carol even though scared and
dusty is a most beautiful young woman, long yeller hair and the
deepest blue eyes I had ever seen on a woman, a couple inches over 5
ft., with a figure that would turn most men's heads, mine included.
From behind me Tex says, "took a bit of a chance their Ranger, I
could be long gone by now", I turn and smile "no chance at all you
old fraud, we both know you would never leave these folks to the
Apache, they will be coming soon, how are you for ammunition?".
Saying he was a bit short I gave him half a box of mine, he takes a
position and piled up rocks to better protect himself, I settle in and
do the same. Looking at Carol I ask if she could shoot, she said she
could but was not a good shot, so I handed her my shotgun and two
extra shells, showed her how to load and cock it, smiling talking soft
hoping to calm her and young Billy "all you need to do is point it
and pull the triggers but make sure you put it snug into her shoulder
or you may break it, then just point and squeeze the triggers, do not
hesitate if need be just shoot".

Then it became a game of cat and mouse, the Apache sniping at us, trying to draw our fire, but we had both been fighting Indians to long to respond to their tricks. I thought it might be fun to shake them up a bit and I called out in Sioux I am Crow Killer, Nephew to the great Sioux Chief Black Hand, Brother to the great warrior and horse thief Grey Wolf, then cursed them out for the cowards they were. I wait about a minute, then mimmick a pretty good version of an owl screech, an owl in the day was bad medicine for the Apache, scares hell out of them a death sign. Billy with big eyes askes if what I said was true, I say it is and I am a full-blooded Sioux warrior. Tex mentions something about how I was full of surprises, now knowing where I learned my tracking skills.

Everyone is on edge waiting for action, and it came real sudden like, not more than 20 yards in front of us the Apaches came out of the ground as if by magic coming at us from 3 sides, Tex killed one and wounded another, I nailed 2 coming directly at me, I hear the blast of the shotgun but before I can look a big brave is on me trying to drive his knife into my stomach, after a desperate struggle I chop him in the throat crushing his windpipe and then drew my six-gun and shoot him twice. Looking around I realize the fight is over, Carol and Billy are alright but Carol was crying, Tex had a cut on his chest but did not look to bad and had already stopped bleeding, we had been extremely lucky, my luck was I was fighting beside a real warrior. When I ask Carol if she was alright, she stops her crying and drying her eyes on her dress, tells me she had to kill an Indian, and had never even killed so much as a rabbit before. "Its alright honey, you did very well and probably save our all our lives, you are a very brave woman". Tex chuckles saying something about a certain Ranger if not careful would be roped and hog tied in matrimony if not careful. I stand up and face Tex, smiling calling him a durn fool but a little red around the ears. Without warning I draw my .44 Russian and point it at Tex's belly" drop your rifle and gun belt Tex."

I look him right in the eye and say, "this is how it is going to work Tex, you are going to give me the bank money back, and I am going to return it to the bank with your apologies, tell the Captain of your heroics today and that you outsmarted me a gave me the slip, and with having to get Carol and Billy to care for had to return to Tucson and could not give stay on the hunt". "But you will be leaving Arizona Tex, I suggest Montana, people know me there, if you need anything just tell them you are a friend of mine". How are you set for water and money"? "Well Mr. Ranger Steele seeing you are taking all the bank money leaves me with an empty sack, good for water got 2 canteens near full". I get Carol and Billy on their horse, shake hands with Tex wishing him luck and I did not want to see him unless it was in Montana, then I dig into my pocket and hand him 50 dollars for travel expenses. As we were shaking hands he says, "Hardin it is more of I break than I deserve, I appreciate the loan and I am good for it pay you back when I see you, but why do you want me in Montana"? "Tex, I will be doing some lawman work in Montana soon, I miss the country, and I will need a good deputy, going to make you an honest man Tex," leaving him still shaking his head we ride away, I want to put some distance in before camping tonight, we were a long still a long way from being out of danger.

I believe that I am guided by chance encounters.
I believe the miracle of chance encounters.
Paulo Coelho

CHAPTER 19

THE RANGER GETS CAUGHT

We ride for about 3 hours in relative quiet until I find a good spot to camp for the night, it would have to be a dry camp with no fire not knowing there were Apaches still around. I grab my saddlebags off Apollo and bring them to where Carol and Billy are waiting I take out some jerky and a couple cans of peaches I had been saving, and we made our supper from it, Billy is plum pleased with the peaches a rare treat on the plains I have weakness for them . Both of my charges have had themselves a very long and difficult day young Billy was almost asleep on his feet, I set up their beds and tell them to get some rest we would be traveling far and fast tomorrow. When they are settled, I grab my rifle and walk out a bit to listen to the night sounds, after I was satisfied we are alone I return to camp. It is a bright moon, I look over where Carol is sleeping, she has the face of an angel pale and perfect in the moonlight, her beautiful yellow hair almost shimmering off the moon beams, it is a vision I will cherish and remember as long as I live. Apollo and Carol's horse are kept in close to camp, Apollo having the instincts of a mustang would warn me of any danger by critter or man, so I doze lightly through the night waking often to listen, all was quiet, I am thinking of Tex hoping he had made it past the gauntlet of savages.

Morning comes quickly, I get up make another check of the area, then start saddling up the horses, Carol wakes up first, sweeping that beautiful yellow hair back from her eyes she starts rolling her bedding for travel, she then gives young Billy a poke to get him moving, still a bit groggy he rolls up his bedroll and puts it on their horse. I tell them we will have breakfast in a few hours, there was a good water hole ahead and we would stop there. Billy said, "I hope we get there soon Ranger I am mighty hungry", smiling, "in couple hours Billy we will have sweet water, good grass for the horses and some thick bacon for breakfast.

I put Billy on Apollo with me him being the much stronger horse, we may need to make a run of it, and are still in unhealthy country. As we are riding Billy is full of questions, I smile to myself reminding me of my younger years with Bear and Ramon, my circle is half turned the student now becomes the teacher.

I tell him of my time with Bear and Ramon, and of the Sioux and how I became a Sioux warrior after the battle with the Crow, I catch Carol sneaking looks at me, and it makes me smile. A short while later we come to the waterhole, I have Billy dismount and get up behind Carol, leaving them I go slowly towards the waterhole, scouting it carefully, waterholes in dry country were always places of constant life and death. When I am satisfied, we were alone I wave Carol in, then I start to gathering dry sticks from underneath a small stand of trees and make a near smokeless fire. Carol demands to do the cooking, and while the bacon is sizzling, I make coffee, I surely did miss not getting my dark brew.

While breakfast is cooking, I take Billy to the waterhole we water the horses and fill the canteens, when we get the fire breakfast was ready and we were more than ready to eat.

After coffee, I put out the fire and cleanup up the area, then back on towards our destination and safety. Riding, my rifle is always out and ready, I ask Carol about her folks, and the farm, I have a bad feeling that the Apache have hit it already. She tells me they were living with her Aunt and Uncle, they had a quarter section about 6 miles from where we found them, my gut feeling got worse as I had seen to much black smoke coming from that direction earlier. I let them know when we got to Tucson the Captain will send a couple Rangers to check on her kin, and they were probably alright and worried more about the 2 of them. Carol forces a small smile, but knowing the way of the land and the Indians held out little hope they were still alive, but holding herself up well showing her grit. Watching her ride sitting the saddle well and her head high I am getting this feeling deep in my chest, it seems a mixture of desire, fascination and fear, I kind of feel like a hooked trout that willingly accepts being reeled in.

Without further incident, we arrive back in Tucson, Billy is fascinated by everything he sees, shooting rapid fire questions at me, we ride directly to the Captains office, after a brief explanation he bellows for 2 Rangers and tells them to immediately ride out and check Carol and Billy's Uncles cabin and any other farms in the area and to get back quick. I ask Carol and Billy to wait for me outside I need to talk to the Captain for a few minutes. When the Captain and I are alone, I hand him my official report, and tell him of the smoke I had seen. Then I tell him the real story about how Tex escaped, "Hardin boy you really pulled a fast one on old Tex, he is probably still trying to figure out how you hood winked him". Before leaving at a bit of a loss I ask the Captain would be the best for Carol and Billy while in town. Looking up with a twinkle in his eye, says "you found them Ranger you look after them".

My first thought is of Manuel's Cantina, we would get a bite eat and I will look for a place for them to stay, Manuel greets us warmly, after ordering Manuel takes a seat wanting to hear all about my trip. I give him a brief description of the events and then asked he had any ideas on where Carol and Billy could stay. Without a word, he gets up and goes into the kitchen and in rapid Spanish he and Mrs. Manuel have a short and animated conversation. Mamma Manuel comes out of the kitchen sweeps up Billy into a big hug, and gives

Carol a motherly hug, Mamma Manuel is a beautiful soul and caring mother. Manuel says, "Mamma insists they stay here, we have lots of room, never to many for Mamma." I ask Carol what she thought, I knew she had been around many Mexican families, but being a woman of good instinct, open minded and understanding said they would be pleased to stay and were most thankful for the families kindness .Manuel sends his gang of kids to get Carol and Billy's belongings, I send Billy along with them, it was pleasant to hear the children's laughter, always makes me smile.

I leave Carol in the capable in hands of Mamma Manuel, saying I will be back later and if he needed anything to call me or Whiplash. I stow my gear back in the bunkhouse, and head straight to the bath house behind the barracks have a long bath, shave, and change my cloths, refreshed I feel like a new man. When I get back to the barracks old Whiplash was there safe and sound, "You beat all Hardin, only man I know that goes on a manhunt, and returns with no prisoner, out of pocket by 50 dollars and returns with a youngster and a very pretty blonde gal". The boys of course found this extremely funny and have a good laugh at my expense, one can only smile. After the laughter died down I tell them the story up to the point of leaving Carol and Billy with Manuel, they all got a chuckle on how I outflanked old Tex. Lanky gets up and walks over to me with a very rare serious face and holds out this hand saying "Thank you Hardin for doing old Tex a good turn, we are pards, we have rode over some tough trails together "shaking his hand," Lanky, that old bullheaded Texican is to good of a man to kill, and I believe he will make me a right good deputy one day soon".

I head out telling the boys I am going to check on Billy, Whiplash said he would join me, I hear knowing laughter from the bunkhouse, them all knowing I was really going to see Carol.

Billy is helping with the cleaning up of the cantina and Carol was helping with the dishes. She has her hair brushed to a silvery shine, she is wearing on the Manuel's daughter skirts, the frilly kind all full of decoration, she was an absolute vision, I can feel my heart trying to hammer itself out of my chest, how the hell can a woman do that to a man? Pulling myself together I introduce them both to Whiplash, he and Billy took to one another right off, pals from the start, that boy was in for some right interesting stories and tall tales.

A couple of days later the Rangers return and the news and it is bad, both the Aunt and Uncle had been brutally killed and the farm destroyed, they buried them as the hot weather made it impossible to bring them back the only thing that they could recover was their Aunts bible. I knew it was up to me to break the sad news to Carol and Billy, it will be one of the hardest things I ever have to do, Whiplash insisted coming along and I am very pleased for his company.

When we get to Manuel's, Carol and Billy are waiting, knowing the Rangers were back, Carol is looking anxious and scared but holding up to it. Whiplash sits and puts Billy up on his lap, being very gentle. I tell them straight out what had happened wanting to get it over quick, sitting beside Carol I put my hand on her shoulder she buries her head in my chest and cries, it sure made me feel helpless, Whiplash is holding and comforting Billy in a quiet voice.

Mamma Manuel is also crying, envelops both of them and leads them back to the living area, I tell Manuel we would be back in a little while, walking away I am thinking what to do next with Carol and Billys later after Carol had time to compose herself we will discuss the matter and make our decisions.

Whiplash and I spend a few hours repairing our gear, cleaning our guns anything to keep busy, then slowly head back to the cantina. Carol being a young woman of fortitude and strong character has pulled herself together, her eyes were red from crying but now had a look of determination on her sweet and most beautiful face.

Whiplash takes Billy for a walk to go see the Rangers quarters and to meet some of the boys, Carol and I sat alone and over coffee and talk in quiet tones. I asked her if she had any other kin, she said she had a Grandmother who ran a cattle ranch just outside of Helena Montana, but they had no money to get there, I told her the money is not a problem and if she wished to go I would make sure they got there safe. Well it is a start I will wire to her Grandmother, explaining matters, and we will go from there, for now they would continue staying with Manuel, I was not going to be the damn fool who tries to take them away from Mamma Manuel.

Love is a game two can play and both win.
- Eva Gabor

CHAPTER 20

SCOUTING FOR THE 8TH

After reluctantly leaving Carol I go directly to the telegraph office and send a telegraph to Emily Holder, care of Helena Montana. As briefly as possible outline the killings of Carol and Billy's Aunt and Uncle, and that Carol and Billy were safe, then requested permission to send them on to her ranch. I get a response a couple days later, it read "Ranger Steele, send them along as quickly as possible, I will meet them in Helena on arrival, I am right grateful to you for saving them, I am good for any expenses, Em Holder."

Telegram in hand I went and found Carol, handing it to her to read, a great look of relieve shows on her face after reading it, knowing she was more concerned about Billy then herself. Carol tells me that her Grandmother was a tough but kindly old bird, was from a large family of mountain folk, could still outride and shoot most men, and has some good and tough men working for her, after her husband was killed by the Bloods she took over the ranch and runs it with iron hand, rustlers and bandits ride wide around Em's range.

With that I start to make arrangements for their travel which would include stage and train travel, Billy is bouncing off the walls excited having never been on a train before. I give Carol some money for clothes and travel items, saying not to worry about it Em would pay me back, Whiplash to Billy mosey over to the store and get the young lad what he needed for the long trip, plus some candy that they are both enjoying.

The stage was leaving in a few days and there is much to do, already getting a helpless feeling of missing Carol, I had already decided I was heading back to Montana after my commitment to the Rangers is over.

The Rangers being good men passed the hat and collected about 60 dollars for Carol and Billy, with sincerity I thank them all, then on the sly gave Billy the money and swearing him to secrecy, telling him to give it to Carol only after they were on their way, fearing she might be to proud to accept the money.

The night before they are to leave Carol and I take an evening walk, we walk arm in arm andtalk of many things, and of my decision to go back to Montana, she is very pleased saying she would miss me terribly and I had better come a calling when I get back. Under the moonlight, we sit under the trees by a slow-moving river, cuddled up, I finally work up the nerve to kiss her, our lips meet her lips are as soft as rose peddles and as sweet as honey, that kiss would remain forever be on my lips. Yep I am goner for sure. We then slowly walk back to Manuel's reluctant to part company, when we get back Whiplash is still there, and Billy had been sent to bed, but I doubt if he was sleeping thinking of the upcoming adventures.

I kiss Carol again and said we would be back early to see them off, as we head back to the barracks, Whiplash said he was surely going to miss them, "not to worry you old softy we are heading back to Montana country soon, but we cannot leave the Captain short handed". He is right happy about it, I know like myself he misses the clean cool air and open skies, we were going home.

The next morning, we return to the Cantina finding it a whirlwind of activity, the gals in a flutter making sure all was ready, all the girls and Mamma are crying and going on, Whiplash and I thought it best to sit out of the way with Manuel and have coffee, but sitting there I could not keep my eyes off Carol, and it seemed the same way with her. When all was in order and ready I steal Carol for a few moments, holding her close to me I profess my love for her, and how much I would miss her, she is crying soft tender tears, I feel like my heart would break when she leaves. But then with a smile I say to her there was and would never be any other woman for me, and she would be seeing me on her doorstep real soon. Just before we have to head back I hand Carol Meg's the derringer, showed her how to use it, and gave her 2 extra bullets, telling her to hide it on her person and always keep it loaded, she promises to do as I said, then hid it in her skirt. Hand in hand we walk to the station, both of us not knowing what more to say.

When we get to the stagecoach, there was a small crowd waiting, Manuel and the whole family were there, Whiplash was of course with Billy, Lanky and some of the boys came over to say goodbye, the Rangers all shook Billy's hand and passed along to Carol their best wishes. Their gear was loaded up on top of the coach, the women again all hugging and bawling again, Whiplash grabs up Billy into a big hug, Billy was crying and Whiplash a few tears in his eyes was complaining of the damn dust getting into his eyes, but fooling no one. He then puts Billy in the Coach and says for him to be good and he would be seeing him soon, I kiss Carol once more, before she gets in the coach in a mock stern voice says" Hardin Steele you take care and do not go and get yourself killed, I will be expecting you to come courting, and I Love you." she then quickly gets in the coach hiding her tears. Looking in the coach I grab her hand," Honey keep the light in the window, nothing is going to keep me from you, wire me as soon as you get into Helena, I love you."

Whiplash and I walk to the front of the coach, I want a word with the driver. The stage driver and shotgun rider were both good men who I knew and trusted. The drivers name was Wildcat Nash, I look up at him and say" Wildcat I know you will take good care of my passengers and I would take it as a favour if you passed it up along the line that Carol and Billy are important to me and I will be right unhappy if anyone caused them harm or distress." Wildcat gives me a big grin, "do not worry Ranger boy, be a pleasure, I reckon no one would be fool enough to interfere with Sudden Steel's woman, with that he cracks his whip and hollers cussing the horses into moving. Whiplash and I watch the stage until it is out of site, a bittersweet day.

The next day the Captain summons Whiplash and myself into his office, it is funny how life's road takes a person on many twists and turns, without a word he hands me a telegram, it was from Washington, offering me a US Marshals position and was needed in Montana to deal with the growing trouble with whiskey traders, rustlers and vigilantes, very pleased by the news, I will be going back to big sky country and Carol soon.

"Congrats Ranger, I know you have to go, but I need you boys for 1 more job before you leave the outfit." We readily agree, he goes on to tell us we would be scouting for a troop of the 8th Calvary hunting down a large party of Pima's that have been causing havoc, the troop would be arriving tomorrow get your gear ready and be armed for bear". Before he dismisses ushe informs me he would wire Washington with my acceptance of the Marshals position and would be delayed needing to finish your present assignment, I said that was fine and thanked him before heading out to get my gear, once more into the breech.

The troop rides into town the next morning and to my surprise I discover it was a totally made up of black soldiers being led by two white officers, the 8th and 9th Calvary are known as Buffalo soldiers by the Indians for there short black curly hair that is like the hair on a buffalo. The patrol consisted of 2 white officers with 16 non-coms, I observe by their manner and the way they go about their duties they were a well trained, experienced and solid group of fighting men.

Whiplash and I walk over to the Captain, he looks to be a competent and experienced officer and has a ready smile, we introduce ourselves and let him know we are ready to go and awaiting his orders. He tells us he was going to rest the men and horses for I couple hours and then we will be leaving, I recommend they use the Ranger area, had water, feed, and bad coffee, he agrees and has the Sgt. Move the troop to the rest area. The soldiers like all good troops took time to eat and rest, knowing what was ahead of them, when I lead out Apollo his blue coat shimmering in the sun, all heads turn, there are very few horses of his caliber anywhere in the west, the Capt. came over admiring him, asking what I called him, when it tell him Apollo and aptly named, he nods saying "you named him good Ranger".

It is time to get going, I mount up and with the Capt.'s order we lead them out. Getting started late we did not make much distance, but it felt good to be on the trail again and busy, I struggle to concentrate on my work and not about Caroli must remind myself if I get sloppy and fail all these brave men could die. I have already picked a campsite and after scouting it out we ride in the Sgt. Begins shouting orders for the camp set up and sentries posted. When all was in order we sit down to chow, I notice the officers did not eat with the men, me and Whiplash have our own spot just back out of the firelight.

After chow, we head down to talk with the soldiers, I do this for a couple of reasons, first I want to know a bit about the men I may be fighting beside in a few days, and I wanted to talk with the Sgt. Knowing full well they were the backbone in any military and a good Sgt is worth 10 soldiers.

We came up to the soldiers and I ask if the if we could join them for coffee, and were invited to sit, one of soldiers bring us over a couple cups of the steaming brew, I take a sip, smiling enjoying the strong trail coffee, I then pass it around tobacco and papers, I light up a thin Mexican cigar I have taken a liking to the strong smoke then hand one to the Sgt. After the smokes trying to lighten the mood I say, "damn you soldier boys got it good, nice sunny rides in the country, picnics, and big pay, you men got it by the ass". Whiplash is greatly amused, as were the soldiers. Relaxing the soldiers begin to open up start talking, this is just what I was hoping for, one the soldiers asked if I was the Ranger they called Sudden

Steele, "Yep I got stuck with that damn handle, and what sticks, stays". Old Whiplash was a delightful story teller, but tends to get a bit windy, as he starts his stories I ask the Sgt for a private talk, the soldiers were already mesmerized by Whiplashes telling of past adventures and did not even notice us leaving.

The Sgt introduces himself as Sgt Bo Washington, "glad to have you along on this trip, Ranger I got a feeling this patrol could get messy, them Pima's is real sneaky and mean". "Sgt, I do believe you may be right, them Pima's are tougher than either the Apaches or Paiutes, if you have no objection I have a few questions about the officers and the men, I like to know what sort of men I have beside me." "No objection at all Ranger damn smart thinking, well the Captain is alright, professional soldier, the Lt is West Point, fresh from the east but knows everything about Indian fighting, so he says, if he lives he may be a good officer in time." No worries about the troops all veterans every man has been In at least one engagement some of the boys been in as many as 6, they will do their duty or die trying." Smiling at the news, now confident Whiplash and I were riding with some of the best, "Bo we hit their lands tomorrow and they will not wait long to hit us, I think we will all have to be sharp and very hard over the next few days." Our meeting over we return to the fire, Whiplash is just finishing his story of our time in Colorado, saying goodnight to the troops we head back to our own camp, we would be taking shifts keeping watch every night until this thing was finished.

The next morning, we come upon many tracks of unshod ponies, I send Whiplash back to bring up the Capt. and Sgt, when they come up I show them the tracks figuring this may be the bunch the Captain was looking for, and they are not running, I reckon them Pima's wanted us to see these tracks. Sgt. Bo askes if I knew where they were going, I figure they were still raiding in the area and when they find we are on their trail and they would lay an ambush by a waterhole or in a valley. The bugler brought the troops forward and the Capt. said we would ride hard today, only short breaks to rest the horses, he wanted them savages to know the 8th was on their ass and were coming for them, cheers broke out among the men. That

Capt. was good to his word, we put in a long hard ride and were quickly closing the gap. I come across a waterhole with just enough water for the men and horses, after the horses were watered and canteens filled, we move to a better spot for defence. I recommend to the Capt. that we make a cold camp and make as little noise as possible, them Pima's may be right close, calling the Sgt over he gave him his orders, going along with my advice. The next day, I keep finding plenty of tracks, but I now know the Indians are aware of us, they had their scouts out, then as if by magic all the tracks vanished now the real hunt begins, it was going to be slow and careful from here on in. I did not pick up sign of them until next morning when I spot where a pony hoof had turned over a stone, it had been done within the last couple hours. Now I just sat there wondering what them Indians had on their minds, and what I would do if I were them, ours is not an overly large troop and the Pima's may not think the black troops would be good fighters, I believed they would try ambush wanting the horses and guns, but where was the five dollar question.

Meeting back up with the column I tell the Capt. I think they will try and ambush trying for the horses first trying to put us on foot, the problem with these mountain Indians they are masters when it came to surprise attacks and concealment. When Whiplash and I head out again every man has his rifle out and ready, the land around was barren, hot and dusty, few places to hide or fight from, we were slowly coming up some rugged rocky country, I figured that is where they hit us. I WAS WRONG.

As the sun is about to set in the west, with the sun behind them and in our eyes they came out the ground, charging, shots ring out, arrows finding targets, 2 troops fell almost at once, I feel the cut of an arrow catching me on my cheek below my left eye, cut to the bone, before he could send his second arrow I shoot him with my rifle holding it like a handgun, catching the savage in the throat killing him instantly. The Capt. and Sgt have done an excellent job of forming a defence, another trooper goes down, it is hand to hand in some quarters, the troopers are fighting well, I drop another Pima when he rose to shoot and then I vamoose back to the group of soldiers. When I get there the Indians had vanished, leaving their dead, I counted 4, and know they had at least that many were wounded, we had 3 trooper's dead, the Lt had an arrow in his shoulder, and a few of the others were walking wounded. I am thanking my lucky stars I was with this outfit, if it would have been green recruits we would have been wiped out. The Capt. and Sgt, both experienced and cool under fire had organized the men into a defensive fighting unit, minimizing our losses.

The Sgt and I check the dead Indians, I was taking no chances I had my greener out and cocked, the Sgt had his revolver out and ready, the leader of this wild bunch was named Two Moons, it pleased me greatly to see him dead at my feet, it would give us some much-needed time they n ow had to choose a new leader, or maybe pull out feeling their medicine was bad, you just never know what a wild Indian will do.

It was getting late the sun would be down soon, we need to skedaddle and quick, we are in a poor position for defence, no cover for the men or horses. The Capt. called us together for a pow wow, wisely asking for input. I speak my peace first "Capt. we need to gather our dead and wounded and vamoose, this is very bad ground to defend especially at night, I know of a spot no more than an hour's hard ride, not much but good water and some grass for the horses, I just hope there is not a reception committee waiting, but we need to move fast Sir, them Pima's are right stubborn Indians. Without hesitation, the Captain orders the troop to get ready to move at the double time, within 15 minutes we were in the saddle heading to what I hoped a safe spot for the night.

When we come within site of the small waterhole, Whiplash and I dismount and slowly scout the area, taking our time, rushing things with savages on your tail gets you dead fast. Finding no tracks other than animals that inhabited the water hole we settled in to watch, I feel certain we are alone but my confidence is a bit shaken after making one wrong and deadly mistake already today. Whiplash and I separate and slowly made our way towards the shaded spot to where the water was, I had my shotgun cocked and ready alert for any movement or noise. We were in luck the spot was deserted,

Whiplash goes and brings the troop up, it is near full dark now, the moon has not risen yet. The Sgt in soft tones starts issuing orders, every man was to take a drink, then give the horses a small amount of water, the hole was near dry after the horses drank but would refill over night. The guard is set for the night, I tell the Sgt, Whiplash and I would take the last shift and would be up through the night checking on things, damn I could use a pot of coffee.

The night passes quietly, with the sky turning the pre-morning grey and the morning birds welcoming the day the Sgt wakes the troops, sending them first the give each horse a quick drink without the horses our chances of survival were less than zero, then had them fill as many canteens as possible, Whiplash and I had filled ours during the night, and are saddled up and ready to travel.

Whiplash cleans the deep arrow slice on my check getting ready to sew it up when the Capt., Lt and Sgt Bo gather around us and we began discussing our next course of action. The Lt his arm in a sling was for returning to the fort, feeling we had more than accomplished their mission. Looking at me with tired red rimmed eyes the Capt. asks" well Ranger what do you recommend seems to me we run or fight." "Well Sir I have thoughts on the matter but I would like to hear what Sgt Washington has to say." Old Bo looked up with a grin, he knew my intent, "Captain, Sir we still got us a good fighting force with water and horses in fair shape, I say run them to ground and kill them or take them back to the Rez, let them savages know the 8th are whipcord tough and pure stubborn, put fear into their heathen hearts. "Capt., I agree with Sgt keep them on run and fight them wherever we find them, time we became the hunters and them the prey might just might save some civilian and soldiers lives, but it is going to be right dangerous work". The Captain is a fighting man who did not care for running "Sgt get the men mounted and ready to ride we are hunting Pima's and we are not stopping until this renegade bunch is wiped out or they surrender I personally am hoping for a scrap." The Sgt had the troops ready within minutes, each man knowing his duty is doing his share and more.

I tell the Capt. that I was sure the Pima's knew where we were and would have some braves out there waiting for a second ambush,

I am going to light out for a bit and see if I can locate them heathens, maybe we can turn the tables on them. I ride out slowly the greener cocked and loaded my eyes scanning the dry earth, I was determined they were not going to fool me again, old Bear would die of shame. I halt Apollo just below a small ridge then taking my spyglass and crawled to the top, staying low and moving as little as possible I scan the area, mostly flat and dry, light dust blowing, seeing nothing with the first look I rested my eyes for a quick minute and started the search again, this time I saw movement a small mound of dirt had moved slightly, I waited and again saw a very small movement of what I thought was a foot being drawn back. Certain now where they would try to hit us I returned to the troop and brief the Capt., "Sir I figure if I lead off as usual we act as if we do not think them Indians are around, when we get close we charge them with sidearms, slash, trample and shoot them down, get the survivors on the run then we hunt." "Ok Ranger lets try your way, but you know you will be up front alone until we can reach you." I ain't alone Captain got me a shotgun, rifle, smokewagon and knife, if they get me I will not be going to the great spirit alone, but if you hear gunfire or I call you come running right quick and I do mean quick."

When all ids ready I lead off, the scattergun is in hand out and ready it would be close in fighting I keep a leisurely pace and leaning over and studying the ground in case some of them varmints snuck in closer. I am now near the ambush spot, the thong is removed from my revolvers holster off my .44 for quick action. I am now about forty yards from the waiting Pima's, I rein Apollo to a halt taking a quick look to see where the troop is. The blood lust for combat rushes through me I let out my Sioux war cry, Apollo knowing that cry charges, his muscles exploding sending us forward like a freight train. Suddenly two Indians come magically out of the ground not more than 20 feet from me, I let loose the right barrel of the greener nearly ripping one Indian in half, the other Indian made a big mistake of getting to close to Apollo, I hear a horrifying scream and see Apollo has bitten a big chuck of flesh out of the warrior's shoulder and was now going at him with those deadly hooves, I was having difficulty staying in the saddle. Indians were popping out of there holes, I let loose the other barrel of the greener, wounding 2 more, they are all around me I wing the shotgun like a club, I hear gun shots and then see the 8th in slashing and shooting, we caught them flatfooted and they were now paying with their dead. Suddenly it goes quiet, only dead and wounded Pima's remain, the rest maybe no more than 8 remain alive had scattered, broken now and but being intelligent common sense Indians they would now head back to the reservation or deep into the mountains.

The return trip to Ranger HQ is uneventful but before we separated from the soldiers, both the Capt. and Lt thank us, I believe the Lt had grown up some up on this detail, I talk with Bo, and tell him if he ever tired of the easy soldier life to come to Montana, I would find him some honest work. The Capt. said he was going to recommend to his Commanding Officer to write up letters of commendation for our actions. I tell him none was needed we were just doing our duty as Rangers. Shaking hands all around wishing them good luck Whiplash and I leave the soldiers and turn our horses towards Tucson and then Montana and Carol.

There are not enough Indians in the world to defeat the 7th cavalry.
- George Armstrong Custer

CHAPTER 21

MONTANA BOUND

Setting out at a good pace we head back to the ranger station I am anxious to be on my way, it is early spring in Montana and I want to see the rolling green foothills dotted with yellow, purple and blue wildflowers, the mountain tops still showing snow, to drink from the cool clear mountain streams and spend the cool nights under the thousands of stars in the big night sky.

We ride directly to the Captains Office, entering he immediately waves us over to his desk, "welcome back boys good to see you still got your hair, did you get them soldier boys back safe?" "Well boss them Pima's are right good fighters, 3 soldiers were killed and about twice that wounded, but we smashed them, Two Moons and 15 of his warriors are dead." I hand him the report and gave him the story of the battles. "Job well done boys, I hate to see you boys leave but your work here will be remembered and the Territory of Arizona thanks you". Then he hands me 2 telegrams saying he would see us before we left and with his usual wave dismisses us.

Once outside I read the telegrams, the first was confirmation of my United States Marshal commission and I was to report to Helena with all speed, the second was from Carol, saying they made it safe to Em's and were alright and we were to hurry back, Billy sent a howdy to Whiplash,

Seems there is a need for hurry and much to do, I will miss Tucson, not the town or climate but the good and bad people I have met, it is always the people you miss most, leaving friends behind. We pick up a tough mustang pony for a pack horse, there would be few stops in towns on the way, and only to get provisions. We make the rounds saying our good -byes, like with Meg, Manuel and his family were the most difficult, many tears are shed. Said Adios to what Rangers were around, old Lanky teasing me about being a big time U S Marshal now. The Capt. came out just as we are about to depart, I reluctantly hand him back my badge, now feeling a bit naked without it, he shook our hands wishing us the best, "if you boys ever want to Ranger again come on back I will put you to work".

With a wave, we are gone and miles down the road before night came upon us, we encounter few problems during most of the trip, we get caught a quick and violent storm in the open, I am, sure we were going to be done in by the lightning, just scared the hell out of me and the few times I have seen Apollo frightened. We are running low on foodstuffs, coffee and cigars an such so decide to stopover in a town called Salvador to re supply and hopefully get a good home cooked meal and coffee. The town seemed quiet when we ride in I point Apollo towards the general store, we purchasd most of what we needed to include a large amount of arbuckles, we then head across the street to a cafe called the A.J. Eatery to have our meal and hopefully some good coffee. Just as we were to enter the café we hear the Saloon doors smash open and see a man comes flying out landing hard on the ground, he was a black man and by the looks of his clothing an ex Calvary man, a yellow strip down his grey pants and into his high topped black boots. The batwing doors swing open again and four big brutish town thugs laughing loudly pick him up hitting him as they do so, very amused by their own brutality, they then drag their victim back into the saloon. Old Whiplash goes and gets his Shotgun off his horse, he knows exactly what I am about to do, nothing angers me more than abuse, the strong should be defending the weak, I am damn pissed.

Slowly walk over and enter through the batwings, the first thing I see is a big sign behind the bar saying in bold letters, **No** Niggers, **Redskins, Chinks or Spics allowed**. I look over and see the 4 toughs have the black man pinned to a chair and slapping him around and pouring whiskey over him. Well this is why they call me Sudden, I pull my greener from my back and start walking quickly to the front of the bar, telling the bartender he better get the hell out of the way, men are scampering out of the way, about four feet from the sign I let go with a barrel and the sign explodes into small pieces along with most of the mirror behind the bar, I then swing my shotgun and point it at the toughs," I got me a barrel left boys any you varmints want some of it?" my green eyes blazing deep into them. "You will let that man be, I should notch your ears for the cowards you are" I motion for the abused man to go wait with Whiplash who they had finally noticed, but now noticing the shotgun he held.

There is always 1 talker, and this is no exception, he has the look of a townsman about him along with a would-be gunslinger carrying a two-gun rig. "Who the hell are you to be spoiling our fun, this is none of your damn affair, if you didn't have that scattergun I would surely enjoy putting a few .45 slugs in your guts watch you die slow and painful". Well sir my fighting blood is up again, I step back a few paces and lay my shotgun on an empty table. The mouth steps away from the others, smiling and confident "ok stranger your funeral, but I like to know who it is I am going to kill". His hand poised over pistol ready to draw, I smile as I normally do before conflict, and say "my name is Hardin Steele late of the Arizona Rangers, some folks call me Sudden". There were actual gasps, my name stopped them like they ran into a wall, the Mouth wanted out of it but has made his brag and must follow through or be branded a coward. His hand grabs the handle of his smokewagon, my first .44 bullet punches a rib through his lung my second a head shot leaves a small dot dead centre between his eyes but the back of his skull is now missing and a gory mess, I re load and holster my sidearm then pick up my shotgun, as we back out the door I say goodbye to the saloon crowd "You folks got a right friendly little town here, but you fellers need to pick your prey more carefully, you never know when you may run into the he wolf."

I ask our new friend if he has a horse and if he would care to ride along with us, his horse is at the edge of town and would be right happy for the company. We waste no time leaving, I want miles between us and the town, I was am still hungry and in need of coffee, luck would have it that we come upon a Mexican cottage, pulling up in front I call out to the house in Spanish that we were hungry men looking for a meal and have money to pay, the farmer came out smiling greets us then invites us in. To my immense pleasure coffee was served as soon as our butts hit the chairs, minutes later platters of lamb, corn on the cob, tortillas simple but excellent food, I eat my fill and more. After finishing my fourth cup of coffee we get up to leave, I dig into my pants pocket and pulled out 5 silver dollars, much more than the meal was worth but these were good folks treated us kindly and cash money was hard to come by for poor honest folks.

Thanking our hosts, we then move up the road a piece before settling in for the night, now enjoying sitting around the fire talking with our new friend and traveling companion "I want to thank you fellas for pulling me out of that trouble back in town, them boys was likely to string me up just to watch me twitch, my name is Buster Jackson recently mustered out as a Sgt with 9th Calvary. Whiplash replied for us, "I am Whiplash Smith and this is my pard Hardin Steele, recently of the Arizona Territorial Rangers, we are heading back to the Montana country, Hardin has been appointed as a U S marshal but I recon it is that little blonde filly Carol that is luring him back," giving off a loud chuckle. I interject "What are your plans Buster"? If you are footloose you should ponder over the idea of coming with us, Montana is new, big and wild country needs big men to tame it down a might, a man could leave his mark if he played his cards right." William being a man of action, quickly decides he wanted to see this Montana country, it is settled he would come with us, and to our pleasant surprise volunteers to be camp cook, both Whiplash and I agree quick, both of us a bit tired of the cooking duties, and old Buster proves himself to be a top-notch man hand a frying pan.

The miles quickly fall behind us, Whiplash and Buster always swapping stories or lies, Whiplash tells Buster of our fight with the Pima's Buster knew Sgt Bo, been recruits together and each had saved the others life in battle many times over, I am still reading in the evening and would read to the boys, they are good camps shared with good men.

When we start to get close to the Montana border, I start spreading the word with anyone we met that if they come across Tex Fowler I want to see him in Helena and he was not to spare the spurs. One evening we were looking for a spot to settle in, when we come upon a cow camp, we hail the camp asking if they got coffee for some weary travellers, a voice tells us to come on in and break out our cups. There are 6 men around the fire, and a chuck wagon with a cook close by, the other men were out with the cows. "Any chance for grub its been a long day in the saddle, an older cowhand I took as the ramrod invites us to sit and eat, the cookie bringing us plates and coffee. I introduce myself as Hardin, not wanting attention made to my reputation, and introduce the boys. The ramrods handle is Rex Pinder, and his bunch worked for the Bar M spread, he tells us they were moving a herd of cattle to the ranches summer range. I look to the ramrod "by chance you having any trouble with rustlers, we spotted a small fire awhile back but not to far seemed like they did not want it to be seen". "Rex, swore," damn right there's trouble, its probably Bill Mathers gang of cutthroats, the Mathers Mob they call themselves, they have been rustling all over the territory selling to the mining camps. I felt like I had hit by a hammer when I hear Bills name, I ask him if he were sure it was Bill, him and the cowhands all agreed. Damn you Bill, damn you to hell.

I tell Rex I believe they will get hit tonight, but there is only one way to get up here and figure we can intercept them coming up and then read them from the good book. "No offence Hardin "says the foreman "but this not your fight, why would you men want help us?" "Rex an old proverb says if you eat a mans salt you owe him, and besides, I have been appointed U S Marshal for this territory, looks like I am starting the job sooner than I expected". "Rex, I would like you and one good fighting man to come with us" a young slim looking cowboy with fine blond hair steps forward, young looking but has an air of confidence about him, a steady eye and well cared for 6 gun "that would be me boss, been to damned quiet a man needs a bit of fun now and again," Rex did not hesitate, "alright Kid, saddle up and come loaded for bear.".

We ride fast hoping not to be late, we pull up near the top of the path, drawing my shotgun we wait mounted for the rustlers, our position was good had the high ground, they would be caught on the low ground and will be tightly grouped. I am hoping to convince them they have the wrong herd, when they saw their position would ride away quiet and friendly, but it would be their choice. We did not have long to wait, we hear many horses and men talking quiet coming towards us, when they round a bend in the path they are now directly below us. "I cock both barrels of my greener in the darkness the sound carried to the outlaws giving them pause and they pull up to a stop nervous and wary now. I called down to the dark figures, "this is U S Marshal Steele now nobody get nervous and do something to get you all killed, we got you covered from the high ground and enough firepower to empty every saddle". One of the men in the darkness calls from the darkness they want no trouble and were just cowhands looking for work. "Honest men do not ride the night trails, you men are going to turn around and ride away, your plan for this herd is busted the whole camp is armed and ready for you". The same man, knowing they had no choice called back "alright Marshal we are leaving, but I would not want to be in your boots, when we tell the boss of this" I laugh, "you tell old Bill Mathers that Hardin Steele sends his regards and hopes we can have time for coffee before he leaves the territory" With that I tell them to scat, they turn and slowly ride away throwing back insults and threats. William and I would stay a for a bit making sure the rustlers are gone. We wait about an hour, I am satisfied they will not return tonight, we head back to camp for a much-needed coffee.

I tell Rex I did not think there will not be any more trouble tonight, but keep a sharp lookout. "thanks boys you surely saved the herd and probably our lives, that there bunch likes killing". I look at him smiling, "I guess I know why they called me in now, you tell folks around the law is coming, and it will be swift and harsh for any for any that are on the outlaw trail." Smiling Rex laughs, "I believe them varmints should start looking for their holes, if you ever need a favour Marshal you just call on the Bar M, we will come a running."

We get an early start next morning, we now getting close our destination and I want to get to work and more importantly see Carol, I am now thinking to myself of all the damned luck, Bill turning outlaw and leading such a bad bunch, knowing right off there is not enough territory for the both of us.

It has been decided earlier we are going to split up, I am heading to Helena, Whiplash and William were going to Em's I will be along after meeting with the Governor and hopefully finding Tex, I am in real need of his skills now. I write a letter of introduction for Buster, telling Em he was a ex Sgt, a brave man of good character and a good hand all around, I hoped she could hire him on, the next was to Carol telling her I was coming courting, and she was always on my mind, and looking forward to seeing Billy again and meeting Em, I hand Whiplash the letters and leave them now off to see the Governor in Helena and start my new career as a U S Marshal, I had worked and trained hard always has been my dream now I just hope I am man enough and got enough curly wolf to get the job done and stay alive.

Helena was getting to be a fair-sized burg, civilization was slowly coming to Montana, when I get to courthouse who do I see waiting but good old Tex, with a frown looks up "took you long enough" then smiles, "good to see you Tex got some man size work ahead of us, you up for it"" hell yes you knot head, got right bored waiting for you." I told him to follow me and we enter the government building, Tex seems a bit ill at ease in the courthouse, it was most amusing to watch his expressions.

We enter the office of the Governor and are greeted by a young friendly professional looking man, I tell him who we were, returning from the office he says I can go right in, I ask Tex, to stay close I would not be long.

Governor Ivan Reedman, was an older gentleman, with a slim build dressed in an uncomfortable looking suit, had a good smile, and the look of an intelligent and determined man. He comes around the desk in a great flurry and gives me a great handshake, telling me how pleased he is that I got here safe, and in good time.

"Sit yourself Marshal, I just received a telegram from the owner of the Bar M, praising your efforts and saying we need more men like you in the Territory". I give him a brief account with our meeting with the rustlers, and that I had good men with me, just started work a might early is all. Then I tell him of Tex, and that I want him for my deputy, he was the man I needed to cover my back and keep me alive. He agrees readily, and calls for Tex to come in. Then briefs us on the situation in the Territory, how rustlers, horse thieves and vigilantes, whiskey traders and outright lawlessness are out of control, the chaos must end, and we are authorized to use any amount of force needed to bring justice and law to the Territory. He then had us stand and hold up our right hands and swore us in then wished us luck, and hands us our badges, I pin mine on immediately, I did not feel so naked anymore. The secretary lets us know how and where to get supplies, and to report in as often as we could.

As we were walking back to the horses Tex says to me, "one thing about you Hardin you never take on the soft jobs". "Well Tex that would be no damn fun at all" both of us are laughing like school kids as we ride out of town, I am finally going to see the delicious true love of my life sweet Carol.

Racisms still with us. But it is up to us to prepare our
children for what they have to meet, and,
hopefully, we shall overcome.
- Rosa Parks

CHAPTER 22

ON THE SHOOT

Tex and I ride up to Em's ranch house Miss Em walks out with the whole gang in tow to meet and welcome us. Now Em is a wonder has, about 100 lbs of pure fight, fought Indians with her baby on her knee, fought beside her husband against nature, rustlers, and Indians, tough as nails and said what she thought, but a soft heart for those who deserved it, she has never turned away a rider without providing them a satisfying meal.

Removing our hats, we formally introduce ourselves saying how it is our pleasure in meeting her, then I grab up Carol sweeping her off her feet give her a big bear hug, "Hi Honey did you miss me". With typical woman logic, she told me I was a might slow getting there, then smiling that beautiful smile kisses me on the cheek. The arrow wound on my cheek was pretty much healed the stiches are out but still red and a bit raw Carol touches the wound softly concern in her eyes, "ain't nthing but a scratch honey, no need for worry". Just then Buster comes over to welcomes us, saying Miss Em hired him on as a horse wrangler, and was getting on fine with the boys. I thank Em, she waved me off, saying she always needs capable hands, "Hardin I take them one at a time there is good and bad in every race", I told her what I wise woman she is and get a small smile. Billy was very happy to see me, I promised him stories later, he has become Whiplashes shadow and they are both good with it.

We all have supper outside in the backyard, the cowhands were all invited over, they all slicked up best they could, looking forward to a fine home cooked meal. The tables are sagging with platters of beef, mashed potatoes, corn on the cob with real butter and fresh bread, and cake for dessert, everyone eating talking laughing, one of those meals you remember all your life. After the cowhands head back to the bunkhouse, is Billy was forced off to bed, I tell them that we could not stay, the sooner Tex and I get started with this job the sooner it will be done. I tell Whiplash what Governor Reedman said about Bill and his mob and I am afraid I will be on his backtrail soon. Whiplash with head hanging at bit "never figured in a thousand years old Bill would go bad, durn fool ". I then go on to tell Whiplash I have a tough job for him, I need to stay on the ranch be my contact man, gather any information on the bandits in the area, we will keep in contact by telegraph, and most importantly to keep the information close to the vest, not even Carol is to know. "I know I can rely on you Whiplash old pard, you are going to be my ace in the hole." Then looking over at Buster, I brief him that we may come riding in fast and will need 2 of the best horses ready at all times, with saddle bags filled with rations and ammo, I want to be riding out again in no more than 10 minutes, knowing the ex Sgt would have it ready I say no more. It is a nice evening and I ask Carol to go for a walk, that gal just gets prettier every time I see her, its enough to take my breath away, quickens of my pulse and a gives me a hollow yearning feeling in my chest. Arm and arm we stroll slowly alongside a slow moving creek, I enjoy hearing her soft voice in the dark lit only by moonlight, sweet like the pleasant sounds of the night birds. Serious now I caution her I would try and see her as often as I can, but it was a big Territory and I could be away for some time. Being the understanding woman she is, being smart and not only beautiful she knew I had a job to do and it was important to me and the future of the Territory, she then says she can wait for now, showing a teasing smile. I pull her close and kiss her soft moist lips, with every kiss finished I crave another, we kiss and hold each other for a long time, not talking just 2 people holding on to one another, never wanting to let go. Finally,I can delay it no longer and reluctantly take her back to the house, I say good night to Em, and give a quick kiss goodnight to my love, saying I will see them for breakfast, I head straight over to the bunkhouse, I am in real need of rest feeling weary from the road, I recon sleep is going to be a rare thing with this job.

The next morning, I get Apollo ready for travel, and after double checking my weapons and equipment, I grab Tex and we head to the house for breakfast and coffee, Carol already has a pot ready, knowing my love for the evil brew. Over breakfast, I tell Whiplash he is to check for messages every 2 days and be ready to travel at a moment notice, he was raring to go. After bidding, adios and kissing those sweet lips one last time, Tex and I ride out, it was time to go to knowing full well it was going to be no easy task and it is going to get very bloody.

The first thing we are going to do is ride over to some of the bigger ranches and see how hard they were getting hit by the rustling, we know they are stealing cattle and taking them to the meat hungry mining towns, the buyers have a good thing going and did not ask any questions of ownership. We would be paying those buyers a visit real soon, but first we had to find out where the rustlers hung out, I was sure we would find them in some small out of the way towns or deserted farm or ranch.

The second day out we spot 3 rustlers who are doing some brand changing with a running iron, they were so concentrated on their work we get t real close before they notice us, when the cattle thieves look up they were looking down the barrels of my scattergun and Tex's rifle. Not having any death wishes the 3 rustlers give up without a fight, these were not part of Bill's gang, just 3 cowhands trying to make a quick buck. After looking over the cattle they had branded and gathering up their tools of the trade for evidence, we secure their hands to their saddlehorns. The closest town was Medicine Bow, we would leave them with the local law and will send a wire for their pickup. We rein up in front of the Sheriff's office and lead the prisoners inside, I tell the town law we are US Marshals and caught these boys red handed using a running iron. After locking the boys up the Sheriff comes back shaking his head, telling us they were local boys and he isshocked by their actions, never figured them for that sort of thing. Before leaving the jail, I look at the Sheriff, my eyes are hard and serious "Sheriff law has come to the country, if you have any trouble you call on us, and if those boys should somehow escape I will come back and lock you up in your own damn jail." I can tell he is not pleased, and I do not care, it was time to make people accountable for their actions. When we get the telegraph office, I send 2 messages, first to Helena, reporting the arrest and requesting pickup of the prisoners, the second to Whiplash, I wanted to stir up the hornets nest a might, from experience I found warning in the paper or posters works well to get everyone's attention, the wrote out what I wanted him to put front page of the Helena newspaper, it is to read;

ATTENTION VIGILANTES, RUSTLERS AND HORSE THIEVES

THIS IS YOUR FIRST AND FINAL WARNING TO LEAVE THE TERRITORY.

VIGILANTES WILL BE TAKEN AS OUTLAWS AND BE TREATED ACCORDINGLY.

ANYONE CAUGHT IN THE ACT OF RUSTLING WILL BE ARRESTED OR KILLED IF THEY RESIST.

THE LAW HAS ARRIVED AND IS STAYING, VILLIANS CAN EXPECT ROUGH

TREATMENT. BURIALS ON BOOTHILL NO
CHARGE.

Signed
H Steele
U S Marshal

I was chuckling as I send it, Tex also gets a big kick out of it, but
sobering quickly knowing we now would become not only be the
hunters but the hunted and marked for death.

We leave town shortly after sending the messages, we head to the
Bar M and have a talk with Rex and the owner, Pete Miller hoping
to get some information on the other ranches and people in the area.

Somewhat planned we arrive at the ranch just in time for chuck
and coffee, Rex is standing on the porch of the ranch house as
we ride up, smiling I ask "can you feed a couple tired and hungry
lawmen" he smiles back "the boss will feed just about anybody,
laughing, step down and come on in and meet the boss". Pete Miller
was pure Cattleman, survived the stampedes, river crossing and
all other disasters involved with running and driving cattle. Rex
introduced us and Pete walks up and with a firm grip shakes our
hands and thanks me for helping Rex save his cattle, I assure him
it was my duty and I do not like to see hard working honest men
robbed. Looking me over said" you boys will do to ride the river
with, I am thinking outlaws better get while the getting is good, you
need any help Marshal you call on me or Rex". 'Thank you, Pete,
and we just might need it, with your permission we would like to
grab some chow and then I need to talk to you and Rex, I need to
know more about the lay of the land and the people in it."

Pete said he would come over for coffee after supper and we
could talk, a man like myself a man who liked to sit outside by a fire.

After a fine meal of beef and beans, I pour myself a coffee,
cowboy coffee, float a horseshoe in it, and I am enjoying every drop
of it, a few minutes later Pete comes over and the cook pours him a
cup. Pete, Rex and some of the hands come over, a couple I had met
earlier, Tex and I grill them about the other ranchers, where they

thought the closest place was to sell the stolen cattle. I inquire as to where the rustlers would try and hole up, and if any of the rustlers were known to them, and which ones were the toughest and meanest. I already know Bill is the smartest and best of the tough crew, but when names like Blood Cabot, Smash nose Johnson, the Ute, Ringo Rawlins and the Parson are mentioned it got my attention quick, old Bill had with him some of the most brutal vicious killers the west has ever seen, plus there were likely others we had not heard of. We talk late into the evening, Tex then tells them of the notice I was putting in the Paper, Pete smiles and shakes his head, "Marshal I recon you just caught the tiger by the tail, you boys will have to ride careful". Thanking Pete and the boys we head for our bedrolls, it is going to be another long day tomorrow.

It is a sleepless night I am racking my brain thinking of my next move, before I finally dozed off I decided we would ride into the closest mining town where we thought the stolen cattle were being purchased see how things check out. This I am hoping to make it difficult for the rustlers to sell their ill-gotten beef.

Bill Mather's is looking at the newspaper one of his boys brought in, there is a look of part amusement, part frustration in his features, he knew I now meant business, he had seen this set up before. Looking up from the paper says to the other outlaws in the cabin, "looks like old Hardin has made his brag, we are knee deep it boys, he will be hunting us now and with Tex Fowler with him they make a tough pair of aces."

Pony Adams speaks up "lets just kill them boss, only 2 of them, we will dry gulch them and make them plum vanish." "Pony you really are a durn fool, first off he is a U S Marshal, he has more sly in him than a fox it ain't that easy to sneak up on Sudden or Tex, and last he has friends all over the Territory, I do not want men like Bear, Ramon, Panther or the Traveller hunting me. At the mention of the Traveller the room got quiet, this man was a legend and feared by evil men, nobody wanted trouble with him. Blackjack asked "he knows the Traveller? "Bill Smiles "yes good friends I have met him as well, telling all in the room the story of the Evans incident, finishing by saying," and if I know the Traveller, when he hears of this he will be close by, and let's not forget Whiplash, he should be riding with Sudden, that Marshal has something up his sleeve. We will avoid shooting down old Sudden for now, work around him, 2 men cannot be everywhere, our next job will be well scouted out, no mistakes."

When you find your opponent's weak spot,
hammer it.
- John Heisman

CHAPTER 23

CULLING THE HERD

Bill's Mob was not the only outlaw outfit in the territory who were rustling stealing and killing and if that were not enough the hooded vigilantes had to be dealt with, most of them are outlaws themselves, using the guise of the law to destroy or lynch their enemies. On the edge of the camps we come upon a small place with a corral holding about 10 head of white faced cattle, a dirty and bloody man is skinning a cow. When he sees us and stops his bloody work and with a scowl walks towards us the bloody knife still in his hand. Looking down at him from Apollo's back I identify myself as a US Marshal, Tex slides over to the Corral checking brands on the cows and skins hanging on the fence, riding back he tells me it is a mixed bunch of brands, some recently re done, a couple of Bar M cows are in the corral. I demand to see the bill of sale and want to know who it was sold him the cattle. The butcher is beginning to look right uncomfortable, telling us he bought them cows not knowing they were stolen, and he did not know any of the men who brought him the beef. What a load of crap, I am not believing a single word of his story, after he rambled on for a bit and professing his innocence I interrupt him and start laying it out real plain for him. "Mister I could arrest you right now and you would be facing at 3 years' hard labour, in federal prison, but I am giving you a chance and a warning." "Do not buy anymore cows from the rustlers, if there is no bill of sale or there is a question on the brands you will refuse to buy." I will have men in camp watching all the butchers and they will be directly reporting their findings to me, buy your meat legal from the ranchers mister, and do not make me come back" with that we ride off. We come across 3 butchers like the first one, the message is the same, making sure to mention my men would be watching and I would come down hard on them if they failed to heed my warnings. There were more butchers I was sure, a lot of hungry miners who liked meat in the area, but the word is now and will spread like a prarie grass fire, I sure would enjoy seeing the look on old Bill's face when his boys have to bring back them stolen cattle. Now I did not have any men spying in the camps, for every stranger would be suspect and the guilty minds would do the rest, let the enemy do the worrying.

I am thinking it is a good time to touch base at Em's, the horses had put on a lot of miles, even the mighty Apollo has his limits, change horses, re supply and hopefully get a home cooked meal, coffee and kisses from Carol.

That evening as we were crawled into our bedrolls, we hear distant gunshots, there seemed to be a lot of fire coming from one group and the odd heavy rifle or shotgun blast from the other. Takingonly the time to pull on our boots and grab our weapons, we saddle up quick and thunder towards the battle.

Topping a small hill, we look down and see a small ranch house, the moon was bright and showed 8 men in masks holding torches, shooting and trying to set fire to the small cabin. Tex and I pull our long guns, this was going to be the direct approach, with a touch of the spur I put Apollo in to a gallop and when we get in shooting range we started blasting, now Rex is a real magician with his long gun, within seconds 2 were down and 3 were wounded, the rest of the outfit scatter like rabbits. I ride up to the front of the house, Tex goes to check on the wounded and dead. "Hello, the house this is US Marshal Steele and deputy Fowler, it is safe to come out, I believe the cowards have gone." Tex came back with 2 prisoners, the 3rd wounded man had died, total of 4 dead, it is a good start. An elderly man slowly opens the door and comes out still holding his old buffalo gun, his wife stands in the door. "you sure showed up at the right time Marshal, they had us for sure, seems a man can find no peace nowhere." I ask if they were hurt, but both had not been injured, I go over to the 2 wounded vigilantes and remove their hoods, the old man is taken aback, the 2 men are known to him and thought to be good honest ranchers. The settler's wife being a woman of the frontier shrugs it off and goes in to cook up some grub and put the coffee on.

I write up a statement of the attack and had the old man put his mark to it, we treat the wounded men and lay the dead over their saddles, intentionally leaving their masks on, we are going to ride right down the main street of Helena with our dead and wounded, hoping to send a strong message of what to expect if you break the law in the area under my protection. After eating and having damn good cup of Arbuckle's we head out, I want to reach Helena about mid morning when the town was full of people and busy. We enter main street about 11 am with me in the leading the prisoners and the Tex bringing in the recently departed, I ride slowly wanting as many people as possible to see, I am dead tired, seemed like days since I slept. We drop off the prisoners and the dead with the town Marshal and I report in to the Federal Judge his honour Ronald Sanders, I brief him of all events up to present and handed in my written report. He is impressed by our progress and tells me he really enjoyed the newspaper notice and promised me more men but did not know exactly when. Tex and I felt we have been put through the ringer and were going for a bath, and home cooked food and a night on a real bed. Next morning early, we are again on the road, this time to Em's, it was time to re group and try to plan some effective plans of action.

Upon arrival, it was the same friendly greeting, and I get my kiss, they already knew most of the news except the killing and capturing the vigilantes. I mosey over to the small corral and shed where Buster as I already knew had everything ready, nothing better than military training. He has 4 good horses waiting, I chose a big grey, looks like a goer, Buster says damn good horse but a bit wild and rough, I then inform him that we would be leaving in the morning and I liked my horses and women a bit wild." All set to go just throw on the hurricane seat and you are ready to travel." Before I leave Buster, I tell him we going to get together later and I want to have him there, I needed to get input from a good military mind.

Everything seemed pretty much done so I spend as much time as I can with Carol, the day of rest passes way to quickly, over coffee Em, Carol, Whiplash, Tex, William, Em's ramrod Iron Mike Adams and I discuss what needed to be done and how to do it. I give old Whiplash a job I am sure he will surely enjoy, I want him to hang around the mining camps for about a week or so and gather what information he could, be evasive about who he is if asked he was to reply he was doing important work for the government make a point of people seeing him taking notes. I want the meat carvers to think there were spies everywhere and they are aware they were 1 step away from prison. Old Whiplash jumped at the idea, "I got a couple cronies Hardin they would be right tickled to have a hand in this" those poor boys in the mining town have no idea what they were in for". "Ok you old he coon take the boys along but be damn careful some there might not like the idea you boys hanging around, keep a sharp eye and your powder dry". Whiplash grumbles on a bit about being nurse maided, but tells me he and the boys would be careful, but if bullets do start flying he and the boys know how to throw lead back. "Hardin, I got some information for you, heard tell of a group of outlaws hiding out in a deserted mining town, nothing in it but empty buildings, they call it Flintlock, not sure how many rats in town could be considerable". I knew of the place, Rex had spoke of it when we visited the Bar M ranch, figured it a good place for a hideout.

That is going to be our next visit, maybe catch a whole mess of rats in the nest, this I knew it could get right interesting not knowing how many skunks were holed up there, wishing we had a couple more men, but old Tex and I would find a way, hopefully not getting ourselves killed in the process.

There will always be rocks in the road ahead of us.
They will be stumbling blocks or stepping stones;
it depends how you use them.
- Friedrich Nietzsche

CHAPTER 24

GHOST TOWN

Feeling rested and having fresh horses under us we head to Flintlock with new energy and confidence it will be at least a 2 day ride before we can flush the human rats from their holes.

The second morning out we meet up with 4 Sioux warriors, recognizing them as Sioux we turn and ride slowly towards them riding a zig zag pattern to show we are friendly and want to talk, weapons are kept in their holsters. When we meet, I greet them in Sioux and tell them I am Crow Killer, one of the men I knew as Grey Wolves blood brother I then hand them tobacco and papers to pass around. We talk and smoke, then they tell us of the whiskey traders operating a few miles east of us and how they tried to get their people away from there, but the white men said they would shoot them if they interfered. The lowest form of criminal is the scalp hunter or whiskey trader, I have a great dislike for them knowing the many lives they ruin. I tell them to go home and not to worry Crow Killer isgoing to make them go away, and if they saw Black Hand or Grey Wolf tell them I will visit soon, with a Sioux war cry we gallop away. This is the break I have been hoping for, catching them in the act, using the Sioux directions we soon find the Whiskey traders selling rotgut from the back of a wagon, we ride up slow as if customers, but I could see they were on their guard, I pulled my shotgun from the sheath on my back, this would be close in work, Tex had his rifle across the bow of his saddle. There are 4 white men selling bust skull and maybe a dozen Indians, most of them drunk or getting there. Before any of them could speak, I inform them we are the law and they were under arrest for selling liquor to the Indians, one of the men in the front of the wagon brings his rifle up for a quick shot a grab I let him have the left barrel, the force of the shotgun blast at that range just lifts him off the wagon and he is dead before he hits the ground. Tex had the other 3 under his gun and has them drop their weapons. I look at the drunken Indians and in Sioux scold them, it was very bad to trade for bad whiskey when babies go hungry, and I cuss them out good, then I threaten that I will put them in white mans jail if they do not leave now an Indian fears jail above most things like a wild animal hate being caged.

Tex has tied up the traders, they are real peaceful and quiet now wondering what we were going to do to them. While Tex guards the prisoners, I unhitch the horses from the wagon and move them a safe distance away, then I take an axe I find in their wagon and commence breaking open barrels fowl smelling stuff it is, then taking full bottles I smash them against the wagon, making a torch I throw it into the wagon, which ignites I a great ball of flame immediately, great flames rise into the sky, I look back and the Indians are gone. After throwing their weapons into the burning wagon I walk over to the captives and study their faces for future reference, "Tex and I do not like whiskey traders, should just shoot you and bury you shallow for the varmints to feed on, but might make them poor critters sick eating your rotten meat." "We are going to give you each a plug from the wagon to ride, the other stays here for the Indians can use it to eat." "We now know who you are and if we ever see you again we will shoot on site, if you survive your trip be sure to warn the others". We grab the last horse, we will release it later for the Indians to find, those boys were sure going to be sore riding those nags, I like the thought of it. We have no time for prisoners, we need to get to Flintlock, see what live ghosts were haunting the place.

About dusk the next day we find the town, leaving our horses out of sight we crawl up a hill overlooking the town, all looked deserted, just a few unused buildings falling into decay. After a quick look, we return down to the horses, and ride back to a spot where we could not be seen or heard, jerky and water is our supper. We catch a couple hours shut eye and return to our previous spot, sure enough there was light and smoke coming from the largest building which looks to be an old saloon, old habits die hard with outlaws.

We watch the building for a long while, every now and then a man would come out, have a look around and listen, well I knew at least one of them was savvy. I am looking for the guards they must have out, I finally spot him when he lites up a smoke, he was just off the old wooden sidewalk at the end of the saloon, a good dark spot where he is tough to see.

They all seem to be all together other than the sentry, I believe this will be a suitable time to say howdy, we work our way down the slope on foot arriving behind some deserted houses, going real slow and quie nowt, both of us earlier had changed into moccasins for stealth. I whisper to Tex that I will take the guard out and then we would both go in the front, we both had our shotguns, a great equalizer when outnumbered. Leaving Tex I move slow and careful not to alert the guard, I need to take him out quiet and quick. I get to a dark alley and spot him at the other end, now hugging the wall I move in on him silent as a shadow, I think about cutting his throat, but can not bring myself to do it, I am right behind him now with my left hand I cover his mouth and I put the barrel of my six shooter along his skull, he drops quick and quiet without a sound. Quickly I tie his hands and feet then stick his bandana into his mouth, Tex was waiting by the saloon doors, nodding at one another we burst through the saloon doors tshotguns levelled and cocked. In a loud voice, I say "Hands up boys or the devil may take you, I am U S Marshal Steele and you are all under arrest, everyone just take it easy and no sudden moves". Other than the man behind the bar they were grouped up close, looking directly into the four large bores wisely they do not move, motioning with my shotgun I tell the man behind the bar to join the others, there are 8 hardcases in total, I figured on more but they could have men out doing some nightwork. The leader of this band is Buck Stiller, bad man, Rangers ran him out of Texas, a ruthless and evil man. Well sir old Buck is right displeased, Tex steps out and quickly brings in the guard, he is awake but wished he wasn't, and moaning like a new born calf. I did not have any real evidence on this bunch there were no cattle or loot, but honest men do not hang out in ghost towns. We have them all drop their gun belts in a pile in front of the bar, as they are dropping guns I inform them it would go bad for them if we find any hideout guns or other hidden weapons, two more small calibre guns are added to the pile. Moving Buck and his boys away from their artillery I had them sit around 2 tables pulled together. "Tex, I say," take one of these boys down to where they have the horses and saddles, I recon it is the big building at the end and get some light in there, they must have some high beams for the ropes there". Tex without a word points to a man and they walk down to the outlaw's horses were kept.

I look at the outlaws my greener level and cocked, "Buck I gave you your chance to clear out, now you and your fellow rogues are going to have to pay the devil, it will be breakfast in hell for you boys", chuckling. For bad men, they are looking a bit green around the gills, and I want their imaginations going, give them a hard lesson. Buck says we cannot hang them without a trail, I was not judge and jury, and it would be downright criminal stringing them up. I could not supress a laugh "Buck, the Governor for the Territory authorized us to use whatever force we needed, no one is going to care about you and your bunch getting hung." We wait in relative quiet for Tex to return, within minutes he and his prisoner return. I order the men to stand and have them walk slowly ahead to the barn, Tex had it lit well, and a couple ropes are already over a high beam, old Tex does have a unique sense of humour and a flair for the dramatic.

Once inside the barn I order them to stop, looking up at the ropes I shake my head sadly, a few faces have gone white by now, but now it was time we finished it. Tex took each man one at a time to put only a blanket and a bridle on their horses, in short order all the outlaw horses are ready. I tell Buck to step forward, when he was about 3 feet in front of me I have him stop. Time to drop the bomb "Buck this is how it is going to go, you men are going to get on your horses and ride out of the Territory, if after today we see any of you in the Territory we will shoot you on site, is that understood." Old Buck did not know what to say, still thinking he was going to get hung, "What about our equipment Marshall, we cannot go into the wilds without any guns". With that I reply that he was lucky to be getting out breathing, but I am a kind-hearted soul, and they have their chance to leave. I order the outlaws to mount up, we then send them on there way, as they ride away cursing Buck called back "I will not forget this Marshal," Laughing I called back, "you better not forget Buck if you know what is good for you."

Going back to barn we collect all the oil lamps and kerosene we could find starting with the barn we set it ablaze, then we set fire to every building in that town, no vipers would be hiding here any longer. With the heat of the flames at our backs and the sound of the bullets exploding we ride away without looking back, both of knowing there was still a long haul ahead. I am going to send a wire to Whiplash and have him meet us back at Em's, I want to see if my plan to stop the rustling is working.

The more I learn of people, the more I like my dog. -
Mark Twain

CHAPTER 25

———◇◇◇◇◇◇◇———

UTAH FELLONS LAST RIDE

Three days later we all meet up at Em's, it was good to see Whiplash safe and sound, he is still cranky as ever but has some good news and is just chomping on the bit to tell me of it. Buster had Apollo looking good and full of piss and vinegar, brushed to a almost sky blue shine, I have always admired men would do their work well, with pride and without complaint. We need to rest up, I thought 3 days should do it, fatten up on Em's cooking, relax and drink some good coffee, get a few rare nights sleeping in relative safety, but mostly to spend some time with my sweetheart the delicious Carol.

After a fine supper as what had become our custom when we gather together for coffee and bring each other up to date, I thought old Whiplash was going to bust so I let him go first, settling myself in I prepare for a long story. "You got all them butchers right scared Hardin, I did as you told me and even duded myself up a bit, make them think maybe I was a rancher or business man, the boys and

I got a lot of attention anywhere we went, people asking all sorts of fool questions. "I used the note pad as you said, that really got their interest, might have accidently dropped a few hints that I was sent by a very important person to check things out". Laughing," you should have seen the look on them rustlers faces when no one would take their stolen cows, and those butchers now have to go to the ranchers for meat, or they will face some really pissed off miners wanting beef." Well things seem to be coming together, by a show of force and some cunning we had forced some of the outlaws out of the country and the weaker ones will leave soon look for easier pickings, now things would get much more interesting and dangerous. With a grim look, Whiplash tells me" one more thing Hardin, there are rumors that the vigilantes have put a bounty put out for you and Tex, it is a death warrant, and they want proof of death mainly your heads". Tex snorts "let em come I plan on being real stubborn on them not collecting, looks like we will have to take some scalps Pard", I nod in agreement, but in some ways, it is good news it meant they are getting desperate, and desperate men make mistakes.

I let Tex tell them of the whiskey traders and the fun we had in the ghost town, Tex can spin a good yearn when he had a mind to, when he finishes there are smiles and laughter all around the table. Before we break up our little meeting, I tell them I have some serious talk to do first.

Looking around the table I address my friends, "we are making satisfactory progress and the bounty on our heads proves it, you never know what desperate men will do, I want this to an armed camp starting tomorrow morning, everyone including the women will carry firearms at all times" confirming then Carol still had the derringer I gave her, then continued, "always have lots of water and wood in the house, this is a good spot to fight from, solid stone house, hard to burn. Might be an idea to fort up the bunkhouse and barn a bit, extra rifles and ammunition on hand, and no one rides alone, to many people vanish that way, I hope it is nothing but I think it is best to be prepared." Em pipes in "you bet your boots Marshal we will be ready to give them polecats a right fine reception", I believe the old gal is looking for a scrap. Em put Whiplash and Buster in charge of the outer buildings, she has been through wars before this and knew what had to be done.

On our last days stay at the ranch a rider comes thundering into the yard and pulls his horse up sharply said he was sent by the Chief Justice he says he needs to see you both right quick there were new developments with the criminal element, well that left little room for doubt, Bill is shaking the tree to see what falls out. Leaving it to Em, knowing she would crack the whip, mostly on poor Whiplash, who of course secretly enjoyed it all and have things ready at the ranch. Half hour after the rider rides Tex and I thunder out of the yard me giving off my Sioux war cry and Tex giving the rebel yell, sometime we a just big damn kids.

Bill is sitting his back to the wall in an abandoned saloon of a ghost town vacated by the miners after the ore ran out, smoke and the smell of whisky with unwashed bodies fill the room, he looks at his gang with distain, thinking that one Hardin Steele was worth more than all this sorry lot. Utah Frank Fellon is heading straight for his table his a look is one of determination and anger. Utah had ridden in 4 days back bringing 5 tough and capable men, a quiet mean bunch, Bill sensed trouble coming and was anxious for it needing action. Utah and his men had come not only for the outlaw money but the reward on Sudden and Tex. Bill smiled at the thought, Utah would learn the hard way Sudden would not be taken easily. Utah was above average in build, blond with a thick red moustache, confident in his abilities with any weapon, and enjoyed killing.

Taking up a chair looks at Bill with hard eyes begins to speak, "Bill, been talking with some of the boys and have a plan to put down them 2 marshals", Bill takes out a cigar, lighting it slowly looking at Utah with a steady eye, "what do you have in mind Frank, not an easy thing old Sudden is one curly wolf and Tex is a fighter." "Bill, you seem to think this marshal is something special, heard you 2 were friends once, but no matter I will kill him". Fellon then lays out his deadly plan, "I hear that the marshal has a ranch where he gets his horses, grub and picks up information, also has him a gal, me and the boys are going to get him at the ranch next time he comes in, he wont know what hit him until it is to late."

Inwardly smiling Bill takes a few moments before responding as if thinking things over. "Frank, I will not try to stop you, but I strongly advise against it, but a man has to make his own way, good luck to you." Smiling at the unexpected reply, Utah adds that some of Bills men want to join his bunch. One thing that Bill will not tolerate from any man is disloyalty, Bill says to Utah," have the men who want to go with you come over to the table, Utah waved the men over, all 5 men were at a single table and walked over slowly to where Bill was sitting. Intentionally not invitingany of the men to sit he looks at them his eyes hard and full of challenge. "I hear you boys want to join up with Utah and go after the marshals", the biggest of the bunch a dirty brutish man speaks up, "well we ain't making any money sitting here, we believe Utah has a good plan for making some easy money". "Looking Frank dead in the eye, his voice low and with menace s" go if you will but none of you are coming back, if I see any of you again I will shoot on sight, and one more thing, any harm comes to the young gal at the ranch I will hunt and dog you until you are all dead and that goes for you to Frank." Utah is not only astonished but angry "taking on a lot of killing there Bill, I should kill you now, no man talks to me like that." The Utah bunch were so concentrated by the talk at the table they did not notice the men totally loyal to Bill had surrounded them with weapons drawn and would shoot with a nod from their boss. Still looking amused Bill tells Utah to look behind him, Utah is no hero and recognizes at once they were a blink of an eye from the coffin. "OK time you boys hit the saddle, you have an hour to pack your gear and start making dust, the boys will see you off." Without another word, Bill gets up from the table and goes to his room, he has an idea for the next heist and it is big insanely big, he will go to his room he thinks best there. Sudden has ruined a good thing with the cattle rustling, easy money, but there was a big gold shipment going out by train and now all he had to do was figure out how to get it, he is determined to have that gold and give old Hardin a surprise, laying on his bed hands clasped behind his head Bill with a smile begins to think and plan.

Utah is surly as a bear with a sore paw, thinking he will settle Mr. Bill Mathers hash after he and his boys raid the ranch and kill the marshals, he is confident on success with 10 hard and desperate men riding with him, taking the ranch will be easy most cowhands were tough but not gunfighters. Now Utah is not a great thinker and always went in strong killing anything that moves, they would ride in at sunrise just as everyone would be at chuck and mostly not armed. He broke his men into three bunches, one to attack the barn, another to hit the bunkhouse and he and his men would hit the main house, and they would go in fast and shooting. He is going to kill everyone at the ranch including the young gal Bill spoke of but only after he and his men had their fun with her, a cruel smile comes to his thin lips, a spot of drool forms at the corners of his thin mouth as he thinks of the girl. They finda place to camp well away from the ranch to remain unseen, then telling his men to get some rest, tomorrow would be a bloody day, and he was right.

The next morning Tall Bear one of the Sioux horse wranglers is on guard, the view is good and he can c see for miles in almost any direction, all was quiet the morning was near the night sounds dying out, taking a moment looks back at Ems house, it is a good house built by a man who knew how to build things to last. He remembered as a child his father telling him of the times they tried to drive them out, and of the many empty lodges, but he knew his father admired the rancher's for their bravery. Looking back, he notices dust rising still far in the distance, using the spyglass Whiplash gave him he can just barely make out 11 men riding directly at the ranch, without hesitation he runs down and goes directly to the ranch house and tells Em what he saw and says it is trouble for sure time to get ready.

Em had fought Indians, bandits, rustlers and was not a woman to frighten easy, in fact she is a gal who likes a good scrap. Whiplash goes into the house and startes to put rifles and ammunition by the windows and preparing the house for battle. Once the men have gathered she refers to Whiplash to repel the upcoming attack. Old Whiplash is now in his element, he sends the foreman and the cowhands to the barn where logs have been placed for cover,

Buster a cowhand named Red and Tall Elk head over to a spot prepared earlier, rocks piled high for good fire, by placing them in their positions he had set up a deadly crossfire and Buster being a magician with a Winchester it would prove just how deadly for his enemies. Whiplash, Em, Carol, Billy, would fight from the house, shutters with gun ports were secured, bandages water are placed for quick use if needed and a hot fire is blazing, Whiplash feels they are as ready as they can be hoping he has not overlooked anything, thinking to himself now come get some polecats, chuckling. Busters set the other 2 men in their positions, as to his training he inspectes the men, Red is an old hand and had him a big sharps, he looks at Buster "she don't shoot fast but damn she shoots" Buster smiles and nods his approval, Tall Elk has an old second hand rifle with the stock wired together, William goes to the stash of weapons and gets his old Spencer and ammunition still a damn effective killing machine, handing the weapon to Tall Elk he shows him how to load and work the weapon, the Sioux warrior is greatly pleased, "we make big fight today buffalo soldier". Buster with sincerity replies, "today we fight as brothers Tall Elk". Red is smiling, "damndest outfit I ever saw, and I am damn proud to be riding for this brand." The men settle in now double checking their weapons, death would be riding in soon.

Nearing the ranch Utah tells his men to stay in their groups, sweep in fast and hard kill anything that moves no prisoners except the girl, Utah threatened death to anyone who touches her before he has his pleasure first. At 50 yards out the outlaws dig in the spurs and oame into the ranch hot lead finding nothing but empty air. It is Em who fired back first, letting go with her old horse pistol knocking an outlaw clean out of the saddle, dead as he hit the ground, then came a wall of lead from 3 sides, horses and men scream, curse, gun smoke mixed with blood mist fills the air giving off an eerie light. Utah and his remaining men head for the ranch house for cover, but the gunfire from the house was devastating, not a man makes it to the doorstep, Utah dead on his feet is still cursing and firing until Buster puts a 44.40 slug through his black heart. What seemed hours turned out to be only minutes, dead, dying and wounded men litter the yard, 2 horses were dead a third is screaming in pain, one of the ranch hands shoots it. The sudden quiet is deafening, everyone's ears are still ringing from the gunfire, the smell of gun smoke and blood hang heavy in the air. The ranch defenders emerge slowly from their firing positions, weapons cocked and ready, might be some fight still left in the attackers, 5 men were dead including Utah Frank, another 2 would not live out the hour, of the remaining 4 outlaws all were wounded a couple badly. The wounded men are disarmed, Em and Carol comes out of the house with bandages and water to cleanse their wounds, Em sends one of the ranch hands to fetch the doctor and the Sheriff. The ranch defenders incur minor damage, a ranch hand named Crandall takes a ricochet through his calf, not to serious but an ugly wound, Tall Elk had a nasty gash from a wood splinter above his left eye which would require stitches, but all have come out in decent shape, had they not been prepared they surely all would have been slaughtered. Tall Elk went to give William back the Spencer rifle, "A warrior needs a powerful weapon, a gift from the buffalo soldier to his warrior brother Tall Elk.". Tall Elk says nothing just turns and walks away, the next morning Buster finds a beautiful pinto mustang tied up in front of his shed, this cements a lifelong friendship between Buster the Buffalo Soldier and the Sioux warrior Tall Elk.

The only way to have a friend is to be one.
- Ralph Waldo Emerson

CHAPTER 26

COFFEE WITH BILL

Tex and I are returning to the Capitol after being out chasing a couple horse thieves for a week, we are not returning with any prisoners, the thieves because of poor choices are now buried beside each other in lonesome graves on the vast prairie.

We are seated in the Governors office being congratulated on the hard and efficient work in stopping the rustlers mining scheme and the making many of the whiskey traders hunt their holes. "Marshal Steele the miners and banks are going to start moving their gold from Bozeman to the rail hub in Billings, I believe this will be a great temptation to the outlaw mobs, I know you to have a quick and canny mind and we need you boys to come up with a plan on how to thwart any attempts of any robbers looking to get rich quick". I look over at Tex frowning, "Governor how much gold are we talking about?" "Marshal when all is said and done could be in the millions." this was going to be a tough challenge, I am positive this is what old

Bill and his mob had been waiting for, the big score. The Governor interrupts my thoughts "Boys give it some thought and we will meet back here in a couple days for war talk, take a few days off, I have hired 4 new deputy marshals, they can take care of things for a few days". Just then there was an urgent knock on the door and the Aide bursts through the door in a rush handing the Governor a telegram. A look of concern crosses his face as he reads, looking up says "Boys, Em's place was attacked, the telegram doesn't say much, but seems there was a lot of bloodshed." I feel a cold fear spread to my very core fearing for Carol and my friends, the coldness engulfs me, I vow swift and harsh retribution if things went badly at Em's. Shaking my head as to clear it I hear the Governor tell his aide to ride to his ranch and get Long Tom to bring some of his boys and bring his horse Buck, and come loaded for bear, he was going to Em's ranch. "Hardin, you boys get going, me and the boys will be along shortly, Em is a good honest rancher and a close friend of mine, there will be hell to pay if they have done her evil, there will be no place for them to hide." We rise to depart, I look to the Governor, "Sir you damn well got that right, be seeing you at the ranch".

It only takes a few minutes to saddle up and setting a fast pace we head to Ems, praying all are safe, but also trying to prepare for the worst. I know Tex is thinking the same way and Tex is no man you wanted on your trail, there was little talk as the horses sensing their master's urgency gave it their all, eating up ground swiftly. After covering a quick bit of ground, they pull up our horses to give them a breather, even Apollo hsd his limits. Tex was the first to break the silence, "Pard do you think old Bill had anything to do with the attack?" Thinking a moment before answering," Tex, I do not think so, Bill holds all women in high regard, I seen him kill a man at Sandy's place in Billings for roughing up one of her gals, but if he did it will be his downfall and no holds barred" .Nodding his approval Tex responds, "I know Sandy, great gal, treats her girls right and has cut up more than one cowhand for abusing her girls, helps out the town even put in most of the pot to build a new schoolhouse." I knowSandy as well, salt of the earth, but I knew of 2 men who have died by her hand, both deserved their fate. Nodding in agreement

I put Apollo into a fast lope, it is the longest and most anxious ride I can ever remember.

We thunder into the ranch yard guns drawn alert for danger, dust frilling the air, all looks pretty much normal, the bodies of the dead and wounded had been taken into town, the dead now permanent members of the boot hill club. To my great relief, Em, Whiplash and Billy come from the house to greet us, I still did not see Carol my heart was pounding in my chest, but before I can ask she steps out from the corner of the house. I immediately jump off Apollo and ran to her scooping her up into my arms, "Hardin honey I am safe but if you squeeze any harder we may need the doctor after all", letting her go we both laugh, the laughter releases the tension, very much relieved I kiss her softly telling her my love her. She smiles that sweet smile and hand in hand we return to the others, Whiplash is chaffing at the bit to tell his tale,, "Hardin old son you missed a good scrap, we licked them good thanks to you we were ready, Satan has 7 new souls waiting for him on boot hill." Buster and Tall Elk come over and join us, then Whiplash gave a quick account by his standards of the battle. Nearing suppertime I so I ask Buster to have the whole crew gather by the fire later for talk and coffee after chow. It is a beautiful sunset, brilliant oranges and red feathering the sky, Billy isthe last to join the group and I motion for him to sit beside me, once seated I put my arm across his shoulder "story is you stood your ground and fought well, I am very proud of you, you will make your mark in life sure as shooting." Releasing my grip on his shoulder I turn to the others but noticing Billy looking like to burst with pride, just after the coffee is poured and everyone settled in the Governor and 4 of his saltiest hands rode in, Long Tom among them. They dismount and dig into their saddlebags for their cups, western men never pass up a chance for coffee. I knew Long Tom, by reputation a tough loyal man, liked by his men and feared by his enemies, the type of man who could not be killed easy, I get up and shake hands all around. We then gather Indian fashion around the fire, the Governor knowing now all is well seems to be enjoying himself, teasing and flirting with Em much to Whiplashes displeasure. I look around the circle before I speak

"I want to apologize to all of you for putting you in harms way, it will be my fault if you are killed or harmed, I misjudged the enemy and that will not happen again." Em looks over at me, "now Hardin Steele do not worry yourself about it, we can take care of ourselves, and besides was getting to damn quiet and civilized around here, you prepared us and we overcame., enough said". The rest of the group vocalized their agreement with Em's statement, with Whiplash the most vocal, I think mostly to impress Em.

We are quietly drinking our coffee many conversations going on within the circle when a voice came from the darkness, "Hello the ranch would old Hardin be there?" I recognize the voice immediately it is Bill, "I get up and move away from the fire towards the voice, "I am here Bill, why do you not join us for coffee, no tricks you have my word you can leave anytime no one will try to stop you." that got a chuckle from Bill, "Hardin is that tough old he coffee boiler Whiplash with you?" Whiplash joins me "I am here Bill and watch who you are calling old, I can still whip both you boys would not even work up a sweat", all of us started laughing, for a moment it seemed like old times. "Ok Hardin I am coming in your word has always been good." Bill appears out of the darkness leading his horse he does not look as neat and trimmed as he usual and his facial feature a bit haggard by stress, leaving the horse ground hitched he joins us at the fire, once seated with a steaming cup of brew says to the group" Boys I want you to know I had no part in the attack on the ranch, I even told poor old dead Utah it was foolish, some just got to learn the hard way, and putting them under was damn clever work." "Damn Bill I knew this was not your doing, you may be riding the wrong side of the law, but I know you would never harm women and you do your shooting from the front. "Bill, give it up and turn yourself in, the Governor is here I am sure we can talk it out and work out a deal, we both know if things stay as they are we must face each other, it would give me no pleasure in killing you". Another small chuckle from Bill, "you take on a lot Sudden, but I hope that day does not come either, killing you would sadden me as well, we crossed to m any rivers together old son." Before he could leave Em and Carol tell Bill not to leave just yet saying they would be right back with a surprise. A few minutes later they emerge from the ranch house with 2 huge trays heaping with bear sign or known to some as donuts, it is said a cowboys would ride days out of their way to get a chance at some, a rare treat, I can tell you those plates emptied fast with the Governor inhaling a giant share of them. For a few minutes, it was quiet and relaxed all enjoying, some small talk quiet and comfortable. Bill with hesitation rose "Well it sure was a nice visit, good to set with good folks again, Miss Em thanks for the bear sign, been along while since I et them, and Carol a pleasure to meet you I think that old knot head Hardin got himself a real fine woman to walk beside him. Before he could leave I gave him fair warning, "Bill I know you will be going after that gold shipment, and they are paying me to stop you, and stop you I, and I damn well will, leave the territory lots of good country out there to see, think it over Amigo." After shaking hands Bill walks over to his horse and mounts "Pard I am after much more than the gold, it is an all or nothing game now, be seeing you boys make sure to keep your powder dry, "I listened as the hoofbeats faded away, I had the feeling the next time we met it would mean hot lead and gun smoke.

After the trays are empty including the crumbs with a fresh cup of coffee I address the Governor, "Sir I know sure as shooting old Bill is going after the gold shipment and my gut tells me it will be a well planned and tricky heist, he is a fox and plans everything down to the last detail, but we will outfox the fox or die trying". "I could use another good gun and a man who knows how and when to use it, be a pleasure if Long Tom agrees to hook up with Tex and myself but do n ot want you short handed." The Governor thinks it over for a few minutes, Long Tom was his Segundo, fighting foreman and a needed man, he looks over at Tom, "well Tom what do you say, remember there is still a bounty out on these boys and anyone who helps them." Long Tom needed no time to decide, "be right proud to ride with these boys, and if these so called bad men want my scalp let them come and try and take it, one thing about riding with these 2 itain't going to be boring" smiling hugely.

So, it is settled Long Tom was joining us, I advise the Governor the 3 of us would be at his office in 2 days to discuss a battle plan. The group breaks up and everyone heads for their beds, I was thankful to hit the hay I had not have a good night's sleep in weeks without the threat of danger, I barely got my boots off before I fall into a deep sleep.

Waking late in the morning, I am feeling better than I had in days and hungry as all get out, when I get to the kitchen, Em with a smile scolds me about sleeping the day away, smiling back, I gave her a hug which she gently shoos away with mock protest, I am ordered to sit breakfast was ready. After a huge portion of steak, eggs and fresh bread Em brings me a huge slice of fresh apple pie to go with my coffee, she knows my love for pie, Em is certainly one of the good ones. Billy comes into the kitchen having already eaten I sentd him on an errand to fetch, Tex, Whiplash, Long Tom, William, Tall Elk and have them meet me over by the corrals, then come back to the house and we would go meet them together for war talk. Billy is off in a flash, feeling honoured to be included in such a select group of men.

Within 20 minutes we are all gathered, I had selected everyone there for their individual talents, Tex and Long Tom were of the same mold and thought alike experienced and proven fighters, Whiplash had the experience and was down right inspirational at times, Tall Elk was a master of ambush and cunning, Buster being a soldier had a regulated and excellent milirary mind and is an excellent tactician, Billy is there to listen and learn.

Looking around I address the gathering, "Boys we got some man-sized work ahead, we are going to palaver, think, and come up with a way to stop the gold thieves, and there will be other gangs wanting to take their chances, with that much gold its going to attract outlaws like flies to shit".I give them a moment to think it over, Buster broke the silence, "Hardin do you think Bill will take your advice and leave?" Shaking my head in a negative manner, "no it is a personal thing now, he needs to prove he can beat me, I think he would trade bragging rights over the money, wish he would though, things would be much simpler."

The discussions went on throughout the morning with little progress, one thing we did decide is that Whiplash would be our man in the Governor's office, gathering intelligence and keeping us informed of all outlaw activities. Tall Elk stood, proud and serious, "Marshal I would like to join you, will fight strong." "You have proven your courage Kola, it will be an honour to ride with a strong and brave warrior but the ranch work still needs to be done, and I ask you as a brother to stay and protect my friends and family." Tall Elk disappointed but knowing the logic of it nods in agreement, "not worry Marshal, I will give my life to protect Ems lodge". Thanking him I proceed, "Buster you will be Segundo, and handle any gun trouble if need be, no one goes out alone and all go armed." "Hardin, the old Sarge will handle things here, no harm will befall the ranch while I live, this is my family now." The meeting breaks up for chuck, I have zero solutions and really did not expect any, but things would be alright at the ranch now I can now focus at the task on hand, I know already secrecy and adaptability would be the keys to success, plus a shit lot of luck.

Before the Governor and his men leave I brief him that me and the boys I are going to ride the rail line, and I will be seeing him in a few days time to plan our strategy, Tex and Long Tom will start from Billings and I the Bozemen, meeting in the middle figure the territory we need to cover, there was no need to tell the boys what to do, as old hands they knew what was needed. Whiplash would go into the Capital and set up shop in the governor's office and start gathering information, and he is just the man for the job, has many friends in the area and is well liked by most, and did not miss much. The dangerous and possible bloody game ha begun, I just hope I am man enough to get er done.

You got to be brave and have courage, believe in yourself, because that it is the first thing to success is the belief in yourself. - Louis Riel

CHAPTER 27

BILLY TAKES ACTION

Apollo is well rested and sassy, as I am getting my gear ready and saddling up Carol and Billy walk over to me I can tell they have something on their minds. Carol gives me a sweet hug, "Hardin honey, Billy would like to go on the ride with you, he is close to being a man now and he fought well when we were attacked." With my most serious look, I say "Carol do not forget there are a lot of folks out there who want me dead and would not blink an eye to kill Billy as well", looking at Billy seeing the disappointment on his face and against my better judgement relent. "OK buckaroo go and see Buster and get ready to travel, we are leaving leaving right after coffee, be here in half an hour or I leave without you, now scat." With a huge grin, he takes off like a shot, I noticed Buster already had a fine roan horse ready to go, smiling I knew I had been played like a fiddle, good thing I am not chasing this sneaky bunch.

Billy was back and ready to go before I was halfway through my coffee and visit with Carol, she still has that innocent smile on that fools no one. After finishing my Arbuckle's, I walk out to check his gear, the horse is a good one, lots of bottom and speed if needed, Tall Elk had selected him and that Sioux knew his horseflesh. I check to make sure he had a canteen and was filled, had his slicker, looked like it may be a wet ride, Billy had his Winchester in the boot and extra ammo, satisfied with I nod of approval tell him to mount we are hitting the trail, I give Carol a long hug and kiss then saying goodbye to the family I slip my shotgun into the scabbard across my back and crawl up on Apollo, with a wave we head out.

Once down the trail a bit we fall into a smooth travelling rhythm I start to tell Billy as Bear did for me the things a man needed to know when travelling, I talk of flowers and plants that the Indians use for medicine, what wild plants you could eat if you were out of grub, how to judge how fresh a hoofprint was, about reading sign, not only tracks but how to think like the prey ahead, things to look for when picking a campsite or escaping bad weather, always watch the wild animals for signs of trouble or to find water. I tell him many more things as we ride, how to use cover for approach and escape, and never skyline yourself in dangerous country. The most important thing we talk about is in trouble no bad how it is, remain calm, use your mind, if there is life there is hope. I find that I am enjoying passing on my knowledge, and it dawned on me that I am now like my hero's Bear, Ramon and the rest, I was now the teacher, who would have guessed. We are having a comfortable ride and the weather is holdind, but I am constantly on the lookout for trouble and likely places that the gold train may be attacked from. Billy is quickly becoming a good scout with sharp eyes and is proving himself well on the trail. That evening I have Billy select the campsite, does an excellent job of it, good water and grass for the horses, cedar trees for fuel and cover, and good ground with approach difficult not to be seen, with a slap on the back "you will do to ride the river with old timer". The evenings fire is put out, laying in our bedrolls we talk I tell him stories of Bear, Ramon, Black Hand, O'Shea, the Traveller and many great men that I met including the old rascal Panther.

"Hardin who do you recon is the toughest and most dangerous of the men you have come across, I hear that John Ringo and Billy the Kid are right bad hombres." "Billy them two would not come up to a real tough mans bootheel, there is a big difference between a gunfighter and a man who fights with a gun." "If it came to gunfighters there is no better than Hickok and Wade, but when it comes to tough and man killing I would say Jerry Potts rules the roost, word has it he has killed a man for every year of his life and he is no button well over 30 I am guessing." Bear once told me this story of Jerry. Jerry was visiting in Montana his mother's tribes Chief has a celebration but fearing trouble his mother and sister do not attend, this insults the Chief and he sends two of his bucks to teach them a lesson, but they go to far and kill both Mother and his sister." When Jerry gets word, he heads back to Whoop up country with blood in his eye, he starts to hunt the killers who were known to him." "As luck, would have it he comes across the two killers as they are riding back to their camp, and gives chase, Jerry is an excellent shot from horseback and punches one of the braves off his horse to die on the prairie with a single long shot, the second almost makes the camp which was at the bottom of a ravine, again Jerry's rifle speaks death and the brave falls and rolls to the bottom of the hill almost at the Chiefs feet." "the braves are angry and want to charge up the hill but the old Chief says no, looking up at Jerry who was calmly sitting and waiting Winchester ready," his medicine is to strong today not one of you would live to m ake it to the top of the hill and he was right Jerry would have killed every last man." "After a bit, Jerry just rides off, no sane man would want Jerry Potts dogging his trail, well Pard I think we best get some shuteye got a lot of ground to cover tomorrow, no need for a guard old Apollo will keep watch". With that we both pulled up the blankets, it is a beautiful night, calm, the moon bright, countless stars winking, nights like these always give me a feeling of freedom and mystery."

As we are getting ready the next morning I begin to feel restless and a bit uneasy, I have a hunch there was going to be trouble and it will be soon, hoping I am wrong having Billy riding along with me. Sure, enough my instincts are right, just before we are to take a breather we come over a small rise and find 3 tough dirty men waiting, the 2 outside men have heir rifles out and over the saddle ready for quick action, the man in the middle did not have a weapon showing but is holding his hat off holding it in front of him. I know instantly this was a trick the Mexican bandits use and he has a gun in his hand ready for use, I have just enough time to take the thong off the hammer of my 44, I have the other Russian in my belt hidden by my jacket for a side draw, the belt draw is one of the fastest ways to get a smoke wagon into action. Without looking at Billy in a whisper I tell him to stay loose and this is big trouble. We pull up in front of the men acting unsuspecting, smiling I say, "Howdy boys, how is the trail treating you?" The man in the middle has the look of a stone-cold killer with a scarred-up face, looks like an axe was taken to it, his sneer indicated he was enjoying his moment, the other 2 both had hard looks about them and they were on edge, the man in the middle did the all the talking "Well if you are Marshal Steele, real fine, going to be a right prosperous day, your worth a thousand dollars dead and we uns plan to collect. I respond telling him I was Steele and asked who he might be. "They call me Hilltop Charlie, and these be my brothers, rode all the way from Kansas just to get a chance at you and make some easy money. "Looking directly at him my green eyes hard and steady "No such thing as easy money Charlie, and not all of you boys are going live to collect, and the boy has nothing to do with this, I was just taking him back to his folks. Hilltop gives a nasty chuckle, just his bad luck Marshal, the boy has to die no witnesses." Billy's roan takes a shift to the left, looked accidental but I know he did it intentionally to spread us out, good lad. I could tell the talking had ended and it was killing time, I knew I could not get them all but lucky might get 2, giving Billy time to get away. Out of nowhere came 2 loud pops and the bandit in front of Billy grabs his throat, instinctively the 2 other killers turned their heads, within the blink of an eye I had the .44 out and being in close I hold the trigger down and fan the Russian, within a couple heartbeats I pump all six sounds into the two bandits, dropping he handgun I pull by belly gun, I can see both men in front of me are out of action, the 3rd brother is sliding off his horse bleeding bsdly from his throat but trying to raise his weapon to shoot Billy, the gun bucks in my hand and the top of the killers head explodes showering the air with bone, brains and blood. All three brothers now lay dead on the dry grass the ground greedily soaking up their blood.

With a look of amazement, I look over at Billy who is holding the now empty derringer and looking a bit shaky and green around the gills but holding up well, "Pard you really saved our bacon, very cool work it took a lot of grit." Billy is shaking but with a steady voice says" well Hardin I owed you one and more, Carol gave me the derringer for luck, it sure did come in handy".

We dismount before I speak again, "you proved yourself a man today, Carol and the rest will be proud, but no more Billy, the boy is gone in his place a young man who one day you will be the pride of Montana". "The lesson here Bill is if your going to do some shooting, shoot first and fast, those men were over confident and smug and wanted it to last, that's why they are dead and not us, remember it Bill. "I surely will Hardin, I see now why they call you Sudden you got your gun out lightning quick."" It is not all about speed Bill, got to make the first one's count, miss the first and you may not get a second, well we better load up these men and will drop them off at the next town, still got a job to finish, you up to it Pard?" "Smiling now having calmed down says "lets get er done Marshal". We continue our scout watching for points of concealment or any spots that may give an advantage to the outlaws, after I believe I have seen enough we head for home thinking of good vittles and coffee, time for counsel and decisions. Unknown to us at the time is that we would be returning to a sad and angry ranch, one of our own has made the ultimate sacrifice.

Show respect to all people but grovel to none.
- Tecumseh

CHAPTER 28

A TEXICIAN DIES

Long Tom is sitting on the front steps of the ranch house when we ride into the ranch yard, Em, Carol, and Busterwere waiting with him, I know immediately by their expressions there is something terribly wrong. Long Tom rises as we near the house, with his head down and look of sadness and shame tells us in a faint voice "They kilt old Tex Marshal, the cowards shot him from ambush, there were at least two shooters I think one was to take me out but missed and hit Tex as well, I got off a couple shots at them but doubt if I hit anything. I took his body to the undertaker in Helena, told him you would be around shortly and to start the arrangements. "That Texas boy died game Hardin, before he died he said to tell you thanks for being his friend and how proud was proud he was being a Deputy marshal admitting a pretty lousy bank robber, then he died in my arms."

"I swear Marshal that I will have them polecat's hides patched to the barn door it will not be justice it will be revenge." I sit very still on Apollo, shock, sadness and quilt hits me to my very core.

"You did really good Tom, I am pleased to see you with the living, I swear to you these men will pay, when I catch them I just may give them to the Sioux squaws to play with, but we do not have time for Tex now, I think that's why they killed him, to distract us from out duty and keep the focus off the gold shipment." Looking around and seeing Tall Elk I ask him a favour, "I heard old knot head Panther is in the area does you think you could find him for me brother." "Yes, Marshal I can find the Cat, he is close, what you want I me tell him?" "Tell him I would be right pleased if came to see me, I have some work he might like and tell him to come quick." "Leave at first light, Busterw ill go with you so that Panther does not shoot you, he can be right touchy, Red was there and asked, "mind if I ride with the boys Marshal, since the shootout we have sort of become a team." I told him if it were ok with the foreman it was fine with me and all were to be damn careful.

With that we dismount one of the hands takes the horses, Carol brings coffee, we all sit quiet for a few minutes sipping our java a quiet and solemn group. Looking over at young Bill I tell them tell them of our encounter with the Kansas boys and how young Bill had saved our lives, showing his sand and savvy, proved himself a man sure enough, Billy some thrilled when the old hands give their nods and gestures of approval, today he learned what respect is all about, then I move on to some of my findings. "I need someone to fetch Whiplash and bring him back pronto." Long Tom said he would go, had to talk to the Governor and make sure is all good at the ranch. Before we split up I say we will all get together tomorrow morning, bring your thinking caps, we have got to get this one right. I am worried to many damn questions with not enough answers, hopefully a good night's rest will bring some inspiration.

Young Bill leaves with the hands, they all want to hear the story of the killings, Em, Carol and I go into the kitchen where they start getting supper ready, I grab a fresh coffee sat at the table and enjoying the smells of the cooking the chatter of the gals, a rare moment to be of peace, damn my gal makes great coffee. Weariness and sadness envelops ome I sense that it will be the showdown and soon, it is going to be dirty, vile and bloody, both good and bad men are going die.

Em sure can cook, heaping plates of ham, potatoes, corn on the cob with fresh bread and butter fills the table, later some apple pie made with real apples, refilling my coffee mug I struggle to my feet and gently grab Carols arm leading her outside by the back door, we walk in silence, coming to an old bench we stop and sit. Within seconds I am once again feeling her sweet lips on mine and enjoying the softness of her body as we embrace, never wanting it to end, now being both of us are near full grown things were get heated, desire and lust consume us, finally with great reluctance we separate, after sorting ourselves and regaining some composure Carol snuggles into my shoulder and we soft talk looking at the universe above.

I walk Carol back to the house and kiss her goodnight then I head straight to my room and into bed, although exhausted I can not stop thinking of the events to come, all I could bet on is Bill and his gang would do the unexpected, now how to fool the fox was the question. Next thing I know it was morning, I could smell breakfast and coffee, low conversations could be heard in the kitchen. After I washing up and dressing I enter the kitchen and find old Whiplash chowing down and sweet talking Miss Em, "Getting lazy in your old age Hardin, damn near half the day gone", finding himself very amusing. I am a bit embarrassed as I am normally the first one up. Smiling over at him "your old goat I was on the hard road while you were sitting on a purple cushion in the Governors palace" the room erupted in laughter, I sat down next to him, "good to see you Pard, have any luck with your investigating?" "I got plenty, but some is just hunch and guesswork, I will say my peace at the meeting". ""Sounds good to me old timer now who does a man have to hug to get a coffee around here". After a stern look from Em she sets a fresh cup in front of me grumbling something of how useless men are.

With Whiplash, back we can get started, the gang is already gathering and it is a quiet group, doing their thinking before their talking, and like most men of the west they like to say it short, loud, and only once. With everyone settled into the circle, I get the meeting started by asking Whiplash what information he got from the Capital.

As was Whiplash he humps and frumps a bit clearing his throat liking being the centre of attention, I looked over at him," maybe sometime before the rainy season Pard", amidst snickering and with a sour look laid out what he knew.

"Well Hardin I done what you said, made myself right at home in the Government building, some of the boys did not like me intruding but the Governor read them the scripture and that settled it, I found my old pards Moose Morrison and 10 Jewel Jonny in town and we all set to watching and listening, Moose is keeping an eye on the train station, telegraph office and any stagecoaches coming in, Jonny was hanging around the stables and saloons, Jonny listens real good. I talked with Jim Meadows the city Marshal and that newspaper man, looking any information that would help. I interrupted, "damn fine work old timer now let's hear what you and your gang of spies have found out."

"Don't rush me youngster, I am a getting there. Ok first off there is lots of talk about this here gold shipment, the whole Territory is abuzz, bets going on in the saloons if and who it will get it." I chuckled, "I recon I may have to put a few dollars down on that wager, I'll be damned if anyone is getting that gold." Continuing, "seems to be more hard cases drifting in getting supplies but not hanging around town very long, I figure the wild bunch is gathering. Old Moose spotted one of the railway men trying not to be seen but talking with a couple local hard cases, goes by Digby and is assist manager, Moose figures he has seen this Digby before but can't figure out where but you can be damn sure it wasn't church. That ain't all, crime has suddenly gone down in the territory, no reports of rustlers or holdups, only trouble is in the towns and not much of that. Now the last bit is more suspicion I cannot prove it but I smell a polecat in the Governors officer, a gent named Harpin caught my eye, always around listening, asking to many questions, being real sly about it, but gets my hair itchy like when there are injuns are about". Looking over at me says "about all I can get Hardin hope it is of some use." "I knew I had the right coon hound on the trail, this gives us much needed information, 1- we can be pretty sure we are dealing with two or more spies, 2 -Bill is gathering a tough crew and keeping them low and out of trouble 3- with that many guns could be more than one attack on the train or they could have more than I robbery planned to knowing we are short of men. I then take out 2 maps one by the railroad surveyors and cruder one I had made with the route and landmarks, I was pretty much thinking that first we need more men and this action is to be run like a military campaign, tactics and stratagem are the key. I break up the meeting and ask the men to stay close I may have need of them.

I am worried, it is big and complicated job, I always like things simple, I go to my room and take my boots off, laying on the bed with my hands behind my head I start to formulate my plan and thinking of Tex, wishing he was riding beside me. Surprisingly I drift off and wake with a start but refreshed, after a quick wash and grabbing a coffee I head back to propose my intentions, at least the people with me would be honest with me and point out any flaws.

Once everyone was back and settled leaning against the fence I begin "now to the rat killing, as I see it we have the following problems to get settled, first we must get Digby and Harpin out of the way, somehow secure the most likely places of the attack and try to outguess Bill, that SOB has an ace up his sleeve or I will eat my hat. "Em I would like you and Carol to go see the Governor, tell him our suspicions and have him send Harpin out of town on business or something, then get the Governor and the Railroad Manager together privately, make an excuse to get Digby out of the picture, if it comes from you Em I am sure he will comply but everything has to be very hush hush. What do you think Em can it be done? ""Do not fret yourself Marshal we women can handle our load and saddle our own broncs" in a softer tone said we will do everything we can Hardin." "Now you gals be careful some of these villains will kill anybody for that much money even women, but I pity the bandits who tangle with you two wildcats."

Just then we hear the panther scream looking down the road see the boys coming back with Panther, he was making a show of it, flapping his gums to all his greatness. Those old mountain men love their brag these men through skill, bravery and a lot of luck earned their praises venturing into unknown and often hostile lands.

Panther slides off his Indian blanket saddle coming together we shake hands that old man still has an iron grip, "Sorry to hear about Tex, he was one of the good ones, a man to ride the river with."

"Thanks Panther, it is about Tex's murder I asked you in, I am going to deputize you and have you find those two lowdown killers and take their scalps, this time it is no quarter, I want them dead and left for the varmints to feed on, but first I need you to ride over and tell Bear and Ramon I could use their help for a few days, and come ready for an all-out war." Laughing and happily rubbing his hands together Panther, "You can count on the Cat Marshal, I will fetch the big lunkhead and Senor Valdez, them cowards that put Tex under are dead men they just do not know it yet, I will have some Arbuckle's and vittles and head out." "Thanks, pard I knew I could count on you, we will set you up with any supplies or any ammo you may need, I got a good mountain horse if you care to take him along, now you be careful old timer, these men are dead sure killers take no chances with them." With a smile and a wink, he heads into the house happier than a kid at Christmas time.

"Whiplash you think Moose and 10 Spot Jonny might want in on some of the fun?" Laughing and jumping up, "you bet Hardin them boys love a scrap, and damn good fighters to." "Good, Em will pass the word to them to meet us at the ranc"h. Whiplash askes, "Hardin do you know couple young mountain boys, look like brothers from Tennessee I recon, they said they knew you and holler if needed they are right close by." "Damn that is good news, those boys are tougher than wang leather and deadly with their long guns, send one of the hands to ask them see if they want to join the posse, but tell him go gentle, those mountain boys don't take chances and they play for keeps." Long Tom said he would bring back Cal Smith and the Panhandle kid, both good men and fighters, Cal hard and skilled fighter and the kid has got unreal gun savey. Ok "I said let's get started, the rest of us will get supplies and ammunition together, young Bill you are going to be my Aide and scout, I need you to go with the women and when they have news get back here lickity split, it is a most important job Pard are you up to it?" "Standing tall looking proud of have been chosen for a mans Job replies," you can count on me Marshal, I can do it." Putting my hand on his shoulder said," Go rope yourself a fast horse, remember the things I taught you, always be wary", then I handed him Hickok's .38 with the shoulder holster, always keep it fully loaded and ready for use, after helping him adjust the holster and secure the revolver I suggest he better go help the gals get ready.

~

No battle plan survives contact with the enemy. -
Colin Powell

CHAPTER 29

MATHER'S MOB

Bill is sitting by the campfire sipping his coffee and looking around the camp, missing nothing, men were riding in, 63 by last count, a few were good steady men but most were a dirty mean lot, cut their mothers throat for Indian whisky, but their guns were clean and rode fast horses. They were in a short valley with good water and grass very remote, chances were good they would be undetected. He is not in the best of moods missing the soft beds, fine cooking and bad women, but he thought soon, very soon, he will cross the ocean to Europe living a gentlemen's life. His thoughts are interrupted by a voice of a man demanding to see the man in charge, the voice belongs to a weasel faced creature, had a meanness and brutality look about him, and thinking he is the he wolf in this pack. Bill gets to his feet and takes the thong off his 6 shooter. In a soft voice, said "I am Bill Mathers and it is my show, what can I do for you?" "My name is Drake Smyth" saying it like it meant something, Bill knew the name and knew him to be unstable, devious but most of all very gun slick. "I done brought 6 good men with me now I want to know the setup and how we split the gold and I better hear some good answers we rode a fair piece." Bill calmly looks over at Drakes men, mean but not tough, back shooters mostly, he turns his attention back to Drake, eyes now hard, ready and even wanting trouble, then moving about 20 paces directly in front of Drake leaving no doubt about what was going to be between them. "Smyth, you will be told your job and where to do it when the time comes and not before, as for the split any man alive at the end gets an equal share, if that don't suit you ride out." Thinking himself a big man Smyth does not like it one little bit to be talked to like that, he decides then he would kill Mathers after he got his money. Puffing up the sneer on his face responds "must be some tough competition if you have brought in all these men for one little train, taunting, somebody got you scared Bill"?

"As a matter fact, I am not scared but cautious, we are going up against the best Marshal in the west, Hardin Steele and he will have some men with hair on them, smart hard men." Drake laughs, "I heard of him, he ain't nothing, just all brag behind his badge." Many of the men in the group who knew Hardin and Tex laughed at Drake, making him furious inside. "Drake, Bill replied, "there is no brag on old Sudden, I rode with him for a time and I have seen his graveyards, you and all your men would not reach the top of his bootheel." It was meant as an insult and it hit the mark with Smyth, Drakes hand went up over his gun, ready to draw, "you calling us no good Bill?" Bill standing relaxed but poised said "I recon I am you floor flusher." Drakes hand flashed to his gun, he knew it was the fastest draw he ever made, that was his last thought just before two .45 slugs tear his heart to shreds, with a look of surprise Drake crumples to the floor. Bill ejects the 2 spent bullets and replaces them before holstering his colt, looking over at Drakes riders, "you boys can stay if you follow orders." All of them are looking at Smyths body, one of the group says "figure we will stay boss, got no other place to go. Bill tells them to go bury Smyth well away from camp then get settled in.

Things are nearly in place the chess game has started, Bill knew Hardin would ride the route and know the likely spots for the grab, he figured old Sudden would stick with his habits, and be watching the likely spots to hit. Most the men here were going to be his pawns and keep the lawmen off balance and busy. Only a few of his most trusted men knew the full plan, he was going to hit the train injun style about 2 miles from its destination, last place anyone would expect, there is a thicket about a quarter away from the rail line to hide the horses and wagons. With a few hand-picked men, they were going to blow up some track and telegraph poles. Shallow holes would be dug out close to the tracks and they would cover themselves with sod, when the train stops they would pounce and have the train within seconds. The only law close would be in Helena and will be a small party, the rest would be far away. Smiling and thinking to himself, I got you beat this time old son.

Overconfidence is the most dangerous
form of carelessness.
- Star Wars; The Clone wars

CHAPTER 30

BLACKFOOT FIGHT AND THE TRINITY KID

The word was going out and my friends and allies to all gather at Em's soon as possible, in the mean time I must ride over to the small community of Brenner, there has been a killing and money stolen from the Blue Duck saloon, with the bandit escaping. I am the closest Marshal so I decide to ride over and get some information from witnesses while their memories were still fresh. It will take me a little over 3 days there and back, as soon as I get back will be laying my friend Tex Fowler to rest, we are going to give a good man a right proper send-off.

Apollo is enjoying the ride, we both had a love for open country, I noon near a small creek enjoying a couple cups of coffee and a thick beef sandwich Carol packed for me, Apollo was enjoying some thick rich grass. I pour the remaining coffee over the small smokeless fire, put the coffeepot back in the saddlebags and am back in the saddle, after only a few minutes riding I am getting edgy, therreis a feeling I am being watched and tracked, smells like Indian trouble, Apollo seems to agree, his ears are up his mighty muscles tense ready to fight or flee. We are riding through rolling country many small groves of trees with low places for concealment and ambush. By now I knew we were riding into an Indian ambush, which Indians I do not know, showing no sign that I suspected any traps I pull up Apollo and get down pretending to check his hoof, looking over the terrain I fall back to my training by Bear and Black Hand, I now had to be Crow Killer, the Sioux warrior. I have a pretty good idea where the enemy is, waiting to my right in a low area behind a small stand of ash trees, I figure my best bet is to find some high ground or cover to fight from there, there is not much cover, things were looking grim I prepare myself for a mounted battle, but just then I spot a small rise to my left looked about the best spot in which to make my stand. It was going to be a race, the Indians I am sure are in position to cut me off before getting to it, but I have the best horse in Montana and we were going to prove it. I crawled back into the saddle and start off at a normal gait, I pull my hat down tight, talking to Apollo I get him ready, then I pull my Winchester from the boot and with a Sioux war cry I let him loose, for a big horse he has incredible speed, off to the right six braves came riding out at full speed whooping and waving their weapons and as I figured setting a course to intercept me. Apollo was running hard his hooves thundering gathering speed with every step, I know now I was dealing with the Blackfeet, now brother let me tell you them Blackfeet are right tough and skilled fighters, a fierce race. Apollo's speed got us to the mound with about a minute to spare before being set upon, I grab my saddle bags and canteen, smacked old Apollo on his butt and told him to get. He would run until just out of rifle range and would wait for my call, and no one was going to capture him, I could hear him snorting and challenging the other horses. I find a good spot I pile some deadfall and small rocks in front as a small barricade, the scattergun I remove from my back and place it close to my right side.

The Blackfeet are just getting in rifle range and closing fast, I pick my first target, one warrior was a bit out front, eager for the kill, I laid my sites on him and squeezed off my shot, the warrior grabs his chest and falls from his horse, I then start pumping out lead as fast as I could lever, I saw another pony go down and then there was nothing to shoot at. Coughing from the gun smoke with ringing in my ears I reload the Winchester, all was quiet, true to the warrior way, I called to the Blackfeet and tell them I am the Sioux warrior Crow Killer, nephew to the great chief Black Hand and Brother to the great horse thief and warrior Grey Wolf, I curse and taunt them, dare them to come fight for it was a good day to die. I can through much practice can make the screech of the owl hoping to unsettle them a tad, I wait a few minutes and cupping my hands to my mouth let out another screech, now let them ponder that over that for a spell. It is near sundown and there were at least 5 Blackfeet warriors only yards from me, it is to my advantage it will be getting dark soon, I knew that the Blackfoot did not like fighting at night, fearing their spirits will get lost forever in the darkness. I very slowly and carefully study the scene in front of me, after a spell I believe I located the position of one of the braves, when it got dark I was going to try and turn the tables and steal them Blackfeet's horses, walking Indians are unhappy Indians.

No more shots were fired or sounds from the enemy but I knew they were out there, after a long nervous wait I put the Winchester down, quietly as possible I take my boots off and put on my moccasins I had in my saddlebags, the shotgun I slid back into its in its sling, leaving the thong on my six-gun I pulled out my knife, before I leave my shelter I rubbed dust on my face hands and the knife blade, I need to be invisible and will need all my skills and more than a little luck getting to their horses, to make things more interesting I suspect they will have a sentry watching the horses, he would have to die and it had to be a quiet kill.

It is a good dark night lots of clouds blocking the bright moon. I got to tell you I am scared clean through, this is where only death wins, I knew I had to kill myself if there was a chance of being captured, those Blackfoot women were cruel, torture a man for days to test his strength, I heard a great man once say "courage is being scared to death but saddling up anyway", with that thought I begin to move, I had decided my route before it got dark and will try to swing around and come up behind the warriors.

I slowly back down on my belly off my small rise making sure I made no scaping sounds to alert the enemy, once down I get to my feet but stayed bent over, with my moccasins I can feel the ground before planting my foot so not to snap a branch or twig, sounds travel far at night and those heathens have sharp hearing. Once I figure I am out of hearing distance still staying low I moved quickly, twice I must stop and lay in the tall grass as the moon breaks through the clouds. Patience is the most important thing if you rush you make mistakes and you die, when I figure I am behind the Indians I start in. I have mis calculated a bit and am much closer to the horses than I figured I immediately drop to the ground, moving in a bit closer I search the area for the night guard, within a minute I spot him, he is sitting on a tree stump half asleep not more than 20 yards from my position. I could now make out 3 still figures by a small fire, the remaining warrior would be looking forward watching my previous position, they never dreamed a white man would try such a thing as stealing horses from some of the best horse thieves in the world.

I lock in on my target, but did not look directly at him, men of the wilderness a man can sense when they are being watched, my 10-inch razor sharp Spanish steel knife is firmly in my right hand I now am crawling on me on my knees and elbows moving with agonizing slowness in for the kill. The brave appears half asleep I can see he is not alert for danger, I am now only a few feet from the brave I can smell the smoke and bear grease on him. When one of the ponies snorts loudly the guard focuses his attention to the sound, it is my chance, in one swift move I lunge and put my big left hand over the Indians mouth and with a quick swipe I cut that mans throat the razor sharp blade cutting deep like a hot knife through butter, with his throat cut the Blackfoot could not call out, I pressed myself on top of him holding him down until the movements stop, it did not take long for him to bleed out with his head near cut clean off, looking over to the sleeping men I make sure no one had stirred. I am lucky to find a sage brush and rub the spice on my clothing and with some of the grease off the dead Indian I took as much white man smell off me as I can. Now horses are horses most times a little sweet treat bribe will have them following you like your pet dog, I had put a small pouch of sugar in my pocket, I now pour it into my hand and started to walk slowly towards the horses my sugar-coated hand outstretched in front of me. Talking low in the Sioux tongue I was getting near them hoping they would not spook, I stop with my hand out hoping one would come for the sugar, a white mare started to advance towards my hand, I suspected she had been stolen off a white man and remembered treats. As with most women of any breed they never make it easy, I could have grown a beard by the time she decided it was safe to take the sugar. With the mare licking my hand I began to slowly walk away from the camp the white following looking for more, quickly looking back I could see the other horses following I just kept walking straight out into the night my little horse herd following. When we get about a quarter mile out I pull out my shotgun, with a war cry I let one barrel go then the next, in the night it sounded like cannon fire, let me tell you what them horses vamoosed in a hurry, those Blackfeet will have themselves a time getting them back.

I then start to make my run to get back to my shelter before the braves get their bearings, like the horses I skedaddled not liking being in the open, as I near my camp a couple shots rinhg out but nothing was close, I take a long dive and land beside my Winchester I pick it up and I let loose at the spot where the Indians had been sleeping, firing fast to the left and right hoping to get in a lucky shot, after the Winchester clicks on empty I reload it and the shotgun.

I am certain them Blackfeet will be gone by morning most Indians are smart enough to know when their medicine is bad and it is better to flee to fight another day. Resting my back against a tree I doze but not deeply listening for any misplaced sounds, after settling in and get comfortable I did hear some really pissed off Blackfeet walking look for their horses, gives me cause to smile and a feeling of pride by taking on this tough bunch but not only surviving, I whipped them.

Morning finally arrives, the Blackfeet had left taking their dead with them, after carefully checking the area I call Apollo in within seconds I can hear the thundering of his hoofs racing towards me. The Blackfoot although beaten respected courage and skill and this story would be told and re told in the lodges and at the fires Starman Crow Warrior will now be regarded as a mighty warrior and any Blackfoot brave who slays him will have big medicine, although on the other side of the coin I will now in constant danger in Blackfoot country I felt honoured to be known as a strong and mighty warrior and worthy enemy to the great Blackfoot nation. The Indian telegraph will spread the word and Black Hand will hear and be proud of my victory, my status will now grow now within the Sioux community.

Soon I have my gear re packed and am continuing my trip to Brenner, it was getting on mid afternoon as I ride down the main street, it was very much like many other small western towns, regular folks just going about the business of staying alive. I pull up in front of the Sheriffs office and leave Apollo ground hitched as I enter I see two men, the one behind the desk a bit older but looked capable and the other a slim young man, has a look of an aggressor about him, his smile was neither warm or friendly more of a sneer, seemed like he figured himself a tough hombre gunfighter wearing two tied down guns in a fancy silver studded rig.

Addressing the sheriff I ignore the kid, "Sorry I am late Sheriff had a run in with some Blackfoot devils, it was a very close thing, them Indians are right sly and tough, lucky to get here with my hide." A nasty chuckle come from the kid, I knew he was pushing me and I was right short of patience I put the hard gaze on him, "Do you find something amusing about this boy, and just who the hell are you?" "Well Marshal, they call me the Trinity Kid, I recon you heard of me, talk is you are a ring-tailed terror the he coon of the territory, I think you are all brag and I ain't seen any of your graveyards. "I just wanted to size you up before I kill you Marshal Steele, I will be the big man when I put you under."

This was gun talk, the challenge was there, this smart mouthed would be gun fighter needed a lesson but not killing, remembering Mr. Li's training my right hand snaked out and I grabbed the kids pinky finger, the sound when it broke was like breaking a live branch, without hesitation I grabbed his thumb and dislocate it, he was screaming in pain and fear. I then with my left hand I grab his collar and began to slap him hard with my open right hand, hard vicious slaps snapping his head back with each time, blood was now running from his mouth and nose, removing his fancy gun rig I put it on the sheriff's desk, I then grab him by the back of the collar and seat of his pants I throw him into the street and closed the jail door.

The sheriff is looking a bit unnerved and shaken remarks, "you are a very hard man marshal better if you killed that boy, you destroyed his pride." "Sheriff that kid needed a lesson not killing, when you kill a man you take everything he has or will ever have, now give me your report and a description of the robber I need to be getting back." *Once* finished with sheriff I head over to the saloon, there was no sign of the Trinity kid, I get some eye witness accounts, seems it was a fair shooting over a card game, but the winner got nervous and grabbed about 600 dollars in cash and ran. I had the witnesses write out statements, just before leaving I address the men in the saloon in a sarcastic tone, "Now if any you boys by chance run into the desperate bandit you tell him for me I am not coming after him for the killing sounds like a fair shooting, and if he returns the money or works it off I will forget him, but if that money is not returned you let him know he better watch his backtrail because I will be coming for him"

Without another word, I leave the saloon and head across the street to the Rose's cafe, I needed a meal and a lot of coffee, I will be back in the saddle and heading back within the hour. Two things of major importance are waiting for me, Tex's funeral and send off and the protection of the gold shipment. I would be taking a different route back staying wide of Blackfoot country, I have had enough of those tough bastards for a spell.

Even the seasons form a great circle in their changing, and always come back to where they were. The life of man is a circle from childhood to childhood, and so it is in everything where power moves.
- Crowfoot, Blackfoot warrior and orator.

CHAPTER 31

SAYING GOODBYE

The trip back to Em's ranch is uneventful and I even manage to catch up a bit on my rest but I am sorely in need of a bath, some good cooking and strong coffee and at least one night in a soft bed under a roof. All is quiet as I ride into the ranch, the first person I spot is just the man I wanted to see, my old Pard Whiplash. I turn Apollo and we ride into the barn ducking as we go through the door Whiplash follows me in and as I am unsaddling and rubbing down Apollo the old know it all fills me in on what's been going on in my absence. I quickly tell him of my encounter with the Blackfeet and of the Trinity Kid. "Good to have you back Hardin, we were beginning to worry a might, everything is quiet now and Em and the Governor have everything arranged for Tex's funeral, be at 11 o'clock tomorrow morning, going to be a lot of folks there, I sure do miss old Tex he was one of the good ones." "Most of the folks are in town already, Carol says to come a running you have been falling behind in your courting duties." Tempting as it to head to town I decide to stay at the ranch I can get a bath and my Sunday going to church clothes are up in my room, I would get an early start in the morning. "Pard anyone here to feed a man and make a good pot of coffee?" I recon will stay the night and get an early start, need me some cleaning up, I still got the dead Indians blood all over me." I finished up with Apollo and before leaving him give him a bait of corn, then we head back to the house. Lucky for me one of the Mexican ladies was in the kitchen, when she saw us come in she gives me a great big smile and brings coffee and cups to the table, I ask her in Spanish in jest if she will be my kitchen wife and I would be grateful for some hot food, my stomach feels like my throats been cut.

Damn that woman can cook, fried steak big enough to cover a plate, heaps of mashed potatoes, fresh bread and real butter, and to top it all off the best damn chocolate cake I ever ate, with that and about six cups of coffee I was near ready to burst. The last few days were catching up with me, I am extremely and pleasantly stuffed and tired so bidding goodnight to Whiplash and my Mexican wife I head up to bed and barely had my boots off before I fall into a deep sleep.

I wake before dawn dress quickly and go downstairs, there was no one in the kitchen but the coffee is on, I put water on the stove to heat up for my small bath, while waiting for the water to heat I sit drinking coffee and enjoying the quiet of the morning, I always enjoy this time of day before the world came alive. When the water I is ready I have a quick bath more of a washing off and a shave but I feel cleaner than I have in ages, I return to my room and bush off my black suit and Stetson and put a bit of shine on my high top black boots. Once dressed I pull to my dresser drawer a beautiful pair of silver Mexican spurs that I treated myself to in Arizona, looking in the mirror I almost did not recognize myself, I feel I did clean up nicely though. I leave the house carrying my saddlebags and long gun I find good old Whiplash has the horses saddled, he knew Apollo needs some rest he picks me out a big black gelding with a touch of attitude, good gait smooth riding animal. I mount and that black tests me out to make sure I was man enough to ride him, I stayed glued to the saddle waving my hat and called for his best, soon he settles down he knew who was boss, with that we head out. It is a quiet ride each of us feeling the sadness of a close comrade passing and remembering a real man.

There are a lot of folks in town for the funeral, Tex was a well-liked man with his easy humour, fair and honest nature, even most of his enemies respected him, in fact the telegraph office was working hard just trying to keep up with the telegrams of condolences with almost half sent from known outlaws. We head over to the Governors house where Em, Carol and young Bill are staying, as we dismount Carol comes running from the house and flew right into my arms her arms tight around my shoulders kisses my long and hard, she then she un tangles herself and we both smile with pleasure being together once again, then true to nature she gets that look and stating that an engaged man should have the manners not to worry his love, he must make more of an effort. Smiling again we hug and kiss again, I will never tire of my sweet Carol's kisses, just then Em young Bill and the Governor come out of the house it was about time to be heading to the grave sight, being close we walk over as a group Carol and I hand in hand.

By the time, we arrive at the cemetary there is already a large crowd, looking around the crowd I could see big cattle ranchers, a few diplomates, some railroad big wigs, mixed in were regular farming folk, townspeople and a sizable group of Mexicans, I spotted at least two known outlaws neither wearing their hardware, they knew today everyone was welcome here, there will be no trouble.

We slowly work our way to the front talking quietly with people as we pass by, once we were at the grave I move over to stand by the padre, I notice the casket it really is something, made of a shiny dark wood almost black, with brass handles, it is a thing of beauty and some sweet soul had gathered wild flowers and put them on top, Tex would have liked it.

The Padre starts the service with a hymn and then a prayer, his words are soft and with meaning, Carol and Em are crying along with many other women and a few hard men were struggling not to shed a tear myself included. When the padre finishes the Governor makes a speach on the sacrifices good men make must bring law and order into the Territory and that Tex was one of the very best and he will be missed by many. After he has his says I step forward feeling a need to say my goodbyes, I start off by telling the congregation the story of my man hunt and how I met Tex, the fight with the apaches and how Carol and young Bill came into my life, then how I lost my prisoner and was put the touch on for 50 dollars, this got some quiet laughs from the crowd. I went on to say," I am right proud to have ridden with a man of Tex's high calibre, he was always there to cover my back, saved my life more than once, and never shirked his duties. I and others will be missing you Pard, and I promise that the cowards who killed you will be dealt with- harshly, I will have their scalps hanging from my belt, this I promise you. Be seeing you down the trail Amigo, Adios", I look up and in the distance, I see a lone figure on a far hill, I know it is Bill paying his respects in his own way.

I put on my Stetson and take Carols hand together we leave Tex to his rest, we then walk slowly back to the Governors house, I tell Carol I have to leave her for a bit, I promised to go have a drink with the boys to honour Tex, but I would be back shortly, and make sure to keep the coffee hot, with a quick kiss I head for the saloon with full intentions of having a couple then sneaking away, but as we all know to well plan A rarely works.

When I enter the saloon by the batwing doors the place was already filling up, Whiplash, the Governor and Long Tom had a table and waved me over, as I sit Whiplash pours me a big double and puts the glass in front of me. Now I am no tea tootler and grew up drinking white lightning made in the hills but I rarely overdid it, I do not like loosing control or hangovers. I pick up my glass, "boys a toast to a friend, a damn good man and dedicated lawman, here is to our Pard old Tex," then together we knockback our drinks. Whiplash is already about half in the bag pours me another big one, then he gets up takes his pistol and bangs it on the table demanding everyone's attention, once quiet he delivers his toast and demands everyone have drink to Tex.

The Governor orders another bottle, the drinks were going down easy now and we laugh and tell many stories, old Tex would have been right pleased to be joining us. Before I know it, I am shitfaced drunk, the saloon was very noisy and filled with smoke, I push my drink away a light up a cigar, someone was now standing in front of me and places a big steaming cup of Arbuckle's in front of me. I look up and through bleary eyes look into the intense green eyes and smile of the Traveller, "wrap yourself around that coffee old Hoss see if we cannot sober you up some." Old Whiplash was passed out head on the table, the Governor for some unknown reason wants to hang all the dentists in town and is making a real ruckus in the street. That is until Em got a hold of him, she scolds half him severely and then had two sober men take him home, wisely he complied but was heard saying as they departed, "boys I truly love that woman but she just scares the hell out of me."

I am a bit sloppy from the booze but could still make some conversation, Wade and I talked in hushed tones as I drank my coffee and enjoying my cigar. The coffee finished I put out my cigar, time to be getting home, my first attempt to rise was not successful, Wade helps me out of my seat and putting his arm around my shoulder guides me out of the saloon and home, that was my last memory of the night.

The noise of pots and pans rattling wakes me, I open my eyes and the morning light rips through my eyes stabbing deep into my brain, with a pounding head and a severe case of dry mouth I very slowly get up and dress. When getting to the kitchen the Governor and Whiplash are already at the table, they both looked like I feel, and they were real quiet. Looking towards the gals it did not take a genius to figure out were about as popular as a skunks at a Sunday picnic, but my angel Carol brings me coffee, thanks to that rascal Tex the boys were in the doghouse, I can almost hear him laughing down at us.

Life is tough, but tougher if you are stupid.
- John Wayne

CHAPTER 32

THE RENDEVOUS

Em's ranch is filling up, men are beginning to filter in, things are busy, horses, food, ammunition and medical supplies are being gathered and readied for the upcoming battle. I am helping Buster mending some tack when I hear a great ruckus coming towards the ranch. Walking out side I see Bear and Ramon riding in, and to my great surprise Black Hand and Grey Wolf are riding with them, I thought to myself this was akin to the old-time mountain men's rendezvous, men like Bear and old Panther were involved with but a much tamer bunch here. Some of the men are looking a might nervous seeing full Blooded Sioux War Chief and the best know horse thief in Montana in camp, Black Hand is known by all to be a fierce and deadly warrior, they all knew Grey Wolf as well, he was the most known horse stealer in the territory, the Sioux hold him in high regard, smiling to myself I figured the boys would be bringing their horses in closer to camp tonight. Just by pure chance they were at Bears cabin doing to trading and telling some tall tales when the news arrived with my request for help, both Uncle and Brother said they will go, Crow Killers enemies were their enemies.

I walk over to the unusual group and before I know it I am struggling for air as Bear lays one of his back-cracking hugs on me, Ramon and I embraced as gentlemen I tell them how pleased I am to see them and that they were still above the flowers. Naturally an old mountain man, a tough looking Mexican and 2 Sioux warriors would grab anyone's attention men were meandering over toward us, many just curious it is not everyday a man can say he shared coffee with one of the most famous Sioux of recent memory.

Before anyone canspeak I move over and stand beside Black Hand, "Gentlemen I would like the present the great Sioux war chief Black Hand who is with great pride I call my Uncle, this is my Kola my Brother Grey Wolf known everywhere as the finest horse stealer and a brave warrior counting many coup." with ceremony we shake hands, Black Hand puts his large brown hand on my shoulder, standing with great dignity commanding instant attention looking around the group he lifts his arm showing his intent to speak, everyone goes t real quiet you could hear a pin drop, most of the men are leaning forward to hear his words, there would be great stories of this to tell their grand children. Most folks think the Indian just grunts words but many men the likes of Red Cloud, Chief Joseph, Sitting Bull and others would have been accepted as great speakers even in the halls of Greece along with men such as Plato and Socrates.

"I am Black Hand of the People and my son Grey Wolf we have come to help my nephew Crow Killer in fighting his enemies for his enemies our enemies, It makes me happy to be with him again, he stands tall and is only of one tongue, we will make it a much remembered fight." I see you men who help my nephew and know I in my heart I am fighting with the wolves not the coyotes, I see strong magic you warriors, may the Great Spirit protect you."

Without another word, he steps back, the men look at him in awe, and I was sure vest buttons would be popping them now being all swelled up on themselves. That settles the matter of differences we are one lodge working fighting and maybe dying for one purpose, it sure is good to have the Uncles around, gives me a renewed confidence and strength. I tell the boys to get settled in and I would be around later, and there will be a powwow tonight.

After making my rounds checking on everything I could think of including extra water, there was not much water at some spots and a man gets mighty thirsty after battle or wounded, latching on to old Whiplash we amble over to the Uncle's camp. Bear has the coffee on and I go right for the pot, his coffee has not changed, black as tar, horse shoe floating brew, but I had grown up on it and drank it with relish. After settling in I give the boys the layout, my plan and my thoughts that Bill still had that ace up his sleeve, I ask them to ponder on it and we would talk it over at the meeting tonight. Just as we about to leave the group Bear asks, "now who would that be riding like a prairie fire is chasing him? ""That there is young Bill, Carols brother, I had him do a job for me, the boy takes it serious, I just hope he does not break his young fool neck"

Bill rides up to the group and dismounts now looking around mouth open amazement at the assorted men, mostly he is looking at Black Hand who stone faced is looking right back at him dark eyes revealing nothing, once he comes out of his trance he gives me the scoop. "I have the news you wanted Hardin, Carol told me to hurry." With a chuckle, I said "well done Bill, but you got to slow er up a bit pard, you know Buster is going to be right put out you are riding a horse hard like that. But glad you are back, now get yourself some chuck and a bit of rest if you can, we will hear your news at the pow wow tonight, off you go buckaroo."

During the afternoon, the Hennessy brothers Peter and Paul from the Smokey Blue mountain arrive in camp, still wild looking in their buckskins, I notice that they are now both are carrying new Winchester rifles, we shake hands and I thank them for coming. "Hell "Marshal says Peter smiling "it is our pleasure, would be right selfish you boys having a good scrap and not letting us in on the fun."I walked the boys over to Bear's camp and do the introductions, I knew the Tennessee boys would be right at home talking with the mountain men.

Late afternoon the Traveller rides in, dismounting his big beautiful gray horse we shake hands, smiling at me says, "you look a sight better than the last time we met Hoss, quite a crowd you have here Marshal, should be a right interesting, hope I am not to late for supper I could eat a horse hooves and all."

With supper done we all gather behind the ranch house, the Mexican ladies put out coffee pots and a couple heaping platters of bear claw on the outdoor tables, again I damn near got trampled in the rush for them, them Mexican ladies knowhow to spoil their men. Over coffee and donuts, the men gathered got re acquainted or introduced, good humoured laughter fills the evening, I look over the group feeling good to have them here with me, good men all but granite hard when it came to skinning the coon. The old and the new were here, men of different races, places and upbringing, it may be the most famous and deadly gathering of men the west had ever seen or would ever see again.

I get everyone's attention and get by asking young Bill to give us his information from the Capital. He is a bit shy about it with all these great men in attendance, but Whiplash gives him a pat on the shoulder, nodding it is alright. In a surprisingly strong voice tells us that both Digby and Harpin had been sent out of town for at least two weeks they were not happy about it, but it was go or lose their jobs. That was good news one less problem to deal with. Bill continues on saying Em and Carol are watching and talking to the locals, a great many rough men with many guns have been passing through town almost like a taunt, Em figures Bill could have up to 60 hard cases, ending his briefing with Carol sends her love and says be damn careful and do not get yourself all shot up. The group of course got a chuckle from this and I get a bit red around the ears. As usual Wade comes to my aid, "Marshal how much gold are we talking about here I figure it must be a goodly sum to bring that many bad men together" "Boys, I said, "in two days a train will be leaving the Bozeman with near a million dollars worth in gold bars to be delivered to the bank in Helena ", a few low whistles and noises of astonishment are emitted from the group, "all the miners have put their eggs in one basket and they have put their faith in me and the law to get their gold through. I recon many a man will be ruined if that gold is stolen, I also believe Bill and his mob want to be running the territory and that means killing as many of us as they can, with the law gone they can rape the whole territory, Bill always did think big."

Looking back over the group I begin to voice my thoughts and plan of action. "Boys I believe this is going to get bloody, so let's make sure its their damn blood soaking in the grass," there are nods of agreement and men swearing in low serious voices their solemn intent, "I believe Bill will be sending out killing squads their sole purpose to kill as many of us as possible and keep us busy while he puts into action his plan for taking the gold." "Now if anyone here sees it different speak up, I ain't against suggestions, my ideas rest mostly on my gut feeling and knowing old Bill. "It is going to be an open warfare a Calvary battle, no quarter to be given and winner take all, well men I never took to losing so if it is death they want I for one will be happy to oblige, death they will have." A roar of battle cries burst from my fellow warriors so intense it sends chills down my spine, my blood is now hot and pounding, the Mathers Mob are going find out the hard way what a few hard-determined men with right on their side of the law can do.

After things calm down and get quiet, Traveller breaks the silence," I did a bit of scouting before coming in, talked with a few folks I know well and trust, I believe old Hardin here has it figured right, they not only want the gold they want to nail our hides to the barn door". Hardin what is your plan to stop Bill and his mob, we only got once chance at this pard so we better be right.

"I have put much thought into it Wade, we will be greatly outnumbered but we have here the very best, skilled and proven fighters, survivors of many battles, and the meanest SOB's in the territory, most of Bill's men will hardcases not warriors nor will all stand when the lead flies, Old Bill has made his first big mistake by under rating us."

"I plan fighting fire with fire, we are all going to be in the field working in groups spaced along the route, this is not a defensive action, we will attack any armed groups on sight, you are all experienced fighters you decide how you want to tackle them." Taking out a map I had drawn from the scout I lay on the table, 3 red X's were marked where I wanted the squads.

"We will be in four groups, the first unit will be Buster, Tall Elk and the Hennessy brothers, I put you fellers together because Buster and Tall Elk are both Calvary experts and damn fine rifle shots, you Hennessy boys are just a pair of curly wolves and do right fine work with them long guns." "Any objections men? the time to speak up is now "Paul who rarely did not do much talking looks over at me, "no objections Marshal, we uns respect a good fighting man no matter the colour of his skin, not to worry boss them varmints are going to find it hotter than a whorehouse on nickel night".

Pointing at the second x on the map, "this is a hilly area with some thick brush, I am going to have the toughest, meanest and most experienced woodsmen at this location, Bear, Ramon, Black hand and old Panther who I recon should be back anytime now".

"Winking to the boys "maybe I should send a few young fellas along give you old timers a hand maybe to help you on your horses and such." A smattering of chuckles arose and old Bear was up raring to go, standing and looking very imposing responded "youngster we pulled down them britches when you were a button and gave you some tannings and I recon we still can, "and damn it I knew they still could. "after the laughter died down and with a serious look I respond "You old boys be careful I will be damned upset if any of my Uncles or friends was to get himself killed, but it should be a wingding of a scrap, a remembered fight."

Turning my attention to Whiplash pointing to the 3rd x which was by the water tower and wood station, "Whiplash, you Moose Johannsson, Johnny Diamond and Dakota Smith will be protecting this area." I was right pleased Dakota is riding with us, some say he at times rode the outlaw trail, but he seemed to always on the right side when the shooting started, a very tough hombre and a survivor of many hard-fought battles, there was no backup in any of these men, fighters all. "Whiplash you keep a sharp eye, and your ass down when the shooting starts, if anything happens to you Em will surely skin me." Whiplash sputters and frets making the boys laugh even harder, cursing me out in a somewhat friendly manner, then serious I said, "no fooling boys take care and watch over one another."

My mounted escort will be Traveller, Grey Wolf, and Long Tom, I still suspect Bill means to hit the train where no one would expects it, that to me meant closer to Helena, flat country with little cover, I was sure I had the area pegged but damned if I knew how old Bill was going to pull it off. The train itself would have its own protection, there were to be two US deputy marshals, and a couple good and tough railroad trouble shooters, and a somewhat elderly baggage clerk railroad who had been a ring tail terror in his day, probably still the toughest of the whole bunch. All the train defenders would be carrying double barrel shotguns, the railroad had modified the car by putting hidden shooting slits two on each side, wooden slides covered them to hide them, set up like the cover on a ships cannon port, pull the rope and the cover is pulled up opening the whole, if taking heavy fire lower the rope and the heavy oak shield is back in place. Whoever got near the train would pay hell trying to get that baggage car.

"I would appreciate it if all you fellas think this here puzzle out and if you think I missed something I want you to come to me right off, we are going to be bucking some of the toughest men this side of hell being lead by a smart and determined leader, we all know old Bill don't miss much and I need all the help I can get and hope to get lucky and draw that ace". "Well boys tend to your weapons and equipment if you need anything see Buster or Tall Elk, see you at chuck." I walk away worried, this certainly is my biggest challenge and the stakes are high the Territory of Montana is the prize the if we loose this fight the Territory will be lost and Bill and his outlaws will run it using terror and guns to take anything they want there will be no one to stop him. Well I will know in a couple days, now comes the hard part the waiting, I much prefer action but the teaching of my uncles have taught me that patience will keep you among the living. I had not practiced the skills Mr. Li taught me for a spell now,

I would have a hard workout relieve the tension then take the time to calm my mind before battle. I will be ready.

You may have to fight a battle more than
once to win it.
- Margaret Thatcher

CHAPTER 33

PRELUDE TO WAR

Not so many miles away Bill is laying in his dirty cot, hands behind his head, he is getting tired of waiting and in real need of a bath and shave, some clean clothes and a fine meal. He comforts himself in the fact in a couple days he would be a very rich man and he will finally get see and enjoy the luxury and rich lifestyle of a gentleman visiting all the great cities of Europe. A frown comes over his face, in a moment of conscience he knew to succeed he had to kill many of his friends including his oldest and best friend Hardin, shaking his head as to rid himself of the thought, swore," if they stay out of my way they live, fight me and they die in the prairie dirt." Bill eventually falls asleep, but it is restless filled with strange dreams, Bill feels fear, stronger than any before, he was standing in the middle of a town street waiting for someone, there was a fog at the end of the street, not a normal fog, it has a dark evil look about it slowly out of the mist the shape of a man appears, his mouth gets dry as the shape turns into Hardin, saying nothing his friends deadly green eyes lock on him, Bill yells at him to stop, Hardin is as silent as death, the distance closes swiftly, Hardin then gives Bill that famous smile, and draws his .44 Russian, Bill can see the flame of the gun and feel the hot lead entering his body, Hardin keeps walking closer firing every time his right foot hits the ground, Bill is on his back looking up into the big bore of the .44, Hardin cocks the pistol and points it at Bill's face, green eyes blaze into Bill's soul, still smiling Bill watches as his executioners finger as it tightens on the trigger, Hardin with a voice not his own, deep, terrible and menacing utters alaugh of a madman more like a chilling scream, in slow motion Bill watches the hammer of gun fall. Bill's eyes burst open as he explodes out of bed, disoriented for a few seconds then before realizing it was a nightmare, looking at his bed he sees it is wet with his sweat and fear, after a few minutes later the shaking stops.

Bill takes a long pull off the bottle of rye beside his bed, putting the night's thoughts away he grabs some coffee and breakfast, damn beans again, but the coffee was good, not as good as old Whiplashes, that man sure could make coffee.

Sitting and savouring his coffee in his mind goes over his plan again, he had planned it for months leaving nothing to chance. He will be sending out his killing squads their job is to attack and kill any groups of men along the route and assault the train by hitting the baggage and passenger cars with barrages of lead, but they were not allowed try for the prize that was going to be Bill's pleasure. He had already made his choices for who would lead the assault death squads, those he chose were the most ruthless, vile and savage men in his mob, kill anything that walked with pleasure and lust.

Each mounted unit would have 8 to 12 men. Bill would set up the trap just outside the city, taking with him the best and the worst, Cim Smith 2-gun man liked working in close, and lusted to use cold steel. The Ute, pure evil, kill you for the gold in your teeth, but great scout, tracker, enjoyed toying with his victims, fire being his favorite perversion. Known by no other name but Nolan, never mentioned his last name, and no one dared to ask, lighting fast and accurate with both .45 and rifle, quiet, but his guns were loud and he could be trusted. The last member of Bills band was his only friend whom he totally trusted, Nevada Jones, wild as a maverick tough and strong as oak, next to Sudden and himself probably the fastest gunman in the territory. He had carefully handpicked the leaders of the 4 assault parties, picked for their ruthlessness, men who enjoyed hurting and killing, mean clean through who would spit in the eye of the devil, the killing madness stronger than their fear of death. The first group of vermin were to be led by a scoundrel named Blood Cabot, his name well suited as people's blood flowed whenever he was about, a smallish dirty man, not a clean spot on him except his weapons, well used and cared for, his greasy hair pulled back and tied, his face distorted by a knife scar from the corner of his eye to his earlobe, the eye drooping and an unpleasant ooze was ever present. But no man would dare say anything or joke of it, Blood would kill without warning even men who know him walk wide of him. Blood is not a man of vision, he will surely have a large man advantage and he will do as Mathers said hit any group they come across and smash them making sure none are left alive he hopes he can catch a few live ones to play with. Thinking to himself how much he would enjoy leading his bunch in for the kill and the money that came with it, a small and evil leer comes to his scarredface.

Flat nose Johansson is leading the second group, Flat nose was a mountain of a man, almost as big as Bear. His name was derived from him having his nose broke so bad it could not be reset proper making it a displeasing site to look upon, he lives to kill with his hands or steel, but it is the feel of the blade slicing through the flesh that pleasures him most, his favorite weapon a wicked looking razor sharp Arkansas toothpick. More than one poor captive was skinned alive by Flat noses hand, he had an Apache last almost 3 days once, the only man that Flat nose ever respected. Only the bad hombres would have any truck at all with him, and not a single man wanted him close at night. Flat nose looked over at the men that he would be would be riding with, proven killers everyone, but he knew they all feared him and he wanted it that way, they all knew he would shoot them down if they did not fight or tried to run. The blood lust was riding him now, it was almost overwhelming, licking his greasy lips, with fever in his eyes he smiles insanely, knowing it would be very soon.

The man Bill picked to lead the third bunch of rabble is pure wicked a scalp hunter and back shooter for hire named Scars Fornier, half Metis, Half Ute and all bad. Scars got his name from the many cuts on his body, his Metis Father in a drunken state would cut on the boy, laughing as the boy cried and bled. When Scars was about 11, his father came home drunk and again worked the boy over, watching his father passed out in the chair something snapped in his head, he picked up his father's knife and cut his throat deep, then stabbed him until his arm grew tired. By morning he was well down the road, realizing now how it is killing he killed to live and lived well. He would have a devil's posse of eight men including himself, at least 3 were Texas gunman run out of Texas by the Rangers, leaving a trail of death and rapine behind before escaping.

The last of the Leaders was grim and gray skinned man, tall, slim, skin plastered tight to his face giving him an evil and haunting look, known to his comrades as Gabriel. It is his habit to dress in black down to his gun belt and pistol grips, not a killer for pleasure, killing is a job like any other, with guns as his tools. Gabriel loved his work, but his ghosts were starting to appear in his dreams, and he is beginning the drop slowly into madness. His party would consist mostly Mexican bandits and cowboys who had fought in a couple cattle wars, all gun savvy and a rough lot but not warriors.

The plans are set, all the players in the drama of gun smoke and hot lead are coming together for a bloody showdown, very soon it would be known if the Territory would be a place of civilization and order or lawlessness and terror, either way it was going to be a very long, mean and bloody day.

A believe in a supernatural source of evil is not necessary;
Men alone are quite capable of every wickedness.
- Joseph Conrad

CHAPTER 34

THE CHARGE

Peter, Paul, Buster and Tall Elk are getting ready to leave they had the farthest to travel, the rest of the boys are there to wish them well, and giving them some well intentioned advice. Old Panther is back, he had found out who Tex's killers were, a couple of cowards from Arkansas that got out of the Nations just ahead of the Judge Parkers Marshals, went by the name Irving, they would be with one of the assassination squads.

I walk over to the departing men, at times it is difficult to adjust my mind and accept what I was seeing. Buster had his Calvary campaign hat on and his Calvary boots at a high shine and spurs, Tall Elk now the Sioux warrior, hair braided, both he and his appaloosa horse painted for war, his spencer was in the boot, in his hand a long and deadly looking spear decorated with eagle feathers and no less than six scalps. Peter and Paul are in buckskins and moccasins, looking relaxed with never any wasted movement almost as if they glided when walking, the ever-present rifles in their hands looking like an extension of themselves. All of them are mounted and ready, I put my hand on Busters' horses neck, stroking it, "Good luck men, if in doubt follow Busters lead he is Calvary clean through", looking up at the soldier, "you will have to be very hard and stubborn today, Sgt. the men out there want your lives and you will likely be outnumbered." Laughing Buster looks me in the eye," hell Marshal ain't nothing new, would not know how to fight if the odds were even" his manner now more serious, "no need to fret Hardin we will hold up our end, old Sgt Bo has a special prayer, Though I walk through the valley of death I shall fear no evil because I am the meanest son of a bitch in the valley." With that Tall Elk lets out a yell and the four horsemen thunder out of the yard, all yipping and yelping like the wild men they are, leaving the rest of us to cough on their dust.

I call across the yard to young Bill to get old Sam and meet me at the house, the ranch still needed protecting and it would be up to young Bill to see it was. Now old Sam ain't that old but no longer a young man the gray showing, he is quiet and unassuming except for his eyes, deep blue like a summer sky, missing nothing. I believe I am the only one who knows who he really is, his name is known and respected all over the west by both honest men and outlaws. The man could not be over 5 foot 8and weigh 160 pounds but he is a holy terror in battle, heard tell a story of him and 3 other trappers getting ambushed by a large party of Bloods, old Sam like a Viking berserker tore into them Bloods, hacking, slashing smashing skulls with rocks, it was to much for the Indians they believed he was possessed and thought best he be left alone.

Old Sam is lying low there is a reward for his scalp, the charge against was murder but I know for a fact it was a fair fight, the deceased a nephew of town official, the kid just took on more than he could handle .Young Bill and Sam come into the kitchen and after grabbing coffee sitt down both looking a bit concerned, I did not have time to beat around the bush so I begin to lay it out plain. "Bill, I know you want to be riding with the boys but now you're are the owner and protector of the ranch, I suspect their will be some that will try to escape, they will need horses and supplies, this ranch is right smack in the middle of it all, these men will be desperate and that means very dangerous." Sam, I am making you Segundo, I know who you are and although Bill has the sand he is still between the grass and hay, needs a fighting man beside him, you will be shorthanded there will only be six of you on the ranch." Looking at me those blue eyes locked in on me, "are you sure Marshal if you know who I am you know I am a wanted man." "Sam, I know it was a good shooting, so I have no need of you, but Bill does, what say you old Hoss?" Give me a minute Marshal will be right back", with that he heads to the bunkhouse, after a few minutes he emerges from the shack but now with a well used six-gun tied to his thigh another in his belt for a quick draw, and a new Winchester 73 in his hand, Old Sam was gone and it is now the gunman who stands before us, "Marshal I am right proud to take a hand if its ok with Bill here, he is the boss." "Bill had a look of pride and confidence, "Hardin them outlaws will be getting nothing from this ranch but dead and a burial, Sam and I will make sure of it."

Smiling I get up and head to my room retrieving my spare greener and shells, returning to the kitchen I hand it to young Bill, "When the shooting starts Pard you listen to Sam, these men are killers, shoot first and let God sort them out." With that I leave them there was still much to do, but I know Sam would give his life protecting young Bill and I could think of no better man for it.

Blood Cabot is content, riding slowly they were almost to there assigned area, he smiles as he listens to his followers talk about how they were going to spend their share of the money, damn fools he thought, Blood was not real bright but he did know many would not live to collect, he may just kill a few himself, the fewer the bigger his take

The Blood gang are now insight of the tracks they were going to ride close to the tracks and when the train goes by they were going to empty their guns into the train cars and kill anyone who tried to stop them. The landscape showed no signs of activity, and he can spot no dust trails, but his coyote instincts tells him the enemy is near and it would be a scrap.

He did not have long to wait, a few minutes later directly ahead of his mob 4 men ride up a small knoll about 300 yards away 3 of the men had their rifles out but one had a large and menacing spear, he realizes he is looking at a full-blooded Sioux warrior painted for war, the sight made his blood run cold giving him a sense of foreboding. With the Sioux was a black man who looked like Calvary and 2 young men in buckskins, all just sitting their horses showing Blood and his gang this is as far as they go.

One of his men got nervous and takes a shot at the Sioux but it came up way short, as if on a signal Tall Elk gives a war cry and with spear leveled charges the enemy, his comrades half a stride behind, their horses at full gallop their rifles barking with deadly accuracy. Blood sees nothing but the big Sioux charging directly at him the spear tip reflecting in the sunlight, he empties his rifle trying to bring down the big Indian but as if protected by magic no bullets touch Tall Elk, Blood drops the rifle and with hands shaking makes a grab for his six shooter, as his hand grabs the butt of the weapon he knows he is to late. Blood mesmerized is looking directly into the dark savage eyes of the Sioux, he feels a hard blow to his stomach as Tall Elk thrusts the lance through Blood's stomach and out of his back, Tall Elk quickly let's go of the spear but as he passes Blood he grabs the bloody shaft from the back and pulls it clean through the outlaw's body. Blood feels himself falling from his horse but feels nothing when he the ground, Tall Drives the gory spear tip into the ground and uses it to swing off his still fast moving horse, looking up Blood sees the big Warrior take his scalping knife out and with a pull of the hair and a quick cut Talk Elk holds up his bloody trophy, with one last terrified scream Blood dies, the flies already starting on his gaping wounds.

The rest of Bloods bunch were not fairing any better, men and horses were falling to the accurate and continuous rifle fire laid down by the three attackers, Tall Elk mounts again to rejoin the fight, lance forward he charges the remaining enemies. Buster and the brothers ride full speed into the rabble clubbing and slashing with their rifles, the Hennessey boys then drop their rifles and pull their hog legs, blasting death at arms length, with Tall Elk charging screaming his war cry it becomes just to much for the cowards the ones that were able break free hightail it out of there like the devil himself is chasing them. Eleven men lay on the prairie grass dead or dying, only 3 escape, every victor is covered in blood either theirs or the enemies, Buster is hit by a rifle barrel receiving a nasty gash under his right eye, laid clean open to the bone, Paul takes a rifle bullet through his calf but luckily goes straight through and did not hit the bone. Each man now is sitting quiet on their mounts, all breathing heavy, ears ringing, thirsty with the taste of brass in their mouths, Tall Elk breaks the silence displaying his two scalps, "damn good fight, we ride now find more men to fight." Buster and the boys get a chuckle from that, then he rells Tall Elk, "it was a great honour to fight with my Brother the great warrior Tall Elk, you have counted much coup today, but we will give the horses a rest, have a coffee and tend our wounds. "besides I recon the other boys would take it right unkindly if we interfered with their fun, we will gather the weapons and head after the train, you never know we might get lucky and come across another pack of vermin."

War means fighting, and fighting means killing.
- Nathan Bedford Forrest

CHAPTER 35

MOUNTAIN GAINTS CLASH

Flat nose Johannsson looks back at the men riding behind him, a sorry bunch he thought, not a man worth fighting in the whole bunch, gunfighters not fighting men, he is hoping the enemy had some good fighting men to give him a challenge but he doubted it, not many of the real tough ones left.

Moose is a giant of a man, almost as big as Bear, a bit shorter and wider, powerful and very strong, has killed many men, more than 14 at last count, using every type of weapon including his hands, but he loved the cold steel best, feeling the razor-sharp blade slide through skin into the vitals, lusting as his victims screamed, then watch as the soul leaves their eyes. Only one man ever bested him a big man named Macdonald, the other men called him Bear, it was at a rendezvous, Macdonald caught him in the attempt to rape a squaw, the man was a monster, giving Flat nose not only a thrashing but his nickname by breaking his nose so badly it could not be fixed and disfigured him for life. He swore to kill that son of a bitch Macdonald, but as the saying goes be careful what you wish for you just may get it.

A sparsely treed hill came in sight between him and the railway tracks, Flat nose halts and pulls from his saddlebags a sailors telescope he had stolen off a old miner he had killed, putting it up to his eye 4 men came into focus, his mouth opened in disbelief in what he was seeing, removing the scope shook his head, it could not be, then looking through the glass again, saw what appeared a damn big mountain man in beautiful buckskins, a well armed Mexican, another man in worn buckskins and a very big Indian in war paint holding a large spear, he could not make out their faces but he knew this type of man. The defenders were standing out in the open looking towards him and his men unconcerned, Old Flat nose actually smiled, thinking to himself this is going to be a very good day. "Turning to his men he informs them there appears to be 4 men up there on yonder hill, we are all going to ride up slow and friendly to parley, pointing to 3 men, you ride on my left, you other 4 will be on the right, the big un is mine, none will shoot until I give the word, and I will kill any of you cowardly skunks that fail to follow my orders." As he suspected there were no objections, leading off slowly Flat nose is riding towards the hill and its defenders, his beady eyes shining with a pent-up desire for blood.

The 4 warriors on the hill watch as the rider's approach, without a word the men separated themselves putting about 12 feet between them with Bear in the middle facing the advancing threat all heavily armed and wired tight for the anticipated conflict. Flat nose brings his men in real slow, all but himself had their long guns out and over their saddles. Flat nose pulls up in front of Bear, 4 of the riders split off to face Ramon and Panther, sitting in a tight bunch, Ramon just turned a bit to be face on with the so-called gunman, smiling to himself how considerate and foolish these gringos are to be such nice easy targets. The other 3 attackers faced Black Hand, none looking very happy about it, all knew of Black Hand and his reputation, his war paint bright yellow and raven black, holding a huge spear that no average man could wield, eagle feathers and 9 scalps hanging from it. Black Hand made no move but looks directly at the men, his black eyes are hard and steady his face a stone mask.

Flat nose looks over the 4 men but focuses on Bear, recognition came to him, this was the man that disfigured him. Looking to Bear "I recon I know you, pointing to his face, I swore an oath that I would kill you one day for this, looks like I will have your scalp after all." Bear looks up at the big man and "I be knowing ye Flat nose Johannsson, knowing you for a low-down thief and back shooter, with a stink no honest man can ignore, mean and low down, you just try for this child's scalp, choose your weapon woman killer I will give you all the fight you want." Flat nose could not believe his luck, he was going to cut the Bear up real bad before finishing him off, "I says knives unless you are scairt, taunting, Bear who just smiled, he removes his huge walker colt and hands it to Black Hand then placed the big 50 against a nearby tree, turning he faces Flat Nose who is flexing his huge muscles under the buckskin to loosen up, this will be a brutal fight to the death no mercy could or would be shown.

Both men pull out their razor-sharp knives about the size of short swords, then start to close in, their knives held low with the razor edge up, as if on a silent single both men charge each other Bear yelling the Sioux war cry. The collision is violent, sounding like a couple big buffalo bulls clashing heads, their big blades clashing, each man trying to drive the other back or get him on the ground to make the kill. Bear went to move his foot back to pull Flat nose off balance but his foot caught on a small stone putting him off balance and open to be cut he instead of fighting to get up and be at a disadvantage he continues to fall back just saving him with Flat noses knife making a long but not deep cut across his chest drawing first blood. Both men close in and fast again but this time Bear came in low a smile on his face then with a quick feint at Flat noses belly steps back and with a quick overhead slash cuts off half of Flat noses ear opening a bloody gash slicing clear through the cheek, bleeding badly Flat Nose is shaken, he knows now he will die this day his opponent is too skilled and powerful. In sheer desperation, Flat nose makes a rush in screaming like a madman his knife high hoping to knock Bear over and bring his knife down into Bears chest, he knew he was going in to fast, he felt himself being tripped and falls forward a huge hand hammers him into the ground. Before he can rise Bear slammed a knee deep into the middle of his back, knocking the wind out of him. Flat nose feels himself being turned over, Bear now places his large knife against the throat of the doomed man, the palm of his hand on the end of the handle ready to push the big blade through the defeated mans throat. Bear his eyes blazing and terrible says to Flat nose, "this world will be much better off without you Flat Nose, have the devil keep a seat open for me, Adios Asshole, "Bear then pushes down hard the knife, the dead mans throat opened like splitting a ripe tomato, after a few gurgles and a lifeless nerve twitches, Flat nose Johannsson got his wish.

All the other players in this deadly drama have been so engrossed watching the violent struggle had forgotten the job at hand, the 4 gunman started to swing slowly towards Ramon, now Ramon for all his calmness can be a very quick moving man, the man on the right Ramon knew was going to make the first move, his hand flashes to his pistol is faster than the eye could follow his 2 quick shots so fast sounding like one his first shot notches an outlaws ear the second mutilates another man's shooting hand "Amigos I have many bullets left would you care for them?" Panther steps forward and points out 2 of the men facing Ramon, "them 2 is the low down cowards who shot Tex, pointing his big .50 cannon at the 2 back shooters, "you boys drop your guns and do it slow I got me a real itchy trigger finger, I promised Marshal Steele I would deal with you, now laddies now put your hands on your saddle horns, and I would do it right damn now." As if hot the 2 outlaws dropped their rifles and sit real quiet, one of the man Ramon shot was one of Tex's killers the other looked to be kin. The men facing Black Hand tried to look tough and remain calm but when Black hand threw the blanket from his massive shoulders and pointed that giant spear at them screaming his war cry it was to much for them they folded like house of cards and bolted faster than a rabbit with a coyote on its tail, Ramon after disarming the remaining men to the told them to leave and stay gone this was not healthy country for outlaws. Only the dead Smash nose and the 2 prisoners remain it is deathly quiet.

The hostages are taken off their horses Ramon ties their hands behind their backs with leather pigging strings and he is none to gentle about it. The executioners are in a quandary the trees being small ash were not suitable for hanging, shooting them was letting them off to easy. The old cagey wolf Black Hand solves the problem, raising his spear calls across what seems empty prairie, as if by magic two of Black Hands older and trusted warriors appear just yards from us and are coming over to parley.

Black Hand and his warriors move off a short distance and started to speak in rapid Sioux even Panther can not catch it all of it but getting the gist of it starts cackling. The Sioux chief turns to his companions, "We take bad men, will give them to the Blackfeet as a gift from Crow Killer, ask they die long time." Other than the 2 prisoners who were both about to wet their pants thinking of the horrible fate awaiting them if the Blackfoot got a hold of them there were smiles all around it was agreed the braves should take the luckless men. The Sioux braves now mounted and with leather ropes around the necks of the doomed men give a wave and are off, the pleas of the desperate men can be heard for a long time, but falls n the deaf ears of hard men who administerehard justice.

Shortly the sound of the train is heard approaching, so far so good, 2 large squads of men destroyed and not a single bullet shot at the train, but how long could their luck hold.

Float like a butterfly, sting like bee.
- Muhammad Ali

CHAPTER 36

HOT IN THE BAGGAGE CAR

Scars savage riders are the first to hit the train, not encountering any opposition they catch up with the train just as it was pulling out from the water tank and wood filling station gathering speed. With a whoop and a wave of his hat Scar's mob start peppering the baggage and passenger cars with rifle and pistol fire. Other than some windows shot out of the passenger car there is little damage, in the passenger car the ancient conductor was banging away with his big horse pistol with a damn big smile on his face. Inside the express car the 2 marshals were about to spring their deadly surprise, with a nod the portals are opened and the barrels of 2 double barrel shotguns appear, all four barrels were fired together creating a solid wall of hot lead, like a sickle through hay it mows down the raiders. The barrels withdraw and the portals shut again securing the defenders, Scars looks back and sees 4 horses with empty saddles, with no need to pursue the train any longer he turns and rides over to the fallen. It was not a pretty sight even for the heartless Scars, those shotguns at close range just tear up a man something awful, with himself he has six men left one which had caught some pellets in the knee, which looks damn painful.

The rider with the shot-up knee is the first to notice four riders riding directly for them closing the distance fast, their intent crystal clear. Whiplash and the boys had just missed intercepting Scars riders by a few minutes, hearing the gunshots they lit out fast towards the ruckus, the outlaws concentrating on their dead failed to notice them until it was to late, they have no chance to run, it is now going to be close in and bloody work for both sides of this deadly conflict.

Whiplash his smoke wagon is blasting and is charging directly at Scar, he is so close now he could see the hideous disfigurement of the man he faced, Whiplash figured he is looking at one of Satan's soldiers it gives him a shiver. Spurring his horse forward Whiplash slams his horse into Scars mount, both horses and men smash hard into the dirt all struggling to rise, Whiplash gets to his feet first but has lost his six-gun in the fall, his hand quickly reaches for the handle of his steel tipped bullwhip, uncoiling it from his body. Scars rises fires to quickly at his target and misses, before he could fire a second time with a loud crack the tip of the whip takes two of Scar's fingers on his gun hand, a second later a second bite and his left ear evaporates into a red mist.

Scars already damaged mind is now completely broken, he falls to the ground and curls up in the fetal position, drooling, whimpering and repeating one single word, "Da, Da, Da"

Whiplash looks to his comrades, Dakota is wounded but alive, the two men in front of him were now buzzard meat, Jonny Diamond is cleaning his double-edged knife on his victim's shirt, Jonny was one of the very best with a knife the outlaw with the shot-up knee just sat his saddle hands high in the air having enough fighting for one day.

Moose was in a hand to hand struggle with a very big Irishman, neither combatant holds a weapon in this struggle, it will be won on strength and skill. The Irishman is tough and a good fighter, knew all the dirty tricks, but he had never fought the likes of

Moose, old Moose had fought just about every critter up and down the river. When they broke the Irishman lets go a wide haymaker at Moose's head which if connected might have taken it clean off, but he overextended himself, Moose lets go a left hook to the ribs, the sound of the bones cracking could be heard from all that are watching. With a powerful right hand, he hits the Irishman with a brutal shot to the solar plexes, the big man doubles up, with a leg sweep Moose takes the hurt mans legs out from under him, the big outlaw falls forward on his face. Moose then slams a knee into the downed mans back then with his huge hands l he locks them under the Irishman's chin and starts to pull the mans neck back, the Paddy has a neck of a bull but it was no match for Moose's strength, with one mighty heave the outlaws neck is put in an impossible angle and snaps loudly ending the struggle. Moose stands and looks around sanity now returning to his eyes, nothing is said about the killing it was known by all it was a death match. Whiplash looks up at the remaining outlaw hands still raised and looking right pale, "Get you polecat, never come back, ever, now go," the bandit did not need to be told twice, within minutes you could only see his dust.

The men then go over to Dakota to check on his wounds, he has been hit twice, one hit his shin and broke his leg, the other a through and through just above his hip, neither to serious but he is losing blood. As the men tend his wounds best they can old Dakota lets out a nervous laugh, "damn boys that got right interesting there for a few minutes, you fellas alright?" Whiplash who was splinting his leg, "of course we are alright you lunkhead only a durn fool gets his self all shot up, we more experienced fighters feel no need to go get ourselves all full of lead", then looks and smiles that devilish smile at the wounded man, his two comrades stifling chuckles. "Well you sinners only had one each I had twice the trouble and I will tell you what serious like, them boys was good, now get me on my damn horse, time to be riding."

Scars is still in the same position and it isobvious his mind completely shattered never to be right again, the men gather and look down at him not sure what to do with him, without notice

Jonny draws and puts a .45 slug just behind the killer's ear ending his torment, without a word the men mount and follow the rails no one looks back.

*Conflict follows wrongdoing as surely as flies follow
the herd. - Doc Holiday*

CHAPTER 37

THE 4 HORSEMEN

I am scanning the landscape for enemy activity trying to concentrate on the task at hand and not worry about how the other fellas are making out, I suspect there was a killing squad between me and Bill's ambush spot and I figured them to be near. Grey Wolf spots them first, we were behind them still to far away to make out anything but that there were 8 horsemen grouped together, riding slowly not seeming to care about their backtrail. Looking over at the boys I nodded and nudged Apollo increasing our pace, hoping to close most of the distance before we are spotted.

Gabriel is worried they should have encounter their competition by now it is far to quiet, nothing but a few buffalo were moving on the plains, his concentration is broken by one of the Mexican bandits, "Senor Gabriel, the posse men are behind us, I theenk". Gabriel pulls up and turns his mount to face the oncoming men, he can see the sun shine off Marshal Steele's badge, he counts 3 white men and an Indian, as they ride closer he recognizes the members of the posse and even though he outnumbers them two to one he knows he does not have enough men. The 4 horsemen coming towards him are by far the deadliest men anywhere in the west, he knew the Marshal on the big horse was Sudden Steele, he reckoned that the Indian with him was Grey Wolf, he had heard many stories of the Sioux's savagery and bravery. He recognized Long Tom right off, he had seen him at the hole in the wall when Tom was riding in amongst the outlaws to retrieve horses stolen from the ranch, when the smoke cleared the two horse thieves were dead and Tom rode out with the horses, very tough man would take a lot of killing. The last man Gabriel knew it must be the Traveller, the most dangerous of the posse, when his guns spoke death answered the call, Gabriel was wishing he was a long way from here, he looked to his men all had their weapons out and ready but he could tell they were scared might even bolt.

I call a halt, "That preacher looking bad man would be the one they call Gabriel, a killer who hires out his gun to the highest bidder, right and wrong mean nothing to him, the rest look like Mexican bandits and cowboy would be outlaws. "Ok boys from here Grey Wolf and I are going to veer left and you boys veer a bit right have them worried on 2 sides, when I give the signal we charge guns a blazing, I figure they will not be able to take the heat and I want this ended quick we still got old Bill to catch". "Gentlemen if you are all ready we will now proceed to smite these evil men and send Gabriel back to hell where he belongs." With that Grey Wolf and I start slowly swinging left, Wade and Tom to the right, Grey Wolf although an excellent rifle shot was going to fight with his bow, in which he was very skilled he would have been right at home riding with the Mongol hoards of the old times. I wrap Apollos reins around the saddle horn, I have a six shooter in each hand I could feel the mighty animals blood pounding and his lust for battle, Traveller has the reins in his teeth and a .44 Russian in each hand, Long Tom a short-barrelled Winchester with a wide loop lever in his right hand and a long barrelled .45 in his left, with a Sioux war cry we charge.

Gabriel watches as in slow motion as the riders split up and get themselves in position to attack, his men are waiting for him to act and take the lead, but for the first time in his life he was uncertain what to do. To late his decision is made for him when his competition suddenly charges them, he has his rifle up to his shoulder and is firing now, knowing he is hitting only air, the others are not doing not much better their horses are frightened and hard to control. The incoming fire is deadly accurate, only one other time did Gabriel encounter such heavy fire power and that was during the war, he had now been hit twice both minor wounds, quickly he drops his rifle and puts his hands high in the air, it is to nice of a day to die.

What is left of Gabriel gang of killers wisely give up, I count the dead horses, 3 men lay deathly still on the grass, the survivors were all wounded in some way, I ride up facing Gabriel with Traveller beside me, "you and your men shed the rest of your guns, and if I spot any hideouts I will shoot to kill, now slow and easy boys no need for more killing."

Well them outlaws are right obliging, they know what we would do if crossed, and with Grey Wolf an arrow notched in his bow dark eyes locked on them they are seeing the light. I look over at Wade he was looking at Gabriel with a terrible deep gaze, green eyes to like burn through the man, "Something personal Wade? "Yep", "well I will leave it to you then, finish it and we will go hurrah old Bill." I back Apollo up a few feet to give Traveller room for what ever play he is planning to make.

Traveller never took his eyes off a nervous Gabriel, "I know you killer been hoping to come across you, I also know the evil you have done, do you remember the Riess family, nice couple had a nice farm near Grassy Lake, 2 sweet kids, you was paid to run them off but you found it easier to just kill the whole family and put the bodies in a cave".

"Frank Reiss did me a good turn, fixed me up after a gun battle, I swore you would pay, and now you will", without notice and faster than the eye can follow Traveller draws firing 2 quick shots, but Gabriel was not dead he was much worse, the trigger finger and middle fingers on each hand had been shot away, both Angels hands are now useless. "I was going to kill you but that would not be punishment enough, you ain't going to be good for anything now Gabriel, must beg for your food, every day you live will now be filled with regret you dirty son of a bitch." Gabriel looked down at his now useless hands, the realization of it all flowed through him, the fear panic and frustration overwhelms Gabriel he screams in panic and insanity Looking over at the remaining men I say," We do not have time to deal with you, get out of the territory right soon and if I ever come across any of you assholes again I will shoot you on sight, now get and take this piece of shit with you."

We do not wait we take off at a fast pace the real battle is yet to be fought, it beginning to be a long day, already so much blood in the dust, knowing there would be much more before this day was over, damn you to hell Bill.

Revenge is a confession of pain.
- Latin Proverb

CHAPTER 38

BILL'S TRAP

About 8 miles from the gold trains destination is a turn in the track where the train has to navigate around a small set of rocky hills and would be out of site of the rail line for a brief time, Bills trap is all ready, when the train comes into view they would set off the dynamite blowing up the tracks and telegraph poles cutting the line to the Capital then forcing the train to stop directly in front of him and his men. Bill and his crew are cleverly camouflaged, he and his men lay in shallow trenches, sod has been removed and using short sticks to prop up the sod front they crawl back under the sod making them nearly invisible to bee seen but also gives his comrade and himself the ability to see out. Bill is not enjoying his time beneath the grass although it was cool it gives him an eerie feeling of being in a grave, to add to his misery, dirt and small bugs were falling on his back getting inside his shirt, he must struggle to keep from moving, but not long now he thinks, a little discomfort now and much comfort and pleasure to follow, you never get anything for nothing.

It will not be long now, he is getting more uncomfortable by the minute laying still under the sod, but he knew old Hardin was out on the scout and settled in still once again. His mind falls into fantasy as he thinks how it will be being king of Montana. Bills mind is on the good food, women and wine awaiting him and by the time the politicians got the facts together and made any decisions to send troops in he would be on a big ship sailing first class to Paris, and nothing would stop him this time, no matter who if they get in his way they must be eliminated.

I am laying flat on my stomach using my binoculars to search the area in front of me knowing Bill was out there somewhere and close by. "Boys I figure this here is the spot but damn if I can figure how old Bill is going spring it on them, I ain't exactly positive on this but it is where I would be." Traveller nods his approval, "I think you got er pegged pard, we must be quick if we are going to upsets old Bill's wagon." Grey Wolf, not taking his dark eyes off the country in front of him slowly searching turning his head never looking directly at any point, I see his movements stop and focused now like an eagle on its prey then he smiles "it trick, Indian trick, men hide under grass, blow up train quick ambush." I knew in a moment that that had to be it, Bill would hit fast and hard, the lawmen in the baggage car would have to be very strong today. Looking again through my binoculars sure enough there were some uneven mounds that should not be there, I sure should have seen it the first time. Traveller after making a thorough sweep of the area looks to me "they are out there alright, I am guessing 6 or 7 but could be 30 no way to know until we flush them out charging them would be suicide. As Wade is talking I am looking out over the prairie, about a half mile or so I noticed there was a small slough with about 20 head of cattle around it, looking at them I was wondering what old Bill and his cohorts would do if 20 full grown cattle were stampeded right over his hiding spot. Smiling at my friends I nod my head toward the cattle, the men catch on right right off and smile back, we all then turn back to get our mounts. Long Tom, looks over at me and chuckles "I don't recon old Bill figured on this in his planning, then in a more serious manner, "as those varmints leave their holes we will have to be ready for anything, that Bill will have his best with him and he never seems to run out of tricks." I nod in agreement, "Well boys lets give er a try and see if we can serve up some beef on the hoof, we best get going time is short and I am plum out of ideas." We mount up and in a large circle and come in slow behind the cattle not to startle them and then get them pointed in the direction of the concealed outlaws, with our saddle ropes we haze them cows out at a slow pace, as we got closer we urge the herd for more speed, we all have our guns out and ready, about 200 yards out I let out an eagle scream and fire off a shot, the small heard bolts directly where Bill and his mob are waiting, shouts and gunfire had those old cows in a panic and are running full out.

Bill is shaken from his day dreaming by the sound of guns and shouting, he looks out and his heart skips a beat as he sees the cattle heading directly for him and his men, he knew at once it was that damn Sudden and he also knows he better get out of his hole right fast before it becomes his grave. It was damn near comical watching them outlaws jump from their holes like prairie dogs, Bill only had four men with him which said to me these men are extremely dangerous and it would be his best against mine, this was going to be savage bitter fighting each and everyone now just fighting for survival, the thought of riches gone for the moment.

Bill has always been lucky and it was with him again, his sod hideout happened to be the closest to the tracks, if he went fast and low he might just get to the stand of trees the were the horses and wagon were hidden, but he would have to make the run of his life over open country, it his only chance escape and he takes it, with the thought of his probably dying in the next couple minutes he makes his dash. None of the outlaws were trampled, but it got them out in the open and put off balance, we now mixed in amongst them each man finding his target.

Grey Wolf spots the big Ute, with a scream of challenge he throws himself off his horse crashing his body into his enemy, they go down in a tangle. The Traveller has dismounted and is now facing the man known as Nolan, "never figured you to be riding with this bad bunch Nolan, always figured you to be standing on the right side when it mattered." "I know Wade but got in some money and law trouble awhile back but getting paid good for this job, gold or no gold and my only job is to kill you, and that's what I am to do."

I had just jumped off Apollo when I feel the burn of a bullet that came so close the friction burnt the skin on my thigh, I look and see a man I find out later is Cim Smith, cocking his smoke wagon for another shot at me, with the shotgun in my right hand I tip the barrels up and let go the right barrel just as flame shoots from Smith's gun. Long Tom and Nevada just went to fighting each walking towards each other slamming shots at each other like 2 boxers slugging it out, both men have been hit and are reloading.

The Ute is confident he can kill this scrawny Sioux, he was much stronger and had killed many men, he would take his time play with the Sioux pup before gutting him. As the Ute was to find out he had never fought anyone as skilled in warfare as Grey Wolf, although smaller he was much faster and deadly with the Spanish knife his Kola Crow Killer gave him. The Ute was confused and angry he has not so much as touched his enemy and he was bleeding from more than 6 deep cuts, the Sioux was like fighting smoke, in desperation he takes a mighty swing at Grey Wolf to end it, faster than the eye can follow Gray Wolf's blade flashes opening up the Ute's throat deep red blood now spurting out, his life draining, the last thing he felt was Grey Wolf's blade taking his scalp.

The Traveller knows there are no options left to him and adopts his gunfighting stance hand close to the butt of his .44 Russian, he sees Nolan's eyes flicker and makes his draw, Nolan's first bullet knocks Wades leg out from under him throwing off his aim hitting Nolan high in the shoulder, then the Traveller goes to work, pumping shot after shot into Nolan's chest, the outlaw was still firing but his nerveless fingers fired into the ground, he sways and with a small smile at Wade lets his hog leg fall to the ground and then follows it .

My load of buckshot takes Cim in the neck and face throwing off his last shot, it was a gruesome sight, the soft lead nearly tearing the mans face off, it is not a good way to die but he drew cards in a tough game. I look over to see Long Tom just as he is putting a killing shot into Nevada's skull, there is a Winchester by my feet I pick it up and jack a round in the chamber now looking for Bill. I see him running hard towards the protection of the trees, the rifle is now snugged into my shoulder and the sights locked on Bill's back, a sure kill all I have do is squeeze the trigger, just then he turns, I can see the son of a bitch is smiling he holds up his beautiful black hat which with great pleasure I shoot it ripping it from his hand from his while still in the air I put another bullet through it. Bill is running again grabbing his ventilated hat on the way he is now in the bushes and trees there is no chance for another shot.

The boys are looking at me with some concern, "Boys I just could not shoot old Bill in the back, I know he needs killing but not that way." Wade looks down at me, "you know he has to meet you in the street now, you have shamed him, and I do not think it will be long before he comes hunting you." I knew he was right but did not say anymore on the matter changing the subject asking about the wounds of Long Tom and Wade, both men were lucky and not hurt to bad, Tom had one go through his shoulder and another took a chunk from the top of his left ear, Wade took a bullet below the knee, bouncing off his shin and tearing a fair-sized gash but looking worse than it was.

After tending our wounded, we head towards town, the train flies by us the conductor blowing his whistle in victory, I am most anxious for news on the rest of my posse, hoping our losses are not to great and we have ripped apart the Mob. My thoughts are dark and troubled thinking over Wade's word's and I knew them to be true, the next time Bill and I meet one or both of us will die.

You miss 100 percent of the shots you never take. -
Wayne Gretzky

CHAPTER 39

SMOKE AND THE EAGLE

We were the first to arrive back in I make directly for the Marshals office, getting down off Apollo I feel like I have been rode hard and put away wet, but there will be no rest until every man is back and accounted for. The young doctor had an aid station set up close to the jail with nurses assisting him, I send Wade and Tom over, Grey Wolf left us before we entered town, I suspect the sly devil would be gathering the dead outlaw's horses increasing his already impressive horse herd thus boosting his status even more among the tribe.

I am just about to sit when Carol and Em burst into the office, I can see the fear leaving Carol's face as she can sees I am not hurt, throwing her arms around me she weeps into my neck, the strain releasing. Em asks if I have heard anything on the coffee boiler Whiplash, then started cursing him for a fool, but it was Em's way if she was angry it most often because she is scared she is very fond of Whiplash but to damn stubborn to admit it. Unwrapping myself from Carol f I tell the girls what I know which is not much, but I will be here to meet every man jack coming in, and a mans gal should have the Arbuckle's brewing by now I kid her. Slowly the groups are coming in, and I go out to meet each one, sending the wounded to the doc and others to where there were sandwiches and coffee provided by the Cafe owner.

The last of the men arrive well into the night, from the stories of the men we did very well and that Bill's Mob are finished dead or scattered all over the prairie, the scavengers will feast this night. I send the men for rest informing them I will take their statements in the morning. I can almost feel the tension evaporating from my body it is an intense and horrible feeling that makes me queasy I must duck into an alley to throw up, not sure how but we pulled it off, who would have thought. I feel much better after that, I walk back into the jail and fall into a cot in one of the cells asleep before I can get my boots off.

I come awake with a start by a thunderous pounding in the office area, of course it was Bear, "You going to sleep the whole durned day away nephew, get your ass up and moving we are for breakfast and coffee." Laughing I get up and already dressed I join the boys, the cafe is just packed with people, poor Mrs. Lofton the cafe owner was being run off her feet but a few of the local women were helping Carol of course one of them. Mrs. Lofton with a tired smile says, "no more room out here boys must eat in the kitchen, but they are the best seats in the house."

The cafe was abuzz with talk of each of the groups well of their adventures heroics and horrors of the clashes, Bear, Ramon, Whiplash and myself are in the kitchen also telling our tails, but the bottom line is that law and order will lead Montana into the future.

The next couple days are pure chaos in trying to get statements from all the riders, most had decided a celebration was in order but I finally get enough of the facts to write up my report, the Governor and the man in Washington are most pleased and the story of what was now being called Mathers-Steele war spreads across the nation.

Now only one more horse to rope before this roundup is over, I have not forgotten about that curly wolf Bill, the drama has yet to reach the final act.

Young Bill and Sam came to town to report, seems a couple of desperate men in trying to escape made a couple tries at stealing horses and supplies from Em's ranch, a very bad choice, Sam put them down quick. Sam would not take the credit said young Bill stood up to them tall with not a step back, high praise from a man of Sam's calibre.

The next morning, I am sitting outside my office coffee in hand and enjoying the quiet of the morning when I see a young Navajo man who appears to be in his 20s riding a splendid black spotted appaloosa down the street towards the jail, right off I knew right off he was looking for me. Watching him as he rides down the street towards me I see he is a handsome fella his jet long black hair that is clean and shining like a crow's wing, had himself on a colourful patterned shirt and a beautiful belt of silver and turquoise handmade by a true artist, hanging off his belt is a serious looking knife with an Elkhorn handle and a well used henry rifle close to his hand. I can see that he was alert to trouble and his senses miss nothing, he pulls up directly in front of me but does not dismount, looking me over, "Morning I am US Marshal Steele can I help you with something, come on down off your horse I got some fresh coffee on the stove."

In excellent English, better than most of the white men I know hereabouts answers, "Marshal are you the one the Blackfeet call White Crow Killer, if so I would advise you to stay out of that country, their young men all want a chance for your scalp and the big medicine it will bring them." "Yep that's me alright and I have no desire to tangle with anymore of them Blackfeet they are a tough and mean bunch, by what name are you called?" "I am Atsa, I come to you because I need the law, men try to force me off my land, kill my sheep, frighten my family, my land is filed and registered and legally mine." "But we must go quick my family is alone and the enemy is near, will you come now?"

As I was listening to Atsa I notice Sam across the street in front of the general store, I hail him and ask him to join us. I introduce the 2 men who nod and look the other over, "Sam, Atsa is being forced off his land by his neighbor and needs my help which of course I will dhelp, but with Tex gone I need a good deputy to cover my back, and I recon you and Traveller are about the best I know, how about riding along?"

Sam rubs his jaw in deep thought, "I recon you know my real name and my past, but if you are serious marshal, I will be damn proud to ride beside you, just how long have you known who I really am?"

Giving off a laugh "about 5 minutes after you rode in, Bear pointed you out once when I was a youngster, "tossing him a deputy badge I told him to get his gear and meet me at the office in an hour, we would be heading out directly, I did not like to think of Atsa's wife alone with enemies all around.

I send one of the town boys to go to Mrs. Lofton's cafe and ask her to pack some food for 3 hungry men hitting the trail and bring it to the stable. I stuff my saddlebags with extra ammunition and grab 2 canteens, my greener is slung down my back, I grab the spare to give to Sam, sawed off shotguns at short range will make many any sinner a believer, no sane man bucks a scattergun. Satisfied I have everything Atsa and I head to the livery to get Apollo ready, upon seeing Apollo the Navajo is in awe of him, having superior knowledge of horses he knew immediately that this incredible horse was a beast of strength, stamina, cunning and was a vicious war horse in battle.

The town boy delivers the food and I give him 4 bits for his assistance, Sam is already mounted and ready, I hand him the scattergun and some shells, Atsa turns his beautiful Appy and we head out of town, I feel I have made a wise choice in picking Sam, and it would prove out in the days ahead. I talk with one of Em's riders before leaving asking him to tell Carol I would be away for a few days maybe a week and Em that I borrowed Sam to lend me a hand, and make sure that old stubborn mule Whiplash stays out of trouble. The rider was happy to do it and tells us to take care, I give him a couple bucks to have a few drinks before he heads back to the ranch.

Before the time of the destroyer Kit Carson and the trail of tears the Navajo were a mighty race, and in some ways still are. They were many and feared warriors not even the Apache wanted a dust up with the Navajo, but contrary to other tribes the Navajo were also farmers and sheep ranchers, talented and creative silversmiths, the women making the most beautiful blankets a treasure to the lucky few that owned one.

As we ride Atsa tells us with great pride of his ranch which was in a long narrow valley foothills and mountains natural barriers to keep the sheep from straying, a couple clear cold running streams, filled with trout. He had dammed the closest to his house, and made runoffs for his corn fields and a reservoir back of the house, deer and elk to hunt for meat, sounded like paradise to me and when I saw it I am not disappointed, the only other place that came close to being this beautiful would be Bears cabin.

We talk as we ride I tell him of my Uncles and my fights with the Crow, Pima and Blackfeet, the war with Bill's mob. Sam had at times lived among the Indians, fought with them and against them but held no malice as the native warrior he respected bravery. Atsa tells us his name means Eagle and he was a Prince, he brought his family to his valley to hopefully start something that will be his legacy for future generations. For his years he had done a heap of fighting, tangling with the Pima, Paiute and Apache, thinking to myself, him surviving those battles left no doubt this Navajo is one tough Hombre.

Atsa informs us the rancher he was having trouble with had no interest in the land until Atsa started showing the lands potential and profit, he did not need the valley he was already ruling over 4 thousand acres, a case of the rich wanting to get richer, the sin of greed. I ask him what this man's name might be, his brand and how many riders he had. "The owner is a man called Lon Gentry runs the double L brand I figure he has close to 20 riders and at least 6 getting fighting wages, Tulsa Tom would be about the worst of the bunch. "Before I could speak Sam jumps in, "Did you say Lon Gentry, a big man blond haired galoot, likes to push his weight around, got a scar along his cheekbone?" Atsa confirms that this is the man. Sam chuckles to himself, "Things are going to be right fine Marshal, I know Lon, in fact I gave him the scar, with a little luck we might just be able to show the big jackass the error of his ways, without bloodshed" still chuckling to himself leads off, only couple hours now and we will be at Atsa's ranch.

Riding over the hill and looking down on Atsa's valley if I live to a hundred it will be a sight I will never forget, if it was not paradise but close enough, I can see Sam feels the same and said so. When we ride into the yard 2 sheepdogs came running out barking up a storm, Atsa spoke a word and they both settled down and sat quiet, a good sheepdog is worth its weight in gold and prized by all sheep owners.

From the house emerges a beautiful young woman dressed in the Navajo fashion holding her hand is a fine-looking lad about 4 with large dark brown serious eyes, Atsa introduces us, his wife's name is Kai and the little fella was Niyol. She speaks to Atsa in Navajo and just sounded like any other wife, Atsa nods then turns to us, "the boss says we are to go put up our horses then come in for supper, she says she is grateful you have come to help us."

Looking over the ranch yard I am more than a little impressed by the work done, wisely Atsa built his house from stone, the stables and corrals were secure and solid, wild flowers adorned the front of the house with a nice sized garden in the back, if left alone these nice folks will get along right fine.

After finishing with the horses, we head to the house for supper, now I find out just how lucky that Atsa is, it was a dinner to remember, platters of lamb, chicken, corn on the cob with real butter, flatbread and ice cold buttermilk, I ate until I was ready to burst, and old Sam is doing his fair share, fried dough and honey served as dessert along with some damn fine coffee.

Sam not surprisingly speaks a few words of Navajo and was trying them out on Niyol, getting the boy to smile and laugh honestly as only children do, I never trust a man who does not like kids or dogs. Almost having to be lifted from my seat I thanked Kai for the wonderful supper and told Atsa to rest well tonight Sam and I would keep night watch, I knew he had not been getting much sleep being only one man, I could tell he is grateful, the stress of fear for a mans family is a hugs burden to carry.

I do to the stable and fetch Apollo and my bedroll, under a big oak near the barn I picket him close but on a spot of fresh green grass and I lay out my bedroll under the tree, Sam was spreading his out on the other side of the tree. "Try and catch some shuteye Sam, Apollo and the dogs will warn us of any trouble and I always sleep light in enemy country." "Ok boss I could use a few winks ", you should get some your own self nothing going happen tonight, but I figure it might get right fun, real soon" with a soft chuckle he turns over and is softly snoring in minutes. I look through the branches of the big oak at a soft moon and stars without number, thinking of Carol I drop off into a light sleep.

It is a quiet night I snatch more than enough sleep, couple times I get up and listen as was my habit, I notice Sam was up at least once through the night listening to the night sounds then satisfied rolled back up in his bedroll. We are just washing up when Niyol came to fetch us for breakfast in no way shy grabbing Sam's hand leads us to the house, the two them jabbering away. I swear if I was married to Kai I would be fatter than a bear in late fall, to my great pleasure coffee was already on the kitchen table, Atsa being a wise man kept some chickens so they would always have fresh eggs, a man out in the wilds could go a long while without even seeing and egg. It is a fine way to start the day with a feed of fresh eggs, beans and biscuits with honey and damn fine coffee.

With breakfast finished Sam and I clean and check our weapons, around mid morning Atsa said riders were coming 4 or 5 men riding slow and will be here shortly, after some discussion, it is decided Atsa would meet them and Sam and I with shotguns would be on each end of the house, staying unseen until we knew the men's intentions. Kai and Niyol we put in a backroom away from the gunfire, Atsa with his Henry in hand stands strong and fearless waiting for the visitors.

The horsemen pull up in front of Atsa, they are 5 very hard and fierce looking men, but only two had the look of gunfighter the others were just tough cowhands riding for the brand. The spokesman of the group is a big shaggy unkempt man, larger than the rest of the men I suspected him of being a bully using his size to intimidate.

"Injun, we warned you to get off this land, the Boss says you go and you go today, we are going to give you one hour to get your possessions if you are not on the trail by then we are going to hang you right in front of your sweet wifey and brat. I had heard enough as if on cue Sam and I show ourselves both cocking our sawed offs shotguns, well brother that got them cowboy's attention, casually pointing my scattergun at the shaggy mans belly I introduce myself. "My name is Steele and I am the United States Marshal for this Territory and there will be no hangings today, my deputy and I just enjoyed a fine breakfast and I would hate to ruin it by blowing your guts all over the yard". I will tell you what with 2 scatterguns at no more than 20 feet those cowboys were sitting real quiet and respectful.

Sam then interjected "I hear you fellers ride for a scoundrel named Lon Gentry, is he big and ornery with a scar on his left cheekbone?" The shaggy man growls back, "Mr. you got him pegged, but marshals or not Lon is going to have your hides pegged to Atsa's barn when he hears of this."

Sam smiles at the big man, "now who do your recon gave him that scar, best listen real close boys, you are going to ride out real peaceful like and tell Lon, Smoke Kellerman from Amarillo way sends his regards and says he is to leave these nice hard working folks alone, they own the land legal and the polecat has more land he can use." "Also, tell him if he does not heed this warning I will come calling and my guns will be doing the talking, you boys got that?"

I am inwardly enjoying myself, Smoke was a known man from the Nations to old Mexico, a man who lived by the code, a fine friend but a hard-unforgiving enemy, a man whose word when given would die for it.

The shaggy leader answers "We hear you and its your funeral, there is no backup in Lon once he gets his mind set on something, we will see how tough you boys are without then shotguns." Well I had enough I always disliked bullies, I believe the strong should protect not harm those weaker than himself. This big gunman is no real fighter, maybe winning a few fights against farm boys, but he has never gone up against a skilled fighter, I was feeling mean, and I mean to punish the big man before I take him out.

Handing my shotgun to Atsa I then remove my gun belt, "ok bigmouth you want some come and get it, time you took a beating." Smiling and rubbing his hands together he comes for me, I knew by his eyes if he got the chance he would kill me, without warning he throws a haymaker that if connected would have landed my head in the next county, but I seen it coming before he throws it, now I got to work, it is brutal and ugly, I attack pressure points, kidneys, causing him extreme pain, with fingers extended I sliced both cheeks to the bone, finally I was tired and sick of it all, throwing an uppercut from the ground I hammered him on the chin, he drops like he had been hit with an axe.

"I do not like bullies, you men pick this piece of shit up and you get, anymore trouble with you and we are going to get short tempered and mean." They quickly throw big Shaggy on his horse and hightail it out of there, Sam comes over, "damn Hardin remind me never to piss you off, never seen a more efficient and brutal beating, you have been well trained."

I give him a quick explanation on my training by Mr. Li, Bear, Ramon, Black hand and William, then I asked, "ok Smoke what's the deal with you and Lon Gentry, I think there is more to it than just you being Smoke Kellerman."

"Pard, old Lon and I go back to being wet behind the ears, he ain't really a bad man just gets to big for his britches and likes to be bull of the woods. That scar on his face I gave him last time he thought to hurrah me, and he knows I will do as I say, I am hoping he will come to his senses and makes peace."

We spend the rest of the day helping Atsa with some chores, I sharpen the axe and began to work on a big wood pile, enjoying the feeling of using my muscles and working up a good sweat, Smoke and the Eagle are fixing up the corrals reconnecting loose rails. After I cut what I felt was a good bit of firewood I went to the shed and grabbed some harness that needed mending, we all kept busy until supper time.

Supper again is delicious and it had a quiet peaceful feeling, everyone talking in quiet tones all a bit tired from a good day's work, Niyol was on Smokes knee they were witling away at making a flute, human nature is so amazing in how people connect, it is just an instant click which I am nowhere near smart enough to explain, like Bill and Whiplash Niyol and Smoke took to each other right off.

We were just puttering around the yard the next morning waiting for Lon to make a call, we did not have to wait to long, riding toward us is an older man going a bit to fat but still looking strong and dangerous like the old tiger with him 2 men both looking like cowmen not gunfighters. They stop at the gate and Lon Gentry hails the house, saying he was here for peace talk and is coming in friendly. Atsa welcomes him and tells them to step down and grab their cups coffee is on. Lon smiles when he sees Smoke, "damn boy it is good to see you, could not believe it when the boys told me, man, we really raised some hell back in the wild years, but never figured you for the law. I recon you are still a second-string checkers player, might be fun to get in a few games like the old days."

Smoke steps forward with a smile shaking hands with his old pard, "hell you never seen the day you could beat me with the discs, ok Lon time to fish or cut bait is it peace or war? be smart you knot head, Atsa and his family would make great neighbors honest hard working and Kai has got some damn fine honey." Lon looks over at me, "I recon you would be marshal Sudden Steele, heard allot of you, from the tales I figured you were at least 8 feet tall spit fire, that was some beating you gave Dave, he will be abed for weeks, but I guess old Dave needed a lesson getting to big for his britches, but damn you are one hard son a bitch Marshal."

Then turning addressing all in the yard, "it will be peace, you will have no more trouble with my outfit, Smoke is right I have enough and we need good folks settling here, Atsa has done some damn good work here and I think you can be a help to one another." Kai speaks to Atsa asking him something, he then speaks to Lon, "my wife asks if you have a woman a wife?" "Why yes, I have my Mary a woman to good for me, old Smoke and I both courted her, but Smoke was always footloose and needs to see what's over the next hill, leaving me with most special loving gal." Kai goes to the house and returns shortly with a beautiful bright coloured Navajo blanket and gently hands it to Lon, Atsa translates her words, the blanket is for his wife from a neighbor and friend, may it bring warmth and comfort to her.

Well old Lon is just flabbergasted he had never seen anything so beautiful, Mary would surely love and cherish it, red faced he removed his hat and thanked her for it struggling for words which made her giggle. "Well we better be going, been good seeing you Smoke will you come see Mary before you head out, she would be very disappointed not seeing you." Smoke a man of never ending surprises laughs, "Well you old jughead you better get used my mug because I talked it over with Atsa and I am sticking around and we are partnering up, it is quiet and peaceful here, time I was putting away my six guns and picking up the plow." "I will be heading back to the ranch with the Marshal to pick up my gear and thank miss Em for hiring me off and say Adios to the boys you tell Mary I will be around for Sunday supper and dust off the board been awhile since I had me a good game."

Atsa and Niyol handed each cowboy and Lon a jar of honey as they were leaving, them boys were right tickled pink, anyone bothering the Navajos now would have Smoke Kellerman and Lon Gentry to deal with, I don't recon there will be no more trouble over Atsa' claim to his ranch and the Eagle and Smoke will fly and prosper.

The next morning, I finish another fine breakfast then Smoke and I saddle up, Kai packs us a huge lunch for trail. It is times like this I get great satisfaction being a lawman and peace officer, the conflict ended with no bloodshed, two old pards are re united and Smoke can hang up his guns, but sadly this type of outcome is very rare. It is time to go, I miss Carol and I have not forgotten Bill, I want it finished between us no matter the outcome.

Ah, how good it feels! The hand of an old friend.
- Henry Wadsworth Longfellow

CHAPTER 40

BLOOD IN THE DUST

Smoke and I split up, he heads for the ranch and me my office to get my report written and see if there was any news of Bill's activities. Before we split up we shake hands ", can't thank you enough Hardin you putting your trust in an old gunfighter, now I got a chance to live like regular folks, it feels right good. ""Well Mr. Kellerman I never had a doubt about you, Bear told me years ago, that you were a man who would live or die by his word and you lived by the code, also you stood by your friends. "I am right pleased to see how things worked out, need a favour Pard, could you give Carol my regards and tell her I will be out to the ranch soon as I get finished at the office and have the coffee on." Good luck Amigo keep your powder dry."Smoke smiling readily agrees to deliver my message, with that we part, now to town, get my report in and catch up on the scuttlebutt, I give Apollo a nudge putting him into a ground eating trot. My satisfaction at getting back was short lived, the moment I see Wade sitting outside my office I know things cannot not good damn just 1 damn beak.

Traveller is rolling a quirly as I pull up to the jail as he lights it greeting me, "Howdy Hardin old son nice to see you back in once piece, I hate to be the one to have to tell you but Bill is somewhere in the city and he is making his brag about gut shooting you on site. "You also must keep a sharp eye out there are some new faces hanging around the saloons they have the look of trouble and it appears they are waiting for something to happen". "Hardin, I know how it is with you and Bill I could take care of this for you if you like." "Appreciate the offer Wade but you know I have been saddling my own broncs for some time now, and fate or destiny have determined Bill and I must meet for one last time." I was thinking to myself the Gods must have a very strange sense of humour and a thirst for irony pitting two best friends closer than brothers against each other in a final struggle where one or both will die.

Nodding thoughtfully informs me, "do not concern yourself about them hard cases, Red, Shorty and myself will keep them off you, you concentrate on Bill, he is desperate and I believe a might insane which makes him a very dangerous man, you must be very good and make sure your first shot scores a hit." ""Be seeing you Hoss, Get er done Marshal."

Nodding at his statement I turn Apollo towards the stables, the Traveller turns and makes his way back towards the saloon and pleasure palace district, I am feeling fear, dry mouth, sweaty hands wanting to flee scared as hell. If someone ever tells you they are not afraid of battle he would be a liar, fear is needed to keep you on the edge, pump you up getting you ready for action, but it must be mastered and tamed so not to take control.

The Tombstone Doc was deadly because he had no fear of dying he was a lunger with his time becoming short, fought without fear hoping for that bullet which never came, old Doc ended up passing over in bed, was never even scratched by hot lead, strange world.

I am taking my time with Apollo, giving him the royal treatment, hoping this had not been our last ride together, after giving my animal brother a bait of corn I gather my gear and return to the jail,

I need a coffee and time to prepare. With coffee poured I place both my Russian .44 and Colt Peacemaker on my desk then I empty all the chambers and give both weapons a good cleaning and oiling, then I carefully inspected each and every shell making sure it is not damaged before re loading both weapons, with both smoke wagons ready for action I then take my gun belt and lightly oil both the belt and leg holster making sure the guns would come into my hand smooth. I return both weapons on the gun belt and then hang the belt up on the wall, there would be no fight tonight, Bill will know I was back in the capitol by now but still needs his audience he will wait until the town wakes up before making his play.

I am getting a might hungry just as I was about to mosey over to the cafe when to my great surprise, Carol, Em, young Bill and Whiplash burst in with a big tray filled with supper, they had got the news on Bill long before I did. I hug and shamelessly kiss Carol, she always feels just perfect in my arms, never wanting to let go, finally after a spell Em breaks the embrace telling me they did not bring this food all this way to be eaten cold.

It took little convincing I sit and remove the cover off the plate, I am looking at a heaping plates of steak mashed potatoes and gravy, cornbread and a half a real apple pie, I then had a dark thought invade my mind, am I a condemned man and is this my last meal. The dark moment passes quickly with all the talk in the office, it sure is comforting knowing even if I am killed tomorrow I had a damn good run and a large circle of people which I love dearly.

Carol asks, "is there no other way honey, must it be guns and death with you and Bill, maybe you can talk him out of it, I am so very afraid for you Hardin, Bill has gun savvy and is a stone cold killer clear through?" "Carol, you know yourself this has gone as far as it can, it has to be to the finish this time, and do not be fearful not even Bill can separate us, I believe this very strongly." Holding unto each other we spend a fitful night but taking comfort in having each other close, looking out the window I could see it close to sunrise with the sounds of the morning birds saying good morning to the day I rise and go the stove going it was not cold but a day should never start before coffee.

Carol is up straightening her skirt and pinning back her hair, she gives me a weak smile worry heavy in her eyes, but being a western woman she stands up to it, after a hug and morning kiss she leaves to go pick up breakfast from Bon Ton. I watch her walking away head up and firm step of a determined woman, I notice old Smoke joined her as she was nearing the cafe, I smile and go back in the office in to get my first taste of Arbuckle's, if Smoke is with Carol there was no fear for her safety. I take this time to meditate as taught to me years ago by Master Li, breathing slowly I clear my mind of all distractions, I can feel the fear leaving my mind and a calmness and sense of purpose flow through me, after a few minutes I say a prayer in Sioux asking for strong medicine and courage, looking out at the morning sunshine I feel it is a good day to die.

Finishing my meditation, I feel better and go back to my coffee waiting for Carol and breakfast, she is back shortly and bringing Smoke and Wade with her. After the morning howdy's the boys pour themselves some brew, it was quiet as I eat, the boys were casually watching the street and are trying to comfort Carol, but I can feel a tenseness within them as well. I know it will be awhile yet, Bill will not make his challenge before the streets were full of witnesses, taking my gun belt from the hook I strapped it on and make one final inspection of both my revolvers, satisfied I returned them to their holsters, the weight of the weapons was reassuring I knew I am as ready as I can be. Throughout the morning folks are dropping by to wish me luck, Bear and Ramon have that hard look they got when there was trouble, Em, Whiplash and young Bill as expected were there with me and Carol, with not knowing what say the room took on an awkward feel filled with deafening silence and tension.

Suddenly there was some commotion on the street I knew before I hear Bills voice it was time, I tell Whiplash and young Bill to keep the girls in the jail away from the windows, Wade and Smoke wished me luck and said they had better be getting over to the saloon.

The street empties quickly people hereare smart enough to know that bullets have a habit of making victims out of bystanders, I now hear Bill's challenge, "Hardin I have come for you, all these people will know soon that I am the best man in this Territory you know damn well its never been near big enough for the both of us, now quit hiding in that jail and face me, I am saying plain for all to hear you are a lowdown gutless coward, come, time to play for blood".

I give Carol a last hug and kiss and then I step outside, standing just outside the door I light up a fresh cigar, I look down the street and see Bill standing ready in middle, no longer is he the sharp dressed man, his white shirt was marked with stains and his black coat wrinkled and dirty, he also has 2 bullet holes in his hat.

I know I must do the walk down, once I step into the street and start towards Bill there can be no hesitation, to show weakness now would brand a person a coward. Before I step into the street I call to Bill, "Bill you are under arrest it would be better if you came peaceable, I can talk to the Governor get you off with a couple years, how about it pard?" Laughing loudly Bill gives me his answer, "Hoss you damn well know I am not the peaceable type, you want me Marshal you come get me and you better come a shooting". "Ok Bill you drew your cards now you must play them, I wish it could be some other way. Adios Pard I will be seeing you down the trail, "with that I step into the street and face Bill I remove the Russian .44 from its holster and hold it down by my side, with my eyes locked on my opponent blocking everything else out I begin my long walk.

The street is graveyard quiet but I can feel the eyes of the spectators on me, the walk down towards Bill is becoming surreal, time slows, I can hear nothing but the beating of my heart, my senses and reflexes are on a keen edge, it will only be seconds now the distance is closing fast, I know Bill will shoot first I always warned him about hurrying his first shot. Even though the distance is still to far for accurate pistol fighting I see Bill's arm raise and fire, a buzz goes by my ear, damn fine shot, as Bill cocks his .45 for another shot I bring up my smoke wagon and fire, I get lucky and nick Bill's left shoulder causing his second shot to go wide then all hell breaks loose. Bill lets go a rebel yell and starts running at me blasting away, I give my war cry and charge the air is now full of screams, curses, gun smoke and hot lead. I empty the .44 knowing I had hit Bill at least twice, quickly I replace the .44 and draw the .45 a perfect weapon for close in killing, I come to an abrupt stop as I am hit just above my hip, felt like a red hot poker had been slammed into my side, I see the buttons on Bill's white shirt and aim for the 3rd one down and fire, Bill is hit hard, I can now see blood on his shirt, I am hit again my left leg knocked out from under me, both on our knees only feet apart are firing the gun smoke makes my eyes water and hard to see. My .45 clicks on an empty chamber automatically I try to reload but my body will not respond to my minds command, I look up and directly into Bill's eyes, I watch unable to move as Bill struggles to bring his gun to bear, I now am looking into the business end of Bill's .45. With one last smile from my friend the gun slips out of his hand and he crumples in a heap on the street, unable to walk I crawl to him, to my amazement he is still breathing, but his life's blood is draining fast from no less than 6 wounds at least 4 mortal.

Holding his head without shame I am crying for what I have done to the man I called Pard and brother, "Bill, I am sorry, oh Bill I never wanted any of this to happen, is there anything I can do for you Hoss"? Bill looks up at me and gives a weak smile, "My fault Pard, always was to prideful, tell the boys good bye for me and hoping no hard feelings, one last thing Amigo could you bury me proper I think I would enjoy my peace under a big shade tree down by Bears creek, you were the best......" I can see the life has left his eyes, my friend is dead.

People start crowding in mostly gawkers my grief was replaced by an intense anger, waving my gun around like a madman I threaten to kill anyone who comes near us, through the fog I hear Bear, "do not fret Nephew you will not be bothered." On Bears signal, Ramon, Traveller, Whiplash, young Bill, Buster and Long Tom made a circle around me, I continue to hold Bill lost as to what to do now. "Bear I would be obliged if you and the boys to bury Bill proper and do not let anyone disrespect the body, no hair cutting, stealing clothes and such, I swear I will kill anyone abusing Bills body" and I meant it.

I did not hear Bears response my mind was now dealing with the shock of the wounds, blood loss was making me weak, through bleary eyes I see my beautiful Carol, I can see the fear for me in her eyes, "Hardin honey you cannot do anymore for Bill but you are hurt really bad we have to get you to the doctor." She motions to Whiplash and Buster to come over and carry me to the doctor's hospital, leaning on the boys my head starts to spin it is like a whirlwind sucking me down, I feel my head fall forward, unable to fight it any longer blackness envelops me, my last thought is wondering if this is what it feels like to die, I then fade to black.

He who conquers himself is the mightiest warrior.
- Confucius

CHAPTER 41

SUNDOWN

The sun is setting behind the western mountains, I always enjoy this time of day, as the town is quieting down folks getting to their suppers. I lower myself into my old wooden chair in front of jailhouse, leaning back propping my heels on the rail I light a thin Cuban cigar, enjoying the strong fragrance of the smoke.

Been four years now since the shootout with Bill, it was a close thing they almost buried us together, three of Bill's shots tore up my body his last shot bouncing off my thick skull giving me a new hairline and putting me in a coma for over two weeks, I was abed for over three months, it was almost a full year before I fully recovered, but one thing I am real good at predicting the weather now. There has been a lot of changes over the years, I am no longer a US Marshal, but Marshal of Cutknife County Montana, a nice quiet town inhabited by hard working church going folks, those that would do evil tend to ride wide around my county looking for easier pickings.

Only once since I took on the job of Sheriff have I had to use my guns to kill, three Eastern thugs thought it would be a simple matter to rob my hicktown, I spot them gathering in front of the bank, I grab my greener and hightailed it to the front of the bank. The first robber bursts through the door and sees me, I do not hesitate I let him have both barrels nearly tearing him in half, I drop the sawed off and pull the Russian, before I can shoot again the remaining two would be outlaws were being shot to pieces from all directions, western men have little patience with these matters, tend to shoot first and let God sort it out.

Before the undertaker took the bodies, I gathered up the men's hats, returning to my office I made up a sign, smiling to myself as I wrote it. When finished, I headed to the train station, taking a hammer and nails I nailed the dead men's hats to the railroad station building, underneath the hats I put up the sign.

THESE HERE HATS BELONGED TO THIEVES WHO ATTEMPTED

TO ROB OUR BANK AND PUT OUR CITIZENS IN HARMS WAY.

WHATS LEFT OF THEM CAN BE FOUND ON

BOOT HILL, BADMEN TAKE NOTICE. MOVE ON

> H. STEELE
> Marshal CUTKNIFE COUNTY

Carol and I are married now and very happy, we are expecting our first child in a couple months, Carol is healthy, happy and heavy, got a little duck walk thing going on I kind of like. We have talked about names and agreed if it is a boy he will be known as Angus Ramon Steele and if I girl Emily Anne, Uncle Grey Wolf will give our child its Sioux name I do not give a hoot either way, teach the boy spoil the girl. Young Bill is at Harvard studying law, but is coming back with a degree and determination to make Montana a great state, he will bring civilization run by law and organization, not with lead and gun smoke, the gunfighter lawmen are becoming rare and it is a positive step.

Old Bear has gone over to the other side, he was killed by a huge grizzly as he was cleaning a deer he had just shot. That behemoth weighing close to 800 pounds stalked him so quiet Bear was only able to get I shot into the silverback's shoulder before the beast was on him. Bear never a man to take a step back tore into his foe his huge blade slashing and stabbing steel against teeth and massive claws, both savage animals tearing and ripping each other to shreds. The two brothers were found lying dead next to each other, Bears knife buried in the beast's throat, I recon it was the way my uncle would like to go out.

Bear never looking the part was a right smart man, had some education in Scotland, and knew how to squeeze a silver dollar until the eagle screamed. He had filled on 1000 acres of land surrounding the cabin leaving it all to me, a paradise filled with trout streams, beaver ponds, timber and grass plenty of game for hunting. We try to get out there as often as we can it is only a day's ride from Cutknife, got old Buster and Tall Elk looking after the place and breeding mustangs with some high-grade Spanish and Morgan stock.

The Sioux found Bears body and buried him with great ceremony and honour the Sioux way, placing his body on a platform above the ground wrapped in a Sioux blanket his possessions were then placed beside him, now giving himself back into the arms of mother earth, Bear would have been right pleased, I surely do miss the man.

Black Hand and the Sioux are having a rough go of it, a conquered people and are at the mercy of the of the most corrupt government system in America's history, I try to help taking Blankets and food to the Reservation, Buster and Tall Elk, take over a few beeves when food gets short but it is never enough.

Old Panther and a couple of his cronies went into Blackfoot country for pelts and like many before them never came out, I heard from a Cree that they were wiped out by the Blackfoot, Panther fighting until his last breath taking more than a couple Indians with him, out of respect for a brave man the Blackfeet did not desecrate his body. Like most tribes, the Blackfeet respect a brave fighting man, by killing him their medicine became strong, he will be a remembered man among the Blackfoot tribe.

Ramon is in New Mexico, rumour has it he was just riding through a village when he spotted some ruffians roughing up a parish priest, big mistake. Being a very religious man, he acted and those he did not kill he run off, now he stays to help the priest and teach the children. Known throughout the territory as the Shepard, he is a living legend, and part of a very elite group, men who dealt out justice and when needed came to each others aid, even the Apaches avoid his village knowing to many would die.

The Traveller is still as mysterious as ever, stories abound of his exploits are exaggerated in saloons and around campfires. I saw him some time back, he was looking fit and confident as ever, a touch of gray starting around the temples. Said he was heading to Alaska needed to see some new frontier, he heard Wyatt Earp was heading up that way he just might see the sights and get in a few hands of poker with a real card player. Old Whiplash is companion and ranch boss for Aunt Em, they still fight like cats and dogs, but are never very far apart, and totally devoted to one another but neither one will admit it, love is strange.

Checking my pocket watch I see it is time to head home Carol will be putting supper on the table, she worries if I am late. I remove the 5-pointed star from my vest, after checking it over I rub some shine on it with my sleeve smiling I pin it back on the vest. Time for supper.

Wyatt says to Josie, "some people say it didn't happen that way", to which she responds "Never mind them, Wyatt. It happened that way."

Be seeing you down the trail.
Adios

CPSIA information can be obtained
at www.ICGtesting.com
Printed in the USA
LVHW020913200121
676960LV00003B/173